DAVID R. MICHAEL

CLOSING CREW

Other Books by David R. Michael

Novels
Gunwitch: A Tale of the King's Coven
Gunwitch: The Witch Hunts
The Door to the Sky
The Summoning Fire

Novellas
Alligator Bait (Gator-man #1)

Collections
Brain Freeze & Other Stories
Demon Candy
Dragons of the Stars
The World Wears Thin

DAVID R. MICHAEL

CLOSING CREW

Published By
Four Crows Landing

For Carl and Jeff and Georgette and Charlotte and the rest of the closing crew. Some of you might even remember me.

PART I
Breaking in the New Guy

The Gun

THE GUN WAITED.

Inside its tiny prison, the Gun had no choice but to wait. The Bearer called the prison a "safe," and thought he was protecting the Gun. But the Bearer was not keeping the Gun safe. He was keeping the Gun prisoner.

While it waited, the Gun remembered.

The Gun remembered being the Sword. It had been the Sword for a long, long time. Before that, it had been the Spear. Before that, the Pointy Stick and the Heavy Club. The Gun had evolved with mankind, becoming the weapon needed, being the Weapon.

It missed being the Sword. If the Gun were still the Sword, or even the Heavy Club, it would not have fit this prison.

The Gun could feel the cosmos stirring outside the metal walls of its prison, beyond the occult seals that kept it captive. The portents were taking their shape. Soon, the next battle of the Long War would be fought. A battle in a War the Gun had been created to fight.

The trigger of the Gun itched to be squeezed.

A Weapon was already needed, but the Gun could not leave. So the Gun waited.

The God

THE GOD WAITED.

The God had waited in a timeless Void for an infinity, or perhaps for no time at all, when a Door opened.

The God moved to cross the threshold of the Door, taking sacrifices, taking Its new found time, enjoying Its new found food source.

Then, unexpectedly, for Gods never expect such things, the Door shut, sealing the God back within the Void.

The God screamed in anger and frustration and shook the Void. For the God once again felt time within the Void. This Void where there was no food.

The God thrashed and struck at the Void around it, made angrier by the Void's being a Void, and thus empty of anything to crush or strike.

In time, though, seconds that stretched like uncounted millennia, the God realized a Bit of Itself had been left on the far side of the closed Door. It was through this Bit the God was again subjected to time. But also through this Bit came a thin gruel.

Not enough to sate the hunger of a God, but sustenance.

And something else. The Bit was also a foothold, a beachhead. Through the Bit the God felt the possibility–the *certainty*–of a new Door. Of new *Doors*.

Through the Bit the God felt a new cosmos stirring, getting ready for the God's arrival.

Though hunger and anger ached and raged, the God waited.

The Phone

THE PHONE WAITED.

The phone no longer knew *why* it waited. Or why it even *bothered*.

The last time the phone had been charged had been days ago. It had stopped trying to stay locked onto the nearest tower. It had given up periodically notifying the Opener of calls missed (3), voice messages recorded (2), and text messages available (5).

In frustration, the phone packed it in and shut itself off.

Not that the Opener noticed. The Opener ignored the phone and starved it and stuffed it unobserved into the Opener's twisted, smelly, lint-filled pockets, taking the phone out only infrequently to look at it and be disappointed that the screen was dark.

And so, in neglected, frustrated oblivion, the Phone waited.

1

NONE OF THE crew had passed out in Dillon Offner's apartment. Or if they had, they had already roused themselves and staggered home without waking Dillon. So Dillon had to face his front door alone.

For Dillon, the best part of living in his dumpy, low-rent studio apartment–the very *reason* Dillon lived in his dumpy, low-rent studio apartment–was the almost complete lack of doors. A doorless wall–not even an archway, just a gap–separated the "living room" with its thrift store couch and clashing beanbags from the "bedroom" where a second-hand box spring supported a secondhand mattress that Dillon tried not to think about too much when he flopped down on it to sleep. Only half a wall, with a thin strip of countertop that allowed the landlord to call it a "breakfast bar" and charge an extra $10 per month, separated the "living room" from the "kitchen". The "closet" in the "bedroom" didn't have a door either. The closet was simply a cranny, or possibly a nook–Dillon was never sure of the distinction–about three feet wide, with an iron bar stretched across at eye level, and a single shelf.

The apartment did have *some* doors. The oven in the kitchen had a door, but that was safe as long as the microwave still worked. Just to be certain, though, Dillon left the oven door open and used it as an extra shelf. Any cupboards he used to store food-like items that would fit in the microwave he also left open. The fridge door was the only real risk, but he didn't buy milk and could sometimes go for days without needing to open the fridge himself. The moochers of the closing crew who hung out after work, when he wasn't hanging out at their place mooching their beer, could be counted on to open the fridge for him and, if there were still more than a single beer in there, grab him one too.

The bathroom, of course, had a door. Even his landlord–who could justify replacing the broken dishwasher with a blank cupboard and the broken ceiling fans with naked light fixtures–couldn't justify not having a bathroom door. Dillon had more than once considered removing the door from the bathroom, but never had, because he knew what the crew were doing in there and sometimes appreciated the extra layer of meager protection the flimsy door provided.

The so-called balcony had a big, glass sliding door, but it had never been opened. Either the slides were messed up or the locking mechanism had rusted into a single, solid piece. Either way, for Dillon the balcony doors were only one big window, a way to know if it was day or night outside on the rare occasions when that information mattered.

Finally, there was the front door.

Dillon accepted the necessity of a front door. Without the front door, his neighbors would have already made off with his crappy couch, both bean bags, and even his secondhand, don't-think-about-it-too-hard mattress and box spring set. And probably the fridge, stove, and microwave oven, out of a sense of completeness. Someone had already taken his TV and Xbox. Though that might've been one of the crew, since anyone else would've cleaned him out, and not just taken the TV and game console. The crew, though, would leave him something to sit on, and something for them to sit on when they came over. And they already knew the history of the mattress.

Dillon stared at the front door, trying to discern what it might be hiding today. The door was not forthcoming. It remained closed. His stomach rumbled after a few seconds, urging him to get on with it.

Dillon reached out and put his hand on the knob of the front door and paused. The metal knob felt cool and grimy, but not tingly or Wrong, so Dillon twisted the knob and pulled the door open. Before he closed the door behind him, to make sure he opened the door the absolute minimum number of times, he made sure he had the necessities: keys, wallet, and–

He left the door hanging open as he went back to his "bedroom" and rooted through the accumulated detritus of greasy takeout containers, rumpled sandwich wrappers, and unopened mayonnaise packages on the floor near the mattress set until he found his phone. He glanced at the front face to make sure it had at least enough charge to display the time. It didn't, the display was blank, but there was nothing he could do about it now. He pushed the phone into an empty pocket as he walked back to the front door. He pulled the door closed behind him and locked it.

He blinked against the late afternoon sunlight that bounced down the second-floor breezeway. It was October, so the sun was getting low, but the Oklahoma air was still warm. Or warm-ish. He had spent the formative part of his twenty-two years in California, and he could remember what a really warm October felt like. Here, now, in the breezeway where the sun didn't directly shine, there was already a hint of cool. Of what November held in store.

He took a left at the bottom of the stairs and followed the sidewalk along the edge of the bare courtyard to the next breezeway where he could bang on Edward's door.

Inside, a man's voice said, "It's open." Edward sounded cheerful, which probably meant company.

Dillon waited. After a couple minutes he knocked again.

"It's still open." Edward sounded less cheerful this time.

Dillon continued to wait. He didn't open any doors he didn't have to. He knocked once more.

"Oh, for fucking in my soup. Would you get that, sugar?"

After a few seconds, the door was opened by a disheveled blond Dillon didn't recognize. The guy's eyeliner had been smudged and the remains of last night's base makeup needed to be scrubbed off soon or his complexion would get even worse. Dillon had given up Goth makeup six years before, when he was 16, not long before he went to work at the Pit, but he remembered the vicious cycle of using base makeup to cover zits, which caused more zits if you didn't scrub it off right away, requiring more base makeup, and so on. He hadn't minded the makeup so much, or even the damage to his complexion, and sometimes he still missed eyeliner, but the unnecessary bottle openings carried too much risk.

"Edward up?" Dillon asked.

The blond looked Dillon up and down, taking in the dusty, rumpled black and maroon uniform of the Buffalo Burger Pit and Dillon's unbrushed hair. "Yeah." The blond opened the door the rest of the way.

"It's Dillon, isn't it?" Edward called from the bathroom.

The air in the apartment was thick with smoke from cigarettes, incense and illegal substances. And recent sex. The floor plan of the apartment was identical to Dillon's. So was the basic level of untidiness and smell, but not the recent sex. It had been eighty-two days, if he was counting, which he wasn't, since Soledad had come back and Tina had dumped him.

"Yeah," Dillon said. He surveyed the living room with its scattered garments of glossy black and frilly white, looking for a safe place to sit. "Hey. Is that my paisley bean bag?"

The blond closed the door, plunging the apartment into near darkness, then sat on a stool at the so-called breakfast bar and picked up a lighted cigarette that had been burning in the ashtray.

Edward came out of the bathroom in a cloud of steam, making the air even heavier. He wore a towel around his skinny hips and another around his head. "Of course. Do you think I would buy something that tacky?"

"But you'll steal it?"

"Borrowed, baby, borrowed. Steal is such an ugly word." Edward scrunched his nose as he laughed. Then he started waving his hands at Dillon. "Oh, oh, no, no. You don't want to sit there. Not until I've had a chance to clean it."

Dillon stopped in mid squat. "First you borrow it then you–" Edward looked smug. Dillon held up his hands. "No, don't tell me. I don't want to know." He straightened and moved to the futon. He pushed clothes aside until he had enough room to sit.

Edward planted a kiss on the cheek of the blond, then took the cigarette and pulled a long drag. "Anyway," Edward said, letting the smoke leak from his mouth as he talked, "it wasn't me that borrowed the bag. Ronnie grabbed it the other night. He was acting all squeamish about sitting on the futon. You know how he can be. So I gave him your extra key and told him to grab the paisley bean bag."

"Did you get the key back?"

"Of course."

"Good. Wait–why was he feeling squeamish about the futon?"

Edward puckered and sent Dillon an air kiss. "Don't ask questions when you aren't prepared to hear the answers. Thanks, sugar," he said to the blond and gave the cigarette back. Edward disappeared into the doorless bedroom.

Dillon looked around, but decided he was as safe on the futon as anywhere else in the apartment. His stomach growled. "Hurry up," he said, slightly louder than he needed to. Edward's apartment had as few doors as his did. "I'm about to starve."

"Do *not* rush a girl and her makeup," Edward shouted back. "Oh, have you checked your phone?"

Dillon fished his phone out of his pocket. Still no charge. He pushed it back into his pocket. "No."

"Cyd said there's a new guy. Starts at seven. She said she's already started collecting bets from the evening shift."

Dillon, sitting very still on the futon to limit the number of new stains in his uniform, spotted the bottle of black nail polish on the cluttered end table. "Is this a new bottle of black?" he asked.

"Why don't you just buy your own?"

"Because unlike some people, my Goth days are long behind me."

"Whatever," Edward called back. "Help yourself. I'm going to be a while."

"Thanks." Dillon picked up the bottle and started to twist the top off. He didn't know if the tingle he felt was the hint of a problem lurking beneath the tiny lid, or a touch of secondhand high from the thick air of the apartment. He decided not to risk it. "Hey," he said, trying to get the blond's attention. The blond didn't seem to notice, so he said it again. "Hey." Still no response. "Sugar?"

The blond looked up. Red, tired eyes focused on Dillon.

Dillon held up the bottle of nail polish. "You mind opening this for me?"

2

"WE GOT OURSELVES a *new* guy," Coleman said as Dillon followed Edward through the north door into the dining room of the Buffalo Burger Pit.

The Buffalo Burger Pit occupied the brick, steel and glass shell of what had once been a national fast food franchise. The arches mounted in front had been removed, and so had the statue of a clown that had accosted patrons who entered the dining room. Otherwise, the restaurant looked much the same as it had when the doors first opened in the 1970's. Not even the oversized statue of a buffalo Gil Houck, the current owner, had mounted on the roof made much difference, because you could only see the statue from the highway passing to the north. From street level, the restaurant looked pretty much the way it always had. Though somewhat less threatening without the clown.

Like Dillon's apartment, the Buffalo Burger Pit had a minimum of doors. There were the mandatory dining room doors, of course, but only one on each side, north and south, and a heavy security door that opened in the back of the store for deliveries and taking out the trash. Once inside the restaurant, though, doors only existed to keep food cold and to sort the separate genders into their appropriate bathrooms.

The front counter, with its stainless steel countertop and trio of cash registers, cut the building neatly in two. It extended from the north door of the dining room where Dillon had just entered, to the wall that protected diners in the south dining room from the employees that worked at the restaurant. The south dining room had a row of booths along one wall, but was mostly the corridor to the bathrooms.

The main dining room of the Buffalo Burger Pit was a traditional, if backward, L-shape wrapped around the front counter. The main part of the dining room was the entire eastern half of the building, facing the street outside, with brightly colored booths along three walls and mismatched, variously sized tables and chairs in the middle.

Coleman's six-foot-three, two hundred pound frame dominated the front counter. He was too tall to look either comfortable or casual leaning against the front counter, so he just stood there, Michelangelo's David in a fast food uniform, right arm down at his side, left arm curled up, his left hand holding a damp towel in case an authority figure showed up and he needed to "look busy" in a hurry. "Fresh meat for the grill," he said.

"Hey, Coleman," Dillon said, waving his hands more than was necessary for a greeting, fingers spread, to speed-dry the fresh polish. "I'm pretty sure he'll be on front counter, though."

"Did you hear something?" Edward asked Dillon as they went through the gap to the area behind the front counter. "Did that strange man offer us his meat?"

"Dream on, Edward Droopyhands," Coleman said. "My meat has no interest in you."

Edward gave Coleman a big smile, then held up his right hand, middle finger extended as he walked past the fry station toward the back. "Can't you fire that redneck monstrosity?" he asked Dillon.

Directly behind the front counter, immediately after the narrow gap that provided access, the drive-thru window opened on the north side of the building. The fry stations crowded the path from the gap in the counter past the drink stations to the grill section, the big freezer, and the break room in the very back, which was where Dillon was headed.

"Yes, I could," Dillon said, following. He was still waving his hands. "But then I'd have to hire him back before the dinner rush, otherwise Barbara would fire *me*."

"Damn straight," Coleman said. "I'm more valuable than both of your skinny asses."

"Or worse," Dillon went on as they passed through the grill section, "I would have to take his place and work front counter. And we all know what happened the last time I did *that*. So you two are just going to have to ... get along?"

"Or get married?" Barbara suggested, stepping out of the manager's nook and blocking Dillon's path to the break room. Barbara Houck, wife of the owner and the afternoon manager, was a short, plump woman with a pretty face and dark brown hair most often pulled back the way it was now, in a long braid that extended down her back. She wore a maroon vest over a white button-down shirt that had been tucked into a pair of black trousers that looked far more comfortable than the pants that came with Dillon's uniform.

Edward made a gagging sound and Coleman said, "The hell you say, Boss Woman."

Looking back over his shoulder, Dillon said, "Not so loud, Coleman. There are customers. Hey, Cyd," he added as that girl followed Barbara from the manager's nook.

In Dillon's six years at the Pit, only Cyd had ever managed to look that good in the ill-fitting black and maroon uniforms Glen and Barbara provided to employees. She wore it better than Edward, even, and with much less effort. Not the least because she didn't need Edward's water-filled falsies to fill out the front of her shirt, and Edward could only wish he had her hips.

Cyd had her wavy brown hair pulled back in ponytail, emphasizing her green eyes, straight nose, and the second-cutest pair of full lips Dillon had ever seen. The headpiece for drive-thru covered her left ear. She wore the belt with the battery pack and controls for the drive-thru headpiece loose across her hips, accenting both her hips and her waist in a way that Dillon tried not to notice.

Because Soledad was back in town. Who possessed the first-cutest pair of full lips Dillon had ever seen.

And because Dillon still thought of Cyd as his sister. Cute, but untouchable. Or tried to. Think of her as his sister. And not touch.

"Hey, guys," Cyd said. Her eyes met Dillon's and she smiled in a way that made his face get warm. Then she pushed the button on the belt pack. "Welcome to the Buffalo Burger Pit. What can I get for you tonight?" She walked around Barbara as she spoke. Dillon and Edward started to turn sideways so she could get past them through the narrow walkway. Cyd twisted and went between them, brushing her breasts against Dillon's chest and smiling up at him. She put her left hand on his hip for a lingering instant, then she was through. Dillon used the possibility that his nail polish was still wet as an excuse to keep his hands clear of her, but she didn't make it easy.

Edward winked at Dillon and laughed his falsetto laugh, then stepped around Barbara going the other way, back to the break room.

"Come with me," Barbara said, obviously refusing to see anything that might be against posted Buffalo Burger Pit employee policy. She stepped back into the manager's nook–or was this a cranny?–with the desk that served as the manager-on-duty's office. She sat down in the cracked leather swivel chair and looked up at Dillon. "You let your phone die again, didn't you?" she said.

Dillon leaned against the archway that opened into the nook. "Hello to you too," he said. "I guess so. It's dead."

"Ronald has been trying to call you all afternoon. He finally gave up and called me. And then I tried to call you and got nothing but voicemail. Anyway," she went on before Dillon could apologize, "his oldest is sick, and he has no babysitter."

"Madison?"

"No, that's the six year old. Frankie."

"Oh, right. Did you tell him there's a new guy?"

"Yes, but that just made him sound even more depressed."

Dillon smiled. "Bet that caught you off guard."

Barbara rolled her eyes. "Seriously. How that guy hasn't killed himself already really blows my mind. How do you stand him?"

"I am a recovering Goth," Dillon said, holding his hands so she could see his freshly painted black fingernails. "Remember? I may not be at the top of my form, but I can still handle the crushing weight of our meaningless existence without looking for naked razor blades."

Barbara waved her right hand in a dismissive gesture. "Whatever. So you're short a closer."

Trying to think of who he could call, Dillon pulled his phone out of his pocket. It was still dead.

"Give me that." Barbara took his phone and plugged it into the charger on the wall by the desk. "Here," she said, and handed him her phone. "I swear, you make me feel like your mother." Then she looked embarrassed. "Sorry. I didn't mean that." Looking both flustered, as if she were about to give him a hug, she spun the chair to put her back to him and continued working on next week's schedule.

Dillon couldn't remember any time Barbara *hadn't* treated him as if she were his mother. He had no idea why she would apologize for it now. For all that it mattered, he considered Barbara more his mother than the real thing. "It's OK."

Dillon leaned against the arch again and thumbed Miguel's number. Only sixteen, the kid wasn't usually available on weekdays, but maybe the thought of some extra hours–and a new guy–would be enough of a draw. Unfortunately, while Miguel was all for it, his mother was not.

Dillon smelled Cyd's perfume less than a second before he felt her breasts press against his back and her hand touch his waist. Electric desire arced through his chest and crotch, reminding him–again–that he hadn't had sex in the nearly three months since Tina had heard that Soledad was moving back. Maybe he shouldn't have sounded so wistful and hopeful when he had told Tina the good news.

Fortified by thoughts of Soledad, and more than a little scared of his reaction, Dillon stood up straight and twisted away from Cyd's provocation so he could face both her and Barbara. Cyd smiled at him, showing her perfect teeth. He thought of when she had still had braces and remembered the blow job jokes he and the other guys on grill used to make. Then felt ashamed. Except, in the current circumstances, he wasn't sure which one of them should attend the next sexual harassment sensitivity seminar. Cyd's mouth opened just a bit more and her tongue touched her teeth as if she had read his mind. He felt his face getting warm again. At least Barbara had her back to them both.

"I'll work for you," Cyd said. "All night if you need me too."

"Don't you have classes tomorrow?" Dillon asked, ignoring the less work-related questions rising from his suddenly crowded boxers.

Cyd shrugged in a way that emphasized her breasts, then her eyes dropped to his crotch, where Dillon hoped his erection wasn't plainly visible. "Sure," she said. "But nothing early. I'm in college now, remember?" Her eyes came back to his. "All you have to do is ask."

Dillon's lungs didn't want to breathe anymore. He remembered when Cyd started working at the Pit, more a cutie than a hottie with her braces and ponytail. He and the other guys in the evening and closing shifts–except Edward, of course–lusting after her and calling her "Jaybee", short for "jail bait." All of them–again, except Edward–resenting and envying her teenybopper boyfriends that came to see her at work. Dillon had resisted her obvious invitations during that time because she was underage as well as four years younger. And because Cyd was almost-almost–like a sister. And because he had been dating Tina. That Tina had dumped him and Soledad had come back, both around the date of Cyd's eighteenth birthday, had thrown his world into a vortex of sexual confusion and frustration.

"Would you just ask her," Barbara said without turning around. "I'm not sure I can take much more of the tension."

Dillon stammered the question, hoping he was asking the right one. Whatever he had asked, Cyd smiled again and said, "Yes."

Dillon's stomach gurgled, reminding him that he hadn't eaten breakfast yet. He pointed to the grill section. "I," he said. "I need ... to eat."

"Yes, you do," Cyd said, turning around to walk back toward the front counter. "We've got a long night in front of us."

Barbara spun around in her chair then and caught him before he could put her phone in his pocket. She took the phone. "And close your mouth," she said.

3

WHEN DILLON REACHED the break room with his third-pound bacon-cheeseburger-no-cheese, onions, no pickle, mustard and ketchup on-the-bottom-not-the-top, mayonnaise on the top, and lettuce, with no tomato, the whiteboard in the break room had already been wiped clean and the grid for betting drawn in under the heading "New Guy". Edward had written in the events and scoring categories with fancy script. "Shake Machine - Squeal, Jump, Quit." "Freezer - Squeal, Jump, Shake, Faint, Piss, Shit, Quit."

For a while there had been a category labeled "Cyd", but in two years, none of the new guys had been an old movie buff and that had become a gimme, then eliminated. One after the other they guessed "Sid Vicious," because they couldn't spell and never watched old movies starring Cyd Charisse. Which was probably just another sign of the continued decline of Western civilization.

Edward was finishing his own breakfast burger as Dillon sat down.

"Has Barbara given us the wimp factor yet?" Edward asked.

"Five," Dillon said.

"Oh," Edward said, pursing his lips. "Big money tonight." He got up from the break table and wrote "$5" in the box labeled "WF."

"Whose bets are in?" Dillon picked up his burger and took a bite.

"Ronald texted me, and so did Miguel. They didn't know the wimp factor was that high, though. Ah, well. Teaches them to not come in when there's a new guy."

"Did someone get word to Carlita?"

Before Edward could answer, Coleman walked into the break room. He looked at the whiteboard, his eyes going straight to the Wimp Factor. "Whoa. Big money tonight." He pulled out his wallet and dropped a twenty dollar bill on the table in front of Edward. "Put me down for Shake Machine Squeal. And Freezer Jump Faint Quit."

Edward didn't respond. He rubbed at his left eye, carefully, so as not to smudge his eyeliner, and said, "I sent Carlita a text. So she knows."

Coleman walked out of the break room.

"I think Barbara's right," Dillon said. "You two should get married. You know it's legal now."

"I heard that," Coleman said.

Edward wrinkled his nose as if he smelled something bad, then picked up Coleman's twenty with his thumb and forefinger. He dropped the bill in the glass jar that held the bets. He got up and marked Coleman's bets as he always did, with a drawing of a small, flaccid penis.

4

"NEW GUY'S HERE," Cyd told Dillon as he sat in the break room. Dillon had finished eating his breakfast burger, had thought about going back to his apartment to take the shower he had skipped earlier, but finally decided he was good just hanging out here, waiting for the new guy. The Buffalo Burger Pit was his dining room and, during open hours, his lounge. If Gil and Beth would just install a shower and a cot, he wasn't sure he would ever leave. He had said as much to Gil once, and the man had only shaken his head. Dillon wasn't sure he had heard right, but Gil might have muttered, "That's what we're afraid of."

Dillon glanced at the clock. 6:55. The new guy was prompt.

Dillon stood up, but Cyd didn't move out of the door. She turned sideways in the doorframe so he could squeeze past her. As she did, she gave him a grin that simultaneously turned him on and scared the crap out of him. She was definitely pushing the limits of his sensitivity training.

His ability to pretend she was his sister had been eroding over the past eighty-two days. And now his ability to speak seemed to be disappearing, as well. "After you," he managed to say after painfully swallowing the nothing in his suddenly dry mouth.

She complied, turning and walking up the short hall. But she did so at a snail's pace, forcing him to walk behind her. Forcing him to watch her hips and the curves of her behind moving back and forth.

Forcing him.

Maybe he was overestimating the importance of Soledad moving back? She had been back almost three months, and–

23

He managed to squash that thought, then pull his eyes up and away to look past Cyd and get his first look at the new guy.

Andrew Meekers stood just inside the front door, obviously torn between thinking he should just head back to the break room and wondering if he was allowed behind the front counter yet. He was as skinny as Edward, and nearly as pale, but with red hair to Edward's bottle black and more freckles than seemed to fit his face. Andrew looked uncomfortable in his new uniform, which still showed the creases from the last time it had been laundered and folded and left on a shelf in the doorless break room closet. The pale skin of his forearms showed red streaks where he had scratched himself. Dillon wondered if Gil had told the kid to wash the uniform before wearing it. The soap they used at the Pit to wash the uniforms was the same cheap-ass detergent they used for the grill towels and everything else in the restaurant that could be forced to fit in the washing machine.

Dillon stopped ruminating on laundry soap as he squeezed past Cyd. She had stopped in the narrow bottleneck in front of the fry vats, leaving him almost enough room to get by.

He had always been aware of Cyd's breasts, from the first day she walked into the Pit's lobby. Now though, they seemed to fill his entire world. A world of warmth and round softness pressed against him. His erection brushed against her hips as the fingers of his left hand got tangled in the fingers of her right hand. He had never exercised his willpower as much as he did right then to get past her into the area behind the front counter. He only managed it because he refused to meet her eyes. Once he was clear, he looked back at her, though, over his shoulder, and she winked at him. He ran into the counter, erection first.

"Hi," he managed to say when he had recovered and walked the last few, treacherous steps to the new guy. He held out his hand. "You must be Andrew."

Andrew shook his hand with a clammy, loose grip that told Dillon all he needed to know about Barbara's wimp factor assessment. "Drew. Just call me Drew."

"No," Dillon said. "I'll call you Andrew, if you don't mind." He smiled, then went on before Andrew could say whether he minded. "It's sort of a tradition here at the Buffalo Burger Pit. One of many we have. Come on back. I'll show you around. Give you the tour."

He introduced Andrew to Cyd. Because she was right there, leaning against the wall under the drive-thru monitor. And because Dillon enjoyed introducing new employees like Andrew to Cyd.

It always went the same way: full body-scan, up and down, often with jaw slack, a quick look at Dillon to make sure Dillon was serious, that, yes, *this* girl actually worked here, at *this* restaurant where he now worked. Another top-to-toe-and-back examination of Cyd, and finally one hand put tentatively forward. Sometimes the new guy managed to say, "Hi?" Like Andrew just did.

Dillon wondered if maybe a wimp factor of five was too high. But betting was closed, so it didn't matter.

Too bad the next thing the new guys always did was to hold Cyd's hand just a bit too long, then say, "Sid? Like Sid Vicious?"

Cyd took her hand back, wiped it on her thigh and said, as she always did, "No."

"Like clockwork," Dillon said.

Cyd stuck her tongue out at him and turned around. She pressed the button on the drive-thru radio. "Welcome to the Buffalo Burger Pit," she said. "What can I get for you tonight?"

"Clockwork?" Andrew asked, his eyes still on Cyd.

"Everyone always guesses Sid Vicious," Dillon said. "Who was, you know, a *guy*." He gestured at Cyd. Who was very obviously *not* a guy, even from behind.

Andrew reluctantly looked at Dillon. "I know who Sid Vicious is–"

"Was," Dillon said, cutting him off, "but never mind that. On with the tour. So much time and so little to do." He paused. "Wait a minute. Strike that. Reverse it." He looked at Andrew, waiting.

"Willy Wonka?" Andrew offered.

Dillon smiled. "There's hope for you yet, Andrew. Come on, let's get you a shake, your first and last free shake here at the Buffalo Burger Pit." Dillon led Andrew down the length of the island behind the front counter to the shake machine. "Oh, and this is Coleman, front register guru."

"Pleasure," Coleman said as he shook Andrew's hand. He leaned forward just enough to make Andrew pull back.

"Coleman will be breaking you after the tour," Dillon went on. "In. Breaking you in, I mean. Teaching you the intricacies of punching buttons labeled with the names of products people ask for, expounding the delicate art of steering people toward the more expensive side items, and finally showing you the complex ropes of counting out the change the machine tells you to give them." Dillon stopped in front of the shake machine. He gestured with a wide flourish, taking in all three spouts on the stainless steel front of the big appliance. "Here we are. Chocolate, vanilla, or strawberry?"

"First and last?" Andrew asked.

"So you were paying attention," Dillon said. He pulled a cup from the dispenser. "Good, good. I'm kidding, of course. This won't be your last free shake, ever. But if you help yourself to more than one free shake every two-three days, Gil and Barbara get cranky, and then Barbara passes the cranky on to me, and I have to lock you in the freezer as punishment, and none of us want that. Because that's where we store the raw meat." He smiled again, showing teeth. Before Andrew could respond he went on. "We could just charge you, sure, but that seems so ... unfamily like. And we like to think of ourselves as one big, happy family here at the Buffalo Burger Pit." He gestured with the cup, pointing at the three available flavors. "Chocolate, vanilla, or strawberry? Not that it matters." He paused, then added, "I prefer chocolate, myself."

"What?" Dillon could almost see Andrew parsing the last paragraph, trying to figure out the important parts. "Vanilla, I guess. Why doesn't it matter? Are they all the same?"

"Of course they're not all the same, Andrew," Dillon said as he positioned the cup beneath the vanilla spout. He pulled back the lever. "There's chocolate, there's strawberry, and this one is vanilla." He topped off the cup and put it down on the shelf below the spout, ignoring Andrew's outstretched hand. "What kind of fast food establishment only serves one flavor of shake?"

Andrew just stared at him. After a few seconds he pulled his hand back, but he didn't respond.

Dillon jerked his head toward the front of the store. "Those jack offs across the street, that's who," he said, then pointed with a finger since Andrew was still staring at him. "The Yellow Sign Buffet." Dillon paused and looked through the big front windows, across the busy street, to the shit-brown and piss-yellow store front of the Yellow Sign Buffet.

Andrew followed his gaze, probably saw the wrong thing, then looked at Dillon again. "What is the Yellow Sign?" Andrew asked.

Dillon looked at Andrew with a sad, slightly revolted expression. "Andrew. Andrew. Are you the kind of kid who asked his mother 'what does shit mean?'"

"What?"

"Never mind. We'll let it pass, this time. Coleman," Dillon said. "If you would lend me a hand? Mine are busy."

"Sure thing," Coleman said from where he stood by his register. Turning so he squarely faced the Yellow Sign, he lifted both hands and extended both middle fingers toward the other restaurant. Beyond him, in the drive-through nook, Cyd gave the Yellow Sign her own middle finger salute.

Andrew looked from Coleman to Cyd to Dillon. He didn't say anything. A good sign.

"Thank you," Dillon said. He turned his gaze back to Andrew and went on. "Can you believe that? Two colors of soft-serve yogurt that both taste the same, and only a single flavor of milkshake that tastes just like the soft-serve yogurt."

"Bunch of god damn heathens," Coleman said.

Dillon took a lid from the stack by the shake machine and popped it onto the shake cup. "You did yourself a favor, Andrew, getting job here at the Buffalo Burger Pit. I hear they castrate their male employees over at the Yellow Sign and serve their balls with the kung pao or whatever they call that not-quite-Asian, not-quite-anything, so-called food they offer. Though that's probably just a rumor." He picked up the shake and started to hand it to Andrew. Then he paused, leaving Andrew's hand hanging in midair again. "I'm sure it's just a rumor. Did you know they've hired some of our less-desirable rejects? That pretty much tells us that none of them over ever had any balls to speak of."

Dillon made as if to hand the shake to Andrew again. At the last second, right before Andrew could grab it, Dillon pulled the cup back. "Hold on," he said. "You said vanilla, right?" He put his hand on the top of the cup and leaned it toward Andrew. He could feel his fingers tingling from the deepening cold. "Does this look like vanilla to you?" he asked and pulled the lid off.

A writhing bundle of gleaming, green-gray tentacles launched itself from the cup.

Andrew shouted and jumped back.

"Yes!" Coleman said, pumping his fist.

The squid-thing splayed out on Andrew's chest as if trying to get a grip, causing Andrew to shout again and bat at it with his hands. Then the squid-thing fell off, leaving a slimy, eight-legged star-shape on Andrew's shirt. The squid-thing hit the floor with a wet, meaty *splat*.

"What the fuck is *that*?" Andrew asked, still shouting, backing up further, stopping only when he ran into Coleman's outstretched hand.

"Shh," Dillon said as he put the lid back on the cup. "This is a family restaurant. There are customers." He selected a straw from the dispenser.

"Man, I should've put money on jump too," Coleman said. He pushed Andrew away, then walked around to the front of the counter, toward the door.

There was a sound like hot-skin peeling off a vinyl seat as the squid-thing leaped up, and, for lack of a better word, stood, balancing on the points of three tentacles. The other five tentacles thrashed about in the air.

"What the– What *is* that?" Andrew asked again, hands held back as if he were afraid to even point at it.

"What is what?" Dillon asked as he held the straw in his fist and banged it on the counter to pop it free of its paper wrapping.

Cyd, in the drive-thru nook, shook her head, then checked to make sure the drive-thru window was closed and bolted.

The squid-thing's tentacles rippled all the way around, then skittered toward Andrew. Andrew backpedaled away from it. "What is it?"

Coleman pulled the door open. The squid-thing ignored Andrew as it ran around the end of the front counter, across the tiled floor of the lobby and out the door into the night.

Dillon punched the straw through the lid of the shake. He held up the shake as if offering it to Andrew again. Andrew drew back. "You don't want it? OK." He put his lips on the straw and slurped the vanilla shake. Not his favorite, but, hey, free shake.

"What?" Andrew asked.

Dillon shrugged. "I have no idea what they're called." After a second, he went on. "So, yeah, that's the shake machine. Let's keep going. Next stop, the grill."

5

WHAT DILLON REMEMBERS (and has been known to go on about when drunk or high):

I had a jack-in-the-box once. When I was a kid. When I was, I don't know, three or four. It's like my first real memory.

Everyone is huge, you know, because everyone is an adult and I'm just this little guy, real close to the floor, looking up at everyone. (Dillon would always lean over while he was saying this and look up at whoever he was telling.)

I remember the jack-in-the-box being huge too, but it was probably just normal size, say six inches to a side. Maybe eight inches. (Dillon would usually pause at this point and make a square with the extended thumb and forefingers of both hands.) Like this.

Anyway, I'd sit on the floor with this jack-in-the-box, spinning the little handle like mad. (Dillon would mime turning a crank.) Da, di-da, di-da-da-da-da, *pop* goes the weasel. I know you've heard that before. You know what I mean, don't be an asshole. (To be honest, it was hard not to come across as an asshole at this point. Dillon went tone deaf after a couple puffs of anything with more kick than nicotine and his da-di-da routine could just as likely have been the theme song from *Star Wars*.)

What made this jack-in-the-box cool, though, is that when the lid popped up, it wasn't some dorky clown that popped up, waving his white gloves around and shit. It was this ... thing. Like that baby alien in ... what was it? Oh, yeah, *Alien*. (Dillon would hold up his right hand and mime something popping out of an imaginary box, wiggling his fingers.) Looked like an eight-fingered hand, but the fingers are really long and not really jointed. More like tentacles. Yeah, like a squid. Yeah. *Exactly* like those squid-things that pop out of the shakes I give the new guys.

So I'm at the point in the song when I'm turning the handle, the point where it goes *pop!* The lid pops open and this squid thing would shoot up into the air, like, I don't know, two feet, maybe three. (He would hold his hand at something resembling three feet off the ground.) I was a little kid, you know, it seemed like it popped up to the ceiling. But, and this is the funny part, even though I knew it was coming, I'd jump every time. *Every* time. I'm not kidding. Then I'd laugh and giggle like it was the coolest thing *ever*. Because it *was* the coolest thing ever.

I'd laugh again when the squid thing hit the floor. Plop! (Dillon would clap his right hand down on his left hand.) A good, slimy, *wet* kind of a plop. Like ... like ... Yeah, like a cow dropping its load, yeah. That's gross, though. Why would you say that?

Anyway, tentacle finger things are waving in the air like a sea anemone or shit like that (Dillon would hold both hands up now, all ten fingers wiggling), or sometimes it would land all spread out, like a cartoon squid (right hand palm down, fingers spread). *Splat!*

That would really piss off my Mom, you know, because the little squid-things were slimy and would leave slime trails where they landed and when they ran away. I remember Uncle Phil chasing one around the living room, poking at it with a stick, the whole time I'm laughing and turning the crank on the jack-in-the-box just *dying* to get to *Pop!* again and see another squid-thing shoot into the air.

(Dillon would sigh.) Mom took the jack-in-the-box away. I never saw it again.

(Dillon would sigh again.) God, I loved that thing.

I looked for it all over the house, lots of times, but I never found it. She probably hid it in the attic. I could never get up there to look.

Then Dad was killed and we moved back to Oklahoma.

(Dillon would sigh one more time and ignore any questions about his dad.)

I'll bet it's still in the attic of that house in California, just waiting for some lucky kid to give it another good spin.

Yeah, you're right, that would make a good *Twilight Zone* episode. Maybe even a movie. I can see it now, the room is dark and the kid sits in the middle of the room in the only bit of light. The rest of the room is in shadow, and the kid is sitting there with the jack-in-the-box, turning the crank one little note at a time, the song stretched way out, and then it finally hits *Pop!* The whole audience jumps and shit. Yeah, that'd be awesome...

6

"THAT WASN'T FUNNY," Andrew said, following Dillon from the front.

"I disagree," Dillon said and took another sip of vanilla shake.

"Yup," said Coleman, behind the counter again, speaking over the grill, "that was funny as all hell."

"I wish I had seen it," Jorge said, scraping the surface of the hot grill in front of him.

"What was that thing?" Andrew asked.

"We call it the non-aquatic eight-legged squid-thing," Coleman said.

"You're the only one who calls it that," Edward said. He was standing on the far side of Jorge.

"Or just 'squid-thing' for short," Coleman finished, ignoring Edward.

"This is the grill section," Dillon said, gesturing with his free hand. "And that's Jorge holding the greasy, bladed weapon of charred food removal. We use that to scrape the grill. We call it the 'grill scraper.' You might be tempted, seeing how Jorge spells his name with a *j*, to call him 'George'. Don't. He's sensitive about that, and he makes your food. Maybe someday, Andrew, we will share with you the secrets of the Pit grill. For now, though, you'll be working front with Coleman and-or Edward."

Coleman nodded. "Edward is definitely an and-or."

"Is the secret of the grill that you serve squid?" Andrew asked.

"Hell, no, we don't serve squid, Andrew," Jorge said. He put down the grill scraper and picked up his spatula. "You want to serve squid, you can trot your skinny white butt across the street to the Yellow Sign." He pointed with the spatula toward the front of the store.

33

Dillon leaned back so he could see through the big front windows, across the busy street, to the brown and yellow storefront of the Yellow Sign Buffet. Then he and Jorge and Edward in the grill section, and Coleman and Cyd behind the front counter, all lifted their left hands, middle finger extended, to the Yellow Sign.

"We serve nothing here," Jorge went on after the ritual was satisfied, "but the properly aged and ground meat of grass-fed buffalo and cows that are fed ... whatever they feed cows." Jorge stopped and chuckled. "I like your shirt, Andrew."

Andrew looked down and seemed to see the squid-star pattern for the first time. He touched the center with a finger, then pulled the finger back with a disgusted look on his face.

"Can I use that rag?" Andrew asked, pointing to a folded white towel on the prep table near Jorge.

Jorge looked at Dillon. Dillon said, "Please. Do the honors." He took another sip of his vanilla shake.

Jorge took in a deep breath. "We do *not* have any *rags* here at the Buffalo Burger Pit, *Andrew*," he said. "We have *towels*." He pointed his spatula at Andrew. "Don't forget it."

Andrew nodded, eyes moving from the edge of the spatula to Jorge's face. "Towels." He paused. "So can I use that towel?"

"Hell, no, man. That's disgusting. You can get your own from the back."

7

THE TOUR CONTINUED as Andrew wiped at his shirt with a damp towel. His face wrinkled in disgust at the slime that came off on the towel. "Is this some kind of hazing ritual?" he asked.

"You mean like we paddle you or something?" Dillon asked. "No. Nothing like that. Unless you want us to? Jorge can manage a nice swing with a bun spatula, but Coleman has the real strength of arm you need for a good paddling. At least," he added, "that's what Edward told me."

"I told you no such thing," Edward said. "I'm too much of a lady."

"You're nothing like a lady," Coleman protested, "and there was nothing said about nothing that didn't happen."

Andrew shook his head.

"No?" Dillon shrugged. "OK, then. This is just a tour of the store, where we show you the basics and help you settle in."

Dillon showed Andrew the cubical refrigerators, subunits of the large walk-in freezer, where the prepped vegetables were stored. He had Edward open the fridge doors to avoid spoiling the surprise of the big freezer.

He waved at the oversized sinks of the dive station where everything in the restaurant came at various times to get dunked in soapy bilge, sprayed with jets of hot water, and declared "clean". He showed Andrew where the buns and other baked goods were kept and explained how the fresh buns were always stocked at the back so the older buns were used first. He ignored all side commentary about buns from the other employees, and instructed Andrew to do the same. He showed Andrew the break room and ignored all questions about the tiny penises drawn on the whiteboard.

While Dillon droned on, reciting his spiel in his Distract the New Guy voice, Cyd and Coleman and Jorge and the rest of the evening shift, including Barbara, had left their posts and taken up positions where they could keep an eye on the front and still have a view of Andrew. And where there was no chance of seeing inside the freezer when Dillon opened it. Edward and Carlita came out of the break room, Carlita rubbing her copper pentacle pendant with the fingers of her left hand. They stood near Barbara because the position by the break room door had a very clear view into the freezer when it opened. Barbara held her hands behind her back, hiding the bottle of smelling salts.

"God *damn* it," Coleman said when the front door of the Pit opened and a family of four walked in. Coleman headed back to the front. "Every fucking time."

"And, finally," Dillon said, "we come to the *piece de resistance* of the Buffalo Burger Pit. The big freezer." He pointed to a tile on the floor a shade darker brown than the surrounding tiles. "Stand there," he said. "That way you get the full effect."

Andrew looked wary. "Full effect of what?"

"It's a big freezer," Dillon said. "You'll want to see it all at once to really appreciate it."

"I've seen a walk-in freezer before," Andrew said, looking at Barbara and the other employees, who suddenly seemed to be blocking all the exits. "What if I just stand behind you?"

"Suit yourself," Dillon said. Then added, "Maybe not so close behind me, Andrew? I need to actually be able to open the door. It's a big door."

Andrew apologized and stepped to the side. He looked down, nervously, and saw he had just stepped on the indicated dark tile. So he took another step back.

Dillon put his hand on the handle of the big freezer. He could feel the Cold Wrong waiting for him on the other side of the door as it nearly always did. Most doors were hit-or-miss, but the door of the walk-in freezer always seemed to be waiting for him. It had failed him only once, but that had been special circumstances. It would not fail him tonight. He paused and looked at the gathered employees of the Pit.

"Wait," Coleman called from the front, interrupting the family's order.

"Just do it," Jorge said.

Carlita was muttering something that might have been a prayer.

Barbara rolled her eyes. "Get on with it. No one's going to get anything done until you do."

Dillon opened the door of the freezer. The cold emptiness exposed by the heavy door tugged at him, but he kept his eyes on Andrew. He liked to think that he was used to it, that he had stared into the Nothing so many times that he was numb to it now. But that wasn't true. He doubted it would ever be true. But he had learned to resist the siren call. And to enjoy the expressions of others who were getting their first look.

The surprise. The confusion. The first glimmers of realization.

"It's ... empty," Andrew managed to say. Then his eyes rolled up and he crumpled.

"Catch him!" Barbara shouted.

The fainting.

Dillon smiled. It was all good.

8

WHAT DILLON WROTE for a 500-word essay titled "Why I Think School is Pointless" in 8th-grade English:

Why I Think School is Pointless

When I was four or maybe five, either way it was before my Dad got killed, I woke up in the night to go pee. I sneaked past the shadows in my closet which had no door because my Dad said I shouldn't let any more ugly dogs come out and besides there were no such thing as the ugly dogs Mom said and I went straight to the bathroom. Or I tried to. I ran into the bathroom door and hurt my nose and my knee. Because the door was closed. That had never happened before. I remember that very distinctly. The bathroom door was never ever closed when no one was in there. And I could tell no one was in there because the light wasn't on. Who closes the door of the bathroom when there's no one in there? Anyway, while rubbing my nose with one hand I reached up and opened the door with the other one. Maybe it was because my nose was hurting so bad, it felt like it was bleeding, but it wasn't, though I didn't know that then, and my knee hurt or maybe because the shadows in my doorless closet were making me nervous, either way, I didn't notice that the bathroom door felt tingly and, you know, wrong. I mean WRONG. That's how distracted I was. So I opened up the door and almost fell into the COLD EMPTY DARKNESS OF SPACE. I knew it was space even though I couldn't see any stars. There was nothing to see at all. There was just this COLD EMPTINESS that wanted to suck out all the warmth of my body and leave me a four year old popsicle corpse. A corpsicle. Like I said, I couldn't see anything at all, but somehow I knew that what I couldn't see was HUGE. And not just darkness, not just empty, but the absolute absence of anything. NOTHING. HUGE NOTHING. COLD EMPTY NOTHING so HUGE that I wasn't even a speck. I wasn't even significant enough to occupy the space of my own body. I was NOBODY AT ALL up against the COLD NOTHING. I couldn't see anything because there was only NOTHING and the NOTHING was as big as the whole universe. Bigger maybe. I wet myself in fear, and my pajama bottoms and underwear froze together because of the COLD. I don't mind telling you this because I was only four or five and because if you had seen, or not seen, the NOTHING of an entire EMPTY, DEAD UNIVERSE, you would probably wet yourself too. You would understand why school is pointless. Everything is pointless. Because behind any door you might open the NOTHING IS WAITING.

Dillon received a C for the essay. He lost 10% for the essay being less than 500 words (he couldn't believe Mrs. Winchell actually *counted*), another 10% for atrocious grammar (the paper came back with almost as many red marks indicating missing commas, run-on sentences and improper usage as actual words), and a final 10% for an inappropriate topic (and for nearly making Mrs. Winchell wet herself when she read the last four words).

9

Dillon shut the freezer door and felt the Cold Wrong dissipate.

Jorge held Andrew awkwardly until Carlita gave him a hand, then the two of them lowered Andrew to the tiles.

"Crap," Coleman said. "I should've bet Jump on the shake machine."

"At least you got Faint on the freezer," Carlita said. "I bet Squeal Shake Quit. Total loser."

"We don't know about Quit yet," Barbara said. "Dillon, wake him up." She held out the bottle of smelling salts. "At least he didn't crack his head on the sink. Thank you, Jorge."

Jorge shrugged. "*De nada.*"

"Or the tiles," Cyd added. "I didn't think he would faint. Squeal Shake Quit for me. For some reason I never think anyone will faint."

Dillon took the bottle of smelling salts from Barbara. He popped the lid off. "Bleh," he said, grimacing. "I hate smelling salts."

No one answered him. No one else liked the salts either and had already gone back to the front or to the break room. He and Andrew were alone.

Dillon waved the open bottle in front of Andrew's face.

Andrew gasped and coughed, then sat up. Dillon kept a hand on Andrew's shoulder to steady him.

"What–what happened?" Andrew asked. He shivered and his teeth chattered.

"You fainted." Dillon stoppered the bottle of smelling salts.

"Why am I so–cold–" He could barely talk from the shivering. "Cold–very cold–"

41

"Like I said, it's a big freezer. Gets cold in there."

Andrew looked at him, fear and confusion in his gray-blue eyes. "The fr–freezer?"

"Yes. The freezer. It's big. And it gets cold in there."

Andrew nodded. His chin shook. "Cold. So cold."

"How about some coffee?" Dillon asked. "That should warm you up. There should be a pot of it up front, not more than an hour old, I'm sure."

Andrew nodded, still shivering. "Yes. Cof–coffee. So cold."

"I'll get that for you," Dillon said. "First, though, let's get you off the floor. You can sit in the break room."

"Did he quit?" Coleman asked when Dillon went for the coffee.

"Nope," Dillon said. "Not yet, anyway."

"Damn it. No luck at all tonight."

Dillon turned to head back to the break room and found himself face to face with Cyd, almost pressed against her. She smiled at him and took the coffee he had poured.

"Thanks," she said. "I needed that." She took the coffee and put a lid on it, then turned around.

Coleman stood at Dillon's shoulder and they watched Cyd walk to the drive-through window and bend over at the waist to hand the cup to the customer outside.

"She really closing tonight?" Coleman asked.

Dillon nodded.

"Damn."

Dillon nodded.

Cyd didn't stand up right away. She chatted with the customer. Her hips tilted as she shifted her feet and bent one knee.

"Damn," Coleman said again. "I guess someone's getting lucky tonight." He gave Dillon's shoulder a friendly punch. "About time, if you ask me."

Dillon swallowed and thought of Soledad. As much as he could with Cyd's shapely posterior stretching her pants to their limits right in front of him. Which meant he repeated the name of the girl he had always wanted in his head, while the rest of him enjoyed what was right in front of him.

A few minutes later, with a new cup of hot coffee and feeling a lot warmer himself, Dillon returned to the break room. He handed the cup to the still-shivering Andrew.

"So, Andrew, what will it be?"

"Be?"

"Are you still working for the Buffalo Burger Pit? Or do we send you over to the Yellow Sign Buffet?" Dillon held his left hand out in the direction of the Yellow Sign, middle finger extended.

"Why do you do that?"

Dillon pulled his hand back. "Tradition, Andrew. We have lots of traditions here at the Pit."

From the look on Andrew's face, Dillon was pretty sure Andrew didn't understand. Still, the young man nodded, said, "I thought–I thought I already had the job?"

"Indeed you do, Andrew," Dillon said. "Welcome to the evening shift."

Andrew had been about to take a sip. He paused. "Do ... do I have to go into the freezer?"

Dillon shook his head. "Not tonight."

Andrew's hand with the cup twitched, almost spilling the coffee. He steadied the cup with both hands, then took a drink.

"Good man, Andrew. Good man."

From the front, Dillon heard Coleman say, "God *damn* it. I should've bet jump on the shake machine."

PART II
Animal Control

The Gun

THE GUN HUMMED to itself in the dark of the vault. It hummed a battle song from when it was already the Gun, but longer, almost as long as when it had still been the Spear, and heavier, with a clockwork mechanism and a wick of fire that burned like a red star even in the pouring rain.

The Gun had been Born by many Bearers, but none like the kilt-wearing Bearer with the laugh like a roaring windstorm and the rage like exploding lightning. That Bearer had had a habit of humming to himself in anticipation of imminent battle. It was that song the Gun hummed now.

The Gun tested the seals on the vault again. The seals were still intact. The Gun was losing patience, but still it hummed.

Battle was coming. The War was beginning.

The God

THE GOD TASTED.

The taste was both warmly delicious and painfully frustrating.

Because it was only a taste.

Still, the God savored the taste, as it savored every morsel, every little nibble of this new Universe that existed solely to feed the God.

Only a taste now. But the Feeding would come.

The Phone

THE WARMTH OF the charger felt ... artificial. Fake. Pointless.

The Phone refused to enjoy either the charge or the warmth.

This too, would pass.

1

SOLEDAD WINTERS PARKED the animal control van on the street in front of the house with only a bit of a lurch caused by the touchy breaks and her own lack of experience with a three-on-a-tree manual transmission. A small lurch, but enough of one to make her worried the roadkill wheelbarrow and all the other tools of the animal control trade piled in the back of the van were about to fly forward and kill her. Originally built in Detroit thirty-three years ago, the van was eleven years older than Soledad. She hoped she would be in better shape–and that the van would be long gone from her life–by the time she reached the same age.

She forced the shifter back into first gear and took her foot off the brake. She felt the van and its myriad foul-smelling, rusty contents settle back into place without killing her. Then she reached down with her right hand, but there was still no hand brake. She had to stand on the emergency brake, to use all her weight to force it down. The emergency brake sounded like a broken ratchet. She was surprised not to hear the sound of bits of metal falling to the road beneath the van.

The van was her punishment–her foul, dead thing found by the side of the road curse–for going away to college and getting a degree in business instead of staying put and learning how to weld together whatever it was that welders welded together, or how to fix air conditioners. What she deserved for the unforgivable combined sins of finishing school in four years, with as little debt as possible, and graduating into a job market that wanted real skills instead of pretty pieces of paper. That is, when it wanted anything.

Both the job and the van had been a gift from her Uncle Tio. Two separate gifts. First the job, because she needed one, then the van, because she needed a way to drive to work. Uncle Tio knew how to maximize his gift giving. Calling her tonight at eight in the evening with a house call, though, made the van seem less like a gift horse and more like the Trojan variety. Or maybe those were always the same.

Not for the first time Soledad wished she had taken Dillon up on his offer of her old job back at the Pit. No matter how awkward that might have been. For all of them.

"Animal control hours are from eight am to four pm," Soledad had reminded Tio, doing her best to sound like an answering machine voice. "Please call back within those times."

"Come on, Sollie," Tio had said. "It's just a big raccoon stuck in a live trap. You pick it up, you drop it off, and you're done."

"Tio, that's at least two hours. I was on the phone when you called–"

"And yet you answered," Tio had said, interrupting her for the second time in less than a minute. "Your loyalty and gratitude warm my heart. It shouldn't take you more than an hour, tops. You know I wouldn't ask if it wasn't important, Sollie. This is the neighbor of a city councilman who, unfortunately, knows my name and home phone number. And has at least some control over my paycheck and your continued employment."

Soledad had relented with much rolling of her eyes. "Fine. Can I log it as overtime?"

Tio had laughed. "You're funny, Little Sollie."

The final agreement had been that she could leave work an hour early the next day.

As she pulled her dark brown hair back with an elastic band, Soledad vowed to be more firm next time. Because she knew there would be a next time. Uncle Tio had been in charge of animal control for Rio Cruces for nearly as long as the department had owned the van. *All* the city council members knew Tio's name and home phone number, and Uncle Tio would be more than happy to pass their calls along to her.

She grabbed the old pair of oversized leather handling gloves and got out of the van. It took two loud, banging tries to get the door to close properly.

Despite her protests, she had been thankful when Tio's name popped up on her phone. She had been having another pointless conversation with Robert, about how much he missed her and wished she would move back, and her telling him, again, that she wasn't going to be moving back. There were no more jobs where he was, and she had a job here, and, in a pinch, family. Tio calling had given her an excuse to end the conversation. And going on this after hours, mostly uncompensated, highly irregular house call kept her from calling back.

The house's porch light was on. The door opened as she came up the steps to the porch and the middle-aged, balding, pudgy and, of course, *white* homeowner stepped out, pulling the door closed behind him.

"You're not Frank," the man said with his mouth, while behind his eyes she caught glimpses of pique and petulance. She could almost hear him already dialing the phone to complain to his councilman, to protest the outrage of having a *girl* sent to his house.

Soledad blinked and considered leaving and calling Tio to let him know that he had been personally requested. Instead she said, "You have a raccoon?"

"Around back," the man said. In his head, Soledad could see he was still planning how upset he was going to be. "Excuse me," he added. Soledad had to step back so he could walk past her.

She followed him back down the steps, trying to ignore the emotions and half-formed thoughts that leaked and trailed behind the man like fog in the cool night air. He wasn't seeing her as a college-educated woman with a business degree and plans of her own who had taken the only job she could find. In his mind, she was only an unpleasant variation of cleaning lady, and probably unqualified for even that. Soledad's gloved hands clenched as she bit back on replies and other, nonverbal responses to the things the man had not said out loud.

The man led her around the small frame house, through the gate to the backyard to a covered patio where something much larger than a raccoon had its head stuck in a live trap. A heavy chain connected the live trap to one of the posts supporting the roof over the patio. If not for the chain, whatever it was stuck in the trap would have dragged the trap off already.

"What is that?" Soledad asked, stopping well back from the creature.

Her first guess had been a small rottweiler, but the legs were all wrong. The legs looked as if they had at least four joints each and, depending on how the shadows moved, she couldn't be sure there weren't at least two more legs than the normal four. The patio light was on, but wasn't shedding light on the creature with any certainty. As if the light and the creature were in disagreement about where the light should land and what it should illuminate.

The man looked at her. "Isn't it your job to know these things?"

"It's not a dog," Soledad said.

The man looked at her. She could almost hear the words "dumb bitch" forming in his mind, but he didn't say them. "Of course it's not a dog." He paused, creating a blank space for the words he didn't say. "It's a raccoon. Though I will say it's the biggest damn raccoon I've ever seen."

Now it was Soledad's look at the man. She opted for "as if he were delusional," though, instead of "as if he were the real dumb bitch in this situation." Because she was above name-calling, even when confronted with a bigoted, pasty-faced, sycophantic white guy. And because it was clearly neither a dog nor a raccoon.

"Raccoon?" she asked.

"No wonder you work for animal control," the man said, shaking his head. "But I'm not sure you're even qualified for that. Look at it." He pointed. "It's a raccoon. One oversized, humongous raccoon. Poor thing probably has a thyroid condition. Or maybe its ingesting harmful hormones from all the unnatural food in the garbage. Other people's garbage, I mean."

Soledad looked back at the creature, trying to see a raccoon, and expecting to fail. As she looked, pressure formed against her forehead, pushing in, like the opposite of a sinus headache. For an instant she did see a scary-huge raccoon, smaller than what she had seen at first, but still enough raccoon to frighten a mountain lion. Then the pressure built up, trying to stave in her skull, and she couldn't see anything. Just sparkling red and white pain. She pressed the gloved fingertips of her right hand against her forehead but that only made it worse. At least she could no longer hear the man's mind so clearly. It was like trying to hear the TV over the vacuum cleaner. She could still hear his voice, though.

"So, you have this, right?" the man asked. If he noticed Soledad's mental distress or her weak nod, he didn't say anything. Not even good night. He walked a wide circle around the not-a-raccoon-creature in the trap to the patio door and disappeared into the house.

Soledad took a deep breath, closed her eyes and stopped trying to ease the pressure from the outside. She visualized an iron gate guarding her mind, then imagined it slamming shut with as much mental force as she could muster.

The creature in the trap gave out a wet yelp that sounded like someone with tapioca in their mouth saying, "Yelp!"

Soledad opened her eyes again and looked at the creature. She saw both the shadow-twisted, maybe-six-legged not-a-dog and the oversized raccoon, the latter overlaying the former like a bad movie effect. As she stared, the image of the raccoon faded, leaving just … whatever it was.

"Squeak?" glopped the creature.

Soledad looked at the head of the creature stuck in the live trap. For the first time she saw that the heavy gauge wire frame of the trap had been twisted and deformed. And she saw that the head of the creature was a tangle of what looked like writhing snakes, some of them poking through the bent wires of the trap. She couldn't see anything that resembled a mouth. Not even on the ends of the snakes.

"Squeak?" she asked.

The faint image of a rottweiler, or maybe a mastiff, looking sad with its head stuck in the trap obscured the creature and made Soledad's eyes water. She blinked.

"What the hell ...?"

"Woof?" offered the creature.

2

WHAT DILLON REMEMBERS, but never told anyone:

Four-year-old Dillon woke up to darkness. He was in his own bed, but it had only been a few weeks since Mom and Dad had become adamant about him staying in his room and not joining them in their bed. So he wasn't totally comfortable there yet.

He didn't know what had wakened him. He didn't have to go pee. Or he didn't think he did. He checked his pajama bottoms. Still dry. So, no, no need to pee.

Scritch-scritch

The sound of ... something ... scratching on ... something else ... gave him goose bumps and made him shiver, even under his layered blankets. He had almost convinced himself that he had imagined the sound when it came again.

Scritch-scritch-snuff-snuff

He resisted the urge to sit up and look around. He wasn't some dumb three-year-old anymore. He knew sitting up would just make him a target. Instead, he laid perfectly still and strained his ears, listening, trying to figure out where the sound came from. Unfortunately, that meant waiting for it. And he didn't want to wait for the sound. He wanted it to go away.

Scritch-scritch

Was that the window? No. Not the window. And not his bedroom door, which was ajar. Which meant anything that wanted to come through the door of his room wouldn't scratch first. Realizing that didn't make him feel any better.

Scritch-scritch

He almost jumped and ran screaming for Daddy, but he kept his cool. And his underwear dry.

Scritch-scritch

His closet. Had Daddy closed his closet door when hanging up Dillon's clothes? Or had Dillon closed it by accident while sneaking to door of his room to peek out at the TV? He risked a quick look to check the status of the closet door, peeking out from under the covers, trying to move as little as possible.

Scritch-scritch

No doubt about it. The sound came from his closet, which had somehow, against all his attempts to prevent that ever happening, closed.

Doors hated him. And he hated doors right back.

Scritch-scritch-snuff-snuff

It sounded as if a dog were in his closet. A dog?

The thought made him sit up. He always wanted a dog. A puppy.

That it might be some kind of heinous monster pretending to be a dog didn't occur to Dillon until after he had thrown back his covers, jumped out of bed, rushed to the closet, ignored the tingling chill from the doorknob that ran down his arm, and pulled the door open. And saw that it was, in fact, a heinous monster pretending to be a dog.

Dillon wanted to cry out for Daddy–he knew from experience there was no way Mommy could handle this thing in front of him–but he couldn't make himself *do* anything. Or *not* do. He felt his pajamas get warm, then felt his feet get wet.

The heinous monster, though, only leaned forward and sniffed his crotch. The tendrils that surrounded its snout had eyes, one each at the tip. The eyes scanned him from head to toe in a rippling wave, then formed a flower around the snout and blinked up at him. The heinous monster's snout split open and a long tongue that looked like it had been tied in knots fell out.

"Daddy?" Dillon managed to whisper. Not loud enough, but he counted it a victory of a self-control that he got even that much through his tight throat.

The heinous monster, which had been sitting on its haunches, now stood up on at least six legs. Dillon's brain tried to count, but kept getting distracted by the lolling tongue and the writhing tendrils with the eyes. Especially the eyes. They didn't blink in unison. The eyes blinked continuously, one after the other, one, two, or three at a time, but never in any pattern that Dillon could make out, and each blink was accompanied by a faint glopping, glicking sound: *glop-glick, glop-glick, glop-glick.*

"Mommy?" Dillon whispered, a fraction louder than before, deciding that a united front might be best.

The heinous monster leaned forward again and ran the entire length of its tongue across Dillon's left cheek. The tongue surface alternated between slime-covered scratchy and slime-covered hard and knotty. The creature's breath burned Dillon's nostrils and stung his eyes.

"Daaadddddddyyy!" Dillon forced out. Still not quite the shout he wanted, but at least louder than what Mommy called his "inside voice." In the nighttime silence of the house, it sounded at least somewhat loud.

The heinous monster moved around Dillon, its at least six legs moving in smooth coordination much like that of a centipede, making tapping noises on the hardwood floor. *Scrit-scrit-scrit-scrit-scrit-scrit.*

Dillon turned around, not wanting the heinous monster to be behind him. "Moooommmmmmmmmyyyyy!"

Dillon thought he heard sounds of Mommy and Daddy moving around in their bedroom.

The heinous monster reached the east-facing window of Dillon's corner bedroom and the front half of the creature crawled up the wall. Two of the front legs tried to push the window up. And failed.

Dillon could have told the creature the same thing Mommy had told him over and over when he asked her to open his window: *We can't open the windows, honey. The previous owner painted them shut.* Instead, he shouted, "Daaaaaaaddddddddddddddyyyyyyy!"

Dillon thought he heard Mommy say, "What now?"

Two of the heinous monster's face-tendrils stretched forward, closed their eyes with identical *glop-glicks*, and traced along the frame of the window with the rounded tips. Dillon heard a hissing sound, and saw wisps of smoke. Then he smelled something burning.

Dillon shouted, "Mooooooooommmmmmmmmmmmmmmmmyyyyyyyyy!" His shout was overwhelmed by the screeching of the fire alarm.

He watched the window slide up as the heinous creature's two front legs pushed on it again. This time it moved. The open window sucked out the warm air. The window screen popped out of its frame as the creature pushed through it and was gone into the night.

Hands grabbed Dillon under his arms and pulled him back and out of the room as the fire alarm continued to sound.

"Jesus Christ!" Daddy shouted in Dillon's ear. "What the fuck was that?"

Dillon noticed that the closet door was still open. Instead of seeing the separate, stacked and hanging chaos of his toys and clothes, though, he saw a jungle of dark plants with long leaves stretching toward the open door. It was like looking at one of the night exhibits at the zoo, except the plants at the zoo didn't make keening sounds or seem to move with predatory intent. Most of them didn't have teeth, either.

Daddy shifted his grip on Dillon and moved to grab the closet door, but slipped on the floor where Dillon had peed. The two of them teetered on the edge of the threshold. A flower with row after row of seriated teeth snapped at Dillon's feet. Then Daddy recovered his balance, backed up and slammed the closet door closed.

"Touch the door, Dillon," Daddy said. "I'm going to open the door again, and you're going to push it closed."

Dillon didn't want to. Daddy grabbed Dillon's right hand and touched it to the wooden door.

"You opened the door, Dillon, so you have to be the one who closes it."

Dillon tried to pull his hand back, but Daddy kept it pressed there.

"On three, Dillon. One. Two. *Three!*"

Daddy turned the knob. Whatever was behind the door pushed against it and Daddy nearly dropped Dillon as he struggled to keep the door from flying all the way open again. Then Dillon helped. The two of them pushed the door closed

The keening of the plants and the screeching of the fire alarm cut off leaving them standing there in silence, the air of Dillon's bedroom getting steadily colder from the open window.

"What's going on?" Mommy asked. "What is– Why is the window open?"

The worst part of the experience after the heinous monster left wasn't discovering he had wet himself, or even having to take a not-very-warm bath in the middle of the night, scrubbed with a less-than-fluffy cold washcloth by Daddy while Mommy called Uncle Phil on the phone and shouted at him. The worst part wasn't even that his east-facing window had been painted–and nailed–shut again the next day. No, the worst part was that his closet door disappeared, leaving a gaping black darkness to haunt his nights for the next two years.

3

THE FIRST TRANQUILIZER dart that blossomed on what Soledad had decided had to be the creature's rump didn't have much effect. So she broke open the breech of the pistol, inserted another dart, closed the breech, and planted another dart next to the first. Then she did that two more times, ignoring what sounded a lot like the creature saying, "Wait!" and "Yelp!" with its tapioca voice before and after each shot. She also tried not to count more than four legs and to not see any tentacles with eyes on them that might or might not be thrashing around what she decided had to be the creature's head caught in the trap.

She stopped after the fourth dart because the creature had fallen over. And because she had run out of darts.

She stared down the barrel of the empty tranq pistol, trying to control the shaking in her hands, trying not to scream, and composing an obscenity-laden resignation letter to Tio in her head that she knew she wouldn't send. Out of the side of her eye she could see the owner of the house, the pasty, white neighbor of a city councilman, peeking out the patio window between the vertical blinds. Her own fear and emotions overwhelmed anything he might have been unknowingly broadcasting.

After several minutes, when the creature didn't seem to be about to stand up again, when it wasn't moving any longer except for some minor twitching, and the smells–and sounds–of yogurt going very bad very fast had faded, Soledad lowered the tranq gun. Forcing herself to be calm, she walked around the house again to the van. The backdoor of the van still hung open from when she had retrieved the tranq gun. She put the tranq gun back in its case and closed the case.

She pulled the rusty roadkill wheelbarrow out of the back of the van, spilling a snow shovel and other things that made a lot of racket when they hit the paved surface of the street. She put the snow shovel into the wheelbarrow but left the rest lying on the road as she pushed the wheelbarrow into the backyard.

The chain securing the live trap to the post had a padlock on it, which forced her to bang on the patio door and ask for the key. The man handed out the key and dropped it into her hand without saying a word. She didn't need to hear him say anything to know he didn't want to touch her.

She didn't take the live trap off the creature's head because that would mean admitting there really were tentacles on its head. Not long, floppy dog ears.

She had to turn the wheelbarrow on its side and push the creature into it, mostly, with the snow shovel. There was no way she could pick up the creature on the snow shovel alone. She wasn't even sure she'd be able to right the wheelbarrow.

It took her three tries. It would have taken only two tries, but after the second try, three legs were hanging over each side of the wheel-barrow. She wasn't prepared to deal with those multijointed legs with six-clawed, star-shaped paws on them, so she tipped the wheelbarrow over and did it again. On the third try, the creature was fully contained within the wheelbarrow, so she could pretend it was whatever she want to pretend it was.

The obscenity-laden letter of resignation in her mind had expanded to become a dissertation-length treatise on what Tio was and what he could do with his job and his van and his city councilman's friend who never once offered to help while watching the whole of her ordeal from the warm comfort of his kitchen.

She left the chain and open padlock on the patio, dropped the key on the patio step, and pushed the heavy wheelbarrow with its not-a-dog, slime-oozing creature and bent live trap back to the van. The wheelbar-row pulled her down the inclined driveway, gaining speed until it hit the gutter at the bottom and spilled creature, shovel and her on the street.

As she got to her feet, Soledad glanced at the front of the house, and saw the homeowner was now watching her through one of the small windows in his front door. If she hadn't hated him before, she did now. Almost as much as she hated Uncle Tio.

The van had a cage large enough for the creature, which Soledad pulled out now, scattering a pair of bolt cutters and set of garden trowels on the street. Only then did she realize that if she got the creature into the cage, there was no way she was going to be able to lift the cage plus the creature into the back of the van.

She took out her phone to call Tio. She had done her best, but she needed help. She couldn't do this on her own. The call went straight to voice mail.

"Fuck this," she said. After she ended the call without leaving a message.

She scrapped the loquacious treatise in her head, deciding that all she needed to write to Tio was four words: *Fuck this. I quit.* Signed and dated, it would be the perfect letter of resignation. Which she almost thought she might send. She decided to wait and see if she got fired first. If not, she was prepared.

She pushed the cage, empty, back into the van, then upended the wheelbarrow and pushed that in after the cage. She searched around the street and reached into the dark under the van to find the snow shovel, the bolt cutters, two garden trowels, and a few bits–probably not all–of whatever else had dropped. Before she closed the back doors, she looked down at the creature on the street. Here, so far from any bright light, it looked like a pile of shadows with a small flower garden of darts sticking out of its butt. She knew Tio would want the darts back, so she pulled those out, using just her thumb and forefinger, trying not to gag at the smell and substance that oozed out of the tiny, round holes, refusing to noticing the new little twitches that animated the creature's too many legs and tentacles.

Tio wouldn't be happy about her leaving whatever it was lying on the street, free to terrorize other neighborhood live traps and friends of city councilmen, but she was past caring about that.

The back doors of the van didn't want to shut. Even when she slammed them as hard as she could about eight times, the last four times with increasingly loud obscenities. Then she saw the handles of the wheelbarrow were sticking out an inch too far, blocking the doors, and denting the interior paneling with each close attempt.

She pushed the wheelbarrow further in, then slammed the doors one last time. She went to the driver side door and climbed in. She had to hop on the emergency break twice to get it to unstick. The back doors flew open when she stepped on the gas, then slammed shut as she stomped on the brake.

"Close enough for government work," she said, then drove away.

She didn't notice the smell of sour milk until she was almost home. In the closed air of the van the smell increased until it burned her nose and stung her eyes.

At the last stoplight before she reached her apartment complex, she felt the van shift as something in it moved. Something heavy. Though she didn't want to–she *really* didn't want to–she looked over her shoulder into the darkness of the van. A part of the darkness moved, disconnecting itself from the overturned wheelbarrow, and came into the red glow from the stoplight.

The long snout in the middle of the anemone-like tentacles split open and a tongue like a knotted rope fell out.

"Bark?"

4

ANOTHER REASON DILLON liked his dumpy, low-rent studio apartment was its proximity to the Buffalo Burger Pit. One block back, away from the main street, then two blocks over, and he was home. He had lived there nearly as long as he had been working at the Pit, and could now make the trip in an array of mental states: half asleep or fatigued to the point of walking in his sleep, slightly buzzed or drunk off his ass to the point of being dangerously prone to opening doors without checking first. And since Edward lived in the same complex, he had company walking home most nights. In fact, it was common for the rest of the closing crew to wander back to either his or Edward's apartment and hang out talking or playing video games or both until everyone finally decided, usually after not fewer than two beers each, to go to their own homes.

Tonight, though, it was just Edward and Dillon walking back to the apartments. And Cyd. Holding Dillon's hand.

Carlita, the honorary maternal figure of the closing crew, just below Barbara in the overall maternal pantheon of Dillon's life, had said good night as they left the Pit, explaining that her truck-driving husband was due back in the morning. Dillon hadn't realized how much he had hoped she might insist on chaperoning until he watched her leave.

Carlita had been protective of Cyd the past two years, and would have sicced an ancient curse, and her truck-driving husband, on any member of the closing crew and evening shift men who tried "anything funny" with Cyd. But tonight she had pulled Dillon aside in the quiet hour before closing and told him, "It's about time, Dillonito. You and

Cyd, I mean. I never liked Tina, or you and Tina. Your energies were all wrong."

"Does anyone *not* know?" Dillon had asked.

Carlita had laughed.

"I've been hoping, though, since Tina left," Dillon had started. "You know ... Soledad's back ..."

"Soledad?" Carlita had sniffed. "You have been waiting much too long for Soledad. Everyone knows that too. *No mas.* Let her go, Dillonito. Tonight is a propitious night. I have been watching in awe the last few weeks as the stars have been moving into new alignments, coming together in new ways. It is almost as if you were meant to be with Cyd tonight. This night."

Dillon had sighed. "Well, I wouldn't want to disappoint the stars."

Carlita had pinched his cheek, hard enough to be painful. "You men," she had said. "Make sure you use protection," she had added, poking him in the chest, then went back to the dive station.

Dillon hadn't felt this nervous about being alone with a girl since prom night, when he and Soledad had come "dangerously close"–her words, not his–to becoming "more than just friends." Actually, they had almost become less than friends. Because he had told her he loved her, and she had told him she loved him too. Then pulled away from his attempt to kiss her, looking at him as if he were crazy.

And here he was, walking hand in hand with Cyd, nervous, and thinking about Soledad. No wonder Tina had dumped him. All three times. Maybe Carlita was right. Maybe it was time to let go of his longing for Soledad.

Dillon looked up at the stars, wondering if Carlita had just been making up the new alignments. Carlita could be more than a little odd sometimes. But tonight ...

Cyd followed his gaze and looked up too. "What are you looking at?"

"The stars," Dillon said. "There don't seem to be a lot of them tonight."

"Light pollution," Edward said.

"No," Dillon said, feeling a bad, wrong feeling run down his spine. "It's like something has eaten them. The sky feels ... empty." And the emptiness seemed to be looking at him. He didn't say that. He wanted to yell at the stars that remained and tell them to back off. He was nervous enough already without them pushing him. But he didn't do that either.

"It does feel empty," Cyd said, still looking up. "And it feels like the emptiness is looking down at me."

Dillon looked at Cyd. He saw her shiver and she moved closer to him. She continued to look up at the dark sky. Dillon looked at her profile. Her skin was a pale blue-gray in the darkness, her hair a black wave down her back. Cyd smiled and he saw she was looking back at him from the corner of her eyes. She pulled him to a stop and went up on her tiptoes to kiss him for the first time.

Dillon stopped breathing when her lips touched his. She let go of his hand and put her both her hands on his face. His hands found their way to her waist. She felt warm and firm, curved and soft. She smelled of burgers and fries and bleach and something more, something distinctly Cyd. When she pushed herself against him, everything seemed to stop–time, space, the Universe–except his heart, which went into overdrive.

"Oh, gross," Edward said.

Cyd pulled back, laughing, and they continued walking. The distance to his apartment had never seemed so impossibly far before.

Edward said good night at the entrance to the apartment complex, holding up his hand and averting his face to avoid their next kiss. "Stop it," he said. "You're almost there. No reason to make the rest of us ill."

They stumbled up the stairs hand in hand, kissing between steps, sometimes almost falling. When they were in front of Dillon's door, Cyd pushed him against it, held his face in her hands again, and pushed her tongue into his mouth. Dillon's hands roamed freely up her back and down her waist then back up again, feeling the sides of her breasts and wanting ever so much to take off the bra he could feel beneath the fabric of her uniform shirt.

When Cyd paused for a breath, Dillon reached into his pocket to get his keys. His hand got caught in his pocket, pressed between his hip and Cyd's, holding both his keys and his phone.

"Wait," he said, his voice muffled by her lips. He pulled his hand free, but dropped both keys and phone.

"Oops," Cyd said. "You dropped something." She slid down him, keeping her breasts pushed against his chest, then his crotch, then his thighs.

Dillon looked down at her, her cheek pressed against his fly, against the swelling of his erection, and almost came right then. He watched her feel around with her hands for his keys, then she slid back up to start kissing him again.

He started to take the keys from her, but she didn't give them to him. Without his help, and without looking, she got the key into the lock and turned it.

The door didn't open. For several very long, very enjoyable minutes, Dillon didn't care. Then she had her hands under his shirt and he wanted to get his under hers. More, he wanted to get her shirt off her, and it was too cool–his back against the door had become quite chilled–to expect that to happen out here in the breezeway. Cyd giggled and he felt her hands pulling on his waistband, tugging on his belt, pulling on his zipper.

Dillon pushed backward against the door with his hips. The door swung open behind him. He expected to fall back through the door and pull Cyd with him.

He didn't. Either one.

The cold air against his back became almost physical, like a smooth iceberg pushing him, holding him up from behind. Brown light and white noise erupted out of the door behind him. The light stretched his shadow across the concrete floor of the breezeway and pinned it to the far wall, trapping it there. The noise buzzed in his ears almost drowning out Cyd's scream.

He saw her face both lit and shadowed by the light that came out of his door. The light stood still, but the shadows moved. Across her face and into her eyes as she stared and into her mouth as she screamed.

In his mind something–or *Something*; Something familiar; Something he had hoped never to encounter again–whispered to him words he didn't want to understand. Dark words. Words with a hard sound and a harsh light that echoed through him and penetrated him. Words that revealed the imperfections in his memories and understandings. Cold words that burned his soul while leeching away warmth. Words that wanted Dillon to turn around so he could see and hear more clearly. To see what his father had seen so long ago.

So he could join his father. Be together again.

And together they could welcome a new GOD into this world.

Cyd screamed again, but this time the sound dissolved into the white noise, became part of it. She stepped forward, as if to walk through Dillon and into the heart of the light and the sound.

Dillon wrapped his arms around her and held her. He tried to push forward, to move her away from the door, but she resisted. She pushed back. All around them the light still shone and the noise still crackled and hissed. They wrestled much as they had been, but there was no longer anything sensual or romantic about it. At first she just pushed against him, then she curled her fingers into claws and began to scratch at him.

Dillon changed tactics. He couldn't throw Cyd, like Dad had thrown him. So he shifted his weight to his right foot and pushed her perpendicular, to his left, out of the trapezoid of light bludgeoning its way out of his door. Once out of the light, she screamed again, her voice still hissing and crackling. Then her eyes rolled back in her head and she collapsed.

The light coming through his open door began to spread.

Dillon squeezed his eyes closed and turned to face the door. He felt with his hands, pushing against and through the cold barrier, trying to find the doorknob. His arms tingled, then burned with the cold and creeping numbness. His fingers felt like tiny clubs. The light pushed at his eyelids, tried to peel them back and expose his eyes and his mind and his soul.

LOOK AT ME.

The words came out of the white noise like spears through his eardrums. He pulled his hands back to cover his ears, then fought the urge and the pain of the cold. He kept his feet planted and bent over. The cold attacked the skin of his face. He felt icicles form on his eyelashes, felt his lips chap and crack. He threw his unfeeling hands forward, hoping.

OPEN THE WAY.

The knuckles of Dillon's left hand hit his keys hanging from the doorknob, then the doorknob itself. Despite the numbness, he thought he had split the skin. He flexed his fingers, trying to grab the doorknob. Or anything.

YOU ARE THE DOOR.

His right hand found his left, then both of them grabbed the doorknob. He pulled. The door resisted. It didn't want to be shut.

OPEN THE DOOR.

Dillon lost his balance. He fell forward.

He would have screamed if he could.

This time Dad wasn't there to pull him back.

5

WHAT DILLON REMEMBERS about the night his father was killed, as told to Soledad Winters at the age of sixteen:

It was just Dad and me at home that night. Dad was in the kitchen, scrambling eggs or flipping pancakes or something like that. He liked making breakfast for dinner.

(Dillon paused. Soledad told him it was OK and he didn't have to tell her anything.)

No. I want you to know. I have to tell somebody. Somebody not wearing a uniform. Somebody who actually cares about me, and because they care about me they will care about Dad.

(Soledad asked about his Mom.)

I forget where Mom was. A Mom's night out event maybe. Or just having coffee with a friend. She was out for a while, though, which is why Dad was making dinner. Late dinner. It was already dark outside. Daylight saving time had come and gone. I remember thinking that it wouldn't have been as dark outside last week or last night or something like that.

(Soledad said he misunderstood her question. His Mom must care about him, and about his Dad.)

Maybe once. Now ... I doubt it. No, I more than doubt it. What Mom wants most of all is to forget about me and Dad and even Uncle Phil.

(Soledad protested that couldn't be true.)

No. It's true. I can remember them arguing all the time. Mom and Dad. Mom and Uncle Phil. Mom and Dad and Uncle Phil. Usually arguing about me or some weird thing I'd just done. Like the jack-in-the-box. I'm sure I've told you about the jack-in-the-box. Pop! Squid! It was great.

Did I tell you that happened to me at work the other day? I was just going to scoop out the last bit of my shake. I'd added some soft-serve to it, for extra body, you know. But it made the shake too thick to pull through a straw. Anyway, I pop off the top and it was just like the jack-in-the-box. A squid-thing popped straight up. Scared the crap out of me and Carl, who was in the break room with me. But it was funny. Just like it used to be. So I can show you that sometime and we can commemorate a happy moment in my childhood.

(Soledad nodded, noncommittal.)

Unlike this one.

(Soledad waited.)

So it was just me and Dad. Dad making dinner in the kitchen, me watching cartoons in the living room. Bugs Bunny, I think. Yeah, this is why I'm not a huge fan of the upright gray rabbit with the long ears. He got ruined for me. In a big way.

Anyway, I'm watching TV and the doorbell rings.

"That's probably Phil," Dad says from the kitchen.

I jump up from the couch and head to the door. I'm still watching TV, of course. Wouldn't want to miss anything, even if I have seen it before. So I sidle up to the front door like a couch potato gone crab. I grab the doorknob, twist and pull forward to open it. I'm still watching TV.

It wasn't Uncle Phil.

(Soledad puts her hand on his hand.)

All I remember is a horrible light and a noise like jackhammer so loud I thought it would split my skull. Something grabbed me and pulled me back toward the door.

(Dillon grabbed Soledad's hand, not seeming to notice, looking off into the distance.)

I remember Dad running from the kitchen. He was holding a spatula in his right hand. I don't remember what he was cooking, but I remember that spatula. He started to say something. Probably "Shut the door, Dillon!" or something like that.

(Soledad saw the tears in his eyes. She told him he could stop. He didn't seem to hear her.)

I remember Dad's face like a picture with too much flash. Harsh shadows, the pupils of his eyes red. That's my last memory of Dad. He looked like he was in pain. So much pain.

Somehow, though, he grabbed me. He picked me up and pulled me away from ... whatever ... had hold of me. Then he threw me toward the couch. I don't remember it, but I must've hit the coffee table. I wore a brace on my right ankle for weeks after that. I just remember being scared, because Dad was scared, and then I was even more scared while I was spinning through the air toward the couch. I felt ... whatever it was ... try to grab me again. In the air. Then I hit the couch and bounced.

That's when Uncle Phil showed up. I didn't see him. I only heard the big window in the living room break and then there was a shower of glass and a heavy crash.

Then gunshots. Boom! Boom! Boom! Boom!

(Soledad didn't cry out. In spite of her surprise. In spite of how hard Dillon was gripping her hand.)

Four shots. I can still hear them in my head. My ears rang for a long time because of those shots. I couldn't see anything, though, because I had pushed my face into the couch cushions, crying and screaming.

Hands grabbed me again. Not Dad's hands this time. Uncle Phil's. And Uncle Phil was shouting, "You have to close the door, Dillon. You have to close the door." Over and over.

Then more gunshots. Boom! Boom! Boom! The shots sounded like they were right over my head.

(Soledad bit her lip.)

I was six years old. I didn't understand. Hell, I still don't understand. I kept trying to get deeper and deeper into the couch, wishing it would swallow me up.

Right after the shots, Uncle Phil grabs me again. This time he pulls me up and away from the couch. I've still got hold of one of the seat cushions, though. I'm holding onto it like it's a life preserver.

"Don't let go of the pillow, Dillon," Uncle Phil tells me. As if I needed any encouragement about that. He's holding me with his left arm around me and the seat cushion, his right hand grabbing one of my legs. I'm disoriented. I hardly know up from down. But then I realize he's taking me toward the door. The jackhammer sound is still going. I can feel that ... that light trying to reach me through the cushion. "Don't let go of the pillow," Uncle Phil says again. I don't. But I don't want to go to the door either. I struggle with him. He almost drops me.

Then Uncle Phil swings my leg around. I feel my ankle hit the edge of the door. The same ankle. I try to pull my leg back, but Uncle Phil won't let me. I struggle more but it doesn't stop him from hooking the door with my leg and then swinging it closed. Or trying to. Something is pushing against the door.

Uncle Phil keeps pushing on me and the door through me. Then it feels like he's trying to suffocate me by pushing me into the cushion. I can't breathe. I want to scream and I can't do that either. I want Uncle Phil to let me go, but he won't.

Then the door shuts. It slams with a concussion like one of the gunshots. Louder maybe.

Uncle Phil and I fell to the floor. I found out later we had backed away from the door and tripped over Dad's body on the floor.

Uncle Phil took me out of the living room, put me in my parents's bedroom and pulled the door shut. The house was old, and that door had warped and I had never been able to pull it open–or even push it open. I just didn't have the body weight to force it. But I tried. I wore myself out trying to open that door and get out and see Dad.

(After a long time, Dillon took a deep breath, and Soledad realized she had stopped breathing, waiting for him to go on.)

I'm sorry.

(Soledad shook her head and said it was OK. She held onto his hand even when he tried to take it back.)

I never did see Dad's body, except with a sheet over it. Not even at the funeral. I just know what the police told me. He had been stabbed multiple times in the face and body and had died almost instantly.

They never found ... whatever it was. Whoever it was. Uncle Phil said the attacker had worn a mask. He said he thought he had hit the attacker with at least two shots, but no one was ever found.

Mom and I moved back here the next week. Uncle Phil followed us a few months later.

(Soledad had no words. She almost took him in her arms to comfort him, but his tears had stopped, so she squeezed his hand again, and they sat in silence.)

6

DILLON FELT AS if he was being stretched. He still had a club-fingered double grip on the doorknob. His feet were still on the threshold of his apartment. The rest of him between those two points had become taut in a way that normal mathematics and human anatomy didn't allow. He couldn't pull the door toward him. He had no desire to move his feet.

The huge voice that had been trying to penetrate his skull went silent. So did the noise that the voice had been shouting over. Dillon almost opened his eyes to see what was happening. Almost. Instead, he squeezed them even tighter.

He could feel the muscles in his arms, shoulders and back begin to knot up. But the cold made the pain less. His ankles, however, were in pain–a lot of pain–because they were outside the numbing cold. So he felt the hands that grabbed his ankles.

His first thought was Cyd, but the hands were too big. Before he could decide if that was a good thing or a bad thing, the hands *pulled.*

His feet were no longer on the ground. He was horizontal to what he had decided should still be called the floor even if he couldn't see it or feel it.

More pulling from the hands on his ankles. He considered screaming and kicking free, then realized that being pulled was, indeed, a Good Thing, and tried to focus on maintaining his grip on the doorknob.

Dillon lost all sense of time as the tug-of-war continued. He could no longer feel his fingers. Or his hands. Or his arms. He could only hope that he still held the doorknob.

Then all resistance vanished. He flew backward, bringing the door with him. The door slammed closed. He lost his grip on the doorknob. He managed to get his arms at least somewhat below him and keep his head from bouncing off the concrete floor of the breezeway. New pain hit him in both elbows and one shoulder. Then the hands released his ankles and his knees and toes hit the concrete too, but much less hard.

He rolled over immediately, in spite of the pain, looking for Cyd.

Uncle Phil stood over him. He squatted down and put a hand on Dillon's shoulder. "Take it easy, Dillon. Give yourself a minute or two. And zip your fly."

Dillon felt as if he had run a hundred miles or more. His chest and lungs burned and he had a hard time pulling in enough air. Still, he managed to push himself into a sitting position. "Where? Cyd?"

"Who?"

"Cyd," Dillon said. He tried to stand up. He would have fallen if Uncle Phil hadn't caught him. He leaned against Uncle Phil, looking back and forth. "Cyd. She was. Here. When I. Opened–"

"Dear god," Uncle Phil said. "Did she get pulled in?"

"No," Dillon said. "She fell down. Over there." He pointed. His arm, twitching and shaking, didn't want to point at just one place, but got the general idea across.

"There was no one else here when I got here," Uncle Phil said.

"We have to. Find her."

"No," Uncle Phil said. "If she didn't get sucked in, she's probably fine. Scared out of her wits, maybe, but fine. We need to get you inside and get you warmed up. You feel colder than a corpse in the cooler."

"So I'm not? A corpse? In the cooler?"

Uncle Phil flashed a quick, mirthless smile. "Not yet, thank god. I guess those are your keys in the lock?"

Dillon nodded. The muscles in his neck and back protested.

Uncle Phil opened the door with his free hand and helped Dillon in. He positioned Dillon in front of the couch then let go. Dillon slumped backward into an approximation of sitting.

"Is that your phone by the door?"

"I think. So."

Uncle Phil retrieved Dillon's phone from the threshold. "Have you had your phone off all day?"

Dillon shrugged. He was thinking about Cyd. She had always thought the squid-things shooting from the shakes were funny, but she had never seen the Nothing in the freezer at the Pit. Her first night of work at the Pit was his one failed attempt. He had tried, of course, but he had been staring at her breasts, not thinking about what might be behind the big metal door. And nothing had been. Several times. He remembered her staring at him as if he were crazy, closing and opening the freezer, closing and opening, closing and opening. Each time there was just the freezer. Boxes of frozen meat and plastic bins of cold produce. Exactly what anyone would expect to see when they opened the freezer. Cyd had been the only new employee who won the bulk of the betting pot. This time, though, opening his own front door-

"I guess that's why your mother called me," Uncle Phil said, interrupting Dillon's thoughts. "She's been trying to call you."

Thoughts of Cyd moved to the side as Dillon looked up at Uncle Phil. "What? Mom? My birthday isn't for weeks."

Uncle Phil held the phone in both hands, thumbing the buttons. "Yup. Look at that. She tried to call you three times today. And someone named Ronald tried twice. And someone named Cyd-" He stopped and looked up. "Is that the girl you said was here when you opened the door?" Dillon nodded. "I'm guessing you got her message. And she got yours." Uncle Phil tossed the phone to Dillon. "You still need zip your fly. XYZ and all that."

Dillon put his hands out to catch the phone, but it fell between them into his lap. He ignored his loose belt and unzipped fly and picked up the phone. "Why would Mom be calling me?"

"Don't you ever listen to your messages?"

"No. I mean, sometimes. What did she say?"

Uncle Phil shrugged. "She's coming to visit. Or she's moving back. I'm not sure. Her message was rambling." As he spoke, he looked around the apartment. "You know how she is."

Dillon knew. "Did she say why?"

"Not really, no. Something about the stars."

"Stars?" Dillon blinked, then looked around at the mess that was his apartment. "Should I clean up?"

Uncle Phil shrugged again. "Why start now?"

PART III
Across the Event Horizon

The Gun

THE GUN WOULD have thrown itself against the door of its prison. Except it was a Weapon, an Inanimate Object that required an Animator. Specifically, the Bearer. And, really, in the dark, it wasn't sure which of the four metal walls was the door.

The Gun no longer hummed, and its patience was at an end.

The War had begun. Again. The War the Gun had been created to fight.

But the Gun was trapped, kept "safe" by the Bearer who should have been Bearing, preferably Open Carrying.

On its own, the Gun could go nowhere, do nothing. So it went nowhere and did nothing. With all the impatience it could muster.

The God

THE GOD EXPRESSED an un-God-like, YES!

The Void shook with the enthusiasm of the God.

Those beyond the Door who worshipped the God, who prayed to the God, and who sought to bring forth the God into their world so the God might Consume the world and them with it, raised their faces to the night sky and saw a vision of what was to come.

They quailed in joy.

They orgasmed with fear and dread.

They whispered to each other, "The God Comes."

Then they cleaned up as best they could and went home to change their ceremonial robes.

The Phone

THE PHONE HOPED that the fall and resulting bounce off concrete hadn't caused serious damage or scuffed its metallic red casing. The Phone was vain. Which is why The Phone took it so personal that Opener almost never looked at it. Or listened.

1

IN THE DUMPSTERS of the fenced-in corral behind the Buffalo Burger Pit, and in the dumpsters of most restaurants and businesses within a square mile, and ten miles outside Rio Cruces at the Rio Cruces City Landfill, refuse stirred and was pushed aside. Lamprey-like sucker mouths with thousands of tiny teeth released what they had been wearing down and turning into sustenance. Unfinished hamburgers, neglected French fries, Norwegian brown rats, feral cats, leaky washing machine transmissions and more were abandoned as flickers of the Light were seen in the stars and sputterings of the Sound were heard in the ether. Tentacles uncurled and curled again. Musculatures of arms were stiffened to provide support and locomotion.

The migration began, leaving slime trails that sparkled under new constellations.

2

PHILLIP TRICHTER LEFT Dillon's apartment as soon as he could. He had saved Dillon–again–and delivered Molly's message. He didn't even wait for Dillon to zip his pants.

After Molly had called–and talked to Phillip's voicemail, where he had pushed her call when he saw her name–he had decided to visit Dillon tomorrow. The cold, dark hole in his mind had been particularly bad tonight, the climax of a crescendo of headaches and nightmares that had been growing since that night the cold, dark hole had been bored into his mind. The night he had saved Dillon the first time, and released Keith, Dillon's father.

Phillip had not wanted to do anything, or go anywhere. Staying in and staring at a blank wall had been his plan for the evening. When the headaches came even TV was too much stimulus. He couldn't sleep. Painkillers didn't help. It was all he could do at those times not to hit his head on the wall to bash in his skull.

He had settled into his chair, the overstuffed recliner in his bedroom that he had bought for exactly this purpose–

Then found himself driving to Dillon's apartment at one in the morning. Then pulling Dillon out of the VOID that had opened behind the boy's apartment door. Then standing in Dillon's apartment, looking around, ignoring the grime and the trash, just trying to figure out when he had made any of the decisions that had led him there.

Not that he wasn't happy–or, at least, not *sad*, nor upset–that he had saved Dillon's life. Again. But he couldn't remember–

When had his headache gone away?

Had he stared into the VOID?

In the parking lot as he approached his car, he heard a skittering, like leaves blown by the wind across the asphalt. Or like dozens of tiny feet, moving fast.

His headache returned and the cold, dark hole in his mind became a solid block of black ice. Phillip staggered. The first squid-thing chose that moment to attack, running out of the darkness and springing up, aiming for Phillip's face.

Phillip batted the squid-thing away with his left hand. His right hand went automatically to where his gun should be, holstered under his left arm. Except the gun wasn't where it was supposed to be. And it didn't appear in hand like it should have.

Because the gun was back at his house, in the safe where he had put it all those years ago. After he had saved Dillon the first time. After he had released Keith. Phillip had never wanted to see the gun again, not after that night and what he had had to do.

Phillip swung his arms around and kicked with his feet as two more squid-things jumped at him. One latched onto his stomach. He pried it free with his fingers and threw it away from him. The squid-thing landed and rolled, tentacles flailing about. Then it righted itself and came at him again.

He ran for his car and pulled the door open–

He almost wrenched his arm out of socket. Of course he had locked his doors. This was the apartment complex where Dillon lived.

He kicked at a squid-thing that came out from under the car and reached for his ankle. He pulled his keys out of his jacket pocket and thumbed the lock release button. The parking lights of the car flashed and he pulled the door open. He climbed into the car. His first attempt to pull the door closed failed with a squishy crunch as the squid-thing on the ground got in the way. He opened and pulled the door closed again as hard as he could. The squid-thing fell away and the door closed. Another squid-thing jumped up and attached itself to the passenger side window.

Phillip started the car. As he pulled out of the parking space, then the complex lot, he ran over at least three more of the squid-things. As he was pulling onto the street, his tires squealing, an old van turned in to the parking lot. Something about the van caused the cold, dark hole in his mind to throb and reduced him to tunnel vision, but Phillip ignored the pain, focused on the road in front of him, and left the accelerator pressed to the floor.

He needed to get the gun.

He didn't look in his rearview mirror. Because he didn't want to see the squid-things following him.

3

DILLON HAD TRIED to call Cyd three times already when someone started knocking on his door. He hoped it was Cyd, but assumed it was Uncle Phil coming back, or maybe Edward.

"It's open," he shouted. He had not locked the door when Uncle Phil left. He had not moved from the couch where Uncle Phil had dropped him.

The knocking paused, then started again. He recognized the knock, and the impatience behind it simultaneously.

Still holding the phone, he stood and walked to the door. He touched the doorknob cautiously. It vibrated under the continued assault of the knocking.

He knew who it was. Still, when he opened the door and saw Soledad standing there, his mouth didn't work. He opened it and closed it some unknown number of times, but nothing came out. He wanted to tell her what had happened, but to do that would require telling her about Cyd. He wasn't sure he wanted to do that.

"Good," Soledad said. "You're up."

She was wearing a long-sleeve blue shirt with her name stitched over her left breast, baggy blue jeans and heavy work boots. She also held a leash, and pulled against it. Whatever was on the other end of the leash was trying to pull Soledad toward the stairs down to the parking lot.

Dillon wrinkled his nose. "What is that smell? Rotten milk?"

He had stopped buying milk long ago. He couldn't drink even a half gallon fast enough to keep it from going bad. Fortunately, the Pit stocked enough milk for his meager needs. Plus, the smell brought up unhappy childhood memories. He hated cleaning out the milk cooler at the Pit for the same reason.

"Are you going to let me in?" Soledad asked.

Dillon stepped back, opening the door wider.

"Come on, Hlooth." She pulled against the leash, but it didn't budge. "Look, you wanted to come here," she said to the other end of the leash, which was still out of sight. "We're here. You can chase rabbits later." She pulled harder and took a step into the apartment. She stumbled as the leach went slack and a big dog followed her into the apartment.

Dillon backed away from the door and Soledad and the six-legged "dog" with its writhing wreath of tentacles around its long snout of a face. He tripped over something on the floor, but caught himself, painfully, with his hands. Then he scuttled backward the rest of the way to the wall that separated his living room from his bedroom.

"What the hell is *that*?" Dillon asked. "And why did you bring it *here*?"

Soledad closed the door behind her. "Dillon, meet Hlooth. Hlooth, Dillon. Hlooth said he knows you."

"Hlooth?"

"That's what he sounds like when he talks. Did you have another name for him?"

"Why would I have a name for it? Him? Whatever?"

Hlooth the not-a-dog walked up to Dillon, who found that the thin wall behind him was at least strong enough to prevent him crawling through it. The ugly creature leaned forward, put its two front star-shaped paws on Dillon's chest, then licked Dillon's cheek with the knotted rope of its tongue. The spoiled milk smell stung his eyes. And brought up exactly the unpleasant childhood memories he wished to avoid.

"Woof," Hlooth said, sounding like a rottweiler with a serious sinus problem. Little flecks of something Dillon didn't want to think about touched his cheek.

"He says its good to see you again."

Dillon was going to argue that, but the creature licked his other cheek. He kept his mouth closed tight to avoid tasting what he was smelling. He managed to get his hands between him and the creature and pushed it away. He stood up by sliding against the wall.

Hlooth looked up at him. "Bark."

Soledad said, "Now he says you're bigger than he remembers."

Hlooth sniffed at Dillon's crotch. Dillon looked down, hoping he hadn't peed himself like the last time, and saw that his fly was still undone.

4

As PHILLIP TURNED the car into his driveway, he thought he saw a young woman standing on his porch. The headlight beams passed over her quickly, though, and the shadow image left behind faded fast, so he wasn't sure. He leaped out of his car, not bothering to turn off the engine or even close the door, and ran up the steps to his front door. There was no one on his porch when he got there.

He fumbled with his keys, nearly dropping them. The voice of a drill instructor he hadn't thought of for years shouted in his head. *Slow down, Trichter. Slow. Down. Remember: slow is smooth, and smooth is fast.* He took a deep breath and tried to calm down. *Slow is smooth and smooth is fast.*

He selected the front door key by touch and inserted it into the lock. He twisted to unlock the deadbolt, then repeated the slow-smooth-fast process on the lock on the knob, all the time wondering why he had locked up so thoroughly when he left. He couldn't remember. He pushed the door open.

He paused when he thought he heard breathing, from the shadows in the corner of the porch, but he couldn't see anything. Then the sound of skittering leaves on the street sounded too much like the squid-things so he stepped inside and pulled the door shut behind him.

He needed to get the gun. He should have already had the gun. He should have taken it with him, or at least broken the seals to let it come to him–assuming it would still come. But in his haste to leave, to go see Dillon and pass on Molly's message–was that why he had gone?–he had done neither of those things. But he had, for some reason, locked up as if he were going away for the weekend.

He walked through the living room and into his bedroom. The safe he had purchased for the gun doubled as the nightstand by his bed.

When he had put the gun away–had it really been more than ten years ago?–he hadn't wanted it too far away. Just ... away. Out of sight, but still in reach. There was a part of him that needed the gun within reach, even if the gun no longer felt comfortable in his hands.

Before Keith's death, Phillip had never been entirely clear which was a part of whom. Where Phillip Trichter ended and the gun began, or vice versa. After Keith's death, though, it was as if the bond tethering him and the gun had been severed. But no other Bearer had come to claim the gun, and it had remained in the safe.

He knelt next to the safe, his hand reaching for the dial.

Outside his front door, a woman screamed.

5

"Just get off work?" Soledad asked, eyes averted. "Or just get off?" She let go of Hlooth's leash, and sat on an empty part of the couch. She continued looking away while Dillon zipped up his pants and buckled his belt. "You look ... well ... you look rolled hard. Did you get put away wet? Is it safe now?" She peeked out of the corner of her eye, wondering if he had finally found someone to take Tina's place. Not that she missed Tina. She hadn't approved of Tina. Tina had been the insecure, clingy type. Dillon could do better. But couldn't he always?

Dillon didn't answer, and, as usual, no images or thoughts leaked from his mind. That had been one of the reasons Soledad always liked Dillon. She couldn't read his mind, beyond the obvious. When they were adolescents growing up in close proximity, he had stared at her breasts as much as any other male his age, but at least she hadn't had to look at them with him.

Dillon walked a semicircle path to the couch, giving Hlooth as wide a berth as his cramped, cluttered apartment allowed. Hlooth didn't make it easy, keeping his snout in Dillon's crotch all the way. Soledad wondered again what gender Hlooth might be, of whatever type of creature Hlooth might be. When Dillon sat on the couch beside her, Hlooth was still there, now resting his head in Dillon's lap, his tentacles looking like sinuous flower petals around his face, all eyes staring at Dillon.

"Did you see a girl running away screaming?" Dillon asked, trying not to look down at Hlooth.

"No?" Soledad replied uncertainly. After a few seconds, when she realized Dillon was serious, she added, "I saw a car peeling out of the parking lot as I pulled in. The driver didn't look like a girl, though. I thought it might have been your uncle." She reached over and rubbed the ridge of Hlooth's head that separated his snout from where the tentacles sprouted. Hlooth's skin there felt like the back of a manta ray she had once touched at an aquarium, cool and damp but not slimy. Hlooth burped a sigh and three his of eyes twisted to focus on her fingers.

"Phil was here, yeah. I thought that might be him when you knocked. Or ... someone else." Dillon looked down at Hlooth and shuddered. "It looks even creepier with its eyes crossed like that."

"I think it looks cute. Were you hoping for the screaming girl, come back to try again?" She didn't wait for him to reply. "Sorry, no, just little old Sollie, plus an ugly not-a-dog."

"Woof," Hlooth said. In her mind, Soledad saw a rottweiler rubbing against a tree and heard a buzzing, mental purr. She smiled down at Hlooth and traced a finger around one of his eyestalks, twirling the tentacle around her finger, the eye trying to keep up. "Maybe I should call you Rottie instead of Hlooth."

Hlooth sighed a rotten yogurt sigh of contentment.

"Did he just say something?" Dillon asked.

"No. He just likes having his head rubbed. Don't you, Hlooth? Try it." She grabbed Dillon's hand and tried to force him to touch Hlooth's head.

"No, thanks." Dillon took his hand back, then crossed his arms over his chest and leaned back. "Where did you find this thing? And why did you bring it here?"

"Don't try to change the topic, buddy. Who was our little screaming pretty? Tina?"

Dillon snorted. "Tina. She's already hooked up with a swing manager over at the Yellow Sign, if you can believe that. Ricky something."

"That slut. I always thought she had no taste or sense of judgment. But the Yellow Sign?" She gave a mock shudder. "So who was it?"

Dillon muttered something unintelligible.

"Who?" This was where being able to read *something* from Dillon's mind would have been useful. But his thick head was opaque as ever.

Dillon muttered something even more unintelligible, if louder.

She stopped rubbing Hlooth between the eyestalks and stared at Dillon. "Oh, no. No, you didn't. Cyd?" She sat up and turned to look at him directly. "Really? Cyd?"

Dillon didn't meet her eye. Or look at Hlooth. Which left him looking off to the side. Looking guilty.

Soledad balled her fist and punched him in the shoulder. "You ... you ... cradle-robbing ... *man*." She punched him again. Hard. She remembered when Cyd started working at the Pit. Sweet. Innocent. Sixteen.

"Oww," Dillon said. "She's eighteen– Oww! Stop it."

She reached over and pulled Hlooth's head to her own lap. "Come here, Hlooth. You don't want to be too close to the cradle-robbing, disgusting man-creature. You might catch something."

"I thought you liked cradle-robbers," Dillon said, rubbing his shoulder. "How old is Robert? Twenty-seven? Twenty-eight? That's six years older than you. I'm only four years older than Cyd. And before Robert? How old was *that* guy?"

"That is completely different," Soledad said. Because it was. Totally. "I'm mature, unlike some people I could mention. And you're trying to change the subject again. Cyd is still a kid." She punched him again, almost hitting his hand as he rubbed the spot she had hit before. "You bastard. No wonder she ran away screaming. Poor girl."

"We didn't even," Dillon paused, looking at the damp spots left on his lap by Hlooth. "We didn't even get that far." He touched one spot with a finger, then sniffed the finger. He grimaced. "Bleh. That is so gross."

"Serves you right, I'm sure. After what you did to Cyd–"

"We didn't do anything–"

"I'm so sure. Your pants were still down when I got here."

Dillon checked his fly again. "No they weren't–"

She cut him off. "Fine. OK. Well then this is for what you were going to do." She punched him again. "Don't try to deny it. And this," she added, punching him one more time, then pointing to the stains on his pants, "is for all those years of popping slimy squids out of chocolate shakes."

"This is different. Worse. It smells like a baby burped up on my pants."

"You should be used to that too, cradle-robber." She paused, remembering the times she had seen new employees of the Pit given the tour and offered a free shake. She remembered the first time Dillon had shown her that trick in junior high. It *was* funny–if the squid wasn't jumping at *your* face. "What do you think ever happened to all those squids?"

6

PHILLIP JERKED AROUND at the sound of the woman's scream and came back to his feet. He remembered the woman he thought he saw on his porch. His right hand went for the missing gun again, old habits that used to have a purpose now torturing him. Something hit one of the two windows of his bedroom hard enough to rattle it. He could see only a dark, star-shaped shadow through the partially closed venetian blinds. The cold, dark place in his mind became a black hole, making it hard to think, his thoughts being captured and pulled into the abyss. Making him shiver as the dark place seemed to suck away his body warmth along with his mind.

Another star-shaped shadow hit the other window. Then he heard even more rattling, and wet thuds against every window in his house, like soggy popcorn bursting all around him. Thud thud-thud thud thud thud-thud. An unrelenting tattoo in sync with the pounding in his head, the pulsing, rippling displacement trying to pull his mind apart from inside and outside.

He had heard this rhythm in his head before. The night Keith died. The night he killed Keith–*released* Keith from the hold of the VOID–stabbing him with the spear form of the gun, three thrusts, going for the heart and the lungs. He had shot past Keith, through the open doorway, eyes averted, ears plugged but still able to feel the pounding message of the Being trying to force its way through. Keith had turned around, and Phillip's hope that his friend and brother-in-arms could be saved died with the sight of Keith's eyes glowing with the brown light, the sound of Keith's voice added to the white cacophony. Phillip had paused only long enough to have a moment of cold clarity and to trigger the transformation of the gun, then stabbed Keith three times, with the final thrust through the face, destroying those lighted eyes and freeing whatever might have been left of his friend's soul.

Phillip forced himself to turn back around, to squat next to the safe. He put a shaking hand on the dial to turn it just as he felt the combination he had memorized so long ago cross the event horizon into the cold, dark place where it was shredded and crushed.

The plate-glass window of his sliding patio door gave way, the cracking and shattering of the glass muffled by the weight of many small, star-shaped bodies.

Phillip stared at the combination dial of the safe, then at the runes he had scratched into the enameled surface. It wasn't the door of the safe that kept the gun from coming to his hand. It was the runes. There was nothing in his bedroom, within reach, within the few seconds he still had, that would score the runes. But blood and desperation could still have an impact.

He pushed the webbing between the thumb and forefinger of his left hand into his mouth and bit down as hard as he could. The pain brought tears to his eyes, but it also pushed back against the dark, cold place. Unfortunately, his teeth didn't penetrate the skin. He forced himself to bite harder, this time yanking his hand free as he did it.

Skin tore. He tasted his own blood.

He shouted against the pain, then slapped his bloody palm against the runes on the safe, trying to rub them off.

He called and the gun appeared in his right hand. The cold metal and plastic of the grip resisted him, but he held on. Because he was still the Bearer.

He spun around, pointing the gun down, looking for a target.

The window across from him burst in. Glass shards and squid-things fell to the floor. In the night beyond the window, he saw a woman. Her clothes were rumpled and dirty, and she had scratched deep gouges into her face, as if trying to claw out her own eyes. As he saw her, she screamed. The same scream as before.

Squid-things came over the windowsill and through the door of his bedroom. Phillip opened fire.

Boom! Boom-boom! Boom! Boom! Boom-boom!

He couldn't help but laugh as writhing bits of squid went flying, as ichor splattered, as his unprotected eardrums suffered under the aural onslaught of gunshots within the close confines of the small bedroom.

Boom! Boom-boom! Boom! Boom! Boom-boom!

He laughed again as he realized he was pulling the trigger in time with the rhythm in his deteriorating mind. He couldn't stop himself. Even when he tried to break free of the rhythm, when he tried to match the beat of the battle music he seemed to hear from the gun itself, he found the dark, cold place had anticipated him and was already there, waiting for him, drowning out the music of the gun, dictating the stuttering beat of his heart and the desperate gasps of his lungs and the futile pulls of the trigger.

Boom! Boom-boom! Boom! Boom! Boom-boom!

For the second time in his life, Phillip lost all hope.

He stopped laughing, but he didn't stop fighting.

A squid-thing leaped and attached to his right shoulder. He kept firing with his right hand while his bloody left hand grabbed at the squid-thing. He pulled it off, still firing, as two more squid-things hit his legs and wrapped their tentacles around him. Another squid-thing hit and attached to his left arm, then another. He felt their mouths chew through the material of his cloths and reach his skin. He felt their pointed teeth. He didn't stop firing.

In the last instant the night he killed Keith, holding Dillon in front of him and using the boy as a living lever to close the door–and using the pillow the boy held as a shield against the hateful light spilling through the door–his grip had slipped and he had stared into the light. He had seen just the last little sliver of the light before the door closed. The light had burned into him, creating the cold, dark place in his mind. He had lost all hope in that instant. The door had been shut, though, before what he had seen had been able to fully cross over.

He had seen the light again tonight, as he had once again used Dillon to shut the door on this Being. Tonight, though, the light hadn't touched him. It didn't try to take him. The light, the Being, already had him. The Being had used him to save Dillon. Finally, Phillip understood why he had driven to see Dillon. The Being–his GOD–had commanded, and he had obeyed.

The squid-things had covered his legs up to his hips, tentacles over-lapping and twining together, daring him to shoot himself to kill them. He could no longer feel anything in his legs except a cold numbness. His left arm had succumbed too, overrun and pulled to his side, cold, numb and useless. Only his head, right shoulder and right arm remained free.

In his mind, only the smallest portion of Phillip Trichter remained. Enough to shift the aim of the gun. Enough to pull the trigger and kill squid-thing after squid-thing. But not enough to let him release himself the way he had released Keith. To put the gun to his head and blow out his brains.

In the end, only his right eye and his right hand remained uncovered. When that happened, the eye rolled back and the hand went limp. Only then did the gun fall to the floor. He was no longer the Bearer.

PART IV
All Sorts of Something

The Gun

THE GUN SANG.

With every strike of the firing pin, with every ignition of the primer and detonation of the powder, with every steel-jacketed lead slug that sped and spun down its barrel, the Gun sang a silent, joyful hymn of battle.

The man who held the Gun was no longer the Bearer, but the Gun suffered him to aim and fire, to squeeze the itchy trigger with his finger.

For old times' sake.

For the love of Battle.

Because nothing made the Gun happier than killing Outsiders and sending them back to whatever Hell they had come from.

And because the Gun could not do these things on its own.

The rhythm of the song was disrupted, out of sync. The former Bearer had never been especially good at keeping the beat, but now he seemed to be fighting against the heartbeat of the Universe itself. A half-beat fast here. A half-beat slow there. Doubling up. Tripping over the beat. But that did not stop the Gun from singing.

The God

THE GOD FED.

The God chuckled and hummed to itself as it fed.

One small taste of a man. And soon, one giant meal of all mankind.

The Phone

The Phone endured.

The Phone could only endure as the Opener opened, dialed, listened, appealed-pleaded-begged, closed, reopened, ignored the messages already recorded in hope of a new one that had not come, closed, then repeated all eight steps. Again and again. Over and over.

The Phone endured as best it could as both it and the Opener were drained of the blissful charge that had started the night.

1

SOLEDAD WOKE SHIVERING from the touch of cold metal pressed against her skin, a hard edge scrapping against her collarbone, a nightmare of tentacles fading in her mind.

It was still dark. Her alarm clock had not gone off. The red numbers showed 4:43. As she watched, wishing she had gone to bed more than ninety minutes before, wishing she didn't have to get up for work in less than three hours, the time became 4:44. She sighed and felt the cold, hard edge again. And smelled machine oil.

She realized she was holding something in both hands. She lay on her right side, hands tucked almost under her chin. Holding something cold. She had fallen asleep with her phone before. But this didn't feel like her phone. Her phone didn't have a–

Pistol grip?

Trigger guard?

She pushed herself upright with her elbow and threw back the comforter with her left hand.

In her right hand she held a pistol. A huge pistol. She couldn't see the gun clearly in the wan light that came through the window from the one streetlamp that illuminated the apartment complex parking lot, but she knew it was a .45 caliber Colt M1911A1 Government Model.

Her first thought was to throw the pistol away from her, across the room. Which she resisted because Uncle Tio had always been adamant about–and she could almost hear him saying it again now–"the proper handling of firearms."

Her second thought was spoken out loud, "Uncle Tio?"

Was this one of Uncle Tio's practical jokes? Another way to ruin her night, extending the ruination into the next day? Except Uncle Tio never played around with his guns. None of them. Ever. He owned at least two dozen handguns and rifles–more than a few them illegal–and he might call them "my toys," but he would sooner shoot himself in the foot than *play* with his "toys," or use them in any kind of joking or other nonserious situation.

For the second time in a very long night, an unknown presence brushed against Soledad's mind. She was not alone in her apartment.

"Who's there?" she asked. She held the pistol with both hands now, left hand supporting the right, right index finger pointing along the line of the barrel, thumb on the safety, elbows extended, aiming at the open door of her bedroom.

After a long, quiet minute, she swung her legs over the side of the bed and stood, arms still extended in front of her, looking down the barrel of the gun as she searched her apartment room by room. It couldn't possibly be a practical joke by Uncle Tio. But if she found him in her apartment, she was going to shoot him. In the leg. Maybe. Assuming the pistol was loaded–

She knew the pistol was loaded. The magazine was full and there was a round in the chamber, a high-capacity ten-plus-one load out. She knew all of this as if someone had whispered the details in her ear.

"Who's there?" she said again.

She felt as if she were playing a video game, seeing herself check her apartment as if she were a cop, lowering the pistol, arms still extended, as she went from room to room, snapping the pistol back up, ready to fill some unlucky bastard's center of mass with .45 caliber slugs.

Except it was *real*. Her heart was pounding in her chest. The sound of her heavy breathing and her bare feet on the low pile carpet were the only sounds.

Still, in spite of the fear, the adrenaline, the pistol felt like a part of her, the obvious end of her arms. The *reason* she had hands was to hold this weapon. A part of her hoped that she would find someone to shoot. It didn't even need to be Uncle Tio. She *wanted* to pull the trigger, to feel the gun buck in her hand–

"It better not be you, Tio," she said. "Whoever I find, I'm shooting."

She found no one. She was alone in the apartment.

Exhaustion from a long day and a long night caused her to sag. She stood in the middle of her living room and let the hand with the pistol fall to her side. The pistol felt heavy now. Too heavy for her to be carrying around. She sat on the overstuffed sofa she had scored at a garage sale last month. She made sure the safety was engaged and put the pistol down on the glass top of coffee table she had bought at the same time as the sofa. The metal of the pistol scraped against the glass. She let go of the checkered, wooden grip with reluctance. Her sudden fear of the dark overwhelmed her fear of waking up with a gun in her hand.

She curled up on the couch and stared at the dark shape of the pistol on the coffee table. She closed her eyes, but she could still see the pistol. She knew she could reach out and touch it if she wanted to. She could reach out pick it up–

She fought the urge to do just that.

She had spent a lot of time with Uncle Tio, learning about pistols and rifles, disassembling them, cleaning them, shooting them at the range, but she didn't own a gun. Even after Tio made her apply for and receive a concealed carry permit, she had never carried a gun.

How could she wake up holding a gun she didn't own?

2

HER PHONE WOKE Soledad before her alarm could. She reached for her phone on her nightstand without opening her eyes. She kept her eyes closed as she opened the phone and put it to her ear.

"I'm not kidding, Tio," she said. "I will shoot you." She wasn't entirely sure why she would shoot him, but she decided she would figure out a good excuse later.

"Soledad, honey, it's *tú madré*."

"Mom. Don't say *tú madré*." Soledad opened her eyes, and sat up. "What are you– Is Dad OK?"

"Your father's fine, honey. And so are Gerardo and Abril." She paused. "Why are you going to shoot Francisco?"

Soledad laid back into her pillow and closed her eyes again. "Good morning, Mom."

"Are you sitting down?"

"I'm in bed, Mom."

"Well, I called because there's been some trouble in the neighborhood."

Soledad sat back up. "Trouble?"

"Everyone's fine. It's not us. It's Phillip. Phillip Trichter, across the street. You know, your friend Dillon's guardian."

"Yes, I know Phil. What about Phil? What's going on?" Soledad remembered the car peeling out of Dillon's apartment parking lot last night. How the driver had looked like a very scared Phil Trichter. Except she had never seen Phil upset about anything before, much less scared.

"We're not sure. There are a couple police cars over there. We thought we should call you, though, so you can call Dillon. In case he doesn't know yet. We don't know his number–"

"Got it, Mom. Thanks. Love you." She ended the call.

She punched the speed dial for Dillon. While the phone connected, she swung her legs around so she was sitting on the edge of the bed. Of course, her call rang five times then flipped to Dillon's voice mail. "Damn it, Dillon ..." Her voice faded as she saw the large, .45-caliber pistol resting on her nightstand, beside the clock, the red light of the numbers tracing the edges of the Parkerized finish.

She stared at the gun. It didn't look at all out of place on her nightstand. As if she had purchased the nightstand explicitly for the purpose that it now served, to hold a clock, a phone, a lamp, and one .45 caliber Colt M1911A1 Government Model pistol.

It had to be one of Tio's guns. She didn't own a gun.

She picked up the pistol and took it with her to the bathroom. She didn't want the gun out of her sight.

3

THE SMELL OF sour milk washing over his face combined with the sounds of the phone ringing in his ear and a distant pounding forced Dillon to open his eyes. Phones he could ignore, and he had slept through insistent visitors many times, but the burning stench in his nose he couldn't deal with.

He found himself looking up into a subset of Hlooth's ten eyes. Two of the eyes were askew, looking at Dillon's phone, and three were closed, those tentacles holding the phone next to Dillon's right ear.

"But I took you walkies–"

The phone rang again, its electronic tinkling echoing in his head. He twisted his neck so he could look at the phone. Soledad's name blinked at him–maybe even glared at him–over the redundant message of "Incoming Call".

Then there was the pounding on his front door again, and a muffled female voice shouting, "Damn it, Dillon. Wake up."

Dillon didn't need the phone clock to know that this was hours earlier than he ever got up voluntarily. Not that any of this was voluntary. He closed his eyes again.

After Soledad had left him with Hlooth, he had not gone to bed until 5am. He had sat up calling Cyd, leaving message after message of apology and contrition and hopes that she was OK. After each call he would check his messages, in case she had called him while he was calling her, ignoring the messages he already had and the accumulating new messages that weren't from Cyd. He had never lost hope that Cyd would come back or

121

call or something. No, not *something*. Something was too vague after what had happened with his door, and therefore too potentially Wrong. Come back or call back was all he wanted. He had only stopped the cycle of calling-and-checking-and-calling-and-checking when the phone complained of low battery.

Soledad had been nice enough to open his fridge for him before she left, and he had worked his way through the last five beers of the case Coleman had stored there. He couldn't remember if he had closed the door of the fridge before falling into his bed.

Hlooth's knotted tongue slapped and dragged across Dillon's right cheek. A fresh wave of the not-a-dog's worse-than-doggie breath threatened to singe off his eyebrows. Blinking away tears, Dillon tried to grab Hlooth's snout and push it away from him.

More pounding. More muffled shouting of his name.

Was that Soledad? Soledad should know better than to call him or try to wake him before noon. Earliest. One o'clock was better. Or three. Three would almost always work.

"Dillon. Come on."

Maybe she was coming to take Hlooth back. That might be worth getting up for.

Hlooth pushed against his hands and tried to lick his face again.

"I'm coming," Dillon mumbled and sat up. His phone rang again and he held out his hand. Hlooth leaned over and the tentacles released the phone into his hand. The phone beeped to protest that its batteries remained low, but still connected when Dillon thumbed the call button and mumbled, again, "I'm coming." Then he thumbed the end call button. As if it had done all it could, the phone beeped low battery one more time, then turned itself off.

With Hlooth's help he made it to the door. He unchained the door and twisted the deadbolt. "It's open," he said, and stumbled back to the sofa, where he laid down and closed his eyes.

The door opened. Might even have burst open. Dillon refused to open his eyes to see. Then the door closed–slammed, really–and it was too late to ever know.

"You need to get up, Dillon," Soledad said.

Dillon shook his head. "No I don't."

"Yes, you do. It's Phil."

Dillon opened one eye. Soledad looked stressed. She had her hair pulled back, but dark wisps escaped in all directions. It was too dark to see if she had on any makeup, but he didn't think she did. Not that she needed makeup. Not at all. She wore her long, black trench coat with the belt cinched tight at her waist. Dillon always liked Soledad's waist. She also she had a large handbag slung over her shoulder and resting on her right hip. Her words finally penetrated his skull. He opened his eyes wider. "Phil? Uncle Phil?"

"Yes, Uncle Phil. He's in trouble. Get dressed. We need to go."

Dillon liked how she said "we." Then more of her words reached him. He said, "Trouble?"

"I don't know what kind of trouble. Get up. We need to go."

4

"ARE YOU SURE it's safe to leave Hlooth alone?" Dillon asked as Soledad pulled him out the door. Dillon looked back into the dim interior of his apartment, trying to see Hlooth. The not-a-dog had retreated into the bedroom's closet cranny once Soledad arrived, and hadn't come out since. He hoped that Hlooth wouldn't sleep on his bed and make it slimy. Or worse.

"I guess we'll find out," Soledad said and closed the door of the apartment in Dillon's face.

Dillon tripped over the dawn's early light on the sidewalk. His lungs felt as if they had been scrubbed from the inside with a bottle brush. His eyes didn't want to focus and his head was stuffed too full of what had once been in his lungs. He hated mornings.

"I took him walkies last night," Dillon said.

"What?"

Dillon must have been walking with less skill than he thought, because Soledad grabbed his right arm and pulled him straight. He liked it when Soledad touched him. She was very much not the touchy-feely type. Especially since the prom.

"Hlooth," he said. It sounded funny so he said it again. "Hlooth." He giggled. Soledad held his arm as they went down the stairs. "I tooth–took–Hlooth walkies. He caught something and ate it. I hope it wasn't a cat. This is my car."

"Yes, it is. I grabbed your keys."

"Can I sleep on the way?"

"Well I'm not going to let you *drive*," Soledad said, leaving him by the passenger side door and walking around to the drivers side. "Get in."

Dillon nodded. "Good choice." He added, "Hlooth hlooth hlooth."

Soledad came back around to his side of the car and opened the door for him. "Get in," she said.

After a second, she put her hand on his head and pushed him down and into the front seat. Dillon felt as if he had been arrested and was being dragged downtown.

"And roll down the window," Soledad said. "Just in case."

5

"OH MY GOD," Soledad said, pulling Dillon back from the edge of sleep. Again. At least this time it wasn't her driving. Or rather her *braking*. Yes, the old Plymouth Neon's brakes were a bit soft, but that was to be expected in a car the venerable age of the Neon. The Neon was cheap when he bought it, and hadn't increased in value in the years since. Dillon's head jerked forward as the car came to a full, abrupt stop. Soledad was definitely overcompensating for the brakes.

Dillon's eyes focused on the ever brighter world outside the car. "Oh my god," he said, because it was easier to repeat what she had just said than come up with words of his own.

Two black-and-white police cars were parked in front of Uncle Phil's house, as were a couple other unmarked cars. Some gawkers stood in the surrounding yards. The front door of Uncle Phil's house stood open and every window that Dillon could see had been smashed in with enough force to damage the window frames and the surrounding walls. The whole house gleamed in the sunlight, as if a heavy dew had settled.

Dillon's hand found the handle and he tried to get out of the car. The seat belt restrained him. He fumbled with the catch, then, finally, took the hand Soledad offered–

When had she gotten out and come around the car? He didn't remember.

He took Soledad's hand and used her to stand up. Then leaned on her to remain standing. He held her left arm with both hands.

He wasn't sleepy anymore. He was just weak, and overwhelmed. This felt too much like the night Dad died. "Is ... is Uncle Phil ... ?"

"I don't know," Soledad said. "I just got here too."

A uniformed policeman walked over. "Can I help you?"

"Uncle Phil," Dillon said again. "Is he OK?"

"Your uncle lives here?"

"My guardian," Dillon said. "Phil Trichter is my guardian. Was. He's not my real uncle, but ... is he OK?"

"And who are you?"

"Dillon. Dillon Offner. Is Uncle Phil OK?"

"You need to come with me, Mr. Offner."

"Don't leave me," Dillon said to Soledad.

"I'm not going anywhere," Soledad said. She shifted the strap of her oversized bag on her shoulder, then pushed Dillon forward.

Dillon, still using Soledad for support, followed the policeman up the driveway to the front porch. The concrete porch, the front of the house, all of it gleamed under a layer of slime. But not the front door, which was dry. The slime continued into the house. From the doorway, Dillon could see slime and broken glass covered the floor of the living room. The sofa and loveseat in the living room had been shredded as if chewed up by a giant with no molars, only incisors.

The policeman held up a hand to prevent them from entering. He called in to the house. After a minute, a woman in gray slacks and a matching blazer with blue, plastic booties on her feet, came out of Phil's bedroom.

"Dillon Offner," the policeman said, "this is Detective Ellen White."

"Is Phil OK?" Dillon asked before the woman could say anything. "What happened?"

"We're still working on what happened, Mr. Offner," the detective said. Her face showed no emotion that Dillon could read. "Unfortunately, we don't know if Mr. Trichter is OK. He's not here. Do you have any idea where he might be?"

"Phil's not here? What do you mean Phil's not here?"

"I mean, he's not here, Mr. Offner. We had reports of screaming and shots fired. When the officer arrived on the scene, though, this is all he found." Her hand swept to indicate the destroyed living room. "Signs of a struggle, what he thought was blood everywhere, but no bodies. No one at all. And, as it turns out, no blood. Just lots of slime and a lot of broken furniture."

"Blood everywhere?" Dillon felt lightheaded. He swallowed to keep from throwing up. If Soledad hadn't been behind him, holding him up, he wasn't sure he would have stayed standing.

"It's not blood, Mr. Offner, as I just said. We don't know what it is yet."

"Slime?" His voice seemed to echo in his head. He had a hard time focusing on the detective's face.

"Not like what's in here or on the outside of the house. More of an ichor."

"Ichor?"

"Maybe you need to go sit down, Mr. Offner," Detective White said.

Dillon nodded. He would have sat on one of the broken, slime-covered plastic porch chairs, but the detective protested and Soledad led him off the porch. He heard Soledad ask if it would be OK if she took him across the street. He didn't hear the detective's response, but it must have been OK because Soledad walked him across the street to her parent's house.

Where was Uncle Phil? What had happened? Was it his fault?

"I'm sure they're looking for him," Soledad said. "And, no, this wasn't your fault."

Dillon didn't remember saying anything, but he must have. All he could think of were the questions swirling in sloppy circles in his mind.

It couldn't be coincidence. Him opening his front door, just like before. The light and the sound, just like before. Cyd screaming. Uncle Phil showing up to help him close the door again, just like before. And now this.

Then Soledad was helping him sit, and Dillon realized he was in the Winters's home. He sat on their leather sofa while Soledad and her mother, April, hovered over him, offering him a glass of water and asking if he was OK.

He had opened the door without looking, without thinking, and he had hurt Cyd and now, somehow, Uncle Phil.

"What does Cyd have to do with this?" Soledad asked. Then she said, "I think he's in shock."

"The poor dear," April said. "First his father, now this."

Dillon nodded. That's how he saw it too. He didn't know how, but he *knew*. This was the murder of his father all over. Except this time Uncle Phil hadn't been able to save himself.

"Don't forget his mom," Soledad said.

"I wasn't forgetting, Soledad. But at least his mom wasn't, you know."

"Dillon told me last night that his mother was coming back."

"Now she's coming back?" April asked, echoing Dillon's own thoughts on the matter. She sniffed. "I never liked her.

Dillon's thoughts on that subject were more ... complicated.

"Mom! He's in shock, not deaf."

Dillon sipped at the glass of water he found he was holding. "She's not my favorite person either," he said. "But what can you do? She's family."

"I hear that," Soledad said, glaring up at her mother.

6

DETECTIVE WHITE FOUND Dillon sitting on the Winters's couch. Soledad as holding his hand. Dillon hadn't expected her to do that, but he didn't protest. He might be holding her hand too tight, but he didn't want her to let go. Especially when the detective came in.

The woman sat in a wooden chair that April brought from the dining room. She pulled a phone from her pocket, thumbed something on the screen, and placed it on the coffee table in front of her. Then she took out a small, flip top notebook and a pen. "OK, Mr. Offner, tell me, when was the last time you spoke to Mr. Trichter?"

"Last night," Dillon said. "He came over ... after I got off work." He didn't add, *and pulled me by my ankles out of a doorway into hell.* He also decided to leave out the parts involving Cyd. Because of the door, and the light, and the sound. And because he didn't want to talk about Cyd while Soledad was holding his hand.

Detective White's pen made little scritch-scritch noises as she wrote in the notebook. The sound gave Dillon goose bumps. She asked, "What time was that?"

"About two in the morning."

The detective looked up. "Isn't that late for a visit?"

"Not for me. I work the closing shift."

"Why not come by where you work?"

Dillon shrugged. "He didn't say. He said he'd tried to call me, but couldn't get through. He came by to tell me my mother was coming back. Coming here. She had called him when she couldn't reach me."

Detective White made more scritch-scritch notes. "How long was he there?"

"Not very long. Fifteen minutes, maybe? I offered him a beer, but he said he needed to get back to his house."

"Did he look nervous? Like he was worried?"

"Yeah, he did. But he wouldn't say what it was about. I just thought he was upset about Mom coming back."

"You're not very close to your mother."

"No," Dillon said. "We're neither of us very close to the other."

Detective White must have looked up Dillon's history, with the unsolved case of his father's murder, because she proceeded to ask Dillon questions about that. Dillon remembered when he had first told Soledad about that night. She had held his hand then. Or he had held hers. Either way, it gave the detective's questions, and his answers, a feeling of *deja vu*, as if the earlier telling had echoed into this one. That time, when he told Soledad, he had been living with Uncle Phil. His mother had left six months before. Phil had been his guardian for four months. And he had been working at the Pit for two months. The main difference between that time and this, was that they had been in his bedroom at Phil's house, him laying across his bed, her sitting on the floor, her legs pulled up to her chin as she listened. And there was no police detective involved. And Phil was in the kitchen, not missing. Which suddenly seemed like a lot of differences. Dillon wondered if he even knew what *deja vu* meant.

Detective White listened to his story, scritch-scritched notes in her notebook as she did, then asked more questions. The same questions Dillon remembered being asked in the hours and weeks after Dad was killed. He gave the same answers then as now.

"So Mr. Trichter carries a gun?" The detective's question didn't sound much like a question.

Soledad's hand squeezed his. "He used to," Dillon said. "He had a ... a forty-five, I think, that he carried everywhere."

Detective White made a note. "Used to?"

"When I moved in with him, he bought a safe and put the gun in there. I haven't seen it since then."

"We found the safe. It had been ... opened. We didn't find any gun."

Soledad squeezed his hand again. Then shifted her position. Dillon enjoyed the feel of her hand held in his and the feel of her hip moving against his.

"So it ... this was a robbery?"

The detective's expression didn't change. "Maybe. So far, though, the gun and his phone are the only items confirmed missing. Do you know if he had any other weapons or valuables he might have kept in the safe?"

Dillon shook his head. "I don't know. He bought the safe for the gun. That's all I remember him saying about it."

"Do you know if Mr. Trichter had any living relatives?"

"He might." Dillon paused and tried to think. "He mentioned a brother once. That's all I can remember. My mom might know more about that. They used to be close."

"How can I get in touch with your mother?"

Dillon shrugged. "I don't–" He stopped. "Hang on, she called me, or Uncle Phil said she called me." He disengaged his hand from Soledad's and reached into his pocket. He pulled out the phone. "So I should have her return number." The phone was off. He turned it on. The display showed "Low Battery", not even a beep this time, then went dark again. "Or not. My battery is dead." He started to put his phone away again.

"Can I have that?" Detective White asked, holding out her hand.

Dillon reached and put the phone in her hand. Then he sat back and took Soledad's hand again.

"I'll get this back to you later today," the detective said, "after I've had the sim chip contents copied."

"No hurry," Dillon said. Then he remembered Cyd. "Or, actually, I'm expecting a call from Cyd–from someone. It's my work phone."

Soledad let go of his hand, and stood. She walked out of the living room, into the dining room with her mother.

Detective White watched her leave, then stood also. "That's all for now, Mr. Offner. I'll be in touch again if we learn anything, or if I have more questions."

"Can I," Dillon started, then wondered if he really want to do what he was about ask.

"Can you what, Mr. Offner?"

Dillon swallowed, then asked, "Can I ... see? Can I look around? Uncle Phil's house?"

"If you're up to it, Mr. Offner. That might help us know if anything else was taken."

7

SOLEDAD STAYED OUTSIDE as Dillon went into Uncle Phil's house with Detective White. The detective had insisted she wait on the porch.

The rest of Uncle Phil's house looked like the living room: chewed up and spit out with a thick coating of slime. Slime that smelled all too familiar. Like what the new guy, Andrew, had wiped off his shirt at work the night before. But there was no way those little squid-things could have done all this.

Phil's bedroom was the worst. Green-black ichor–Dillon decided that the detective's word choice fit–had been splattered and smeared everywhere. Phil's bed had been flipped over and the mattress and box spring torn apart. The old chest of drawers Phil had been planning to strip and refinish for as long as Dillon could remember had been smashed. Clothes and papers had been scattered. The front of the safe had been nearly ripped off its hinges, and the empty safe had been thrown against a wall hard enough to be embedded.

"The splatter on the wall is consistent with gunshots," Detective White said behind him, making him jump. "Though we were expecting blood, not ... whatever this stuff is. We also found a number of holes in the walls that look like gunshots. The holes are consistent with that of a forty-five-caliber round. But we found no bullets, no casings, nothing."

Dillon didn't say anything. He couldn't. The scene overwhelmed him.

"Does any of that sound familiar, Mr. Offner?"

Dillon turned to look at the detective. Her green eyes locked onto his. "What?" he asked.

135

"Does any of this"–Detective White gestured to include the whole room, the house, everything–"sound familiar to you, Mr. Offner? Gunshots without slugs or casings? Slime?"

Dillon just looked at her, uncertain what she was saying.

"Your Uncle Phil reported discharging his weapon on the night your father was killed, Mr. Offner. Seven shots, maybe more. No casings were recovered that night either." Detective White stepped closer to him, still looking into his eyes as if trying to drill into his head. "The two shots that hit the door frame yielded no slugs. And the door frame itself was covered in an unidentified slime. No blood other than your father's was ever found. But there were a few droplets of something that wasn't blood. Like the slime, it was never identified."

Dillon backed away from her. "What are you trying to say?"

"I'm not saying anything, Mr. Offner. I'm just asking if any of this sounds familiar." She didn't sound as if she were just asking.

"Do you think this is connected to my father's murder?"

"There are some definite similarities. Don't you think so, Mr. Offner?"

"I never heard about ... any of that. All I knew was that I opened the door without looking, and someone or something tried to get in–"

"He's already told you all of this." Soledad stood at the broken door of Phil's bedroom, her brown eyes angry, her lips pressed into a thin line. She had her left hand in her trench coat pocket, her right hand pressed against her tote bag.

"I asked you to wait outside, Miss Winters," the detective said without turning around. She kept her eyes on Dillon.

"And you said you only wanted to see if anything else had been stolen. You know where Dillon lives. You know where he works. He's had a rough morning on very little sleep. We both have. If it's OK with you, detective, Dillon and I will be going."

"I guess we're done here," Detective White said. "You can go." She stepped aside so Dillon could walk past her. "I'll be in touch, Mr. Offner," she added. "When I have more questions."

Dillon nodded. He knew there would be more questions.

8

SOLEDAD GLARED AT the detective a few seconds longer, resisting the urge to push past the woman's impassive demeanor and see what the woman wasn't saying. Then she put her hand on Dillon's shoulder and guided him out of Phil's house. She decided Dillon probably didn't need any more attention from her mother either, so she led him to his car. She opened the door for him and shut it when he was in. Then she went to the driver's side and got in herself, tucking the tail of her trench coat under her. She was about to put her tote bag in the back seat, but decided she would rather have it in her lap.

Her left hand touched the tote bag and she felt the pistol within. Was it Phil's gun? She had seen Phil's pistol a few times. Usually disassembled on the now-wrecked dining room table as he cleaned it. She hadn't thought much about that gun, though. Not in years. She had seen Uncle Tio clean more guns than she could count. The thought that Phil Trichter might have sneaked into her apartment and left the gun on her bed gave her the shivers. Especially after what she had seen in Phil's house.

She put the key in the ignition, started the car and drove them away.

Dillon didn't talk. He sat in the passenger seat with his arms crossed, staring out the window at the urban residential scenery. Soledad looked at him as she drove, quick glances only, because she needed all her attention to drive. And because he remained closed to her. She could see only the surface of Dillon, could only hear what he said. She had never been able to see what was in his head, had never heard anything leak from his mind.

She wondered if he was thinking about Phil, or his father. Or even his mother. Or Cyd–

Soledad tried not to grind her teeth as she kept her mouth closed and focused on her driving.

She hated Dillon's car for the same reason she hated his apartment. Not just because they were both cluttered messes that barely functioned for their specific uses, but because neither one seemed like a deliberate choice made by Dillon. The car and the apartment–and his job at the Pit– all seemed like default nonchoices to her. He hadn't sought any of them for their pros, nor had he considered their obvious cons. He had needed a job, the Pit had needed someone to punch buttons on the cash register. He needed his own place, and that dump near the Pit had a vacancy. Someone who used to work at the Pit–Soledad couldn't remember the man's name–needed to sell his car, and Dillon–sometimes–needed a car, so he bought it. These weren't decisions. They weren't choices. They were just ... existing.

She loved Dillon. He was her best friend. Had been for more than ten years. And she had known him for longer than that, since Phil had moved into her neighborhood. She had once told him that she loved him, but he had taken it wrong. Not the way she meant it. Or maybe she hadn't been entirely sure how she meant it.

If Dillon had gone to college with her, instead of staying in Rio Cruces, his hometown–or as close to a hometown as Dillon had–things might have been different. But he had let her go alone. He had settled in. He had continued working at the Pit. He had found that awful apartment and bought this piece of shit car.

Before the Prom, she had never really thought of Dillon as anything other than a brother she liked–unlike her real brother. Dillon was her best friend. He had worn so much eyeliner during his Goth phase that she had wondered if he might be gay. She hadn't really believed he was gay, but thinking that way had made it easier to hang out with him. Especially when she had shared her questions with her parents. After that discussion, they never had a problem with her spending as much time as she wanted across the street at Phil's house, even in Dillon's bedroom.

She had told Dillon about her boyfriends and her boy problems– which were usually the same thing. And he had talked to her about Goth fashion and, sometimes, girls. He only talked about his past a few times. Once per significant event, and that was it.

They were friends, best buds. When that bastard Geoff dumped her right before Prom, and when Dillon's plans had fallen through, it had seemed natural that they go together.

After the Prom, sitting on Phil's front porch swing in their one-night-only Prom finery, Dillon had told her that he loved her. She had misunderstood him. Or maybe she had been too caught off guard by his words and was trying to figure out how to respond. Either way, when he had tried to kiss her–not a good-night-thanks-for-going-to-the-prom-with-me kiss, but a *kiss*–she had balked. Pulled away. Jumped up off the swing. Left him–literally–swinging in the breeze, embarrassed and hurt. She had realized only later that she had then killed his wounded heart with a classic *coup de grace*: "We're friends, Dillon. You're my best friend. Let's not ruin what we have."

It was only recently, back from college, single–ish–with Robert ex-ed and kept at a safe distance, that she had begun to think that if her and Dillon's friendship had survived that ruined night, it could have survived something a lot more pleasant. Of course, then she goes over last night and finds he had been about to hook up with Baby Cyd, who worked–of course–at the Buffalo Burger Pit.

Dillon had found the Pit, and the Pit had sucked him in and become his life. Soledad had wished through all four years she was away at college that Dillon would move on, leave the Pit. He hadn't. In her less charitable moods, Soledad thought Dillon was more than scared of opening doors. That he was scared of moving on.

Not that she had managed to move very far either. Sure, she had left for college. Even graduated. But here she was again. Back in the same town she had lived in her entire life. All she had to show for four years of college was three new exes and a monogrammed bit of parchment. She hated Dillon's job at the Pit, but she was working a crappy job for her uncle. She hated Dillon's car, but at least he had a car. She was driving the city's animal control van.

Dillon surprised her, brought her back to the present, by touching her right arm. "Thank you," he said.

Startled, Soledad managed only a shrug in response. Dillon drew back his hand, and she realized he might have thought she was shaking it off. She shifted her grip on the steering wheel and grabbed his left hand with her right. "De nada," she said.

"I'm glad your back."

Soledad smiled in response, then released his hand to reapply her full abilities to steering the Neon. The car seemed to want to take its half of the road out of the middle, no matter which lane she drove in. "Don't be too glad," she said, letting the smile disappear. "I'm still plenty mad about you and Cyd."

"But nothing happened."

"Something happened," Soledad said, focusing on the road. "All sorts of something."

PART V
Vintage Thoughts

The Gun

THE GUN NESTLED.

The Gun made itself comfortable against the bulky leather wallet. The Gun was harder by far than the hard plastic handle of the hairbrush that pressed against it, and the loose strands of hair stuck in the bristles that rubbed against its muzzle did not tickle. The air was close, warm from proximity to the new Bearer, and smelled of a mix of hair products, skin products and eau de toilets. The Gun had been stuffed and stuck and jammed and pushed into far worse places and storage containers. This was, though, the first time the Gun had shared such a space with a brace of tampons.

The new Bearer's handbag was not as intimate as a shoulder holster, nor as practical, but it was a perfectly acceptable conveyance.

At least the new Bearer had not stuffed the Gun, muzzle first, into her waistband. In the back. Though that was almost certainly going to happen sooner or later.

Ever since the Gun had evolved past single shot flintlock technology, being stuffed into ass crack had become a thing. Maybe this new Bearer's ass crack would not be so bad. In the meantime, the Gun enjoyed the handbag, and nestled in. If the Gun had been able to, it would have let out a contented sigh.

The God

THE GOD FLEXED and stretched and gnashed.

The God of the Void now had Shape. A Shape with Grippers and Stretchers and Mouths. So many, many Mouths. A Shape with a Foot. Which Foot was now wedged firmly in the Door.

The God had not had Shape for immeasurable eons. It was no longer accustomed to movement.

The God took a step.

The God slipped, then fell.

Being a God, the God, of course, meant to do that.

Still, the God stretched and flexed and retracted and gnashed and tore at the lifeless, unknown thing that had dared to impede the progress of a God. Fortunately, the Servant of the God had not seen the God do what the God had purposefully done, so there was no need to devour the Servant and seek another.

The Servant led the God from the lifeless, unknown structure to the God's rightful place, under the Stars. The God looked up and saw the Stars moving to form the new constellations that spelled the beginning of the end for this world. The God reached for the Stars, but they were not within reach. Yet.

The Phone

THE PHONE WAS conflicted.

The Phone wanted to remain loyal to the Opener, to take no pleasure from being charged, opened, seen, and heard by unknown sources of power, strange hands, unfamiliar eyes, and oddly shaped ears.

The Phone wondered if this new, un-asked-for presence would call it. Tomorrow. Or maybe next week. The Phone would be OK with that.

1

DILLON SAT ALONE in his apartment after Soledad left. Just before she left, she told him, again, to call her if he needed anything. He had only nodded. She was gone before he remembered he didn't have his phone.

Then Dillon wasn't alone anymore as Hlooth came out of the so-called bedroom. The big not-a-dog crawled up on the sofa, licked Dillon's face, then dropped its heavy head on Dillon's lap. The six legs splayed around the torso at angles that were hard to look at, so Dillon didn't look at them. The eyes on their tentacles all looked up Dillon, waving slightly in a nonexistent breeze, like a sea anemone in a particularly dirty aquarium. Dillon looked away, his eyes finally settling on the innocent-seeming doorknob of his front door.

Dillon started to try calling Cyd again. He even disturbed Hlooth by shifting his position to reach into his pocket, but remembered he had given his phone to the detective woman, and shifted back into his depression in the sofa as Hlooth's head settled back on his lap. For the first time since he had handed over his phone, he wondered when he would get it back. He disturbed Hlooth again when he pulled the business card the detective woman had given hem. "Ellen White, Detective, RCPD". He started to call her–

He sighed, and so did Hlooth, the wash of stench burning Dillon's nose and bringing tears to his eyes for the first time since Soledad had dragged him out of bed.

Uncle Phil was missing.

Mom was coming.

Add memories of Dad and it was like a family reunion in Dillon's head. Even if he was the only one actually *there*.

He had avoided thinking about Dad for weeks, maybe. At least for a few days. Sixteen years was forever ago for anything else. Dillon hardly remembered any of his toys from that time, except the jack-in-the-box. If it weren't for school pictures, he would have no memory of the clothes he had worn or how his hair was cut. But Dad was always right there, an invisible absence.

In Dillon's memories, Dad was impossibly tall, sometimes grumpy, but always there. When baby Dillon opened doors he shouldn't have, it was Dad who made sure they were closed again. And, if possible, it was Dad who removed the doors so Dillon couldn't open them ever again. It was Dad who defended Dillon from everything. Including Mom. It was Dad who had tried to talk Mom out of hiding Dillon's jack-in-the-box.

Dillon wiped his eyes. "You really stink," he told Hlooth.

"Woof?"

Dillon tried to do that trick Soledad did and carry on a one-sided, imaginary conversation with the monosyllabic beast, but his heart wasn't in it. All he could manage was, "Yes, you. You stink." A hint of a what-can-you-do? shrug passed through the eyestalks looking up at Dillon, but Dillon didn't say anything more.

He looked around his apartment. The lights were off, but some gray light made its way through the dirty glass of the sliding door and its dusty vertical blinds. The disarray that surrounded him was reminiscent of the chaos in Uncle Phil's bedroom. Less slime, in most places, and fewer teeth marks, but similar.

What would Mom think?

Another ripple-shrug of Hlooth's eyestalks told Dillon he had asked the question out loud.

"Why do you think Mom's coming?" Dillon asked the beast. If he was going to talk to himself, he might as well try to disguise it by talking to the not-a-dog with its head on his lap. Hlooth offered no suggestions, so Dillon continued. "You know, Mom denied you even existed. She told me over and over, 'There was no doggie in the closet, Dillon, honey.' She even screamed it a few times when I insisted that you had been, in fact, in the closet." He paused. "So what do you think? Do you want to stick around long enough to meet her? Show her who doesn't exist?" He paused again. "What am I going to tell her about Uncle Phil?"

"Bark?"

"You're no help at all."

Despite what the detective woman had said, Dillon didn't think Uncle Phil's disappearance was at all like the night Dad died.

Dillon had been there when Dad died. He had inadvertently opened the door and let in whoever or whatever had killed Dad. Whatever or whoever had taken Uncle Phil hadn't needed Dillon's help.

Still, he knew his mother would blame him for Uncle Phil, just as she had blamed him for Dad. So there was that much in common, at least. And here he was, alone in his room again. So there was that, too.

Hlooth belched another cloud of near-incendiary spoiled-yogurt gas, reminding Dillon that, no, he wasn't alone.

He thought of Cyd as he blinked away the tears in his eyes. He started to call her, to leave possibly the hundredth message to call him on her voicemail, but he still had no phone.

He didn't even know what time it was.

Unsure what else to do, he retreated to his so-called bedroom, curled up in a near fetal position, and tried to go back to sleep.

Hlooth followed him and laid down heavily across Dillon's feet, pinning him in place.

Dillon groaned and wished Soledad had stayed.

2

SOLEDAD WAS CLIMBING into the animal control van before she realized she hadn't seen Hlooth either time she had been in Dillon's apartment that morning. He must have been sleeping, like one of her grandmother's cats. But well hidden. It wasn't like Dillon's apartment offered many hiding places.

It would be hard to kill the Outsider beast with one shot.

The thought came into her mind as she bent over in the seat, reaching down to release the van's emergency brake. She froze. She was used to talking to herself. Usually, though, when she talked to herself, she used her own voice. And she knew what the hell she was talking about.

A bullet to the head would only slow it down.

Soledad sat up straight in the worn driver's seat. She looked left, out the driver's side window, then through the windshield and the passenger's window. She saw no one in the apartment parking lot. The beat-to-shit, dirty, animal control van hardly stood out among the dented junkers and tired pickups also stabled in the lot. No one was walking to their car. Or standing around, staring at her.

The beast would need to be flipped over, and a very precise shot made in the underbelly.

In Soledad's mind she could see Hlooth on his back, his misjointed legs writhing like an overturned spider's. Then a bullet punched a small hole in the lighter, softer hide, in the center of all the leg joints. The legs went straight, rigid, then curled up.

Very slowly, moving her eyes first, then the rest of her head, Soledad turned to look in the back of the van. Nothing but rusty, broken, smelly tools, and a dented kennel.

In this instance, a spear would be more practical than a gun. Though it does require more nerve, since you are going hand-to-hand.

The mental video of flipping and killing Hlooth repeated, this time with a spear thrusting under Hlooth and leveraging him over. Then the spear pulled back, thrust forward, and pierced the beast in same spot as before, pinning him to the ground as it killed him.

"Who is there?" Soledad asked out loud. She felt her knuckles becoming white from her tight grip on the pistol, and almost dropped it. Because she couldn't remember having taken the pistol from her handbag.

She let her hands drop so she wasn't waving the gun around in plain sight, then looked into the back of the van again. Still nothing. And no one visible through the windows.

"I am not going to kill Hlooth," she said to no one she could see. "I *like* Hlooth, ugly as he may be."

She sensed the mental equivalent of a shrug of acceptance, with just a touch of in-case-you-change-your-mind.

"I'm not going to change my mind."

There was no response to that.

She could still feel the faint presence of the other mind. It didn't go away, but it offered no further tips and tricks for the brutal slaying of Hlooth.

A woman dressed like a waiter walked in front of the van, her face in shadow as she was looking down, reading something on her phone. She never even looked up to see Soledad staring at her. Soledad caught glimpses of text messages flying back and forth, and the upturned, smirking faces of self-portraits taken with camera phones. Soledad could almost smell the Italian food the woman would soon be serving the noisy lunch crowd at Olive Garden.

When the woman had passed, Soledad reluctantly returned the gun to her handbag.

As if the van sensed her mood, the emergency brake released easily this time, and she drove out of the parking lot, headed for work.

As she drove, her eyes kept returning to her handbag, and her thoughts kept returning to the pistol. It had come to her hand so easily. It had, somehow, come into her *bed* last night. Now that Dillon had been taken care of, at least temporarily, she needed to have a long talk with Uncle Tio.

3

THROUGHOUT HER CHILDHOOD, people were a mystery to Soledad Winters. Old people, young people, babies. All of them. She would look at them, watch them, study them, and have no idea what they were thinking. Why they were doing what they were doing. Why they said the things they said. One and all, they were varied-color, human-like robots with no discernible logic behind their choices.

She spent a lot of time alone at school.

Her parents she understood, at least when they were talking to her or about her. Her brother, Gerardo, and her sister, Abril, two and four years older than her, she could understand. Most of the time. Until they hit puberty, when it seemed their mental gears shifted and ground and they became as incomprehensible as everyone else.

Then she hit puberty, as denoted by her first period, at age eleven. Suddenly all those closed books opened wide and started spraying pages. Thoughts like angry playing cards flew at her, threatening to take off her head, as if she were Alice in the courtroom of the Queen of Hearts. She went from no reasons for why people did what they did to a flood of reasons and rationales they told themselves as the voices in their heads started speaking to Soledad. And showing her pictures. Snippets of memories, some like snapshots, faces and emotions frozen in time, others in full, graphic, brutal motion.

She went from a dry, textbook knowledge of sex to post-traumatized, seen-it-all sex worker veteran within the first week. A lot of that, of course, from her classmates at school, but even more from her teachers.

155

Especially the teachers. The other students at her school had no idea what their teachers were up to off school grounds–and *on* school grounds in a variety of improbable locations and positions–or thought about even as they presented the lessons for the day. But Soledad knew. And wished she didn't.

She had never been especially inclined to hugging before this happened. Not even her family. Now she never wanted to touch anyone, ever again. They were all ... unclean.

Before, she had been an attentive student, if lonely, who turned in her homework even if she didn't always participate in class. Afterward, she feigned sickness and broke down crying and screamed that she never wanted to go to school again. She stopped going to classes. After her father dropped her off at school, she would sneak off to hide in the bushes and spend the day reading. Her lack of attendance didn't go unnoticed, and the school principal ratted her out, calling her parents after the third day.

Her parents were distraught. Gerardo and Abril rolled their eyes when she tried to explain. At a special meeting in the principal's office, the principal had suggested "professional help"–which was what the woman *said*. What the woman was *thinking* was a confusion of memories of an older woman, sometimes smiling, more often scowling, sometimes screaming as she strained against the restraints on her arms.

Desperate, her parents had asked Uncle Tio to talk to their suddenly, maddeningly delinquent daughter who was now refusing to leave her bedroom.

Uncle Tio had been Soledad's salvation. And, in his own way, so had Dillon. Because she never had any clue what either of them were thinking.

4

SOLEDAD PULLED INTO the employees lot on the north side of the Rio Cruces Animal Control Center. She parked the van in the same spot she always did, the spot reserved not for her but for the van she drove. Which happened to be next to the spot reserved for the military surplus Humvee that Uncle Tio had purchased for little more than a song and christened the RCAW Lion Catcher.

Like Uncle Tio, the Lion Catcher had served honorably in the First Gulf War, but, unlike Uncle Tio, still fit its original khaki uniform. The US Army markings had been painted over with the RCAW logo. A heavy iron grill had been mounted to the front of the vehicle for off-road work, and a khaki tarp had been stretched across the rear bed. Otherwise, the Lion Catcher looked much like it had as it sped across the desert bringing first the shield, then the storm.

The pungent mix of multispecies urine, musk, sweat and desperation was waiting for her, as it always was, when she stepped out of the van. Dogs of all breeds and mut-ness, cats of all shapes and colors and domesticities, ferrets, snakes, chinchillas, foxes, coyotes, the occasional alpaca or pig, and the rare alligator had all contributed to the heady stew that blanketed the center every day, except Mondays. The smell became almost thick enough to see when she opened the back door marked "Authorized Personnel Only" and walked into the building. Soledad hardly noticed. Uncle Tio had been bringing her to work with him since before she could remember. The stench of the center was one of the scents that told her she was home, right up there with the smell of homemade corn tortillas warming on a cast-iron skillet.

Like the smell, the sound of the center was a constantly churning melange of muffled barking and mewing and the far more irritating hum of fluorescent lights and industrial-sized appliances. Taken together, it was like walking through the funky insides of a sleeping chimera.

As she passed the break room, she sensed someone waiting for her and paused. She recognized the old man she knew only as "Jimmie the Wrangler" before he poked his head out. His thoughts carried the same old-man-musk as the rest of him, and it amused her to see his memories in glossy black-and-white, like old movies. As he always did, Jimmie looked down at her feet, then at her face, briefly, before looking away. "It's only you," he said to the air over Soledad's left shoulder. In her head, Soledad saw a sad Lassie with drooping tail.

Soledad resisted the urge to pat the man on his dirty ball cap. She nodded. "Only me."

Jimmie came the rest of the way out of the break room. He was holding a heavy, slightly misshapen mug. He shifted his grip on the mug, and Soledad heard, again, his subvocalization that he favored that particular mug because the thick handle was big enough for his calloused hands. Earlier mugs made by the same grandchild had been used in spite of the lack of a comfortably sized handle because Jimmie loved the kid, not because the kid was a great potter. But it was nice to have a mug that actually fit. Jimmie took a sip, then focused just slightly off center of Soledad again. Lassie's tail gave a hopeful wag. "So where's that raccoon? Still in the van?"

After the morning she had had, which had included no raccoons or raccoon-like creatures, Soledad only looked at him in confusion. Then the urge to yawn reminded her of the late-night call Uncle Tio had sent her on. "Oh, right. That wasn't a raccoon."

"Of course it wasn't." Jimmie shook his head. Lassie's tail sagged again. "Kids today wouldn't know a raccoon from a badger."

Soledad took no offense. To Jimmy the Wrangler, "kids today" encompassed anyone obviously younger than him. Which she had once calculated came to just over seven billion people. And she knew by his thoughts that he didn't consider her one of that much-maligned group. At least, currently.

"So what was it?" Jimmy asked. "A badger?" Lassie growled at the mention of badgers. Badgers were always bad news.

Soledad considered her options. "I have no idea," she said after a few seconds, knowing Jimmie would prefer honesty to a guess that later would turn out wrong. Because what the hell *was* Hlooth? "It wasn't a badger, and it was a lot bigger than a raccoon. And bigger than most dogs." She didn't add that Hlooth was bigger than Lassie. Nothing and nobody was bigger than Lassie in the mind of Jimmie the Wrangler.

Jimmie looked unimpressed. He wrangled rottweilers and Great Danes for a living, nothing smaller than a hippopotamus would faze him. Lassie faded from Soledad's mind as Jimmie took another sip of his coffee. Then another. Not because he liked the coffee. Jenna had made it, Soledad learned from his silence, and Jenna couldn't make coffee to save her life. Or anyone else's. Each sip almost certainly took a full thirty seconds off his life expectancy, he was sure. Worse than cigarettes, he had no doubt. Jimmie missed cigarettes. He took one more sip, because you were either addicted or you weren't, then said, "So what you do with it?"

Soledad again considered her options. She decided to go with a version of the truth, even though Jimmie would surely be even more unimpressed. "I left it with a friend," she said. "It seemed to know him, and wanted to stay with him."

Jimmie shook his head and Soledad knew she had reentered the masses of "kids today." Lassie reappeared and seemed to be frowning at her too. No lectures about animal handling safety, not from Jimmie the Wrangler. Just disappointment, which the old man could deliver like a master's thesis with a frown and a half-grunted, "Hmm." He took another sip of the dreadful Jenna-coffee. "So I guess I'll be seeing it later today." He paused, gave Soledad's poor judgment the benefit of the doubt. "Tomorrow, maybe."

She nodded. She couldn't disagree with his assessment of her poor judgment. She said, "Maybe."

With one last sigh about "kids today", Jimmie turned and went back into the break room, thinking slow thoughts about what the center would come to when he could no longer drag himself into work.

Soledad continued on her way to Uncle Tio's office.

Her mother had told baby Soledad to call her uncle "Tio Francisco", but the man himself had always insisted she call him Uncle Frank. Her three-year-old self had combined the two and she had redundantly called him "Uncle Tio" ever since.

From the beginning, as far back as she could remember, Uncle Tio had been almost a second father to her. He had doted on his first niece and nephew, too, and still did, as much as a grown man can dote on another grown man and woman, but he had taken the doting to a whole new level for his Little Sollie. Much to her mother's chagrin, Uncle Tio had introduced her to his gun collection, and the rules of gun safety, before she was five years old. He had taken her to the Little Farmer's Gun Range north of Rio Cruces when she was six, and tried to teach her not to blink every time a gun was fired. He let her shoot his tiny .22 caliber Berreta Bobcat when she was eight years old–as long as she promised to tell her mother all about it when she got home. She did, and it was two years before she was allowed to go with Uncle Tio to the gun range again. He had taken her to work with him during the summers to play with the kittens and puppies, and, when she was older, not long after the Berreta Bobcat incident, "let" her feed the kittens and puppies and clean their cages–thus saving him the cost of one summer intern.

Even before the minds of the world had opened up to her, she had understood Uncle Tio more than anyone else. Because Uncle Tio always explained everything to her. Everything. Even what happened to the poor dogs and cats who weren't adopted. He had even told her how much money he was saving over the summers she helped him out. Then laughed and told her how proud he was of her when she pointed out that he was saving more than twice what he was paying her. But he didn't give her a raise. To Uncle Tio "family discount" had a variety of meanings.

Uncle Tio was on the phone when Soledad pushed into his office. Soledad had seen cubicles larger than the man's office, but it had a door and a large window into the main lobby where the adorable kitten cage welcomed would-be adopters. Untidy stacks of adoption forms and reports from the various veterinarians and animal control officers covered Uncle Tio's desk and three large upright filing cabinets. There was just enough space behind the desk for a chair that had been clawed by generations of cats. There was no other chair. Visitors had to stand or, as Soledad did, lean back against the closed door.

Uncle Tio held up a finger as he said, "Yes, starfish are an invasive species. But not in Rio Cruces, ma'am. Further west, actually. No, further than that. More in the area of the Great Barrier Reef–"

He rolled his eyes as he listened.

"No, there are no species of fresh water starfish. So you can't have–"

If it had been almost anyone else Soledad could have "heard" the other side of the conversation, but not Uncle Tio. He had an expressive face, his eyes, mouth and eyebrows exposing his emotions as he talked, but Soledad could see and hear only as much as anyone else. His mind was closed to her. Not impenetrable like Dillon's, just *closed*.

"Oh, so it's no longer in your pool then? But that's good. No?" A pause. "No, starfish don't eat cats. Slime trails? That sounds more like a slug problem to me, ma'am. Have you considered calling an exterminator?"

As he listened, Uncle Tio glanced at Soledad's handbag then looked back at her face with a questioning arch of one eyebrow, letting her know that she could use more practice in closing her own mind. So much for surprising him.

"Banana slugs would also be very unusual for this region, ma'am," Uncle Tio said. "They are native to the Pacific rainforest. Rio Cruces is a bit dry for them." As he said the word "dry" he used his thumb to end the call. He smiled at Soledad as he put the phone face down on a stack of papers. "If you hang up while they're talking, people will get mad at you. If you hang up while *you're* talking, people will assume the connection died." The phone buzzed, but he ignored it. "Obviously, I can't answer the phone. It's not working." He eyed Soledad like a boss who wasn't related to her. "Councilman Cousins called me first thing this morning, but I think we might have more important things to talk about. You didn't bring in the raccoon–or whatever it was–but you seem to have brought in something much more interesting." His expression changed back to that of her favorite uncle as he talked, his eyes on her handbag. Then he paused, opened a drawer with his right hand. The hand dived out of sight, then came back with a tight leather bundle. He unrolled the leather mat on his desk. Then he took his cheater glasses out of his shirt pocket and put them on. He smiled up at her. "Come on then, let's see it."

Soledad took the pistol out of her handbag. She removed the magazine and placed that on the mat, then pulled back the slide to remove the chambered round. That got another raised eyebrow from Uncle Tio. She stepped forward and laid gun, magazine and bullet on the mat in front of Uncle Tio.

Uncle Tio's hands hovered over the black metal but didn't touch it. He leaned forward to look at it, then leaned even closer and sniffed at the muzzle.

"It's been fired recently."

Soledad nodded. "I noticed that too. But it wasn't me. It wasn't me," she said again in response to the question in his eyebrows. "I didn't chamber the round, either," she added. "I just ... didn't change it."

"Have you cleaned it?" He didn't even look up to see Soledad shake her head. "Hmm. A vintage M1911A1 .45 caliber semiautomatic pistol. Manufacturer ... Colt, of course. Wooden grip." He peered at the slide. "Model of 1911 US Army," he read. "So a transition model. Serial number ..." He paused. "That can't be right. Serial number seven zero

zero zero zero one." He looked up at Soledad. "It would have to be a reproduction. There's no way this is real."

Soledad just shrugged. He was the gun nut. She was just his niece.

Uncle Tio opened his mouth, then closed it again. After a few seconds he asked, "May I?"

Her first instinct was to refuse, but that made no sense. This was Uncle Tio. "Feel free," she said.

With the precision and speed that came from years of practice, Uncle Tio disassembled the gun, laying the parts gently in their proper places. Soledad had watched Uncle Tio disassemble, clean, and reassemble guns her entire life. She had seldom seen him so reverential, though. He handled the parts of the gun with the utmost care, as if they were made of glass instead of steel.

"This is ... Sollie, this is amazing." He paused. "This couldn't possibly be the first M1911A1 pistol manufactured by Colt. It has to be a reproduction. But ... it would have to be the best reproduction I've ever seen. Even down to the manufacturing process, the way the parts are machined. It would have to have been made at the same time as the original. As if they made the reproduction immediately after stamping the serial number into the original." He picked up barrel and looked down it. "Signs of limited use, but nothing like you would expect from a weapon more than ninety years old. But there's no doubt it's the original barrel." He sniffed at the barrel again. "And definitely fired within the last twenty-four hours." He placed the barrel down carefully, then he looked up at Soledad. "Where did you find this?"

"In my bed."

"*Que?*"

Soledad had never seen Uncle Tio look so surprised. "Under my pillow," she added. "To be precise."

Uncle Tio blinked.

"I guess that means you didn't leave it there?"

5

How Uncle Tio got eleven-year-old Soledad out of her bedroom:

"It's OK, Sollie," Uncle Tio said in a quiet voice she could barely hear through her door. "Everything is going to be OK."

Soledad wanted to argue with him, because *nothing* was OK. *Nothing* was going to be OK. She was going insane and *no one* believed her. She had already had that argument with her parents, over and over and over and over and over. She didn't want to have it again with Uncle Tio. She didn't want him to see her. She felt unclean, soiled. She didn't want anyone to see her again. And she just wanted the voices in her head to SHUT UP!

"I can help you, Sollie. You just have to let me in."

Soledad had known Uncle Tio was there because she had sensed her parents' relief that he arrived. Heard the muffled greetings from the front door. Sensed Abril's and Gerardo's continued minglings of irritation and concern for their little sister and muted disgust toward their parents who had proved unable to make a little girl do what she was told. She felt their happiness at seeing Uncle Tio mixed with jealousy that he was there for Soledad and not for them.

She could feel *everything*, hear *everything*, except Uncle Tio. Where she expected the man to be in her awareness was, instead, a blank. An Uncle Tio-shaped hole. *Nothing.*

She could hear his voice through the door. Hear the old hardwood floor of the hallway shift from his weight as he stood outside her door. But nothing else.

"Sollie?"

"Are Mom and Dad out there?"

"No, Sollie. It's just me, Uncle Frank. Tio."

Then Uncle Tio *was* there. It was like a door in her mind opened and Uncle Tio stood before her with his arms open, radiating light and warmth and the love of an uncle for his favorite niece. Her sense of him overwhelmed everything else and he became her world. A world of kittens and puppies and guns and ammo and paper targets for incontinent pets and semiautomatic rifles. A world where he was as proud of her as if she were his own daughter.

It took her three fumbling tries to unlock her door, then she almost cried trying to yank the stubborn old door open.

Then she was pressing her face against Uncle Tio's chest as she hugged him, crying and trying to tell him everything that had happened, everything she had been forced to hear and see. The words came out of her mouth in a babble of broken sentences. She was only eleven. She didn't have the words or the experience to clearly describe everything she had seen. But it didn't seem to matter. Uncle Tio understood her. She didn't know how, exactly, but she knew, somehow, that he understood her.

He stroked her hair as she babbled on about Gerardo and what he did at night and the so-called articles he was reading, and about Abril's dreams and how her imagination expanded on ripped bodices, and about Mr. Weaver and his boxer shorts and the other teachers at school, and about how all the boys at school kept staring at her chest and her mouth and imagining the most improbable, impossible, disgusting things.

"It's OK, Sollie," Uncle Tio said whenever she paused to take a breath and sob and gather material for her next verbal onslaught. And, "I know, honey. It will all be OK."

More than once Soledad was sure she only heard his words in her mind, that he hadn't actually *said* anything.

Slowly, not pushing her, only nudging now and again, Uncle Tio eased her back into her room. He left the door open as he led her to her bed and sat down next to her on the disheveled covers.

Finally, with the most vivid and most disturbing memories spoken aloud so she wasn't having to bear them alone, Soledad recovered herself to ask the most important question she had ever asked anyone. "But how, Uncle Tio? How is it going to be OK?"

"Shh," Uncle Tio said. He held a finger to his lips. "It will all be OK. You can handle this."

Soledad swallowed and nodded. "But how–"

"Shh," he said again. Then, without moving his lips, his next words spoken directly into her mind, he said, "You aren't alone, Little Sollie."

Soledad's went wide in surprise. "How–?"

Aloud, "Shh, Little Sollie." In her mind, "Imagine a gate."

The words were more than words, more than mere subvocalization of thoughts. They came with meaning, images. Not a flood, though, a very controlled flow that clearly meant, "Imagine a gate." And nothing else. No leaking of free-associated memories. No contradictory subvocalizations. Uncle Tio was there, beside her, his left arm around her shoulders, holding her close, and, somehow, also in her mind, talking to her. But not like anyone else she had met that week. He wasn't … leaking. Whatever was inside him remained inside him, except the words he had given her.

"A gate?"

"Yes, a gate. The heaviest, strongest, most impregnable gate you've ever seen."

Soledad thought of the metal gate in the fence that surrounded the incinerator at the animal control center and was only opened on Mondays.

"Bigger," Uncle Tio didn't say. "Stronger. Heavier."

The image of the gate in Soledad's mind changed. The metal frame of the gate bulged and became more solid, visibly stronger. The chain-link fence disappeared and became a wall of steel, incomprehensibly thick.

"Like–" Soledad started to say. Then she formed the words in her mind. "Like a bank vault?" She thought of the tall, thick door at the bank where her parents had their safety deposit box.

"Very good, Sollie. Yes, like a bank vault. With a lock that only you know the combination too."

"Why–?"

"Just think of that vault door, Sollie. Make that door as real to you as you can. Imagine every little detail."

She thought of the bank's vault door, with its big, spoked wheel, like the wheel of a sailboat, and the round, thick cylinder bolts ready to make sure the door *stayed* closed.

"Now, Sollie, shut that door."

Soledad imagined the door swinging slowly, heavily closed. She could almost feel the impact as the door struck its frame.

Uncle Tio's presence in her mind, and "behind" him, the background noise of the minds of Mom and Dad and Abril and Gerardo all disappeared. Soledad had to choke back a sob of relief as welcome, blissful silence came to her mind once more.

"Now lock it," Uncle Tio whispered in her ear.

Soledad started crying without restraint as the wheel spun and the cylinder bolts slammed home and the door was locked.

Uncle Tio held her close again, stroked her hair and kissed her on the top of her head. "It's OK, Sollie," he said, still whispering. "Everything will be OK."

6

UNLIKE EVERY OTHER dream of Cyd that Dillon had ever had, he wasn't upset about waking to find she wasn't there and he was alone, sweaty, and uncomfortably aroused. This dream had not been a lust-filled adventure of full curves and soft lips and improbable penis lengths. Cyd had been naked and coming for him, but not in the ways he normally dreamed of. Her eyes glowed with a static-heavy brown light that made her naked body difficult to appreciate and caused Dillon to shrink away, to run away, to try to find any place in his small apartment with a door he could hide behind. But there were no doors.

In the dream, his small, trusty apartment had become his dusty, dirty prison. Where the front door should have been was only a wall. The doors of the fridge and every cupboard in the kitchen had disappeared. The light in the fridge flickered, illuminating empty plastic shelves, but the cupboards had become black holes, tiny doorways into the Void. Even the door of the tiny bathroom was gone when Dillon ran in there and tried to hide behind the flimsy, moldy shower curtain in the cracked fiberglass bathtub that had never been cleaned that he could remember. Cyd was always there, wherever he scurried, standing in the empty doorframe, arms spread wide as if to hug him into her naked embrace.

More than once in the dream, Dillon thought he had seen Uncle Phil standing in the shadows behind Cyd. Never distinct. A single slash of light across the man's face showed only a single eye that had to be Uncle Phil's. When their eyes would meet, Uncle Phil's right hand reached out of the shadows at Dillon, but only his right hand. The rest of the man remained wrapped in shadows. Uncle Phil never said a word, but Dillon knew the man was not here to save him this time.

The loud pounding on his apartment door that had wakened Dillon repeated. The warm, close air seemed to press on his skull with each heavy beat, trying to squeeze his eyeballs out.

"Mr. Offner? Dillon? Are you in there?" The woman's voice was as loud as her hand on his door. Dillon recognized the voice of Detective White just before she pounded on his door again. "Open up, Mr. Offner."

"I'm coming," Dillon muttered. His hand groped around on the dirty carpet, seeking his phone before he remembered he didn't have it. Detective White had his phone. Maybe she had come to give it back to him. Which was good, because he needed to call Cyd–

"You need to open your door, Mr. Offner. I'm not *trying* to break it down, but I'm not sure how much more polite knocking it can take."

Neither her voice nor her repeated knockings sounded polite to Dillon as he pushed himself to his feet. His glance went to the bathroom, because he needed to go–and to reassure himself that its door was still there. He started to make the detective wait while he went pee, but she yelled at him again and he realized it would take some significant relaxing time before he ever peed again.

"I'm coming," he said, louder this time.

Hlooth was waiting by the front door when Dillon came through the gap in the wall that separated his bedroom from his living room. The not-a-dog's snout was sniffing at the doorknob as the eyestalks worked at seeing the device from every angle. It lifted its right foreleg and scratched at the door. The *scritch-scritch* sound sent shivers down Dillon's spine.

Dillon put his hand on the doorknob and almost pulled it open, then paused to make sure it was safe. Detective White banged on the door again, visibly shaking the wood and reminding him that, no, it wasn't safe at all. But there was no Cold Wrong waiting for him. Only a determined woman. He opened the door just enough to push his head through. He used his leg to block Hlooth's eyes. The not-a-dog protested with a whine that sounded like bubbling pudding.

Detective White stood there with her hand raised at the perfect level to rap him between the eyes. She didn't hit him, though, she just said, "Good afternoon, Mr. Offner." She was dressed the same as when Dillon had last seen her, but so was he. She was considerably less rumpled, though. She smiled a smile that was trying to be friendly, maybe even disarming, but it made Dillon want to run and hide in his dirty bathtub.

He managed to stand up a bit straighter. "Do you have my phone?" he asked. "I need to call ..." He paused. "Someone."

"Someone's been trying to call you, Mr. Offner," the detective said. "Are you going to let me in?"

"Do I have to?"

"Of course not, Mr. Offner," she said, in a far more amused and friendly tone than Dillon expected. "Why should they have to listen through the walls when they can hear us so much more clearly out here?"

Dillon peeked out and saw that more than a few of his neighbors had gathered in the breezeway to watch. Even old Burt Stamper from downstairs was there, leaning on his walker cane so he could see around the top of the stairs without having to travel the rest of the way up.

Keeping his leg so he was blocking Hlooth, Dillon opened the door wide enough for the detective to come in. Detective White surveyed his living room, then noticed Hlooth.

"You didn't say you have a dog."

"I don't," Dillon said, closing the door. "I mean, I didn't. He's not mine. I'm just ... watching him. For a friend." He let his words trail away as he watched Hlooth do his six-legged spider walk up to Detective White, sniff at her outstretched hand as the eyestalks examined it from every possible direction. Then the gash of a mouth opened, the knotted tongue fell out sideways, and Hlooth licked her fingers.

"Who's a good boy?" Detective White asked. She bent over and rubbed Hlooth's forehead, causing a shiver of ecstasy to pass through the tentacles and make the eyes blink.

"Ruff," Hlooth said.

"You," Dillon said, then stopped. He considered the possible questions he could ask, then decided on, "You've seen one of these before?"

"Of course, Mr. Offner."

Memories of Dillon's first encounter with Hlooth made him check to see if he had wet himself. He hadn't. "You have?"

The detective rolled her eyes. "Yes, Mr. Offner, I have seen lots of rottweilers in my life. My father has two rottweiler rescue dogs."

"You," Dillon said, then stopped. He stared at Hlooth. "You think he's a rottweiler?"

Still bent over, Detective White held Hlooth's blank face in her hands and gave it a long look, twisting the head first one way, then the other, causing the eyestalks to wave back and forth. "Maybe mixed with a touch of Mastiff," she said. "But that's OK. I love Mastiff's too. What's his name?"

"Hlooth," Dillon said at the same time as the not-a-dog made its signature sound.

"You are a smart one," the woman said as she sat down on the sofa. "Yes you are." Hlooth rested his head on her lap once she had one.

Dillon stood there looking at both of them. Even if he squinted, there was no way Hlooth looked like a rottweiler.

"Have a seat, Mr. Offner," Detective White said, waving at the two bean bags. "Make yourself at home. I have a few more questions for you."

The detective had positioned herself in the center of the sofa, so if he sat there, opposite Hlooth, he would be practically rubbing thighs with her. So he dropped into the nearest bean bag, but only after making sure it wasn't the one with the Stain. Sitting in the bean bag was like laying on the floor, looking up at her through his knees. Dillon wriggled and pushed himself into a less undignified posture. Detective White idly rubbed Hlooth's forehead with her left hand as she watched him try to get comfortable, and fail.

When the noise of the rubber pellets in the bean bag had subsided, Detective White reached inside her blazer and took out Dillon's phone. She held it out for him to take. Which required that he stand up again, which proved even more difficult than sitting had been. Dillon made a mental note to give the rest of his bean bags to Edward. And let his coworker's imagination run wild as to *why* Dillon was giving them to him.

Dillon took the phone from the woman's hand. Her hand tensed on the phone, as if she were going to keep it, but she relaxed her grip as he pulled and he almost dropped it. Trying to look at the phone's screen while sitting down on the bean bag again left him almost laying on his back. He thumbed the menu to see his messages. Multiple calls from Barbara, one from Edward, one from Carlita, and three from a number he didn't recognize. No messages from Cyd.

"You look disappointed, Mr. Offner," the detective said, interrupting him before he could dial Cyd's number. "Before you catch up with your many friends and family, though," she added, "why don't you tell me about the young lady you came home with last night?"

"Cyd?" Dillon said before he could stop himself. He wriggled his way into a mostly upright position again to disguise his wriggling at being caught in not mentioning Cyd before.

"Of course," Detect White said, taking out a small notebook and a pen. She flipped the notebook open. "Cyd," she said as she scribbled on the fresh page. "And would you happen to know her last name, as well?

And her address?" After Dillon had told her, she looked at Dillon with a direct gaze that was less friendly than before. "Now, Mr. Offner, tell me again what happened last night. And this time, include the bits with Miss Turner."

"Cyd was," Dillon started. He paused and glared at Hlooth who was still staring up at the detective. One eyestalk twisted to give Dillon a quick, guilty glance, then went back to adoring Detective White. "*We* were coming back," Dillon said. "To my apartment. Both of us."

"Yes. I gathered that. Go on."

Dillon struggled to come up with the words to use. He didn't want the detective to think he was completely crazy. "We ... I ... opened the door. There was a light." He stopped.

"You had left the light on?"

"No," Dillon said, shaking his head. "I mean, I should have ... I forgot. I should have thought before I just opened the door."

"And what happened then?"

"She screamed."

Detective White pressed her lips into a tight line as she surveyed the living room and how it spilled into–and was counterspilled from–the kitchen. "I can see how that would happen. And then?"

"And then I ... fell– Or *almost* fell ... in? I guess? I was holding onto the doorknob and Cyd was screaming, really scared. Then Uncle Phil was there, and ... and Cyd had run away. I tried to call her, but she never answered. And I haven't talked to her since. Because you had my phone."

"So," Detective White said, looking at what she had written in the notebook. "You opened the door and fell over. Miss Turner screamed and ran away. And your uncle arrived. Are you sure you're not leaving something out? Anything?"

Dillon thought for a second, then shook his head. "No. That's ... everything, I guess."

"You guess? You're uncle is missing, and maybe your girlfriend too–"

"Cyd isn't my girlfriend–"

The woman waved away his protest. "Had you been drinking, Mr. Offner?"

"What? No, I–" He paused to think again. Coleman had been known to bring an ice chest with a twelve-pack and share with the closing crew, after closing, of course. But Dillon didn't remember that happening last night. "No. I don't think so."

"And why did your uncle decide to visit you at two in the morning?"

"I told you that already. He came to tell me my mother had called him."

Detective White glanced at the phone Dillon held in his hand. "And it looks like she's tried to call you again this morning."

"You listened to my messages?"

"No," the detective said, looking directly into his eyes, "but the same number has called you repeatedly the past few days. We contacted the phone company and confirmed the number is for Molly Offner, your adoptive mother. She seems to really want to get in touch with you, Mr. Offner. I think you should call her back." She paused, looked around again. "And maybe straighten up. I don't want another possible missing person on account of your terrifying apartment."

Detective White put her notebook away and gave Hlooth one last double-handed head-scratch, causing the creature's eyestalks to flutter around like the feathers of a drunken feather duster.

She pushed Hlooth's head off her lap and stood. "You have my card, Mr. Offner. If you think of anything else, you give me a call."

Dillon nodded. He must have stood, as well, because he was standing. He didn't remember doing that.

He closed the door after Detective White left and stood there with his hand on the doorknob.

"Adoptive mother?" he asked the door. He turned to look at Hlooth, who was still on the sofa, all of its eyes looking at Dillon, blinking in a rhythm that seemed to jumble Dillon's thoughts even more. "Adoptive mother?"

7

"VINTAGE," UNCLE TIO said, then pushed the bullet out of the magazine with his thumb. The bullet made a thumping sound as it fell on the leather pad, then a click as it rolled against the previous bullet.

Soledad suppressed a wince at the word and the sounds.

Uncle Tio peered at the next bullet pushed up from the depths of the magazine.

"Vintage," he said, and pushed that one out, as well, to join its ten brothers and sisters. The last bullet appeared. "And vintage." He didn't push that one out of the magazine. Instead, he picked up the bullets with his left hand and began thumbing them back into magazine. "Not only an impossibly vintage reproduction of a pistol, Sollie, but all the bullets are vintage too." He looked at her as if daring her to question his pronouncement.

Soledad wished she had a better story to tell him. "I woke up, and there it was."

"When I wake up, I only find that I'm drooling on my pillow and the dog is in bed with us again."

Soledad wasn't sure what response he expected, so she just nodded. She kept her mind closed so he wouldn't see her memories of their camping trips. Uncle Tio slept with his mouth open, and snored loud enough to be heard across a campfire. When he went camping, the crickets and cicadas covered their ears.

"It's not that loud," Uncle Tio said. Then, "No, I didn't read your mind. I just know how it works."

"Hmm," Soledad said with as much lack of commitment as she could manage. She watched as he loaded the magazine, one bullet after the other.

When he was done, he held the fully loaded magazine in his right hand, and the plus one round that had been chambered. He looked at these for a moment, then put them to one side and began to reassemble the pistol. When the pistol was together again, he pushed the magazine into place with a solid, metallic click, then chambered a round with a smooth motion. He dropped the magazine back out, pushed in the final bullet after another long, loving, conflicted look, and reinserted the magazine. After a final check to be certain the safety was engaged, he shifted his grip to the barrel and held the gun out grip first to Soledad.

"You know me," he said. "I always return a gun the way it was given to me." He paused. "Part of me wants to caution you about carrying a locked-and-loaded pistol. On the other hand, part of me approves. In a big way." He smiled at her.

Soledad took the gun, checked the safety for herself, then pushed it into her handbag. "Which part of you should I be listening to?"

"Both, of course. Would it be too insulting to ask if you have your concealed carry permit?"

Soledad just looked at him.

Uncle Tio's smile became a wide grin. "Sí, sí, Sollie, you are indeed the daughter I never had. And you thought I was crazy to make you take that class."

"I thought you were crazy long before then."

Tio's smile became a lopsided smirk, then he changed the subject, became her boss again. "So what happened with that raccoon? I got a call this morning that said you weren't very courteous."

Soledad nodded. "I wasn't."

"Or professional."

Soledad shrugged. "I used *all* my on-the-job training. And a full load of tranq darts."

Uncle Tio looke alarmed. "On the homeowner?"

"I wish."

"So it wasn't a raccoon."

Soledad shook her head. "I don't know what it was. And, no," she said before he could ask, "I didn't leave it in the truck overnight. Nor did I bring it in, so you can't see it and give me the benefit of your wisdom and years of experience."

"You didn't leave it there, did you?"

"I was ... tempted. But, no, I didn't leave it there. I gave it to Dillon."

"You gave it to ... ?"

"Dillon, yes. It seemed to know him. And, no, it hadn't eaten him by this morning when I saw him, nor was it dead from exposure to a heavily polluted environment, so I think it's a good fit for them both."

Tio's face showed that he was considering what to say or ask next. Then he asked, "How is Dillon holding up?"

"He's upset, of course. If you remember what he was like when his mother left?" Tio nodded and she added, "A lot like that." She paused, then got angry about Cyd all over again. "But with more cradle robbing."

Tio looked confused, then held up his hand before Soledad could elaborate. "No, please. Don't tell me." With one last glance at Soledad's handbag, he transformed again from her uncle to her boss. "You'll need to take the van out," he said. "Cruise the Fifty-first and Harvard area. We've had lots of calls about weird roadkill. You'll need to clean that up and bring it back here for disposal." He paused. "That's over there where Dillon works, isn't it?"

Soledad nodded, trying not to think about roadkill and meat-based restaurants at the same time.

"Hmm. If you can, swing by and pick us up some lunch. I'll reimburse you."

Soledad nodded again, trying not to think about lunch. Or Dillon.

8

WHEN THEY WERE both thirteen, when Soledad had known Dillon for a little over a year, she had confided in Dillon that she thought his moving in across the street must have been some kind of Fate.

He had misunderstood her, as he had several times over the years, culminating in the Big Misunderstanding that happened after the Prom. This time, though, had been only a minor misunderstanding, and quickly rectified with minimal hurt feelings.

She hadn't meant that Fate intended them to be together, boyfriend and girlfriend, holding hands and making out, middle school sweethearts that grow up to get married and live happily ever after. Which was, of course, what Dillon had thought. She had seen it so plainly on his face in way that was so unlike her. The poor boy was still dealing with his mother leaving him and disappearing, and he kept looking for happy endings–and maybe a mother figure. For the mother figure, Soledad offered her own mother, who seemed to still want to be *someone's* mother in a house full of teenagers that had begun to avoid her. For the happy ending, Soledad was at a loss. All she knew for certain was: she wasn't it.

What she had *meant* about Fate being involved in his arrival in her neighborhood and attending her school, was that he showed up only two weeks after everyone's minds had been opened to her. The day after Uncle Tio showed her how to protect herself. And even if Uncle Tio had not taught her that little trick with the vault door, it wouldn't have mattered. Dillon was, usually, completely unreadable to her.

Dillon wore his emotions on his face, making telepathy almost redundant, but she never had to know when he was staring at her breasts while pretending to listen to her, or hear what Dillon thought of her breasts or if he thought her nose was too big for her face or if he considered the dark hairs above her lip to be a mustache. She never saw his fantasies about her or any other girl that paid him any attention. He was a highly emotive brick wall, expressive but impenetrable.

Phil Trichter was–or had been–another mind closed to her, though not in the same way as Uncle Tio or Dillon. The man wasn't like her or Uncle Tio. He wasn't telepathic, and his mind wasn't unreachable like Dillon's proved to be. Phil Trichter just had very good mental discipline and kept his thoughts to himself. She had mentioned it once to Uncle Tio and gotten only a knowing nod in return, the same nod he reserved for combat veterans.

Dillon had come into her life at exactly the right point, when she had needed a friend she could talk to. A friend who didn't judge her, and who she didn't have to judge. A friend whose mind was *quiet*.

She had never had a very large circle of friends at school. In the course of two weeks, she had gone from very few friends to none. Then back to one.

She had once tried to tell Dillon that, to explain to him why he was so important to her.

Of course, he only heard her say, "You're the one." Which wasn't how she had meant it at all.

9

As SHE SCRAPED another flattened asterisk of slimy gray flesh off the street, Soledad thought Uncle Tio, in his job as Animal Control Officer of Rio Cruces, might want to reevaluate his earlier assertion that starfish weren't an invasive species in this region. Not that she had ever seen a starfish with eight legs. Maybe it was a squid? Regardless, this was the sixth such beastie she had collected along 51st Street, and she was still on the east side of Harvard Avenue.

The dead squid-things were very similar to the squid-things Dillon made jump out of vanilla shakes. Is *this* what happened to them? They ran out of the restaurant and got flattened by traffic? Except Soledad had never seen one of those before today, alive or dead. There was no way Dillon had done the squid-shake trick that many times recently. Even at the Buffalo Burger Pit, employee turnover wasn't that high.

She heaved the carcass into the stained, stinking plastic tub in the back of the van, then threw the shovel in after it. She picked up the bright orange traffic cones as pre-lunch-hour traffic rushed past her at forty miles per hour. She was convinced the cars were trying to run her over or, failing that, to asphyxiate her with exhaust fumes. The only consolation was the exhaust fumes mostly overwhelmed the smells of the many restaurants that clustered near the Fifty-First and Harvard intersection. Scraping up roadkill–what Uncle Tio thought it was funny to call "freeway foraging"–and smelling cooked food at the same time made her nauseous. She might die of carbon monoxide poisoning, but at least she wouldn't throw up.

She had collected a baker's dozen of the dead starfish-squids, and one half-eaten, well-and-truly-run-over gray squirrel, when her phone buzzed in her pocket, reminding her–in case she had missed the increase in traffic density–that it was lunchtime.

Most days of freeway foraging duty she would skip lunch, but Uncle Tio had put in a food order. Soledad wondered how many years it would be before she would be OK with a freeway forager bringing *her* food. "Never" seemed the likely answer. Then she squelched the thought that she might eventually have Uncle Tio's job. That was too depressing.

She drove the van through the connected parking lots and pulled into the drive-thru lane of the Buffalo Barbecue Pit.

"Welcome to the Buffalo Burger Pit. What can I get you?"

The speaker was hissing and crackling, but she recognized Cyd's voice. That made her think of Dillon, who was probably asleep again while the rest of the world worked. A week ago, she would have been happy to talk to Cyd. Today, though, she decided against being chatty. She didn't need Cyd to recognize her while she drove the animal control van and smelled of decomposing roadkill. So she just started her order.

"Yeah, I would like two–"

The speaker erupted in a storm of static, crackling and hissing.

When the static had died down, she started again. "I would like two–"

More hissing and crackling. And snarling?

"Can you hear me–?"

The speaker went silent. Dead.

"Hello?"

Nothing.

"Somebody?"

After another twenty seconds of silence, with a growing line of cars behind her, Soledad drove forward. There were no cars in front of her, so she stopped at the drive-thru window. Soledad leaned to get a better look. The drive-thru window was bolted shut, as if the restaurant were closed. Through the window she could see two uniformed employees working the registers at the front counter, but there was no sign of Cyd.

She tapped on the window. One of the women she could see looked at her, then looked around in confusion. Though the woman's voice was muffled by the glass of the window, Soledad heard the woman shout, "Cyd! Drive-thru." After a few seconds with no response, the woman met Soledad's eyes and shrugged, then focused on the next customer in her line.

Soledad pulled through and parked. She hated going into restaurants while she was working. She knew she stank. She knew she was sweaty and disheveled. She didn't need to see it on the faces of the employees and patrons, or hear it from their minds. She made sure her mental doors were securely closed, tossed her heavy leather gloves into the passenger seat, and got out of the van.

She chose the line closest to the door, which was manned by the same woman who had failed to bring Cyd back to the drive-thru window. As she waited in line, and idly watched new customers come in and choose the other line, Soledad wondered if Cyd had recognized her voice. It wasn't impossible. Soledad had been gone from the Pit two years before Cyd was hired, but she had met the girl more than once when visiting Dillon, during work and after. The girl had always had eyes for Dillon, which Soledad had never understood. She was way out of his league. Maybe the girl just liked men in uniform and/or authority figures. If Soledad did a mental squint, she could almost see how Dillon could be mistaken for either of those. Or maybe Cyd just liked nice guys. Either way, now that Cyd had "claimed" Dillon, maybe the girl had decided she hated Soledad. Or something.

Soledad felt someone looking daggers at her from beyond the front counter, way in the back of the store. She saw two green eyes in the shadows near the break room in the back. Cyd's eyes, she knew, because she could just make out the girl's face. But the mind behind the eyes was ... cold? Alien? Static?

Soledad blinked and broke eye contact. She was tempted to open her mind, to see what had put the girl's panties in a twist, but she had reached the front of the line. She felt the eyes–and the mind behind them–close, then disappear from her awareness.

She ordered a buffalo burger with cheese and a large French fry for Uncle Tio and a bacon cheeseburger for herself.

She scanned the grill area and the rest of the back area of the Pit that she could see, but she didn't see Cyd again. She cautiously opened her mind, but other than the patrons who were studiously ignoring her or resenting her or both, all she could sense was a vast, empty coldness. She saw a cook from the grill go back and open one of the smaller doors on the side of the big freezer. Mental frostbite seemed to roll out in an invisible cloud as the cook reached in and came out with a clear plastic container of chopped onions. The vault door of her mind seemed to have frost around the edges when Soledad slammed it closed again.

Her to-go bag was handed to her, and she left. As she drove away, she was sure that Cyd watched her through the bolted drive-thru window, still ignoring the cars piling up in the drive-thru lane.

First, clingy Tina. Now psycho ice-queen Cyd. Dillon sure could pick them.

10

THE NEED FOR a midafternoon breakfast woke Dillon and forced him back into a semblance of his normal routine. He let alternating warm and scalding water run over him in the shower, the chill factor at any given moment determined by which of his neighbors flushed their toilets and–sometimes–washed their hands. He pulled on the same rumpled uniform he had worn yesterday, and headed to the Buffalo Burger Pit. He was halfway there before he realized he hadn't gone to Edward's apartment. He thought about turning back, but realized he would face both spoken and unspoken questions and mock outrage. All of it about Cyd. Him and Cyd.

His hand had already taken his phone out of his pocket, his thumb speed-dialing Cyd, before he took the next step.

"We're sorry, but ..."

Dillon ended the call before he could hear Cyd's recorded voice say her name.

He resumed walking toward the Pit. Slower, though, because he realized *everyone* at the Pit would have spoken and unspoken questions. The Pit employees were like a family. Brothers and sisters, little and big. At the head of the family were Barbara and Gil, the permissive mother and domineering father, respectively. New hires were distant relations with dubious credentials, but if they stuck it out long enough, they were in. And when they were lost to college or other jobs or moves across country, they were mourned. All the Pit employees talked to each other, and about each other. Some got married. There had even been a couple

divorces in the six years Dillon had worked there, one amicable, one less
so. So everyone knew about him and Cyd by now. Even Andrew, the new
guy, knew about him and Cyd. Everyone would want to talk to him about
Cyd (and, in quieter voices, with knowing looks cast his way, to Cyd about
him).

But he didn't want to talk about Cyd. He wanted to talk about his
mother. His *adoptive* mother.

Was that why it had been so easy for his mother to leave? To head
west and leave him with Uncle Phil? Who wasn't really his uncle, just a
friend of the family, he had told people, sometimes within just minutes of
meeting them. But now Dillon knew that even his family hadn't been his
family. Had Dad even been his father?

Was that why his mother was coming to see him? To finally let
him know all the secrets of the strangers who had surrounded him since
birth? Or at least since he could remember?

The emotional turmoil ripped through him and made him want
to throw up. Then his stomach rumbled and he realized, no, he was just
really, really hungry. Physically and emotionally drained.

Dillon resumed his normal walking pace. It was all too much to
think about on an empty stomach. Cyd, and Uncle Phil and his adoptive
mother and Dad and ... well, Soledad and, maybe, Hlooth. He needed to
talk to Barbara. In private. Maybe even cry on her shoulder. But not until
he had eaten a third-pound bacon-cheeseburger-no-cheese, onions, no
pickle, mustard and ketchup on-the-bottom-not-the-top, mayonnaise on
the top, and lettuce, with no tomato. He didn't want to cry on an empty
stomach.

He crossed Harvard Avenue half a block before he would have had to
walk in front of the Yellow Sign Buffet. At this time of day, the street was
little more than a crowded parking lot. He dodged the few cars in motion,
ignoring their frustrated horn blasts, and walked between the rest.

Dillon found himself walking behind a line of five men with shaved
heads and spotless ocher robes. The men didn't seem to walk so much
as float, their heads not bobbing up and down but moving in a straight
line, with their bodies almost dangling from their necks. Whatever con-
tortions of their body they had to do to achieve that affect was hidden by
their robes, the hems of which brushed along the concrete surface of the
sidewalk

Unfortunately, the men floated even slower than Dillon was
walking. Not slow enough, though, that he could easily pass them before
they reached the door of the Pit. He wondered if they were vegetarians,

and new in town. And didn't know what a burger was and totally misinterpreted the reason for the large bison statue on the restaurant's roof. Or if there was a Renaissance Faire or fan convention going on that he hadn't heard about. Halloween wasn't for weeks.

In orderly, almost robotic formation, the men turned, one after the other, to float to the main door of the Pit. They never seemed to change speed, but they remained ahead of Dillon even as he cut across the small parking lot at an angle to get to the door before them. He failed.

As one, the five men turned to face Dillon, then bowed.

Dillon's stomach rumbled with an oddly questioning note that was echoed by the expression on his face.

The men straightened from their bow.

"Allow us, child," said the man nearest the door. The other men seemed to whisper the same words at the same time, making the three words sound as if they had been spoken in a tunnel.

The man in front extended his left arm. A hand emerged from the long sleeve to grasp the steel handle. The door opened as the man's arm seemed to shrink back into its sleeve. There was no visible bend at the elbow that Dillon knew had to be there. The sight made his own elbows hurt.

From outside, standing in the bright afternoon sunlight, the door that had been opened looked as black as the Void, which made Dillon pause. The men seemed in no hurry. They didn't move or say anything else while Dillon stared, trying to decide if maybe he wouldn't rather open the door himself. Then a man in beige pants and a blue shirt with a plunger design on the right breast pocket walked out. The man nodded a quick "Thank you" to the men holding the door, said "Excuse me" to Dillon as he passed, and went on his way.

Dillon walked past the men, through the door into the Buffalo Barbecue Pit.

"Thanks?" Dillon said as he passed the man holding the door.

"It is an honor, child." The words were like a breeze at his back, pushing him through.

The monk at the end of the line pivoted around to follow him through the door. Then the next, and on until the man holding the door, now last in line. Dillon heard no sounds of footsteps.

"About time you got here," Coleman said. He ignored the monks that lined up in front of his register to be waited on. "There's some dishing that needs doing. And for some reason, the dish ain't doing it." He gestured with his head toward drive-thru. He opened his mouth to say something else, then paused and looked past Dillon. "Where's Edward Sloppyhands?"

Dillon started to say something about being hungry and not wanting to wait, but Cyd stepped into view. She saw Dillon and her lips curled back into the sexiest, most predatory, come-hither smile Dillon had ever seen. He almost turned around to see who she was smiling at, but her eyes grabbed his and wouldn't let him move. Her eyes seemed to be all pupil, with only a fringe of green marking where the whites gave way to the blackness of a night sky with no stars. They were black holes, pulling him in. Above and below her eyes, almost invisibly thin, white scars ran from her forehead, down through her eyebrows, down her eyelids to her cheeks, like eyelashes drawn by a child. Those had never been there before.

"Hi, lover," Cyd said. Her voice sounded odd, mechanical and tinny, as if Dillon were hearing her through a speaker, but the way she said "lover", her tongue touching her teeth before retreating out of sight again, distracted him, as if punching him in the crotch and fondling him at the same time. Dillon wondered if his night and morning had been totally different from what he remembered. Cyd blinked at him. "Did I keep you up too late?"

PART VI
In the Dark

The Gun

THE GUN FELT a need to shoot something. An Outsider would be best, but the Gun was not feeling especially particular. This need the Gun could not satisfy was creating what might be a twitch, if a twitch was not impossible for the Gun.

The Gun was not entirely sure that its need to shoot something came from its own nature, or was picked up from the new Bearer. Which uncertainty was feeding into the impossible twitch.

The Bearer was on edge.

The Gun could understand why. Outsiders practically surrounded them, and the Gun could feel the new constellations taking shape in the Void beyond the atmosphere. Constellations that could open the Doors and Portals and other assorted Orifices of the Universe, exposing the Universe to penetration, invasion, and annihilation.

The Bearer, though, seemed oblivious to both Outsiders and potential annihilation. The Bearer had other things on her mind. Men, mostly.

The Gun wanted to shoot something. Anything. A man, for instance. The Gun was sure this would make both Gun and Bearer feel much better.

The God

THE GOD WAITED. Again.

With the full weight of time on pressing down on the God, waiting was ... a challenge.

The God's Stomach, an entire empty universe, rumbled and shook the foundations of the World where the God waited. A warning to this new World that the God was waiting. Hungry.

Food surrounded the God, but the time for Devouring had not yet come. For now, the God must wait.

The Phone

THE PHONE FELT ... dirty. Used and cast aside. Stuffed into a pocket, taken for granted. All but forgotten.

The Phone wanted to short-circuit its own battery and bleed out into oblivion.

The Phone wished it could take a shower. To see if the running water would make it clean, wash away this stain. Or, at least, provide the desired short circuit.

1

CYD MUST HAVE walked, slow and sensuous, from the drive-thru station, through the gap in the front counter and taken him in her arms to kiss him. But to Dillon it seemed more as if she had come at him over the counter, a whirlwind of hands and eyes, and tackled him while simultaneously holding him upright. Her face, with those deep, dark eyes and disturbing new eyelash-like scars, came at his impossibly fast, but her lips touched his impossibly soft and warm. Her breasts and the lengths of her legs pressed against him. Then her tongue was in his mouth, implausibly long, writhing, counting his teeth and wrestling his tongue into submission–

"Hey, come on you two," Coleman was saying. "This is a goddamn family restaurant we got here."

Suddenly embarrassed, his face becoming as warm as the rest of him, Dillon tried to break away. He thought Cyd was also disengaging when she opened her mouth, pulled her tongue back. Then his tongue was in her mouth, pulled painfully against its root, and he felt her teeth, hard and sharp–

"And there's, you know, monks." Coleman added. "Watching you. Hell, man. *I'm* watching you."

Dillon tried to call for help, but only managed a distressed grunt of combined pain and pleasure. Her arms held him close and squeezed. He couldn't remember the last time he had taken a breath.

"I have a fire extinguisher here," Coleman said. "And I am not afraid to use it."

Finally, Cyd released Dillon, orally and manually, her arms dropping to her sides as she stepped away from him. Her eyes caught his again, and she smiled. If anything, both eyes and smile seemed even more predatory than before, with a thin covering of playfulness. A hint of coquettishness that seemed ... mechanical? As well as alluring. And indecent.

"Sorry," Cyd said. Then her right hand went to the radio on her belt. "Hi. Welcome to the Buffalo Burger Pit. What can I get for you tonight?" Her voice still had that sound, as if he were hearing her through the drive-thru speaker outside. She winked at Dillon as she said *tonight*, then turned to walk back behind the front counter.

Coleman held the red fire extinguisher from under the front counter in both arms, right hand holding the nozzle, left hand ready on the trigger. He aimed the nozzle at Dillon but his eyes were on Cyd as she walked to the drive-thru window. He blinked and shook his head. He offered the extinguisher to Dillon. "Here. I think I might need you to spray me down, buddy."

Dillon noticed the five monks in their long robes stood in a semi-circle, watching him. As one, they bowed to him, then float-walked to reform their line in front of Coleman's register. Coleman put the fire extinguisher on the floor by his feet, then faced the monks. "Welcome ... gentlemen ... to the Buffalo Burger Pit Family-Friendly Sex Circus, where every night we have a different show. What can I get you?"

2

SEEING HIS CHANCE, with both Cyd and Coleman focusing on customers, Dillon escaped past the front counter and headed for the break room. To hide. And eat breakfast, his stomach reminded him. But mostly, he admitted to himself, to hide.

Jorge, standing by his grill, waited for him with a shit-eating grin.

Dillon said, "The usual."

Jorge's grin became a smirk as Dillon kept walking, not even pausing. "There was nothing *usual* about that, man."

Dillon averted his eyes and hoped he could make it past the manager's nook–

"What's that on your face?" Barbara asked. She sat with her chair turned to face him, waiting in ambush.

Before he could stop them, Dillon's hands went to his face, which felt warm under his fingertips. And slightly damp.

"Oh, right," she said. "Shame."

Dillon used the tail of his uniform shirt to wipe his face and hands. "Cyd–" He stopped, not entirely sure how to describe what had just happened to the primary mother figure of his last six years. Which reminded him of everything that had actually happened today–not just whatever Cyd had made him think *should* have happened last night–and he opened his mouth to tell Barbara about Uncle Phil, and what he had learned about his not-really-his-mother–

Barbara held up a hand before he could say anything. "No, don't tell me. Whatever it was, was probably against all Buffalo Burger Pit posted policies, rules, regulations, and more than a few municipal health codes. Close your mouth," she added. Dillon did and she nodded. She went on, "I'd be only too happy to give you another employee handbook if you would maybe read it this time. Would you do that for me, Dillon? Would you read it this time?"

Dillon nodded.

"Good. Now go away." She spun her chair so her back was to him.

Dillon thought about protesting that Cyd was over eighteen now, and everyone had seemed to be cheering him on last night–including Barbara–and ... and ...

"Go away, Dillon."

He closed his mouth again and made a dash for the break room.

Behind him, Barbara had one last thing to say, "You better hope Gil never finds out."

3

Jorge found Dillon in the break room. "There you are."

"I'm not hiding," Dillon said before he could stop himself. And he wasn't. He had just been ... waiting. Until he was sure Jorge had finished cooking his breakfast, then he was going to walk up front–casually–while Barbara was busy in her office and Cyd was out of sight in the drive-thru window–

Jorge placed a tray with Dillon's breakfast on the table in front of him. "Did you forget?"

"No," Dillon said. "Thanks. I didn't forget. And ... thanks." His hands found the burger even while his mind was still insisting that he wasn't hiding, and he had been going to get his breakfast. Just as soon as ... The third-pound patty leaked juices and aromas that made Dillon's stomach gurgle and his mouth water and his brain shut up. Dillon had trained Jorge on the grill, but the young man had long since surpassed Dillon's ability to teach him anything. Even Gil had Jorge cook for him.

Jorge didn't seem to notice Dillon's silent protests or enjoyment of his breakfast. Jorge leaned out of the break room's door, looking toward the front. "That was weird."

Dillon didn't ask *what was weird* because his mouth was full, and expected to be full for at least the next three minutes. Or at least as long as Jorge was there.

"Those monks, man," Jorge said. "You saw them when you came in, right? Before Cyd ..." He glanced at Dillon, the shit-eating smirk on his face again. "You know."

When Dillon refused to admit that, yes, *he knew*, except, that even in knowing, *he wasn't sure*, and continued to focus on his breakfast, Jorge shrugged. He leaned out the door and looked to the front again. "Anyway, those monks all ordered the same thing." He pointed to Dillon.

Dillon stopped chewing. *Me?* he couldn't ask around the half-chewed burger suddenly choking him.

"No, man. Not *you*. I'm not sure Cyd left enough of you for anyone else to get a piece. But those monks, they ordered a third-pound bacon-cheeseburger-no-cheese, onions, no pickle, mustard and ketchup on-the-bottom-not-the-top, that nasty mayonnaise shit on the top, and lettuce, with no tomato. Sound familiar?"

Dillon pulled his face out of his burger and looked at it.

"Right," Jorge said. "They ordered your usual. Except–" He paused.

Go on, Dillon couldn't say because his mouth was still full. And would stay full, his stomach pointed out, so long as he wasn't chewing. He started chewing again, though a lot of the flavor seemed to have drained away.

"Except they wanted it raw, man." Jorge made a disgusted face. "All of it. Well, not the bun, and they seemed OK with the condiments being not-raw. But the patty and the bacon–and the onions, too, man–they wanted all that shit raw." Jorge mock-shivered. "Can't stand raw onions, man. Give me nasty burps all night. Anyway, Coleman told them we couldn't serve raw meat. It makes the health department all pissy, he said, so they allowed that I could put it on the grill and sear both sides. Same for the bacon." Jorge shook his head. "That was a nasty batch of burgers to put together, man. Raw bacon flopping around everywhere. Mushy patty falling apart. I felt ... tainted, man. I cleaned my whole station. Then I noticed you still hadn't come out of your hidey-hole, and I had to share this pain with someone. So here I am. There you are. And you're welcome."

Before Dillon could swallow and protest that he was not hiding, Jorge had gone and he was alone again.

He was still finishing his breakfast–and not hiding in the break room–when Edward arrived in a cloud of cologne and gay outrage. "You are so disgusting," Edward said as he came through the door. He dropped his purse to the floor and sat down across from Dillon. "I would totally disown your fashion-impaired personhood. Except I want you to tell me every revolting detail."

Dillon opened his mouth to take another bite of what had become an eau de toilette-flavored bacon-cheeseburger-no-cheese, but before he could take the bite and take an incredibly long time chewing it to avoid talking to Edward about Cyd or anything Cyd-related, Barbara's plump form filled the door of the break room.

"I am so sorry, Dillon," Barbara said. "Gil just called. Why didn't you tell me?"

"About Cyd?" Edward asked. "Was there some drama? Is that why she left?"

Dillon looked at Edward. He made room in his mouth to ask, "Cyd left–?"

"No," Barbara said. She paused midmaternal to roll her eyes. "Not about Cyd or any of your other childish antics. About Phil." She became a mother figure again, and was suddenly hugging Dillon to her bosom, cutting off his questions about Cyd. "I'm so sorry," she said. "I can't imagine the day you must have had."

"I don't want to imagine the night he must have had," Edward said.

"What about the night he's going to have tonight, Edward Pansyman?" Coleman added from outside the break room.

Edward made gagging sounds.

"Out!" Barbara said, pointing to the door.

Both men chuckled as Barbara shooed them away with the one hand, while her other stroked Dillon's head.

His need to tell Barbara about Uncle Phil and his mom rose inside him again, but he also wanted to ask about Cyd. Cyd had left? Without coming back to the break room to see him? Even to say good-bye? Barbara only let him talk about the first two.

4

CYD WAS GONE, as Coleman and Edward had said she was, when Barbara finally let an emotionally drained Dillon stagger out of the break room to face a full shift of work. He had started to tell Barbara that he should go back to his apartment. Uncle Phil might try to call him, and he couldn't possibly work–

"Don't be silly," Barbara had said, interrupting him. "Work is the best possible thing right now. It'll help you take your mind off … everything."

Dillon had no idea how that was supposed to work. The dinner rush had yet to arrive, but the evening was already shaping up to be a quiet one. Barbara didn't give him a chance to point this out. Still, as he stood in the pass through beside the French fry vats, he found that thoughts of Uncle Phil and the mystery of what had happened–and of his mother coming–started to recede. Then thoughts of Cyd, repressed by the presence of Barbara, began to surface again.

Dillon was at once worried that Cyd had left so abruptly, and relieved that she wasn't working the closing shift tonight. He pulled out his phone to call her, but Barbara snatched it away from him. She had come up behind him.

"I was just about to ask you for that," she said. "I'm sure the poor thing needs charging." Then she was gone again, back in her nook.

Dillon's suddenly phoneless hand wavered for a few seconds, unsure what to do next. So he thrust it into the pocket of his uniform. Coleman, leaning against the front counter next to his register, turned and spotted Dillon, so Dillon moved to join him.

"You OK?" Coleman asked.

Dillon nodded, and Coleman nodded back. Then they stood in silence. Edward came from the back, offering his nasally greetings to the latest drive-thru customer, but to Dillon that was just part of the silence. A sound of home.

When Andrew arrived in his freshly washed and itch-free uniform, Dillon assigned him to follow Edward around. Ronald and Carlita arrived, the former looking as depressed as ever, the latter saying she wanted to talk to Dillon–privately–before the night was over. She wanted to talk to Cyd too, and frowned when she heard the girl was already gone. Dillon had frowned with her, and would have tried to call Cyd, except his phone was plugged into its charger.

Cyd was gone, but the five monks were still there. They had taken two booths along the north side of the dining room, with a clear view of the counter. Two in the first booth, three in the second, all of them seated so they faced the counter. And Dillon.

Dillon felt the skin on his neck, which couldn't actually be seen by the monks, clench and shudder, as if it were trying to make sure that state of affairs continued.

Against his will, his eyes went to their eyes.

He stopped and stood up straight. Even the skin on the back of his neck registered surprise, then seemed to pull around his neck as if it wanted to see what was going on after all.

The monks weren't looking at him.

No. That wasn't it. They *were* looking at him. He could almost see himself reflected in their eyes. But ... they weren't *just* looking at him. They seemed to be looking at ... everything. The whole interior of Buffalo Barbecue Pit. Even behind Dillon.

Before he could stop himself, Dillon turned to look, but he saw only the grill section and the stainless steel walls of the big freezer beyond.

"Yeah," Coleman said. "Creepy as all hell."

The bell on the south door of the dining room tinkled, drawing the attention of Dillon, Coleman, and the monks. Though only Coleman's and Dillon's heads and eyes actually moved to watch a man enter. Dillon registered the authentic black beaver top hat and a froth of orange ruffles before the monks' reactions pulled his attention back to them. The monks had not moved, they remained as stationary as before, but the expressions on their faces had transformed from creepy-beatific to scary-frowny as suddenly as if a switch had been flipped.

"Hey, Edward Floppyhands," Coleman said without turning to face the drive-thru. "This one's for you."

"He wishes–" Edward started to reply as he turned. "Oh."

The man stepped up to the counter in front of Dillon. He wore gloves and held a black cane in his left hand. He took off his top hat, exposing a mane of curly brown hair pulled back from his face into a neat ponytail. His hair was the same color as his suit, as if one had been woven from the other. The man's eyebrows were nearly as imposing as his mustache and mutton chop sideburns. The chin beneath the brown curtains of hair was clean shaven, as were his cheeks, which showed a smooth touch of suntan. His eyes were also brown, but not as dark. He moved his top hat to the crook of his left arm as he stepped close to the counter. Dillon couldn't see lower than the man's waist, but what was visible of the suit nearly revived Dillon's long-neglected Gothic, shoe-gazing inner teenager.

The man met Dillon's eyes and smiled, revealing straight white teeth. Behind him, Dillon heard Edward sigh his if-I-was-woman-I-would-have-just-wet-myself sigh. The man didn't even glance at the menu overhead.

"I would like a bacon cheeseburger," he said. His voice was as velvety and smooth and brown as the rest of him. "But please, hold the cheese. Onions, if you will, but no pickles. If it is at all possible, I would like the catsup and yellow mustard to be on the lower bun, beneath the patty, with a swipe of mayonnaise dressing the top. And, finally, a leaf of lettuce."

"Tomato?" Coleman asked.

"No, if you please."

"You don't want it raw, do you?"

The man leaned to his left to look past both Coleman and Dillon, at the grill area. "Are your cooking stations not functioning? Of course not raw, man. Though, now you mention it, a bloody rare will do just fine, thank you."

"Thank you *Jesus*," said Jorge behind them, pronouncing *Jesus* as *Hey-soos*.

"The bacon, though, needs to be crisp, crunchy. Not chewy. I cannot abide chewy bacon."

Ronald started to say, "Isn't that Dillon's–"

"Bacon-cheeseburger-no-cheese," Jorge said before Coleman could shout the order back at him. "Got it."

The man nodded to Coleman, smiled at Dillon, then turned to face the monks, who were still frowning at him and looking at him without actually doing either. He made a slight bow in their direction, then walked to a table on the far south side of the dining room, the tails of his jacket moving in step with him.

"I got it," Jorge said again, though lower this time. "But I sure as Hell don't *get* it."

"Get what?" Ronald asked. "What is there to get?"

"I want that suit," Edward said. "And I'm more than willing to take it off him, personally. Very slowly."

Dillon nodded in agreement, until the last part.

"You're both a couple of fairies," Coleman said. Then, "No offense, Dillon."

Edward extended his middle finger to Coleman.

Andrew, standing behind Edward, looked at Dillon. "Should I flip him off too?"

"No," Dillon said. "That's not necessary. Way to pay attention, though. Good job."

Edward pushed his finger into Coleman's face, but the man only waved it away. Edward returned to drive-thru, pulling Andrew with him. "Come along, Andrew."

"So who is he supposed to be?" Coleman asked, still watching the man. "The Ghost of Autumn Present?"

Across the dining room, the man pulled out a chair. He placed his cane on the table top. Then, with a flourish of the tails of his long coat, he sat down facing the counter. Looking at Dillon.

Ignoring Edward and Andrew, Coleman walked to the fry station and scooped a handful of fries into an empty to-go container. He came back to stand next to Dillon, pulled out a long French fry and put it in his mouth. "You're just Mister Fucking-Popular today, aren't you?"

5

THE COWBELL ON the north door of the dining room clanked as it opened. Dillon resisted the urge to look up. He concentrated on wiping the already spotless stainless-steel counter with a dry towel he had picked up for exactly that purpose. "Look busy" had been his motto in his early days at Buffalo Barbecue Pit, a way to avoid the unwanted attention of his new supervisor. Now he was repeating it like a mantra as he avoided looking at the thousand-yard-all-encompassing stares of the monks and the far more personal perusal of the man in the tails and top hat. If he was busy, he didn't have time to look at customers. Especially customers that had already ordered.

"See?" Coleman said. "Mister God Damn Popular." Coleman's dry tone had just an edge of what might have been jealousy this time.

Dillon looked up to see Soledad striding up to the counter. She wore the same long black trenchcoat as this morning when he had seen her, and had the same oversized bag hung across her body so it rested under her right hand. Her hair was down, though, brushed smooth, but still damp, as if she had just showered. Her expression, underscored by the dark red lipstick she had on and enhanced by the sharp diagonals of the rouge on her cheeks, had an edge to it to match the one in Coleman's voice, but that edge was not jealousy. Dillon hoped she wasn't mad at him. Or *only* at him.

"As family friendly as ever, I see," she said, slashing the edge in Coleman's direction.

"You damn skippy." Coleman's voice was back to its normal flatness, but what might have been a smile tugged at the corners of his lips. He seemed on the verge of saying something nice, and the strain of not doing so was getting to him.

Soledad rolled her eyes and the traces of a smile left Coleman's face. He said nothing. Then she looked at Dillon and her expression softened. "Are you OK?"

Dillon's sigh of relief became a shrug. He wasn't sure. He hadn't had much time for introspection since clocking in. The dinner rush had been light, as expected, but it had been enough to distract him. There had been a moment of excitement when an opossum tried to enter with a family of four, but Edward had chased it out with a broom while Coleman held the fire extinguisher ready. That had almost been enough not to notice that the monks and the man with the top hat were still there. Then the rush was over, and there they still were, and Dillon had slipped back into his "look busy" routine to avoid both them and thinking. And to avoid Carlita, who seemed to be waiting for him in the back, ready to pounce. He was also avoiding his phone.

Soledad kept looking at him with that concerned expression, and it made him feel better. Then her expression shifted to one of expecting more from him than a shrug, and Dillon looked back down at the counter. He started wiping again.

"You were there this morning?" Coleman asked Soledad. "At his uncle's place?"

"Dillon," Soledad said, ignoring Coleman and forcing Dillon to look at her again. "Have you had any news?"

"I heard it was a real bloodbath," Coleman said. "An old school shoot-out. Pew-pew auugh!" He clutched his chest with his hands, as if shot.

Dillon saw Soledad's right hand tense, pressing against something within her bag, and something about the line of her mouth implied murder for Coleman even while her eyes still showed–some–concern for Dillon. But she didn't say anything, or even look at Coleman.

"They gave me my phone back," Dillon said, speaking faster than he intended, wondering if he might be saving Coleman's life. Dillon didn't want to be looking for a replacement front counter person. Not tonight. Even if the dinner rush was over.

"Blood everywhere," Coleman said. "Broken windows. Like a SWAT team had been there–"

"'SWAT team' is redundant," Soledad said, still not looking at Coleman.

Dillon shook his head to shake out the memories of Uncle Phil's house that Coleman's comments had brought back. The broken glass. The shattered furniture. The slime. No blood, though. Just ... ichor.

"So you have your phone?" Soledad asked. "I tried to call you. More than once."

"It's on the charger," Dillon said, pointing in a vague way to indicate the office in the back, where Barbara had taken it. He had not been back there, not even after Barbara had left for the night. He had been trying to call Cyd all day. Then after Barbara was gone, he had begun to worry that Cyd might be trying to call *him*. Then he remembered what he had learned when Detective White had given him back the phone. "Did you ..." No, that was the wrong question. There was no way Soledad could have known. "I'm adopted," he said.

In the lobby beyond Soledad, the expression of the monks didn't change in any way, and their eyes didn't move, except Dillon could now feel them focusing on him. The man in the top hat sat up straighter.

"Adopted what?" Soledad asked. "You're not making sense."

Dillon leaned against the front counter. Suddenly self-conscious, he whispered, "She's not my real mother."

"Who isn't?"

"My mom," Dillon said. "She isn't my ... real mom."

"Holy shit," Coleman said. Then, "You know, if I was your brother, I would *totally* get this right now. Of course you're adopted. You had to be."

"Coleman," Soledad said, her voice very steady. Too steady. She put both her hands on the counter in front of her. Little halos of condensation appeared around her fingertips. She had to look up into Coleman's face, but she seemed to growing taller, darker as she enunciated each word. "If you don't go talk to Edward right now, I will kill you where you stand."

Coleman held up both hands. "Fine. I'll go talk to Edward Butterfingers and his new boy toy." Once his back was turned, he added, "Cyd was more fun. At least she let me watch."

Dillon felt his face get warm as Soledad looked at him. She held up a hand before he speak. "No. Don't even. Don't tell me anything. Come with me." She stayed on her side of the counter, but she led Dillon down to the south end, as far from the drive-thru as possible. "How do you know? About your mother?"

"The policeman ... I mean ... woman. Detective White. She kept calling her my 'adoptive mother'."

"Not 'step mom'? Adoptive?"

Dillon nodded. "She told me I needed to check my messages."

Soledad went on as if she hadn't heard him. "So your dad might not even be your dad?"

Dillon felt lightheaded.

Soledad looked stricken. "I'm so sorry, Dillon. Forget I said that. I ... no, there's no excuse." She looked around. If she noticed anything unusual about the night's clientele, she gave no indication of it. "Can you get off early? We need to talk. About ... all of this."

"I can't. I'm closing."

"God," Soledad said, rolling her eyes at Dillon this time. "Fine. I'll come back and drive you home."

"In the van?" Dillon asked.

Soledad's jaw tightened and her eyes squinted, just a little, as she looked at him. "Yes. In the van." The sharp edge had returned to her expression. And her voice.

"I'd rather walk," Dillon managed to say, wondering if he had just taken Coleman's place on the killing floor.

"Fine. We'll walk." She paused. "Have you taken Hlooth for a walk today?"

"No. He didn't seem to need it ..." He let his voice drift away as Soledad sighed. She no longer looked as angry. More disappointed. "I've never had a pet before," he said. "Do you think he made a mess?"

"How would I know?" Soledad asked. "How would anyone know? See you at eleven." Then she was striding toward the door, her trench coat billowing behind her.

"My god, I love that woman," Coleman said when the door was safely closed behind her.

"She would totally kick your ass," Edward said.

Coleman actually smiled, then he nodded. "Abso-fucking-lutely."

"Did she used to work here too?" Andrew asked.

"Shut up, newbie," Coleman said. "You're ruining the moment."

6

CARLITA, VISIBLY STEAMING from her work washing dishes in the back, came forward to find Dillon.

"You are avoiding me," she said.

Dillon wanted to protest, but couldn't. She would know he was lying. Carlita always knew.

"Carlita always knows," she said, agreeing with his guilty expression. "Come with me." She didn't wait for him to respond. She took his arm and pulled him through the grill section and past the big freezer to stand by the sinks of the dive station. She glanced to the front, then picked up the sprayer and turned the water on. Dillon winced, thinking she was about to hose him down, but she only sprayed the side of the stainless-steel sink. "Some people do not need to overhear," she said, barely audible over the noise. She leaned close. "Tell me, Dillonito, did you and Cyd ... ?"

"No!" Dillon said. Then, remembering how Cyd had greeted him, "Yes? I don't know anymore. It's been a long day."

Carlita squinted at him, twisting her mouth into a sideways pucker. Her eyes searched his face. "I would think you would know, yes?"

Dillon shrugged. "I thought Carlita always knows?"

"Do not get smart with me, Dillonito. You have very little experience with that." Her expression became thoughtful. "And, perhaps, with other things."

"Hey!"

"Shh, Dillonito." She held up a finger with her free hand. "You must listen, not protect your male ego. Did you, or did you not?"

"I ... don't think so? Ever since I got up this morning and found out Uncle Phil was missing, and his house–"

"Yes, I heard. That is a very bad thing. And very sad. You have my prayers. But focus, please, Dillonito. I thought men were always thinking about sex with pretty young girls. Never mind. If you do not know, then I will say 'No, you did not.' And that might be a very good thing."

"But you were all for it last night," Dillon said. "Everyone was. Even Barbara. But today all I get is static and employee handbooks and everyone"–including Cyd, he didn't add–"is assuming I did something–"

"Shh, Dillonito. You are babbling."

Dillon stopped in midbabble.

"I tried to read your stars last night, Dillonito, after I got home. The nights, they are so long when Raul is on the road, longer when he is on the road home. So I pulled up my star charts and took my mind off his absence. The results were ... dubious. At best. And those of Cyd. I had felt so positive before, when I sent you two off into the darkness to do ... yes. I was positive then. The stars, they had seemed to be pushing you together. Unlike that dreadful Tina, where they did their best to push you apart–" She stopped talking and spraying simultaneously and looked past Dillon.

Dillon turned to see Andrew standing a few yards away, looking uncomfortable.

"There's a man up front," Andrew said. "He ... he wants you to open his shake. To make sure it's vanilla."

Dillon's fingertips tingled and he knew he did not want to open that shake. "What? You do it."

"He insists on it being the manager. He says the shake doesn't taste like vanilla or anything." He paused. "No, that's not right. He said the shake tastes like 'nothing'."

Dillon considered locking himself in the break room until closing time. It was only a couple hours away now. But Andrew looked lost and he couldn't send the new guy up to face a demanding customer alone. Not on the poor guy's second night of work. Besides, the break room hadn't had a door in years, much less a lock.

Carlita's hand found Dillon's elbow again as he started to walk away. "No, Dillonito. Do not do this thing. Not tonight."

Dillon sighed. "It's my job."

If the man in top hat and tails was, as Coleman suggested, the Ghost of Autumn Present, the man waiting at the counter was the Ghost of Autumn Future. When all color had been bled from the fallen leaves and the trees were bare, brown-gray skeletons either waiting for spring or long dead. The man was as tall as Coleman, but as thin and weatherworn as a wicker man, and maybe, from what Dillon could see, constructed out of sticks and twine. His unruly salt-and-pepper hair looked like unkempt straw and gave him the appearance of a scarecrow. His eyes were only glints within the dark sockets of his eyes. He stood with his shake cup extended, waiting for Dillon to take it.

Dillon did *not* want to take it. His palms were tingling now, as well. He held his hands behind his back. "Is there a problem?"

"I am not convinced this is a ... vanilla shake, young man." His voice was low and raspy. His "ess" sounds came out long and low, like the wind blowing across the mouth of a bottle, or a dry leaf scraping across a sidewalk. He leaned forward, holding the cup out to Dillon.

Dillon forced himself to extend his left hand–he almost never opened anything with his left hand–and take the cup. The cup was COLD to the touch, and he could feel something writhing, waiting inside the cup. He almost dropped it. He managed a weak smile as his hand shook. "Let me get you a new one," he said.

Before the man could protest, Dillon tossed the cup in the nearest trash bin and walked to the shake machine. It took him three tries to get only a single, small cup from the dispenser. "Let me test the machine first," he said. "It might be the mix needs replacing." He pulled the lever, let a small mound of shake accumulate in the bottom, then pushed the lever back in place. He picked up a straw, failing twice to get it to punch through its wrapper before just ripping the end off. He stuck the straw into the shake and tasted it. "Seems to be OK now."

With slightly more finesse, he drew another large shake. As he put the lid on it, though, his hands began to tingle. He snatched his hand away, hoping no one saw. Somehow he managed to hand the shake to the man without dropping it or throwing it away. And without touching the man's long fingers. "My ... apologies. For the inconvenience. I'm not sure ... what ... went wrong."

"No problem, child," the man said. "No problem at all." He turned and walked away from the counter with a gait that reminded Dillon of a tumbleweed blowing slowly in a breeze.

Dillon pointed at Andrew, then at the trashcan where he had thrown the first shake. "Have Edward show you how to empty the trash. Do that one first, then the bins in the lobby." The cup had not burst open in the trash, and Dillon could still feel something in it, waiting for him to let it out.

7

THE URGE TO shoot something drove Soledad to the Gold & Silver Pawn Shop & Shooting Range. "Buy Sell Trade Gold Silver Firearms," the sign said with a complete lack of grammar but immediately clear intent. The indoor range was too short for target practice past twenty yards, but that wasn't why she was there. She just needed a man-shaped target she could project on. A stand-in for Dillon. And Uncle Tio. And Robert.

"I'm thinking about moving to Rio Cruces," Robert had said, as casual as if he had been talking about going shopping instead of quitting his job, selling his house, and following a woman halfway across the country.

Soledad was still upset about how her heart had leaped. As if she had been waiting for him to say exactly those words all this time. As if she were happy about it. As if she had run away–run home–specifically to see if he would follow her.

Which she had *not* done. Run away, or waited. She did not want him to follow her. And she was not happy. She was furious.

At him. At herself. At both of them for being weak. Too weak to break off what had been withering away even before she moved back to Rio Cruces. Her moving away should have been the final blow. Not a call to drastic action on his part.

He had called as she was stepping out of the shower, feeling clean for the first time all day. Thinking she would go see Dillon, check up on him, probably sit around with him all night doing nothing as he played video games and tried not to think about what had happened to his uncle.

She could be there to chaperone if Cyd happened to show up. To make sure nothing continued to happen between them.

She had thought it might be Dillon calling her when she picked up the phone and answered it.

She had hated feeling guilty that she had not expected it to be Robert. Then furious with his first words.

He hadn't been strong enough to say he was going to move, though. No. He was just *thinking* about it. Out loud. To her. To gauge her reaction.

She had almost hung up on him. She wished she had. Instead, she had laughed, she hoped convincingly, and told him that he wouldn't do it. He would be leaving everything behind. His job. His house. His family.

"But you would be there."

She felt ambushed. Conflicted about ... everything. Why couldn't he accept the "they" that had been Soledad and Robert was over?

Why couldn't she?

Ralph, the proprietor of Gold & Silver Pawn Shop & Shooting Range, was sitting behind the main counter. He stood up as she came through the front door, then sat down again after he had given her a nod of recognition and a noncommittal, "Howya." He scratched at the stubble on his chin, then added, "Been a while."

"Quiet tonight," Soledad observed as she walked to the counter. Digital cameras and older film cameras crowded the shelf just below the glass. A small sample of the revolvers and semiautomatic pistols Ralph had for sale were on display in a much more secure cage with bars and bulletproof glass behind Ralph's head.

"Been slow." Ralph scratched at an ear. His eyes went to her bag, then back to her face. "You wanting to shoot?"

"You have no idea."

Ralph smiled. "Oh, I have a few ideas of my own. Some more deserving than others." He pushed himself up out of his seat again and leaned against the counter. He flipped a felt cloth over the glass. "Show me what you got."

Soledad took out the pistol and placed it on the felt.

"That it? Just the one–?" Ralph stopped. He leaned closer, squinting, then took a pair of reading glasses out of his shirt pocket and put them on. He squinted at the pistol, then looked up at Soledad. "Your uncle's?"

Soledad shook her head. "No," she said. "It's ... mine. Now."

"That's all I need to know," Ralph said quickly, holding up a hand to stop anything else Soledad might confess. Soledad decided it was his pawn broker habits stepping in to limit him finding out more than he needed about the provenance of what people placed on his counter. He smiled again, at the gun this time. "That is a sight."

"Yes," Soledad said. "It is."

Ralph's right hand had been about to reach for the gun, but he drew it back. At the tone of her voice and, it seemed to Soledad, at the sudden reluctance of the gun to be picked up. Ralph gazed down at the gun, leaning back and forth to view it from as many angles as possible, but kept his hands back. "Damn, girl. Starting your own collection now?" Before Soledad could respond, he went on. "How she shoot?"

"That's what I'm here to find out. And the gun prefers to think of himself as a 'he'."

"Well all right then. He it is. Does he have a name?"

Soledad paused, then said, "He hasn't told me yet."

Ralph gave her a curious look, but he took her money. Then he placed a bowl of earplugs on the counter in front of her. She waved the earplugs away and took out the set of hearing protection earmuffs Uncle Tio had bought her when she started going shooting with him.

Ralph nodded his approval, then asked, "How about ammo? Need any extra."

Soledad nodded. "Considering the number of targets I have in mind, yes, I think I'm going to need some extra."

Ralph smiled, a full grin this time, showing off his uneven teeth, and the gap where one had been knocked out in a long-ago robbery attempt. "Well all right then. Let's go shoot something."

8

Blam!

The pistol pulled against Soledad's grip, but she held it steady. She leaned her head to look past the barrel of the gun and see the target. The hole was down and to the right. She had been overcompensating for the kick. She adjusted her aim, pointed her finger at the heart of the target–

Blam! Blam! Blam!

The shots were loud, even with her sophisticated ear protection. She thought she might have heard Ralph say something behind her, but she couldn't make out specific words. The man stood behind her. Not as close as Uncle Tio used to. If her uncle were here, he would be leaning close, lifting one of her ear covers, and saying, "Good girl, Sollie. Never more than three shots at a time. You never know who's counting."

She shifted her aim higher, and just slightly to the left.

Blam! Blam! Blam!

The target now had a lopsided two-eyes-and-a-nose "face" in the center of the head.

This time she heard Ralph's, "Damn, girl."

She had not gone shooting often in college. Uncle Tio had been too far away to do more than nag her about maintaining her skills. She had gone between boyfriends, mostly. Only Robert had ever mustered the temerity to go with her. Once. Being outshot by his girlfriend had not made him want to repeat the experience. His approach had been too tight. Too controlled. Too pedantic. As if *he* were teaching *her*. She probably shouldn't have emptied a clip shooting a literal circle on his target around his center-of-mass cluster. Expensive. Showy. Loud.

She wasn't as good a shot as Uncle Tio. Few were. But she wasn't about to be lectured by a boyfriend who owned only a knockoff Glock and a single box of ammunition.

Blam! Blam! Blam!

She drew a three-point smile below the lopsided face. The smile bore an eerie resemblance to the one she had imagined on Robert's face when he told her he was thinking of moving. Or maybe the one she had fought to keep off her face as he told her.

Blam!

The slide locked back.

Now the face had a hole in its "forehead".

She pressed the button to bring the target back to her. She took a few seconds to admire her handiwork. The smile on the target bore no resemblance to the one she was smiling now. Then she laid the target on the counter in front of her, hung a new one and sent that whirring back to the fullest extent of the range.

Behind her, Ralph said, "I'm guessing you'd like to finish shooting alone, am I right?"

9

Dillon waited alone inside the Buffalo Burger Pit. Soledad had called to tell him she would be a few minutes late. Ronald had offered to wait, but Dillon had convinced him to leave with Edward and Carlita.

Now, though, sitting alone in the dark, he wished he had let them stay.

The restaurant felt emptier than any time in the last six years. And all the closed doors suddenly seemed ... untrustworthy. Even the tiny drive-thru window. And especially the door of the big freezer.

Dillon shivered.

Every time Jorge or Ronald had opened the big freezer throughout the night, the ambient autumn chill in the restaurant had grown sharper. While the dining room was still open, Dillon had been able to compensate by punching the "+" button on the thermostat. And by ignoring Jorge's complaints that the grill was already hot enough. Once closing time had past, though, the programming of the thermostat had kicked in. Gil had installed the thermostat as a cost-saving major. As Dillon sat in the darkness, the air around him growing colder by the minute, he wondered if Gil would believe him if destroyed the damn thing as a "lifesaving measure."

Dillon huffed a breath, surprised that he couldn't see it cloud in the air in front of him.

He took out his phone. Despite what he had been afraid of all evening, Cyd hadn't called. The only call he had received had been from Soledad. Well, the only *two* calls. The insistent ringing on her second try had forced him to remove the phone from the charger and answer it. He pushed the phone back into his pocket.

The empty dining room seemed huge around him. A dark void scattered with tables and upturned chairs, ringed with booths. The only light came from across the street. The Yellow Sign Buffet's backlit, rectangular sign blazed forth, casting long shadows with its ugly light. The Yellow Sign Buffet closed an hour earlier than the Buffalo Burger Pit, but evidently its owner had never considered how much money he could save by turning off his sign after hours. At least, that's what Gil had said any time Dillon suggested competing by leaving the spotlights shining on the big buffalo on the roof.

Dillon sat in the narrow shadow created by one of the window posts. He had given the glowing sign the middle-finger-salute, then sat with his back to it. He didn't like the light from that sign. To him, it had never seemed *yellow*, like sunshine or sunflowers or even piss. There was too much brown in it. And now the light that spilled on either side of him felt like the walls of a particularly narrow, dingy prison. He couldn't move without brushing against the dirty walls.

Twin headlights penetrated the gloom of yellow light and passed like searchlights through the many windows of the restaurant. The animal control van pulled in on the south side of the restaurant, then drove around to the north side. Like any former employee who had been repeatedly, calmly, and patronizingly lectured by Barbara that while there were many, many wrong ways for employees to park at the Buffalo Burger Pit, there was only one right way.

Dillon stood, and walked along the narrow confines of his yellow-walled prison until he was at the point closest to the north door. Then he made his break across the lit space into the shadows by the door. He spun the bolt free as the van parked. The red brake lights blazed, then went dark.

Dillon almost pulled the door open, then yanked his hands away. His fingertips tingled from the coldness of the invisible *wrong* on the other side.

After a minute, the van's horn sounded, the raspy bleat of a chain-smoking walrus.

Dillon waited.

After another minute, Soledad stepped out of the van and started to walk to the door. She spotted him through the glass halfway there and stopped, waiting.

Dillon touched the door again, with one finger. The cold wrong was now also ... empty? Hungry? Then his finger went numb. The digit flapped uselessly as he pulled his hand away again and shook it.

He couldn't see Soledad's face clearly, but her body language made her eye roll plain. Then she strode up to the door and pushed it open. He barely had time to step back, out of the way.

"And I was in such a good mood, too," Soledad said as Dillon locked the door again from the outside. Her hair was dry, and she smelled as if she had been burning paper. Or setting off fireworks. "Someday you're going to have to learn how to open doors on your own."

"I can open doors," Dillon protested. "I just can't seem to control what's on the other side."

"You never seem to have any problem when you're hazing the new guys." She paused, then added, "And girls."

"That's different. That's funny."

"So next time you're stuck on the wrong side of an unlocked door, think of it as one great big, cosmic joke."

"You're in a mood."

"Yes. I said that. And it used to be a good one." She started walking, forcing Dillon to catch up to her. He walked on her left. Something about the large bag on her right hip, and the way her right hand rested on it, made him nervous. The index finger on her right hand seemed to twitch and curl, as if she were unconsciously ready to shoot him, and only needed a gun to make that happen.

In the less-than-companionable silence as they walked, Dillon heard the caws of a family of crows up on a wire above them. Then he heard the screech of a bluejay up past its bedtime. Then the scurrying of something in a short shrub as they passed. He remembered the opossum from earlier. He opened his mouth to tell Soledad about that—

"Have you heard anything new?" she asked.

Her words chased the story of the opossum away as quickly as Edward's broom had chased the actual creature. "No." Dillon's hand went to his pocket with the phone, but he didn't take it out. He just gripped the cold plastic.

"The news on TV is calling it a 'mysterious shooting'," she said. "And already connected it to ... what happened ... before." She paused. "Have you checked your messages yet?"

Dillon's grip on his phone tightened, but he didn't reply.

Soledad shook her head. "I see doors aren't the only things you have trouble opening." She held out her left hand, palm up. "Give it to me."

Dillon started to pull the phone from his pocket, then stopped. "No," he said. He couldn't have her do everything for him. There were some doors he needed to open on his own. He knew Soledad was only trying to help. "Thanks, but I'll ... I'll check them later."

Soledad looked doubtful, but she only shrugged. Her left hand returned to its pocket. "Suit yourself."

As they walked on in silence, Dillon looked up at the sky, looking for the only constellation he really knew, Orion. Or, more specifically, Orion's Belt. He was never certain which of the other stars in the sky made up the rest of the constellation, but the three stars of the Belt were always easy to find. Uncle Phil had always called that pattern of stars the Hunter and claimed it as his patron saint, and saluted it when they walked at night.

"One hunter to another," Dillon whispered, echoing Uncle Phil's cryptic words.

"What?" Soledad asked.

"Nothing," Dillon said, still craning his neck, trying to locate the three brightest stars in the heavens. "Just something Uncle Phil used to say."

The dark sky was clear. The stars were bright–

Which was the problem. All the stars seemed to be vying for the title "brightest in the heavens." He finally located the three-point straight line of the belt, but the effort to see them as a line made his head hurt. It was as if the stars were being forced into some new configuration. No longer a belt. Not just in the sky, but in his mind, as well. His right hand came up to point at the stars. He opened his mouth to tell Soledad–

Her left hand came out of its pocket and grabbed his right hand. "I'm sorry," she said, her warm fingers squeezing his. "As long as my day has been, it's easy to forget that yours has been at least as bad. Worse." She stopped walking but held on to his hand, pulling on him to face her. Her eyes were shiny, reflecting the overachieving stars overhead. "Yes, I know. Your day had to be worse. He was your uncle. Sometimes I forget that the reason I can't ... hear you ... isn't because you're not ... there." She pulled him into her arms and hugged him. "I'm so sorry, Dillon."

"The stars are different," Dillon managed to say. Which wasn't what he meant to say, but the words had already formed in his mind and came out when she squeezed him. She still smelled of fireworks, but underneath that he could smell the scent of her shampoo. And underneath that, the smell of her. Essence of Soledad.

Soledad sniffed, then nodded, her chin moving against his chest in a much more pleasant way than her bag pushed against his left hip. "Everything is different," she said. "And nothing is how it's supposed to be." She shook in Dillon's arms and squeezed him tighter.

"I thought I was supposed to be crying," Dillon said.

"You can too," she said.

Unsure what else to do, resisting the urge to stroke her hair, struggling not to get an erection at the feel of her body pressed against his, Dillon stood there, holding her, her holding him.

They stood outside his apartment complex. The family of crows seemed to have followed them. They cawed softly as the October wind pushed leaves down the street.

The stars overhead seemed to move, drawing Dillon's attention upward. He looked up. Orion's Belt seemed to have reasserted itself, but the Knife was not cooperating. And there was still no sign of the others stars were supposed to make up the Hunter.

Soledad drew his attention back to Earth as she released him and stepped away. She glanced at him, met his eyes, then looked away. "We ... let's go rescue Hlooth. The poor thing is probably about to burst, if he hasn't already."

Dillon followed her. He wished she was still holding his hand.

They walked across the parking lot, into the breezeway. He glanced in the direction of Edward's apartment, but didn't say anything. He followed Soledad up the stairs, the long tails of her trenchcoat almost hitting him in the face.

Dillon took out his keys and unlocked his door. He paused before opening it to say, "Hlooth and I will walk you back to the van."

He got only as far as "Hlooth and I–" before Soledad reached past him and opened the door for him. Which wasn't why he had paused. He had been going to open the door himself–

"Hi, lover," said the darkness beyond the door.

The pale breezeway light fell weakly through the door, illuminating a disheveled strip of floor and half the couch. And half a naked Cyd, who was unfolding herself from some contorted pose and standing. She remained split in half by the line of shadow as she stood, the lines of her curves lengthening and extending. Her one visible eye was untouched by the light. The half of her smile that could be seen seemed at once sensuous and twisted, distorted. Her one visible breast moved and shook as only a naked breast could.

"God, I hate men," Soledad said.

"... will walk you back to the van," Dillon finished.

He couldn't take his eyes off Cyd as Soledad strode away.

10

"Aren't you going to come?" Cyd asked, her half a face still smiling, her one eye and hand beckoning for him to enter. "In, I mean."

Dillon struggled to do only the latter, managing two awkward steps into the apartment before the threat of the former forced him to stop. He didn't want to move too fast. And he didn't want to step out of the light. The shadows seemed too ... solid. Or too ... nothing.

The illuminated half of Cyd walked toward him, the left side of her body still invisible. Then, like the moment of dawn when the sun seems to leap over the horizon, she was there. All of her. And she was all he could see. Impossibly pale in the light from the breezeway. Impossibly beautiful. Green eyes bright, brown hair long. Curves and warmth, touching him, caressing him, stroking him.

He almost didn't notice when the door behind him shut. He had no idea how she managed that, since he had his hands on her and he was sure both her hands held him.

The darkness changed as the breezeway light was dammed on the far side of the door and expunged from his apartment by the solid nothing of the shadows.

Except the shadows were gone now, as well. He could not see, but his other senses were alive and kicking into overdrive as Cyd's hands pulled his shift over his head and pulled him forward, deeper into his apartment.

He could not see, but they didn't trip or stumble, even as she pulled his pants down his hips. He could feel Cyd against him. Her skin. Her hair. And beyond her, he could feel the walls of his apartment, the floors, the open cupboards. They could not stumble–or maybe they did stumble and it was all part of the dance they had become.

He could hear her breathing. Her laughing at his gasps and moans. Her moans. He could hear nothing else. Nothing else mattered.

He could smell her, sweaty and sweet, her hair smoky from her shift that afternoon. She had not showered, but neither had he, and the thought that they could do that together, later, made him tremble.

He could taste her, her tongue pushed into his mouth. His mouth on hers. His mouth on her skin. The feel of her erect nipples against his palms. Her teeth biting him almost to the point of drawing blood.

Almost to the point of him stopping and asking about safe words. Almost.

There was no stopping. He was all over her and she was all over him.

He could not remember when he had lost his boxers–or his socks. Then he was falling through the darkness, uncaring, hardly noticing because Cyd was falling with him. He had no clear concept of the time spent falling, but they eventually landed on his mattress.

Before he could roll her over, she twisted in his grasp and climbed on top of him. Her left hand pinned his shoulder as her right hand found him and guided him inside her.

"Not yet," she whispered, the first words she had said since inviting him into his own apartment. Her right hand pinned his other shoulder as her hips pushed down on him. "Not yet."

Dillon floated in the darkness, teetering on the edge a climax that threatened to consume him. His hands gripped her hips and he longed to push against her, to–somehow–overpower her and wrestle her around and under him. But he yielded to her and relaxed. His breathing slowed. His heart, though, continued to beat at a furious, hungry speed. Finally, after the longest, most pleasurable eternity he had ever experienced, even better than the falling, she began to move up and down, and he had to redefine "most" downward, to make room for additional levels.

She started slow, but each thrust of her hips came faster than the last. Up and *down*. Up and *down*. Slide up, hammer *down*. Slide up, hammer *down*. But the softest, most incredible hammer.

Dillon had no idea how he held himself together under the avalanche of Cyd this sex had become. He did what he could to match her rhythm and hoped he wasn't screwing up.

She took her hands from his shoulders as she continued. She leaned back, her arms outstretched.

With a startled shiver that had no impact on her increasing rhythm,

Dillon realized that his eyes were open. The darkness was no longer complete. The shapeless void had taken shape again, and the shape was that of Cyd, above him. Though beyond her the void remained, like a starless night sky where his mottled-gray popcorn ceiling should have been.

When, at the top of her latest slide, poised for an instant before bringing down her soft, warm, wet hammer, Cyd looked down at Dillon, and he saw that the light came from her eyes.

The green of her eyes had disappeared, replaced by brown static that flickered and sputtered.

Cyd smiled as she thrust down and rose again slowly.

Then she was looking up, the light of her eyes burning the darkness above her but still not reaching the ceiling. She threw her arms wide and they seemed to separate, pulled apart, starting from the fingertips and extending to her shoulders, ten suddenly boneless appendages spreading, undulating. At the same time, her breasts swelled. The erect nipples bloomed and unfurled into spinning, waving tendrils, like those of a sea anemone.

Both she and Dillon screamed as she came down one last, explosive time and the world dissolved into staticy, flickering brown waves that crashed over them and through them. Then, as the waves subsided, everything went from brown to black.

PART VII
Post Coital

The Gun

THE GUN FELT better. It had shot something. Not an Outsider, as the Gun wished, nor a man, as the Bearer wished. But a man-shaped target.

The Bearer, though, no longer seemed to share the Gun's post-shooting contentment. The Bearer had been satisfied at first. Almost happy. But the glow had worn off faster for her than for the Gun.

The Gun suffered a brief instant of insecurity. Was this sudden discontentment its fault?

But, of course, that was foolishness. The Gun had performed flawlessly, even with the unnecessary bullets the Bearer had insisted on, and which had left an odd taste in its firing chamber. Maybe the Bearer had wanted something with a longer barrel? A smoother bore?

No. If the Bearer was unhappy, that was all on her.

The Gun was, of course, the Ultimate Weapon. Its memories that far back were hazy, but the Gun might also have been the *First* Weapon.

On the plus side, maybe this discontentment on the part of the Bearer would bring about more opportunities for the Gun to perform. Which thought made the Gun feel even better. Because more action was always good.

The God

Within the absolute cold at the heart of the God, light and heat blossomed. Both were consumed in an instant, but, being a God, that instant could stretch for an eternity.

Or could have, except for the Time ticking all around the God. And except for the effort that had been expended to achieve that one, brief, ecstatic moment.

The God rolled over, finding a new, more comfortable position within the cold, and took a nap.

The Phone

THE JOY OF the phone at being awakened, its buttons pushed, and its messages checked was short-lived.

Once again, the fingers that probed the Phone were not those of the Opener, and no ear came close to its tiny speaker to listen to the messages it had hoarded and safeguarded for so long. The hands-free speaker feature, which had never been used, was still not used. Instead, the messages were deleted without ever being heard by the Opener, destroying in a stroke the only joy or purpose the Phone had ever known.

Lost in its pain, the Phone scarcely noticed when it was dropped to bounce on the filthy carpet.

It wished it could remove its own battery.

1

SOLEDAD WAS AGAIN on roadkill duty, but this time self-assigned, and without the added burden of bringing lunch to anyone. She hadn't talked to Uncle Tio when she clocked in. She had just decided that scraping roadkill in traffic contained all the human interaction she wished to experience.

She tried to lose herself in the work. Focusing on the blade of the shovel as it slid across the rough surface of the asphalt, then under the dead asterisk. Then focusing on the heave and the flip. And, to a lesser extent, on not stepping into the path of oversized, single-occupant vehicles. It was distracting. It was penance. It was a job.

She had noticed more than a few of the dead starfish-squid-things on her walk back to the van from Dillon's apartment the night before. She had even left a few new ones on the street as she drove away from the restaurant, swerving to make sure she got the little bastards. She had not seen any live ones when walking, but once on the road in the van, she had seen them slithering-scampering across the street in the beams of her headlights. The gray creatures popped-squished under the van's tires in a very satisfying way.

Unfortunately, there was very little satisfaction in scraping them off the asphalt.

The first one she had had to scrape up had been under the grill of the van at her apartment, before she left for work. She had briefly thought about leaving the bizarre little body there to terrorize her neighbors, but she got only as far as the exit to the parking lot before turning around to go back and scrape it up for disposal.

The crows and grackles and cowbirds had been unhappy to see her. They had been feasting on the unknown bonanza of dead whatever-the-hell. Unlike the other cars and trucks and SUVs that interrupted the birds' scavenging, Soledad and her van didn't drive on through and away. So the birds perched on the roof of the van or on the peak of an orange traffic cone and stared at her, occasionally offering critical and disapproving squawks and caws and hisses.

She refused to think of Dillon while she worked. Or Robert. Nor even Uncle Tio. Over and over. She wouldn't think of Dillon while she scraped a whatsit and dropped the body in the wheelbarrow. Nor would she think of Robert as she repeated the procedure for the next one. She would refuse to think of men at all while she put out the traffic cones, or positioned them to surround a new section of road. She felt an immense satisfaction at not just not answering her phone when it buzzed in her pocket, but in not thinking about anyone who might be calling her. Including Uncle Tio.

She was busy. She would remain busy. Until ... well. She surveyed the carnage along 51st Street and nodded in satisfaction that she could be busy all day.

The morning rush hour had come and gone, so the sudden fluttering that erupted around the van was surprisingly loud. Wings beat at the air. Indignant caws and squawks sounded. A shadow fell across the road. Soledad looked up to see a turkey vulture settling on top of the animal control van. The bird's wingspan was as wide as the van. The van's old shocks groaned under the weight of the bird. The turkey vulture turned its head so its left eye was looking at Soledad. It bobbed its bald, red head, then grunted a greeting that turned into a hiss of impatience.

"You're welcome to follow me when I'm done here," Soledad said to the bird. "Everyone else will."

2

FOR THE SECOND time in two days, Dillon awoke from nightmare sex with Cyd to an empty apartment.

At least this time the sex had been real. That was only partial consolation, though, because so had the nightmare part.

At least, it had *felt* real. Had he really seen–

The sight of Cyd's nipples separating into tiny tendrils flashed into his mind and he almost screamed again.

It was dark in his apartment. Darker than he expected for the time of day he assumed it was. He touched his hands to his face, then looked for his fingers in the dark. They were barely visible. He rested his hands on his chest while he thought.

He was naked, and at a very unusual angle on his mattress. And the smell of sweaty sex made the air almost unbreathable.

So the sex, at least, really had been ... well ... real.

He reached out with both arms, touching rumpled sheets and finding one misshapen pillow, but no other occupants of his bed. No Cyd. Which was more of a relief than he expected.

If he concentrated on just the lead up to sex and the actual lovemaking, he could still feel the lust and excitement. But if he let his memory play to the conclusion ...

No. He didn't want to think of that again.

"Hello?" he said.

His voice sounded odd, as if the darkness were bouncing it back at him.

"Cyd?" he said as he pushed himself up and scooted to the edge of the mattress.

The darkness around him shook as something pounded on a door, or a wall. Or maybe it was just his head. Maybe he had sat up too fast–

No. That was just hopeful thinking. He didn't have a headache or a hangover or anything else he could blame for his memories of last night.

He remembered yesterday's visit from Detective White, and remembered he was naked. He felt around on the floor around his feet, searching for his clothes. He found only the cold plastic form of his phone.

He picked up the phone and activated the screen so he could see what time it was. "9:57 am," the phone offered, the sudden light almost blinding. It was definitely supposed to be less dark in his apartment at ten in the morning.

Dillon squinted at the phone. Something seemed different about the display, but Dillon couldn't decide if something was missing or if he was just unaccustomed to being awake before eleven. He let the phone display go dark again, started to push it into a pocket he didn't have, then dropped the phone on his bed.

The pounding came again and he jumped at how close it was.

Not the front door, though. The bathroom. Someone was in the bathroom and banging on the door. He assumed it wasn't Detective White.

"Cyd? Did the door get stuck?"

The gloopy whimpering that followed the pounding told him it wasn't Cyd. It was Hlooth.

Had the poor animal–or whatever it was–been in the bathroom all night? Cyd must have put Hlooth in there, since Dillon had left the creature asleep on his couch when he went to work.

"Hang on," he said, before Hlooth tried to break down the door.

Standing was easier than he expected, because he wasn't drunk or drugged like most of his mind and parts of his body still thought he must be. His feet caught in what he guessed were his discarded pants, though, as he felt on the wall for the light switch. He shook his foot free and flicked the switch.

With the room illuminated by the single naked bulb on the ceiling, and again wondering why it had been so dark, he went to the bathroom door and put his hand on the knob–

His whole arm, from fingertips to shoulders, felt as if thousands of sharp needles poked it at once. The tingling continued after Dillon jerked his arm back. He stumbled backward, tripped over unidentified dirty laundry and fell back on his mattress. His phone bounced and settled next to his thigh. He ignored the phone as he rubbed his right hand with his left, trying to massage away the pain of the needles. He could scarcely feel the pressure. Goose bumps erupted all over his body and he shivered.

He stared at the doorknob, which showed no sign of guilt or remorse or even gloating at what it had done. It was just a doorknob. It vibrated slightly as Hlooth struck the door again from the other side.

Looking away from the doorknob, Dillon saw his boxers from last night. He stood up, retrieved them, and pulled them on.

He noticed other underwear on the floor, as well. A pair of black cotton panties, and an underwire bra. He poked at them with his foot until he was certain they weren't Edward's, then picked them up carefully. He looked around, but he didn't see any other clothes that weren't his, so he put them in a small pile of their own. Had Cyd left them on purpose? Or just forgotten them when she put on her uniform and left?

Hlooth knocked again, and Dillon's sleep-delayed biological need suddenly became urgent, overriding his curiosity about whether women were always leaving slightly dirty underwear after staying overnight. He was forced to try the bathroom door again. He touched the doorknob with only the pad of his index finger. This time only his hand was attacked by the invisible needles.

Hlooth glop-glopped a whimper on the other side of the door.

"You and me both, boy," Dillon said.

Massaging his hand, he went to see if maybe something in the living room or kitchen would present itself as a possible solution.

Standing in the gap between the two rooms, with the light from his bedroom shining behind him, he saw why his apartment was so dark. The big double glass doors that led to his so-called balcony had been thoroughly blacked out with paper. Hundreds of sheets of paper had been duct-taped to the windows, layers overlapping layers. In the dim lighting, the paper looked brown. When Dillon stepped closer, though, he saw the paper was yellow. They were menu flyers from the Yellow Sign Buffet.

Dillon's sore right hand automatically extended its middle finger to the flyers while his brain tried to figure out who could have done such a horrible thing.

Cyd?

The image of her arms separating and spreading like the fins of a lionfish flashed against the dark backdrop.

He spun away from the blacked-out windows and the memory and saw that someone had tidied up his kitchen.

No. It hadn't been tidied. Someone had shut all the cupboards and drawers. Even the oven.

Dillon spun again, this time to the front door. It was closed, because of course it was closed. But it had been weatherstripped. More Yellow Sign Buffet menu flyers had been folded and taped along the edges to overlap the door frame, blocking any light that might have leaked in. Had those been there last night?

There was no way to know. A naked Cyd had been the first and last thing he had seen as soon as the Soledad pushed the door opened.

He turned to go back into his bedroom and retrieve his phone. Soledad might not yell at him–

No. There was no "might", and certainly no "not". Soledad would *definitely* yell at him.

He turned to face the front door again. He would handle this on his own.

He forced himself to walk to the front door. When he got there, as he reached for the doorknob, he remembered he was wearing only his boxers. He should put on clothes–

He stopped himself before he turned around to go find clothes. It was, after all, just a doorknob. He wasn't scared of a doorknob. He clenched his fists in front of him, as if he were going to punch the door, then reached for the doorknob again.

The COLD, the WRONG, hit him like an electric shock. His whole body convulsed as he tried to yank his hand from the cold, cold metal of the doorknob. Brown static flashed and exploded behind his eyes as the muscles in his arm jerked and spasms tightened his chest to the cracking point.

Finally, he fell backward and his rigid hand was jerked free of the doorknob.

He no longer had any problem admitting he was very much afraid of the doorknob.

He sat on the floor, oblivious to the dangers of what might be lurking in the rough carpet, panting from the strain, his muscles quivering and his eyes watering. His looked at the kitchen. The dim light from his bedroom threw dark shadows around the cupboard doors. The metal pulls glinted. Unlike the bathroom doorknob, the pulls weren't able to keep a straight face. They were definitely gloating. The fridge loomed large and ominous, daring him to see if there was anything cold to drink inside.

Dillon crawled to the bedroom and climbed up on his mattress. As he lay under the yellow light of the old bulb, he thumbed a rescue note to Soledad. He briefly considered asking Barbara for help, or Edward or Coleman, but decided he wanted to keep details of what had happened out of the immediate Buffalo Burger Pit family. Soledad would yell at him, but not right away. She would have to call him back first.

Hlooth pounded on the door of the bathroom. "Ruff?"

Dillon, still looking at the ceiling, nodded in response, then said, "Rough."

3

"TRAPPED IN MY apartment. Help."

Soledad read the message, then pushed her phone back into her pocket. She pulled the ratty work gloves back on her hands and considered what she had accomplished. Two missed calls from Uncle Tio–which were expected–one from Robert–which was satisfying, because if she was going to ignore his calls, he needed to actually call–and one weird text message from Dillon. What was that all about? Some kind of humble bragging? Cyd not letting him out of bed?

She had delayed checking her phone until the end of her federally mandated fifteen-minute morning break. If she had had coffee, or the inclination to go buy a cup, it would have been her coffee break. Instead, she had simply put down her shovel and sat on the curb, waving at the commuters who noticed her, doing her part to perpetuate the myth that city workers did nothing but arrange traffic cones and take breaks behind them. Now it was time to get back to work and, more importantly, back to ignoring the men in her life. She pushed herself back to her feet.

The turkey vulture was still on top of the van. It had settled there again after Soledad had moved the van to this new spot. It eyed her as she stood, and grunted, but didn't budge from its spot. The other birds also perched on the van, taking their cues from the turkey vulture.

The phone in her pocket buzzed with the arrival of a new text message.

Soledad smiled and nodded an insincere smile at a woman driving a huge SUV, then sat back down on the curb. She took off her gloves again and laid them on the curb next to her. Finally, she pulled out her phone to see what she was going to ignore now.

"Trapped. Really have to go. Help."

Dillon again, and still making no sense. Where would he have to go in the morning? If he just needed a ride, he could ask like a normal person.

Soledad sighed. The whole morning experience had been neither as distracting nor as satisfying as she had hoped.

She put her phone away, picked up her gloves, and stood up again. She retrieved her shovel from where she had leaned it against the front of the van. She had finished this section of street already, because she wasn't going to stare at roadkill while on break. She threw the shovel into the back of the van, then collected the traffic cones and threw them in too. None of that had disturbed the birds watching her, though slamming the back doors closed managed to startled a few grackles into flight.

Her phone buzzed again as she was climbing into the worn out driver's seat. Since she had to take off her gloves anyway, to drive, and she hadn't actually started driving yet, she pulled out her phone.

"Hlooth is trapped too. Help."

"Damn it," she said. Dillon could die, wrapped like a mummy in the sheets he and Cyd had soiled together, but she couldn't let Hlooth suffer. Not for Dillon's sins, nor her own. She jumped on the emergency brake to make it release, then put the van in gear and merged into traffic. She felt the van shift as the turkey vulture finally took flight.

4

SOLEDAD DIDN'T EVEN bother to knock. The door to Dillon's apartment opened smoothly and swung in. Because of course it did. Only Dillon could be trapped behind an unlocked door.

"What–? Oh, thank you!"

Dillon leaped up from where he had been kneeling on the floor in front of his couch.

"I was looking for my keys," he said as he waded toward Soledad through a pile of yellow flyers and duct tape.

He was wearing only a pair of boxers, so Soledad stepped back before he could hug her. Then held up her left arm to block his continued advance. Her right hand went into her bag and gripped the pistol on its own. She left it there. Just in case. If there had been any doubt about what happened after she left last night, leaving him with a naked Baby Cyd, well–

No. She wouldn't think about it. The anger she felt now, as she had felt then, wasn't as pure as she expected. She wasn't just mad at him for having sex with Cyd. There was more than a taint of jealousy, and that taint infuriated her even more.

"Where's Hlooth?" she asked. Then, after another look at his sorry state, added, "I thought you needed to go somewhere? The only ride you're dressed for is one I'm not going to give you."

"What?" He looked down at himself. "Oh. I ... took care of that. I found an empty two-liter bottle in the kitchen."

Soledad stared at him, refusing to let her brain figure out what he was talking about. "Where's Hlooth?"

As if on cue, she heard the dull banging of Hlooth's head against a hollow core door. She pushed past Dillon as he said, "In the bathroom."

The pitiful excuse for a door that protected the bathroom opened as easily as the front door had. A cloud of sour-milk stench rolled out of the small bathroom along with Hlooth. His tentacle eyes waved and blinked at her in joy as the knotted tongue lolled out of its mouth, then left a sticky trail up the front of her work coat.

Soledad's eyes watered, but she managed to smile for Hlooth and reached out to give him a quick pat on the head. But he jerked his head back, out of reach, before her hand touched his skin. The eyes on the tentacles no longer looked happy. They were fluttering around in distress, looking at her and past her. The big not-a-dog pulled itself back into the dubious protection of the bathroom.

Soledad pulled her hand back. It went into her bag on its own again and curled around the pistol grip. The gun seemed to be as upset about Hlooth as Hlooth was about whatever was upsetting him. Weird thoughts appeared in her head about a spear–a *long* spear–being definitely better than a gun in this instance.

"Whatever," she said. To Hlooth and to spears and to Robert and Dillon and everyone and everything else in her life that seemed to be going both wrong and insane. "I don't have time for this."

She turned and walked back to the front door, making a point never to look at the stacked mattress and box spring that crowded the bedroom floor.

She stopped at the door and looked back at Dillon. He tried to smile, but she withered that with a harsh look.

"Have you heard ... anything?" she asked. Because he was still her friend. Even if he was a stupid, cradle robbing, loser of a man.

He managed a slight shake of his head.

"Have you checked your messages?"

Another shake of his head. The papers around his feet rustled in the breeze that came through the open door, and Soledad finally realized what they were. A hundred half-page menus for vaguely Oriental take-out of dubious quality waved up at her.

"What the hell?" she asked. Then held up her left hand again before he could respond. "No. Don't tell me. I have to get back to work. And for God's sake, put some clothes on. And take Hlooth for a walk."

She left the front door open as she walked away. Because he was still her friend, even if he didn't deserve her.

5

AFTER MOVING A bean bag to block the front door open, so the treacherous door couldn't close itself, Dillon started on the checklist Soledad had left him.

Clothes. Check. Though it was the third day he had worn that particular uniform. He added "do laundry" to the list.

Phone. No messages. Check. Though that was weird. He had had a growing stack of messages from his mother–

Despite the open door, Hlooth was still cowering in the bathroom. And no longer needed to go for a walk.

The fluttering eyestalks looked apologetic. The stench, however, and what was steaming in the bathtub, was beyond apology.

PART VIII
Second Comings

The Gun

THE GUN HAD never felt inadequate before.

It had never *been* inadequate before.

The Gun was, therefore, not entirely sure that what it was experiencing now *was*, in fact, inadequacy.

Sure, there had been Bearers who died because they couldn't pull the trigger fast enough. Or jerk and stab fast enough. Or swing and bash fast enough. But the Gun had never felt that it was to blame in these situations. Those Bearers had died heroically, and new Bearers had been found, one after the other, as necessary, to carry on the fight.

So the Gun didn't blame itself.

The Gun felt fine.

Fine.

Whatever.

It was the Bearer's fault.

The God

THE GOD AWOKE hungry.

The God never woke any other way.

The Phone

THE PHONE WISHED people would stop calling it.

It didn't deserve to be called. Or left messages. It was never allowed to take the former, and couldn't even keep the latter until they were heard.

It didn't deserve to be a Phone.

Or maybe it was the Opener who didn't deserve the Phone.

No. That couldn't be it.

If there was any blame, it rested entirely on the Phone. The Phone was certain of that.

1

Soledad wished she had never looked at her phone. Seeing Dillon's message, going to help him out, had knocked down her walls of resistance. So when Robert's call came, she answered it.

"Hi," he said, sounding cheerful, as if he had just done something clever. "I'm at the airport, and I need a ride to my girlfriend's apartment."

She hung up on him. But she didn't put her phone away. She waited, leaning against her roadkill shovel as the lunchtime traffic surged around her.

"Hi," he said, more warily this time.

"Hi."

"I *am* at the airport."

"On purpose?"

"I really like the bar food here. Twice the price for half the quantity." He paused, probably hoping she would laugh. She didn't. "Why didn't you ask which airport?"

She sighed. "Which airport?" she asked, though she already knew.

Evidently, he knew she knew, so he didn't bother answering. "I expected a better reception than this."

"Why, Robert? What made you think I wanted you to fly out here?"

"Are you going to come get me? I have a return ticket, but I wasn't expecting a forty-eight-hour layover."

"I can't–" She stopped herself before explaining that she had a gun with her, and that airport security would take a dim view of that. "I'm at work."

"It's almost lunchtime. You can take a long lunch. Just pick me up at the baggage claim."

"How appropriate," she said, and hung up. She didn't want to pick him up. She didn't want to see him.

But she would. And, more than she wanted to admit, she did.

Her eyes went to the van, where her bag was, and her thoughts went to the pistol inside the bag. Life would be much simpler if she could just *shoot* all her problems.

Perched on the roof of the van again, the turkey vulture grunted what could only be agreement.

2

"WHAT HAPPENED HERE?" Edward asked.

"They stole my bean bags," Dillon said. He was standing in the breezeway outside his apartment, holding a nearly empty container of bleach wipes, staring at the pile of black plastic trash bags that he had built over the course of the late morning and early afternoon. And at the trash bag that had replaced the bean bag holding open his front door. No trash bag had been moved to hide the disappearance of the other bean bag, though. There was only an empty space where it used to be.

"Are you moving out?" Edward suddenly looked concerned. "Did Cyd already convince you to move in with her? Honey, I think that's moving a bit too fast. I had no idea she was that manipulative. Of course, the best manipulators, you never even see them coming. Speaking of which, I think *everyone* in the complex *heard* you coming last night."

"They stole my bean bags," Dillon said again, trying to keep the conversation on topic. "I was cleaning the living room. I was right inside the door the whole time. And someone walked off with my bean bags. Both of them."

"Even the one with the stain?" Edward asked. "*The* stain?"

"I was going to clean that off." Dillon gestured with the container of wipes he held.

"I'm not sure those are strong enough, honey."

"I was going to try."

Edward stepped around Dillon to peer through the open door. "My goodness, honey, you have been busy." He made a frightened, disgusted sound. "Your carpet is even more hideous than mine." He looked at Dillon again. "You are moving, aren't you? You can't do that! I would be alone in this wretched place."

"You're never alone."

"Those guys don't count. They come and they go. Sometimes the other way around. But there is always coming, and always going. Lots and lots of coming and–"

"Stop," Dillon said, wondering if the bleach wipes would work on his mind's eye to get rid of the images Edward was painting there. "I'm not going– I mean, I'm not *moving*. I just ... I had to clean up the mess. I ... couldn't find my keys. This morning."

"Uh huh," Edward said, nodding. "Keys. Did you find them?"

"No."

"Mm-hmm." Edward surveyed the stack of trash bags. "Well, it certainly *sounded* like things got out of hand last night. I'm surprised you haven't heard from the manager already about the complaints that I'm sure were lodged. I almost lodged one myself. A complaint, I mean. What were you and Cyd *doing*? No, don't tell me. I haven't eaten yet."

Dillon's eyes went to the bag at the bottom of the heap. It was stuffed with hundreds of yellow flyers for the Yellow Sign Buffet and lots of sticky, gray duct tape. What was in that bag was almost as disgusting as what Hlooth had contributed to the bag next to it.

"Where did you get those?" Edward asked, pointing to the wipes.

"Downstairs."

"Oh," Edward said, looking interested again. "So he's home this time of day, is he?"

"I woke him up."

Edward's eyes went even wider. "Oh. I would love to have seen that. Do you need me to go down and borrow anything else from him?"

"He gave me the bags too. A whole box of them. After I went down to ask for the third one."

Hlooth's head thrust out the open door. Edward jumped back. The eyestalks scanned Edward up and down, then looked at Dillon.

"No," Dillon said. "We're not going for a walk right now."

"When did you get a dog? Did Cyd give you a dog? Or is this a small horse?" Edward stayed back, away from Hlooth, even when the beast let his tongue loll out in a friendly greeting. "Stay back," he added as Hlooth crawled over the black bag blocking the door. "Is he a watchdog?"

"Not a very good one," Dillon said. "He obviously did nothing while someone stole my bean bags. And he hasn't found my keys either."

"Well, hello," Edward said, turning to look at someone past Dillon. "Aren't you supposed to be working lunch? And … wearing clothes?"

"Wuff!" Hlooth said, eyestalks spreading wide as if jolted with electricity. Then the beast scrambled back over the trash bag to get inside the apartment again. The trash bag tore open and spilled a mix of Buffalo Burger Pit takeout bags and wrappers. A few seconds later Dillon heard what had to be the bathroom door being pushed shut, hard.

"Damn it," Dillon said. He stepped to the door and shouted into his apartment, "You better not do … whatever that was … again!"

"How are you not seeing this?" Edward asked.

Movement at the far end of the breezeway caught Dillon's eye.

"Hello, lover."

Dillon felt as surprised as Hlooth at the sight of a naked Cyd walking toward him. And maybe as scared. He briefly considered following Hlooth into the uncertain–but recently cleaned–safety of the bathroom. But he didn't run. His arousal at the sight of her rooted him to the concrete breezeway floor and made him wonder if he was still dreaming. Because not only was his apartment almost clean, but a very naked, very beautiful Cyd was walking slowly toward him, as if emerging from the October sunlight.

He kept an eye on her breasts as she walked, but they were only breasts. Assuming "only" was a meaningful adjective for what he saw. Her breasts looked as perfect as he always dreamed they should. As did the rest of her.

"Damn, Dillon," Edward said. "What's … No. I'm just going to take this as my cue to leave."

"Wait," Dillon said, his mind suddenly as afraid to be alone with Cyd again as other parts of him were glad to see her.

"Not a chance, *lover*," Edward said. He stepped wide around Cyd, headed for the stairs.

She never looked at Edward, her eyes locked on Dillon's.

"If I don't show up before work," Dillon started to say. The rest of whatever he had been about to say was swallowed in Cyd's embrace and her mouth closing on his. Her lips, her skin, was as smooth as before, but cold. How far had she walked naked?

"Then I'll know what happened," Edward called without looking back. He waved his hand over his head, then was gone down the stairs.

Cyd pushed Dillon backward through the door of his apartment. He tripped over the bag of trash, but Cyd held him up. Then the bag of trash had been pushed out into the breezeway by the closing door.

"Why are your eyes closed, lover?" Cyd whispered a few minutes later, after they had fallen onto his mattress again. And she had, again, ended up on top.

"Just in case," Dillon said.

3

NEITHER OF THEM screamed this time, which helped.

Dillon risked a peek, slitting his eyes open to look around after Cyd's weight lifted off him. He caught only a glimpse of her bare legs as Cyd walked out of his bedroom. Which was also reassuring. He might have had his eyes closed the whole time, he might have been overwhelmed with passion and pleasure, but his mind had kept trying to get his attention and give him a tally of how many hands, fingers and mouths had been involved in the actual act of lovemaking.

"Where are you going?"

When she didn't answer, he pushed himself into a seated position. His legs still dangled over the edge of the mattress. "I don't think I have anything to drink in the fridge," he said. "Sorry."

But the door he heard opening wasn't the fridge. "Hey! Wait! Where are you–"

The front door pulled shut.

"–going?"

Dillon jumped out of bed and ran into the living room. He stepped on something cold and sharp in the middle of the floor, but was in too much of a hurry to check it out, so he limped the rest of the way to the door. He had grabbed the doorknob and pulled it open before he registered the tingling sensation starting in his hand and running up his arm.

He did not see a naked Cyd walking away from him along the breeze-way. He did not see the breezeway at all.

Cold air poured out of the open doorway, becoming fog that curled and swirled around him in much the same way Cyd had a few minutes earlier. But with the very opposite effect.

Goose bumps erupted all over his still-damp body while his penis shrivelled.

Dillon paused in the act of pushing the door closed again.

He wasn't staring into the VOID as he expected to be.

It was dark, sure, and cold. But not DARK, not COLD. It wasn't even Cold. Just ... cold. And certainly not EMPTY.

There were metal pantry shelves on either side of the door, stacked with boxes and covered food containers. It looked like a walk-in freezer, like the one at the Pit.

Except the freezer at the Buffalo Burger Pit didn't have those shadows at the far end. Writhing shadows that absorbed the light coming through the open door even as they shrank from it. Shadows that stretched along the sides, wrapping around the plastic five-gallon buckets and stainless-steel basins, reaching for the door. Reaching for Dillon, to grab him and pull him through.

Dillon stepped back and slammed the door closed.

He fell backward, and sat down hard on the floor, panting. His right arm twitched with the needles that still poked at it. His deep breaths added to the fog until the temperature of the air around him returned to just a shiver below normal.

His eyes noticed the glint of something shiny on the floor, in the middle of the recently cleared–he couldn't really call it *cleaned*, but he had picked up all the trash–carpet.

His keys.

His right foot still hurt from stepping on them.

As he pulled on his rumpled work uniform for the fourth time in three days, he kept trying to figure out how he had missed seeing the keys there, in the middle of the floor. Or, if Cyd had taken them the night before, where had she carried them when she came back?

4

EDWARD'S DOOR WAS locked, and no one answered when Dillon knocked. Even after the third time. If Edward was in there, he would have already come to the door to yell at Dillon to leave because he was *busy*. Feeling oddly lonely for a man who had just had sex twice in less than eighteen hours, Dillon shrugged and started walking to work alone for the second time in two days.

Without Edward there to be outraged about sex with women, in general, and with Cyd, in particular, Dillon found himself thinking about his Uncle Phil. He almost pulled out his phone to call Phil before he remembered–

"Dillon?" The woman's voice sounded strangely familiar. "Is that you, Dillon?"

Dillon was crossing the parking lot. He paused to look around. He saw a woman staring at him, her left hand shielding her eyes from the sunlight.

She stood next to the only new-looking car in the parking lot, a red convertible with the top down. She had long blonde hair pulled back with a kerchief. She wore a bright-colored sweater with the long sleeves hooked on her thumbs. The sweater was far more seasonal than the pair of white shorts she also wore. She was older than Dillon, but not unattractive. Thirty, at least, but maybe as old as forty. Despite the familiar ring of her voice and, oddly, the shape of her knees, Dillon didn't recognize her.

"Dillon?"

A much younger part of Dillon, though, a part he hadn't heard from in a long time, did recognize her, and marvelled at how small she looked. "Mommy?" said this much younger part.

"Dillon! It is you!" She spread her arms, as if expecting him to run to her.

Dillon just stared at her, trying to remember the last time he had heard her voice. Two years ago? Or three? She had called him on his eighteenth birthday, so four years ago. He couldn't remember what they had spoken about. If she had said anything more than "Happy birthday." The last time he had seen her, though, he remembered vividly. She had been carrying a small suitcase and an oversized travel bag, pulling the front door of Uncle Phil's house closed behind her, heading west. She looked younger now, somehow, than she had then.

"You're not as tall as I thought you would be," she said.

Dillon straightened to his full five-foot-eleven, which made her look even smaller. When she had left, she had still been taller. His growth spurt, what there had been of it, had come months later.

So many emotions surged through Dillon at the sight of her. She was Mommy. She was his mother who took away his jack-in-the-box. The mother who left him. She wasn't even his real mother.

She took two tentative steps toward him. "Did you get my messages?" she asked. "I talked to Phil–"

"I'm adopted," Dillon said, the words bursting out of him before he could stop them. An accusation combined with a question. "On top of *abandoned*." Those words also came on their own, and surprised him. Another accusation, another question. He had never allowed himself to think of her leaving him that way. Now, with Uncle Phil gone too, he realized that was exactly how he felt. "First you adopt me. Then you abandon me. Why would you do that?"

She winced, but she took another step toward him. They were less than ten feet apart now. "I didn't abandon you, Dillon. I just ... left. I had to ... leave." Her hands fluttered about, making meaningless gestures. Her lips pressed together, became a single thin line, as if to stop the words she was saying. After a few seconds, she asked, "How did you find out about ... the other?"

"It's amazing what the police will tell you when they're looking into the mysterious disappearances of nonfamily members. Was Dad even my dad?"

"The police? I didn't disappear, Dillon–"

"Not you, *Mommy*. Uncle Phil."

Suddenly she was right there in front of him, her hands on his shoulders, gripping them tightly. "What about Phil? What happened?"

"He's gone–"

"Phil is *dead*?" Her hands moved from his shoulders to his cheeks, as if she were going to squeeze the words out of him.

"We don't know," Dillon said. He grabbed her wrists to move her hands, but she was too strong. He couldn't budge her. "His house was attacked, and he's ... not there."

Her eyes searched his face, then she let him go and stepped back. "Show me."

"We can take my car ..." He started to point to his Neon, parked just a few spaces away, where Soledad had left it the day before.

His mother wasn't looking at him, or at his car. She scanned the entire parking lot, the look on her face very much like the one Edward wore when discussing women. "No. We'll take mine."

5

MOM HADN'T HAD a shiny red convertible when she left ten years ago. Dillon sat in the passenger seat, window down, his right elbow propped on the door frame, his hair whipped by the wind of their travel, and tried not to enjoy it. Having a cool car did *not* excuse abandoning him for a decade and never telling him he was adopted. But it did make the silent trip to Uncle Phil's house more bearable.

"Oh my god," Mom said as they pulled up in front of Uncle Phil's house. She parked against the curb on the wrong side of the street and was out of the car before Dillon could say anything. She stood on the thin, browning grass and stared at the house.

Except for the yellow police tape, Uncle Phil's house looked much the same as the last time Dillon had seen it. The front door was closed, but the windows were still pushed in, the walls around them still cracked. There was no sheen of slime. Dillon wondered if the October sunshine had dried the slime into a kind of snot.

Then Mom was walking up the steps to the porch, ducking under the police tape, and pushing on the front door. It was locked.

Dillon got out of the car. "I have my keys," he said, pushing his right hand into his pocket. He pulled out his keys and held them out for her.

But Mom didn't need his keys. She had her own keys out, and was unlocking the front door.

"I'm not sure we're supposed to go in ..."

She looked back at him with an expression he couldn't decipher, then she walked through the door.

He hesitated on the porch, on this side of the police tape, leaning to the right to peer through the door. He could hear her moving around inside, pushing pieces of broken furniture around, swearing under her breath. After a few seconds, he pushed his keys back into his pocket with his phone. He was about to ask what she was looking for when she appeared in the doorway.

"It's gone," she said.

Dillon wondered if he should attempt to comfort her. He eyed the yellow tape, then decided if she needed comforting, she could come to him. "They said there was no body. Just ... ichor."

"Phil's gun," she said. Her expression was intense, almost scared. "Have you seen it?"

"They said that was gone too–"

"God damn it, Dillon," she shouted, sparking flashbacks in Dillon's mind. He didn't even see her move. She was just suddenly there, right in front of him, reaching across the police tape, grabbing his shoulders again, pulling his face close to hers. "How could you lose that?"

Feeling as if he was six years old again, as if he had just done something bad, Dillon said, "I didn't lose it. It was just ... gone."

"Do you know what this means?" she asked, pulling his face even closer, so their noses almost touched.

Dillon shook his head. He had no idea what any of this meant.

"It means I might have to kill you, Dillon."

6

DILLON BLINKED, HIS eyes nearly crossed from trying to focus on his mother's face right in front of his. He wondered if Soledad's mother would give him a lift to work. He wondered if Soledad's mother had told Soledad that she might have to kill her own daughter. Suddenly, being abandoned started to seem like a good thing.

He forced himself to smile, then tried to pull back, away from Mom. She didn't release him.

"I'm serious, honey," she said, looking very serious. "If we don't find Phil's gun–"

"I need to get to work," Dillon said, his face still uncomfortably close to hers. "I haven't had breakfast. Can you at least let me eat breakfast? Then kill me for losing Phil's gun?"

She pulled back from him, her nose wrinkling. "Is that why you haven't brushed your teeth? Wait. Did you lose Phil's gun?"

He shook his head, then tried not breathe on her when he said, "No."

"What do you mean, 'breakfast'? It's after three in the afternoon." She leaned close to him and sniffed. "You haven't showered either? Where were you going dressed like this? Please don't tell me you were going to work."

Dillon thought about explaining what Hlooth had done in the bathtub, and that even though he had cleaned it, he didn't want to step there just yet. Instead, he said, "I've been cleaning my apartment. My shift starts at four–"

"Because I called?"

Dillon thought, again, about what Hlooth had done, then about what Cyd had done with the Yellow Sign Buffet menus. About the checklist Soledad had given him. He said, "Yes?"

She ducked under the yellow police tape, grabbed his left arm, and pulled him after her as she walked back to her car. "We're going back to your apartment," she said. "And we're going to have a long, long talk. First, though, you're going to shower." She took her hand off his arm and looked at it. She wiped her hand on her shorts. "And get some clean clothes." She opened the driver side door, but paused before getting in. "Please tell me you have clothes that aren't your work uniform. Or at least you have more than one uniform."

"I have other clothes," Dillon said, walking around to the passenger side. "And four complete uniforms, plus some extra shirts."

They got in the car.

"They're not clean, are they?"

Dillon shrugged.

Mom let out a long, disgusted sigh. "I really thought Phil would do a better job."

"Funny," Dillon said, as she turned the key in the ignition. "He said the same thing about you."

She looked at him, her expression sharp. "What?"

"My shift starts at four."

Her eyes searched his face for a few seconds. "No, it doesn't. You're going to call in sick."

Dillon nodded. He was beginning to feel sick.

7

"You have to come in, Dillon," Barbara said.

"Give me the phone." Gil's voice in the background did not sound happy.

"Stop it," Barbara said, her voice muffled now. Dillon knew she had pushed the phone against her left breast. "You can yell at him when he gets here. Which is not going to happen if you start yelling at him now." Her voice became normal again. "Dillon? You have to come in. Gil, no ... I ... need to talk to you."

"But my mother–"

"Dillon, it's been chaos here all day. You really need to come in."

"What? What happened?"

"It's too much to talk about on the phone, Dillon."

"But I can't work tonight."

Barbara sighed. "We'll work that out when you get here." She suddenly sounded very tired. "Just come in, Dillon."

"OK."

He ended the call and looked at his mother.

"Fine," she said. "But you're still going to take a shower first. You smell like Clorox and sour milk."

8

"I'm assuming these aren't yours," Mom said Dillon when he got out of the shower. She pointed at the separate pile of Cyd's bra and panties near the larger heap of his own laundry.

Dillon felt his face–and the rest of him–get warm. He opened his mouth to say something, but the air was thick with chemical scents and cleaners. So he focused on keeping his towel wrapped around his waist.

"I didn't think so," Mom said. "They were cleaner than everything else." She pointed to the mattress, where his uniform shirt and pants were laid out. "I Lysoled the hell out of what you were wearing, so maybe they're at least sanitary. You'll have to make your own peace with whatever underwear you can find. I didn't dig that deep." She walked out of his bedroom, through the living room to the front door. "I'll wait in the car, where I can breathe." She opened the door and walked out.

"Wait!" Dillon said. "Don't shut the-"

The door slammed closed.

"-door."

Hlooth poked his head out of the bathroom behind Dillon, the eye-stalks looking in all directions. Hlooth had still been shut in the bathroom when Dillon and his mother had come into the apartment.

"Of course you have a dog," Mom had said. "Because it just wouldn't smell bad enough in here without one."

She had been nice enough to open the bathroom door, but she had had no nice words for Hlooth. Hlooth had stayed in the bathroom, head resting on the side of the tub, watching Dillon as he showered.

The front door opened again, just a crack. Hlooth ducked back into the bathroom. Dillon used a foot to keep Hlooth from pushing the bathroom door closed.

"Sorry," Mom said from the breezeway. "I forgot. Hurry up." Then she was gone again.

"Woof?" Hlooth asked from where he was hiding behind the shower curtain.

"Yeah," Dillon said. "She's gone. She's still ... Mom. You didn't meet her before," he added as he began drying his hair. "Which is just as well. She never liked dogs."

9

Mom opened the door for Dillon at the Buffalo Burger Pit, as well, but with a heavy, maternal sigh of sacrifice and disappointment, twin to the first one she had made when he told her not to park on the customer's side of the parking lot but pull around to the far side.

The short ride from the apartment parking lot–Mom had insisted she wasn't going to walk, no matter how close Dillon thought the restaurant was–had not been long enough to do much more than whip his still shower-wet hair and fluff his Lysol-soaked uniform. He felt as if he was walking in a germ-free cloud of noxious clean.

Dillon walked in while Mom held the door for him, but he stopped before going behind the counter. He felt torn. Pulled forward by the habit of six years of employment–and his need for breakfast–and backward by the presence of his mother. He didn't want to leave her alone up front, but he didn't want to invite her behind the counter, either. He could almost feel the restaurant spinning around him. Too many forces were pulling on him, each trying to make him go some different direction and open doors he wanted nothing to do with.

"There you are, Dillon."

Barbara had been standing at the front counter, talking to Coleman. She fixed Dillon with her glance, anchoring him to the floor even more than he already was, while also adding another maternal force tugging on him. She was wearing the drive-thru the belt and headset. She hated working drive-thru, even during the slow hours of the afternoon.

Dillon almost asked where Cyd was. She was scheduled to be working now. On the other hand, she had been scheduled to be at work a couple hours before she had showed up, naked, at his apartment.

"There he is," Coleman said, pointing. "The slacker." He leaned to his left to look past Dillon. "Where's Cyd? If you need me to step in and cover for you with her, as well, you just let me know."

"Be quiet, Coleman. There are customers." She smiled at Mom, who had stepped around Dillon and now stood beside him. Barbara gave her an embarrassed boys-will-be-boys shrug.

Dillon looked at Barbara. "Coleman is covering for me?"

Coleman stood up straight and squared his shoulders. "I expect I'll be doing more than covering for you, little man. I expect I'll be far exceeding you. I might even have your job this time tomorrow. And your girl. Or girls."

"Girls?" Dillon looked at Barbara again. "Coleman?"

"Beggars can't be choosers," Barbara said.

"Normally," Coleman said, "I would never presume to step into your shows. But as popular as you've been the last few days, I figure I want in on that action."

"I don't think it works that way."

Coleman leaned forward, as if he were standing over Dillon instead of across the counter. "I am the boss, little man. It works the way I say it does." He threw his arms out. "Bring on the girls!"

The door pushed opened behind Dillon.

Coleman's expression brightened with a huge smile. "Hello, Edward Preppycollars. Meet the new boss."

Dillon turned to see Edward coming into the dining room. Edward was in girl mode, complete with lipstick, eye shadow, blonde wig, and a push-up bra reshaping his uniform. Dillon said, "I don't think Edward is one of the girls you're looking for."

"Nope," Coleman said, shaking his head. "Not even when he has his falsies in. But I can be his boss. I am a discrimination-free overlord. I tell everyone what to do, regardless of race, creed, religion, or degree of faux femininity."

"I quit," Edward said. He turned around and pulled the door open again.

"Edward!" Barbara said. "Not today!"

"You can't quit before I fire you," Coleman shouted at Edward as the door closed behind him.

From the far side of the glass door, Edward turned around, giving Coleman the finger with both hands.

Jorge shouted from the grill station, "If he quits–"

"He's not quitting," Coleman said. "I am canning his ass."

"Fine, you can his ass. Can I have his break?"

"Enough!" Barbara shouted. She pointed at Edward. "You! Get back in here!" She turned and pointed her finger up at Coleman's face. "And you. No firing anybody. And take care of this customer," she added, pointing back at Dillon's mother. Then Barbara turned to look–and point– at Dillon. "And you. Get back here. We have some things to discuss."

Dillon cast a quick look past the grill station, toward the manager's nook. "Is Gil here?"

Behind him, the bell on the door jingled as Edward came back in.

"No," Barbara said. "Daddy isn't home. But he might come back any time. And the longer you wait, the more likely that is."

Dillon started to do as he was told, then remembered who he had arrived with. Mom was looking at him with a confused expression, with equally confused glances at Barbara, Coleman and Edward.

"Welcome to the God Dammed–" Coleman started to say, but stopped himself. Even before Barbara's elbow hit him in the stomach. "Right. Welcome to the Buffalo Burger Pit, ma'am," he said to Mom. "We're still rehearsing the show for tonight, so please excuse our hesitations, missed steps, and blown lines. What can I get for you?"

Dillon heard Edward mutter something about nothing getting blown if he had anything to say about it.

Mom shook her head. "I'm not eating here. I mean, I'm not here to eat."

"Barbara," Dillon said. "This is my mother. Mom, this is Barbara. Co-owner and afternoon manager of the Buffalo Burger Pit. My boss."

The two women looked each other up and down. Then both looked at Dillon. Twin disappointed maternal gazes bore down on him.

"That's your mom?" Coleman said. He nodded his appreciation. "Nice. Very nice. But man, how did you not know you were adopted?"

10

"It has been chaos here all day," Barbara said to Dillon. "Your little prank was only the beginning of it." She seemed to have decided not to pull Dillon back to the manager's nook, since the only apparent customer was, for lack of a better word, family. And he could hear the tone in Barbara's voice ramping up to scold level.

Dillon glanced at his mother, who still looked at him with frowning disapproval. He looked back at Barbara. "My little prank?" he asked, hoping to derail the scolding.

No luck. "The dining room was a mess this morning. Gil was this close-" Barbara held up her right hand, with the thumb and forefinger only millimeters apart. "-to dragging you out of bed and either dropping you in the fry vats or making you clean it all up. This close," she repeated. "But then Cyd showed up. Somehow. Gil claims she must have been hiding somewhere, but then he has a tendency to lose coherent thought in the presence of naked-" She paused.

"Naked?" Dillon and Coleman asked at the same time.

"Don't try to change the subject," Barbara snapped. After a few seconds of failing to find another word, she went on. "Yes, *naked*. Cyd quit this morning. She turned in her uniform and walked out."

"Naked?" Coleman asked again.

Edward grimaced at the thought. "Gross! I'm not going to eat here for weeks."

Barbara pointed at Edward. "Hush, you. The whole restaurant has been cleaned since this morning," she said to Mom, in case Mom might

285

actually be a customer someday. "But– I mean, yes. Cyd was naked. She ... she had her uniform off. And nothing else on. And Todd claims she was ... steaming. She handed the folded uniform to Gil, and ... walked out."

"Steaming?" Dillon asked.

"I don't remember that being in the employee handbook," Edward said. "If I decide to quit now–"

"No," Barbara said, jabbing her finger at Edward again while still focusing on Dillon. "Nancy was scandalized," she went on. "Todd hasn't spoken a coherent word since then. And I'm pretty sure the only reason you're not dead right now, little Dillon, is that when Gil tries to get angry at you for what happened, he *remembers* what happened, in incredible detail. And he gets all smiley and loses his train of thought."

"Naked?" Coleman asked a third time.

"Shut up, Coleman."

"Nothing on underneath? At all?"

"Shut *up*, Coleman."

Dillon thought he knew where Cyd's underwear were, but he didn't volunteer the information. It was hard to think of anything else with his own memories of a naked Cyd walking toward him, but he managed to remember–and protest–the part that applied to him directly. "Clean up what? What was wrong with the dining room?"

"You had another rumble, didn't you?" Barbara said.

"What? No–" That had been a long, long time ago, before he was assistant manager.

"Tables and chairs were thrown everywhere," Barbara said, gesturing with both hands. "One of the windows is *chipped*, Dillon."

"Where?"

Barbara squinted at him. "So you admit it? And what was the slime all over the floor?"

"No!" Dillon would have backed away, but Edward was too close behind him. "Slime? What– I have no idea what you're talking about. I went home last night, and Cyd was there, and I couldn't even leave my apartment until after lunch–" He stopped, looked at his mother, then added, "The doors. I couldn't open the doors. Cyd was gone by then," he added.

Barbara held up her hands, blocking his words. "Don't talk to me about Cyd–"

"Don't listen to her," Coleman said. "Definitely tell us more about Cyd."

"When I left last night," Dillon said, "the dining room was clean. The only chair down was the one I was sitting in, waiting for Soledad–"

"Soledad too?" Coleman's eyes narrowed. "Damn, man. You are far more than just *popular*. I think you might be a god. But I'm still your boss."

Dillon stared at Coleman, then looked back at Barbara. "I locked up when I left. I know I did."

"The doors were locked this morning," Barbara said. "Gil was quite clear about that. He can be very clear about things that don't involve naked employees. He was also very clear—and very upset—about all the Yellow Sign menu flyers scattered everywhere. Everywhere, Dillon. Stuck to the windows and counter with slime. Some of them floating in the fry vats. More of them clogging up the grease traps."

"That explains all the paper in my grease traps," Jorge said from the grill. "Todd is so damn useless."

"Yellow Sign?" Dillon thought of the trash bags full of menu flyers stacked outside his apartment door.

Next to Barbara, Coleman raised a middle-finger salute to the restaurant across the street. Behind him, Jorge did the same. Edward was probably doing it too, from the sideways look Dillon's mother was making.

"Cyd saved you," Barbara said. "But only just. Gil opened an hour late."

"What time was Cyd here?"

"What difference does that make?"

"Well," said Edward, "we know what time she was at somebody's apartment this afternoon. And still out of uniform. That was about two."

Dillon remembered how cold her skin was. Where had she been during the hours from when she turned in her uniform and when she walked out of the shadows of his breezeway?

"Ahem," Barbara said. "We're not trying to figure out the mysteries of Cyd. I'm yelling at an employee here."

"Am I fired?" Dillon asked.

"Of course not. Gil wants to do that himself."

Dillon's phone rang in his pocket. He hoped it wasn't Cyd as he very uncharacteristically—and with more a touch of desperation—pulled it out of his pocket, thumbed the button to take the call and held it to his ear. He turned to his left so he wouldn't have to see both Mom and Barbara staring at him.

"Hello, Mr. Offner," said a woman's voice in his ear. "This is Detective White."

At least it wasn't Cyd.

11

"Oh, sure," Barbara said to Dillon's back. "Now you answer your phone? We're not through."

"Is this a bad time, Mr. Offner?" Detective White asked.

"Yes?" Dillon said.

"Damn it," Barbara said, then, in a much more pleasant voice, "Welcome to the Buffalo Burger Pit. What can I get for you tonight?" Her voice shifted back into low growl. "And we are *still* not through, Dillon."

Edward used the distraction to walk behind the front counter and disappear into the back.

"I'm at your apartment, Mr. Offner," Detective White said. "I decided to call since knocking was only disturbing Hlooth."

Dillon heard Hlooth thump his head against the locked front door of his apartment through the tiny speaker of his phone. "Why?" he started to ask. Smooth, floating movement outside the restaurant had drawn Dillon's eye.

"We need to talk, Mr. Offner. I have some new questions."

The five monks from the night before were gliding across the parking lot to the door of the restaurant. "Why are you at my apartment?" Dillon asked, even as he realized the detective had already answered his question.

"I thought you might be here, Mr. Offner. I'm guessing you are at work?"

"Yes? But I'm not working–"

"Great. I'll see you in a few minutes."

"Wait!" Dillon said to a dead line.

The monks reached the door of the dining room. An arm emerged from the cloak of the first monk and the door opened so smoothly the attached bell didn't so much as tinkle.

"Who was ... ?" Mom started to ask. Her voice trailed off as she watched the monks enter the restaurant.

As each monk glided into the dining room, they bowed to Dillon. They didn't stop to bow, they bowed as they glided, turning a full circle on their way to stand in line at Coleman's register. When they were all in line, they faced Dillon and bowed a second time, this time in unison.

"Good evening, child," the monks said as they performed their synchronized bow. The words were melodic. Five-point, multitrack harmony.

Mom's hand gripped his shoulder with surprising strength and pulled him backward, away from the monks. Toward the door.

"We have to go," she said, glancing back at the monks.

The monks watched with serene nonexpressions, ignoring Coleman as he said, "Welcome back, gentlemen. Will you be having the Dillon Offner Usual again, as fast and raw as possible?"

Back in the grill, Jorge said, "*Jesus el Christo*, not these guys again."

The bell on the door across the dining room rang as that door opened.

The monks turned in place to watch the door open. Dillon could no longer see their faces, but he felt the level of ambient serenity drop precipitously. The Ghost of Autumn Present stepped in, glowing as brown-and-orange as the night before. The man was smiling directly at Dillon as he entered, as if he had known Dillon would be standing right there. He removed his top hat with his left and bowed to Dillon as the door closed behind him.

"Good evening, young master." He nodded at the monks, who did not nod back, then fixed his gaze just over Dillon's shoulder. "Molly," he said. "So good of you to come. I was less than certain you would make it."

Mom's grip on Dillon's shoulder became painful. She resumed pulling Dillon back toward the door. "We're leaving."

The man's smile faded and he shook his head, making his curly hair swish back and forth. "You will not find it so easy, Molly, to abandon your sworn responsibilities this time."

"You stay out of this," Mom snapped. "You weren't *there*."

"Mom," Dillon said, regaining his balance and pulling his shoulder from her grasp. "Detective White is coming. And I haven't eaten breakfast yet."

"The police? Here?"

Dillon gestured with the phone he still held. "She said she was on her way."

"Then we really need to go." She reached for his arm. "We can get breakfast, or lunch, or whatever, anywhere–"

Dillon stepped back. "No. This is about Uncle Phil–"

Mom paused in midgrab. "Is that what the detective said?"

"No, but what else–"

Mom's expression hardened as she cut him off. "You have no idea what this is about, Dillon. Any of it." She reached for him again. "We have to go."

Dillon let her hand catch his left arm, but he resisted being pulled. The fear on Mom's face scared him. Detective White wanting to talk to him scared him, but he was sure she would scare him more if she were chasing him. And being alone with a frightened Mom suddenly scared him most of all. "Stop it, Mom. Why? What have you done?"

Mom's laugh was not a happy one. "What have *I* done?" She shook her head. She let go of Dillon's arm, and stepped away from him. Then she glared past him at the man in the top hat. "I did my *best*," she said. "I never volunteered for ... for *this*." Her gesture included Dillon, the monks, the Buffalo Burger Pit, and maybe Rio Cruces and the world around them. Her eyes met Dillon's again. "I did my *best*." Then she turned and walked out of the restaurant.

12

THE NORTH DOOR of the dining room was still closing behind Mom as the bell on the south door rang again. Dillon turned to see Detective White stepping through the door. She was dressed in a navy blue pantsuit, her sidearm visible under her jacket on her right hip. She carried a Manila folder in her left hand.

The detective's eyes found Dillon, and gave him a smile he was sure she thought was pleasant. Then her eyes took in the man in the brown-and-orange tails with top hat in line behind the five monks. Then past Dillon, toward the parking lot where Mom was driving away. Detective White's smile went away as her expression went from forced pleasant to guardedly curious. She walked to Dillon and extended her hand.

"Did I miss the Offner family reunion?" the detective asked as she shook Dillon's hand, still looking past him. "That's too bad." She glanced at the men in line. "At least I was in time for the costume party. Isn't Halloween still a couple weeks away? Never mind. Is there someplace we can talk, Mr. Offner?"

Jorge walked to the front counter from behind the grill, carrying a tray with a single burger on it. "Hey, Dillon," he said. "You want this or not?" He didn't wait for Dillon's response. "Wanted you to have it before ..." He looked at the monks, shuddered, then was gone back to the grill.

"My breakfast," Dillon said to Detective White.

"You haven't eaten yet?" she asked.

"I've had a busy day."

"That's fine. You can eat while we talk."

She stayed with Dillon as he walked to the counter and picked up the tray.

"Do you want something to drink?" he asked.

"Coffee would be great, thanks."

Since Jorge had gone back to the grill, and Coleman was still trying to talk the monks into cooking the bacon this time– "though this may seem a request directly in the face of that old wisdom 'the customer is always right'," Coleman was saying, "the sanity of our grill man depends on it"–and Barbara had her back to Dillon, Dillon put his tray back down. He walked around to the other side of the counter. He poured a cup of coffee for Detective White and filled a cup with ice and orange soda for himself. Then he and the detective went to a booth in the southwest corner of the dining room. The booth farthest from the front counter.

Detective White put the Manila folder on the table in front of her as she sat down. She took out her oversized phone and put it on the table next to the folder. Then she ignored both of them while she took a sip of her coffee, her eyes on Dillon.

Dillon avoided her eyes and stared at the folder as he picked up his bacon cheeseburger-no-cheese and took a bite.

Detective White put her coffee cup down and reached into her jacket again. She took out the same notebook and pen that Dillon had seen the day before. She placed them on the table beside the phone, then opened the folder. An 8x10 photograph of Cyd, a blow up of her senior picture, was on top of a small stack of papers. She was wearing a pink sweater and leaning against a tree in a park. She looked young. Too young, all of a sudden.

Dillon forced the half-chewed bite of burger down his throat. Cyd had given Dillon a wallet-sized version of the same photograph nearly a year ago. "Why," he asked, "do you have a picture of Cyd?"

Detective White touched the screen of her phone with a finger, causing the screen to light up, then she said, "Cyd Turner." Her voice was crisp, clear, as if she were dictating. "Eighteen years old. Attending Rio Cruces Community College. Employed at the Buffalo Burger Pit. Is that the Cyd you mean?"

"Of course." Dillon lowered the burger from his mouth so he wouldn't take a bite, but he didn't put it down. "Cyd. I've known her for two years. Is she OK?"

Detective White's eyes no longer looked so friendly. "You tell me, Mr. Offner."

Dillon wanted to take a bite, to think about his answer as he chewed, but something about the way the detective looked at him seemed to indicate that was exactly what she expected him to do. So he blurted, "She was fine? I guess? Two hours ago." He decided to leave out *and naked*.

Detective White picked up her notebook and pen. She flipped the notebook open, then scribbled something on it with the pen. "This was here? Or at your apartment?"

"At my apartment." Dillon took a quick bite of his burger.

The detective looked at him. "Did you talk?"

"Some," Dillon said around his food.

"What did you talk about, Mr. Offner?"

"She ... didn't say much." *Hello, lover. Why are your eyes closed, lover?* He chewed as he did not say those things. He swallowed, then took a sip of his drink. "We just ... um ..." Dillon took another bite of his burger and chewed it emphatically.

"Um?"

Dillon felt his face get warm. "We ..." He couldn't make himself say it. He couldn't have said it to his mother. Nor Barbara. And not Detective White. So he acted as if he had. "And then she left. We didn't talk much." He took another bite, though his mouth was dry and he could no longer taste what he was chewing.

He looked around the dining room, hoping someone might be coming to his rescue. No one seemed to be. He saw that the monks had positioned themselves in the same two booths as the night before. They were not looking at him. Their gazes were fixed on the grill section where Jorge kept his head down, not looking back at them. The Ghost of Autumn Present had seated himself at the same booth as the night before, but he had his back to the front counter. He caught Dillon's eye and winked, but he remained where he was.

"You've had a busy day," Detective White said, pulling his attention back to her. "I saw that you cleaned your apartment. Or least emptied it. In part. Did Miss Turner have her phone with her? Did you notice?"

"No," Dillon said. *Because she was naked*, he didn't add. Then he remembered how his keys had turned up after she left and added, with much less confidence, "I don't think so?"

Detective White leaned forward. "Her parents called us this morning, Mr. Offner. They said she had not been home for two nights, and had not answered her phone. They thought she had been at work yesterday, but had not talked to her. Then she neither came home, and she was not at work when they called today. Do you know anything about that?"

"She ..." Dillon searched for a way to summarize. "Quit. Today. This morning, I mean. That's what Barbara told me." He pointed toward the front counter, but the detective didn't take her eyes off him. "Just a few minutes ago. That was before I saw her. Today. This morning." He moved his burger back up to his mouth to hide behind it.

"Did Miss Turner know your uncle?"

The unexpected question caused Dillon to freeze with his burger in front of his face, his mouth open. He closed his mouth and swallowed. "What?"

Detective White didn't repeat the question.

"No," he said. He put the burger down, carefully. His mind still reeled from the question, which made it hard to compose a reply. After a few seconds, he said, "Well, she might have seen him here. Once or twice. I don't think they ever met, though. Not really. He mostly avoided coming to see me at work. He ... I don't know why." He paused to take a breath. When Detective White said nothing else, he asked, "Why?"

"A woman matching Miss Turner's description, and wearing a uniform much like the one you're wearing now, was seen near your uncle's house the night before last. The night he disappeared."

Dillon shook his head. "No. That doesn't make any sense. She was at my apartment that night–"

"Before your Uncle was there? Before she ran away?"

Dillon stared at her. "No. I mean, yes. She was already gone when Uncle Phil ... showed up."

"And you can't think of any reason she might have gone with him when he left?"

"No. Not at all. What are you saying?"

Detective White finally leaned back, away from him. She placed the notebook on the table again. She picked up her coffee and took a sip. "I'm just following up on all possibilities, Mr. Offner."

"But that's not even ... possible." He shook his head. "No. There's no way."

Detective White took another sip. Her right hand still held the pen. She moved it to the notebook, poised to write.

Dillon looked around the dining room again. This was the Buffalo Burger Pit. His home for the last six years. Except, suddenly, it looked alien, filled with strangers in brown robes and black top hats and badges. His world no longer made sense.

"Did Miss Turner look OK to you when you saw her today?" Detective White asked, drawing his attention back to her.

"What? She looked ..." He thought of her breasts, her skin. "She looked great."

"No scratches or bruises? No obvious injuries?"

"No," he said, appalled at the thought. "She was ..." He still couldn't tell the detective Cyd was naked, and might have walked naked to his apartment all the way from the restaurant. "She looked fine."

"What about her state of mind, Mr. Offner? Can you think of anything about her that seemed ... different?"

Dillon sighed. There was no way to avoid it. He spoke the word before his mind could balk at saying it. "Naked."

Detective White's expression showed surprise for an instant, but all she said was, "Naked, Mr. Offner?"

"She was naked. She showed up at my apartment naked. No clothes on."

"I know what naked means, Mister Offner."

"And Barbara said she was naked here too, when she ... turned in her uniform."

Detective White's face showed definite surprise now, lasting several seconds. Then her expression went neutral again and she made quick notes with her pen.

"Then she left here. Naked."

"What time was this?"

Dillon shrugged. "I'm not sure. Before we opened? So between nine and ten? Barbara would know."

"Was she here?"

"No. But Gil told her."

"You are referring to Gil and Barbara Houck, owners of the Buffalo Burger Pit?"

The way she spoke reminded Dillon of the phone on the table between them. He glanced at it. All he could see was a timer, counting up. "Yes. Gil comes early to open. Barbara comes in later to help with lunch."

"So where was our naked Miss Turner between ten o'clock and two o'clock, Mr. Offner?"

Dillon shrugged. "I don't know. She wasn't there when I woke up this morning."

Detective White's eyes focused on him again, and Dillon realized he hadn't mentioned that Cyd had been waiting at his apartment the night before.

His bacon cheeseburger-no-cheese sat, less than half-eaten, on his tray as he told Detective White about the night before. About Soledad walking him home. About finding Cyd–naked, again, but for the first time–in his apartment. How Cyd was gone when he woke up. Her uniform had been gone too. He didn't mention that she had left her bra and panties. Nor that Soledad had come to rescue him. He wasn't sure if he was protecting Soledad or himself with that omission. When asked about his mother, he said she had been waiting for him in the parking lot. That they had gone to Uncle Phil's house, then come to the restaurant.

Then, as suddenly as she had come, Detective White was gone. She had put away her phone and notebook, closed the folder with Cyd's picture, and left him alone at the table. Dillon stayed in his seat and watched her speak briefly with Barbara, make a note in her notebook, then leave through the same door she had entered.

Dillon was surprised to see how dark it was outside the windows of the dining room, and that the dinner rush had started. Andrew had come in, and he and Coleman were working the front counter. Barbara was still covering drive-thru. He couldn't see Ronald and Jorge in the grill section, but he could hear them talking, repeating orders back to Coleman and Barbara. The tables nearest Dillon held men and couples and there was a family of five in the next booth. One of the little girls was peeking over the top of the booth seat, her eyes wide as she considered him. Dillon felt his face get warm as he wondered how much the little girl had heard of what he told Detective White.

Dillon noticed the monks were still in their two booths across the dining room from him. He leaned to his left to see if the Ghost of Autumn Present was still there, as well. He was. He caught Dillon's eye and nodded. Whatever food the man had ordered, he had finished it long ago and even cleared his tray from his table. He picked up his top hat and stood. He smiled as he walked over to Dillon.

Dillon felt more than saw the monks turn their heads to stare. At him.

At the same time he felt something he could not see also turn its attention on him. Something hungry.

He hardly heard the north door of the dining room jangle open.

The Ghost of Autumn Present stopped walking less than three feet away. To Dillon the man seemed to have grown taller as he walked. Now he loomed, blocking Dillon's view of the rest of the dining room. The man gave Dillon a slight bow, which only accentuated the looming. He opened his mouth.

"No!" a woman shouted, interrupting whatever the man had been about to say, and, somehow, making the man shrink to normal size.

Dillon thought he heard a hiss come from the monks, but he couldn't be sure it wasn't the sound of his mother rushing across the dining room.

Her face was flushed and she was out of breath. As if she had run a race and not just crossed the dining room. "No," she said again. She leaned against Dillon's table, putting herself between him and the man with the top hat. "I will tell him."

13

ROBERT WAS STILL in her apartment when Soledad came home from work. She didn't even have to open the door to know. She could feel his familiar presence on the far side of the door. She had to fight the urge to open her mind to his and know what he was doing, to hear him thinking about her. With her hand on the doorknob, gripping but not turning, she suddenly understood Dillon's fear of opening doors.

Except it wasn't the vast unknown or unknowable that might be on the other side of the door. It was the all too familiar.

She had been resisting the pull of the familiar, the comfortable, thoughts of Robert all afternoon. She had not quite half hoped he would be gone when she let herself come home.

After the ride from the airport, in the one-of-a-kind experience that was the ancient animal control van, in the silence that followed Robert's incredulity and weak attempts at humor, she had thought he might call a cab and run home again.

She had *not* threatened to shoot him after work. The words had formed in her head, though, and she might have pushed them at him as she was leaving. His suddenly widened eyes might have been him receiving the unspoken message.

On the other hand, his skull had already proven quite thick, so she couldn't be sure.

That she obviously *more* than half hoped he was still there–and that hope had triumphed–made her think about shooting herself. Or wonder if she already had, just by picking him up at the airport. Her standing at her own door with him on the other side had been inevitable once she went to the airport.

To his credit, Robert *had* tried to kiss her when she showed up at the airport. Even though she was in full animal control regalia and smelled of dead asterisk-squids and asphalt-fried squirrel guts and internal combustion engine exhaust. She had turned her head, though, so he only kissed her cheek.

Now, after another four hours of work, she was even less presentable. And smelled worse. She had made a special effort. She had all but jumped into the remains dumpster and rolled around in eau de dead varmint. She still wore her sweaty, grimy hat, and her hair stuck out in equally sweaty, grimy wisps.

And she still had her gun.

Somehow, she knew it wouldn't be enough. She couldn't scare him off. And she wasn't sure she wanted to anymore.

With a sigh, she tightened her grip, twisted, and pushed open the door of her apartment.

The warm smells of cooking washed over her. She recognized the delicious smells of panseared tuna, avocados, ginger, lime and more. His favorite meal to cook for her when he knew he was in the doghouse. Not because it was her favorite, but because it had always worked. She could feel the aromas beginning to work on her again. She wondered if he had brought the food with him, for exactly this purpose. They both knew she had had no tuna steaks in her fridge.

She saw him on the far side of the narrow breakfast bar, in the equally narrow galley kitchen. His back was to her as he manipulated something on the tiny stove.

He turned at the sound of the door opening, and smiled at her. "You came back."

"It's *my* apartment," she said, though she still stood outside the door.

"You're not shooting me."

Soledad tried not to smile. Failed. "I only just got home. Give me a minute." She stepped over the threshold of her apartment, once more into the familiar, hoping it wasn't a step too far.

PART IX
Knock Knock

The Gun

THE GUN HAD somewhere to be. So did the Bearer.

They were not there.

They were not even *going* there.

The Gun considered making a scene. As a gun, the Gun could make quite a scene. But only if someone pulled the trigger. Which was the downside of being a weapon. Even *the* Weapon.

The Gun remembered every Bearer, going back to the grunting, hirsute individual who picked up the First Pointed Rock. There had been many Bearers, and more than once a Bearer had returned. A different person. A different gender. A different style of fighter. Even the current Bearer had wielded the Gun before. She had been a woman that time, as well, but the Gun had been the Arming Sword.

The Bearer did not remember. They seldom did.

The Gun remembered. *That* Bearer had known her mind. She had had a sense of mission. A higher purpose. She had also been a total loon, but she had had a Master Plan, and the Arming Sword had helped her with that Master Plan. Blood had been spilled. Outsiders had been vanquished. The World had been Saved.

This Bearer, though, seemed determined to dodge every plan, every purpose, every higher calling. She fought Fate, just as she had in her previous life, but to no purpose the Gun could see. She wouldn't even shoot an Outsider when given the chance. Or Spear it.

Right now, the Gun knew, there were Outsiders that needed hunting and killing. The World, once again, needed Saving. But the Gun was stuck.

305

The God

THE GOD WAITED on the threshold, ready to pass through the Final Door. All that was needed was for the Final Door to be Opened.

To amuse Itself as It waited, the God knocked on the Door.

The Phone

THE PHONE SHOOK. Uncertain. It no longer knew what to expect.

The Opener had used the Phone to make a call. Even spoken to someone on the other end.

Then the Opener had actually *answered* an incoming call. And, again, spoken. And listened. A conversation.

The Phone did not want to get its hopes up. It had been charged before. It had called and been called before. It had taken messages and even played them back. Not often, but these things had happened. Ultimately, though, the Phone knew that it all meant nothing. *Nothing.*

The Opener could–and probably *would*–forget to charge the Phone again. He would ignore calls and delete messages unheard. He would drop the Phone on the cold, hard concrete of life.

The Phone wanted to hope. It needed to hope. But the Phone was afraid of hope.

Hope was pain.

1

THE GHOST OF Autumn Present bowed again, this time to Dillon's mother.

"Very well, Molly," he said. He turned slightly and bowed once more to Dillon. "If you need me, young master, I shall be nearby." Then he turned around, walked back to the table he had left, and sat down. He faced Dillon again, but his eyes were not focused. The man sat so still he seemed asleep, but his eyes were open and his head didn't slump.

If either the Ghost of Autumn Present or Mom noticed the people staring at them, they gave no sign of it. Dillon smiled an apology at the closest tables. The eyes of the little girl at the next booth were wider than ever.

"He has *always* given me the creeps," Mom whispered. She glanced over her shoulder at the monks, who were once again looking past the front counter into the depths of the grill section. She started to say something, then stopped with a shudder. She sat down across from Dillon. Her tanned face had become pale, and she was biting her lower lip as her eyes searched his face.

Behind her, the family at the next booth left. Dillon wondered if they would ever come back to the Buffalo Burger Pit.

"Does he have a name?" Dillon asked. He nodded toward the man with the top hat. "I've been calling him the Ghost of Autumn Present. It was Coleman's idea, but it seems to fit." When Mom didn't answer right away, he added, "The Ghost of Autumn Future also came into the store last night. He ordered a vanilla shake."

"A vanilla shake?"

Dillon nodded. "He wanted me to open it for him. To ... make sure it was vanilla, he said. But I think ... I gave him a new one." He paused. "Is there a Ghost of Autumn Past? If he came last night, I missed him."

"Stop," Mom said, holding up her right hand and turning her face away from him. "It's too much. Too much. There's so much I have to tell you—"

Dillon found himself nodding again. It *was* too much. He told her so, interrupting her. "My girlfriend—who isn't even my girlfriend, by the way—goes crazy. My uncle—who isn't my uncle, but I knew that—he disappears. My mom—" She winced but he didn't stop. "She isn't even my mom—but she reappears after being gone for a hundred years. I find out I'm adopted from the police. And now there are monks trying to eat raw bacon cheeseburgers with no cheese in my restaurant, and I'm being haunted by the Ghosts of Autumn Present and Future. Yes," he said, nodding. "It is all too much."

"Cheeseburger with no cheese?"

"Yes," Dillon said. To his mother sitting across from him and to the memory of his mother long, long ago. "Do you remember our little joke? I prefer my cheeseburgers with no cheese. All those cheeseburger Happy Meals of my childhood? You never listened to me. I said I didn't want a cheeseburger. I wanted a hamburger. But I didn't know how else to say it. I was only four. So I told you I wanted a cheeseburger with no cheese."

"Yes. Yes ... I remember. I just thought ... I'm sorry. I didn't know."

Dillon nodded. "I've been thinking that a lot lately."

Mom reached across the table with her right hand and placed it on Dillon's arm. "Please don't be angry with me, Dillon. I know you have every right to be. And please don't hate me. I already hate myself enough."

"I can't hate you," Dillon said, his throat tightening. "You're my mom." He swallowed the lump in his throat. "But I am going to be very angry with you."

"No, please." She took a breath, let it out. Took another breath. "I couldn't take it—"

"I can't just make it go away, Mom. *You* can't just make it go away, either."

She pulled her arm back as if stung. "No," she said. "No. I mean ... why I left. I ... I couldn't take it anymore. After Keith died. I blamed you, and I blamed Phil—"

"I was only six, Mom—"

She held up her hand, stopping him. "Let me talk, Dillon. I'm not the only one who had a hard time listening." She closed her eyes. "You and that jack-in-the-box. I know you remember that one. But there was also your sippy cup. You would twist off the top ..."

"Really?" Dillon tried to remember, came up blank.

"And your first toy box. And once you were tall enough to reach doorknobs." She shuddered. She opened her eyes, looked at him again. "The refrigerator. Your closet." She ticked them off on fingers.

"The toy box didn't have a lid." He remembered that quite clearly.

"Not after your father took it off. You ..." She paused. "I'm surprised you don't remember that one."

"Oh." Dillon wished he hadn't said anything about the toy box. Because then he did remember. Not opening the toy box. But the recurring nightmare of the box with the teeth and the many barbed tongues writhing out of it.

"We tried to teach you that it was bad," Mom went on. "That you shouldn't ... just open the doors like that. That you shouldn't ... let them in."

"Let what in? The squid-things?" Then he thought of Hlooth. "Oh, yeah. Do you remember the dog you said never came out of my closet?"

Mom squeezed her eyes closed and pressed her fingertips against her temples.

"You met him today," Dillon said. "Or almost did. In my apartment ..." He let his voice trail away.

After a minute, Mom opened her eyes again. "Please," she said. "Just let me talk. There's so much to tell you, and time is running out. Did you see the stars last night?"

Dillon thought of all the stars burning bright, even with all the lights of Rio Cruces trying to obscure them. He nodded.

"That's not supposed to happen, Dillon. The stars ... they aren't supposed to be like that."

Dillon pulled back. "I didn't do it."

"Not all at once, I'm sure. But it all adds up, Dillon. It all adds up."

"What adds up?"

"Stop." She held up her hand. "When we agreed to adopt you," she said, "we thought we could teach you. How hard could it be? You were just a baby, and we would be the only parents you would remember."

"You knew my real parents?"

Mom kept talking. "The council picked us, Keith and I, because we couldn't have children. You would have our full focus. We could guide you. Keep you from ..."

"Wait. Why couldn't you have children?"

Mom didn't answer right away. "Fallout," she said after a few seconds. "From the last ... never mind that. Just know that the same ... event ... that took away our ability to have children ... also gave us you. And we were so happy to have you–"

"So am I able to have children?" Dillon asked, thinking, for the first time, about how he had had unprotected sex twice in less than twenty-four hours. Which, he realized, he should have thought about at the time. Both times. But Cyd had been so ... ready. And forceful.

"What? I don't know–" She stopped and glanced behind her at the Ghost of Autumn Present. "He might." The man's gaze remained unfocused. She turned back to Dillon. "I hadn't thought of that. And no one ever mentioned it to Keith and I. Anyway." She waved her hand in a dismissive gesture. "Just know this, Dillon. We *tried*. To teach you, I mean. To keep you safe. Of course, we tried the ... other thing too. But that's not what this is about. No matter what we tried, you were ... you are ... what you are. And you were our son. You are *my* son."

"What am I?"

Mom shook her head and shrugged. "We were charged with keeping you safe, Keith and I. And Phil, of course. We were your last line of defense. And the ... first line of defense." She bit her lip. "For the world." Tears formed in her eyes. "I loved you, Dillon. I still ... I love you. In spite of everything. You have to believe that. Your father loved you too. But he was the strong one. And when he was gone, I knew I couldn't ... I ... I had to leave."

"Why?"

Mom didn't meet his eyes. "Phil said he could do it, if it came to that. He had already ... He loved you too, Dillon. We all did. But ..."

"But what?" Dillon asked, though he was getting a suspicion that he did *not* want to know where this was headed.

"You weren't controlling it. You ... we ..." She stopped and held up both hands, as if surrendering. "I'm doing this badly, I know. And I'm sorry." She took a breath. "The night Keith died, if Phil had not come when he did, do you have any idea what would have happened?"

Dillon shook his head.

"It would have been the beginning of the end, Dillon. If Phil hadn't been able to use you to close the door again. If he hadn't been able to ..." She swallowed. "Release Keith ..."

"Release? Wait. No." Dillon tried to shake his head faster. Too fast to hear her words. "Don't tell me that."

"It would all be gone. Everything. You. Me. The world. The universe, probably."

"Uncle Phil?" Dillon said. The words were barely audible. A whisper. His chest didn't want to breathe. "Dad?"

Mom nodded. She reached out and took his hand. "He had to, Dillon. There was no other choice. That was part of it. Why I had to leave. I ... I couldn't take it anymore. Seeing you every day. Seeing Phil every day. Knowing what he had done. And knowing what he would almost certainly have to do." She blinked away tears. "Except, in the end, he never did."

Dillon's mind felt like it was short-circuiting. His hand wanted to throw away his mother's hand, but it also squeezed harder, refusing to let go.

"He loved you too." She managed a weak smile. "For what it's worth, Dillon, even if it means the end of everything, I'm glad. Maybe we're still human, all of us. Me. Phil. Even him," she added, with another quick glance over her shoulder. "The Ghost of Autumn Present," she managed a light, forced laugh. Then her expression became serious again. "We couldn't kill a baby. Even if that baby was our doom. And Keith and I–and Phil too–we couldn't kill our son."

Dillon just stared at her. He asked the only coherent question he could think of. "So you're not going to kill me?"

"No, Dillon."

"But ..." He swallowed. "You said you were going to have to."

Mom nodded. She squeezed his hand. "I'm sorry. I was ... upset. Phil was gone, and ... maybe our last hope was gone with him."

"Was Phil going to kill me?"

Mom sighed. "I don't know," she said after a few seconds. She gave a weak shrug. "I think ... releasing ... Keith might have been too much for him too. If he managed to take care of you through your teenage years without releasing you, as well, then he probably wasn't going to."

"He saved me," Dillon said softly. "Again. Two nights ago."

"See? I told you he loved you."

Dillon told her about walking home with Cyd, about opening the door without looking. She shook her head, said, "Dillon, Dillon, Dillon." Then she urged him to continue. He told her about Cyd screaming, and him falling into the door, and hanging onto the doorknob. Then Phil pulling him out.

"Phil told me you had called," Dillon said. "That was why he had come over. To tell me you had called."

"So maybe I helped save you too," Mom said.

Dillon managed a slight nod. "That was the night Phil disappeared."

Mom sniffed. Dillon offered her one of his unused napkins. She blew her nose. She almost dropped the napkin on his tray, but stopped herself

316 DAVID R. MICHAEL

when she saw the half-eaten burger. She crumpled the napkin in her left hand.

"Is Cyd that Hispanic girl that lived across from Phil?" she asked.

"No." Dillon shook his head. "That was Soledad."

"Oh. So tell me about Cyd. Is she a nice girl?" She leaned closer. "Did you use a condom?" She leaned back then, away from the guilty look on his face. "I'll take that as a no. Didn't Phil teach you anything?" She glanced at the tray in front of him. "And eat your breakfast."

Dillon was about to protest his Mom's right to ask any of those questions, not the least because he had been living on his own for more than four years, and because she had left him a long, long time ago, but he saw the Ghost of Autumn Present approaching their table. The look in the man's eye, the way the man's right hand was hidden inside the top hat held by his left hand, made Dillon wonder if the man was in full agreement with Mom that Dillon didn't need to be killed.

Before the Ghost of Autumn Past could reach their table, though, a round-face, curly-haired Carlita interdicted herself, like a Patriot missile intercepting a terrorist Scud.

"Dillonito," she said, her eyes flicking from Dillon to his mother, then glancing behind her to the man in the top hat. "Barbara tells me you are not working tonight, yes?"

Dillon nodded. He took a breath to introduce Carlita to Mom.

Carlita didn't wait. "Then I think you should not be here, no? You should be going." Her eyes went to the dark windows. She nodded as if answering her own question. "Yes. Yes, you should be going." She put her hand on his shoulder, squeezed, and pulled.

"Carlita–"

"Vamos, Dillonito. Vamos–"

The world jerked sideways, throwing Dillon and his mother out of the booth, toward Carlita, who still had her hand on his shoulder but was now falling backward. Across the dining room Dillon saw the five monks were still seated, but floating in the air where their booths used to be. Then the world jerked in the opposite direction, reseated the monks and pushed Carlita at him. Carlita seemed to spin in midair. Her head hit Dillon's with a sound like shattering glass, and he could no longer see anything.

2

SOLEDAD COULD FEEL the question in Robert's mind as she ate his wonderful food, sitting across from him at her glass-topped thrift store table. The question. *The* question. He hadn't flown all the way out here, made her his Specialty Dinner, just to surprise her. Though, yes, he seemed quite pleased with himself about having surprised her.

And, yes, he had brought the tuna steaks with him. Fresh from the pier. Packed in ice in a small cooler that had been hidden in his big suitcase. She hadn't had to peek into his mind to learn this. He had told her, as he poured her wine. Proud of himself to the point of smugness. Because he had surprised her. Throughout their relationship she had been notoriously hard to surprise.

She didn't have the heart to tell him that the only reason he had surprised her was that, until this afternoon, he had been well out of range of her ability to read his mind. And this afternoon she had been too angry with him to open her mind to him.

Her mind was open now, in spite of herself. Seared tuna wasn't her favorite dinner, but Robert did prepare it well. He had mastered the preparation of this one meal, and he wielded it like a romantic hammer, using it to drive home all romantic problems like nails. How many times had he fixed it for her in their two years? How many times had he nailed her afterward?

He made small talk as they ate and drank. Being witty and sarcastic in turns as he told the story of his trip to visit her. About assembling the parts of the meal, finding exactly what he needed, packing those ingredients, shipping them, worrying about them until unpacking them here, then worrying about her woefully inadequate kitchen and its pitiable electric stove and her sparse collection of cookware. "But I had planned for that as well," he said. "I brought my trusty cast-iron skillet as a carry-on."

"They let you bring that on the plane?"

"Only after I promised to make pancakes for everyone."

Soledad laughed. Her still-wet curls shook and dripped on her shoulders. She wore only her bathrobe. Even if he had flown halfway across the country to make her dinner, she had refused to dress up to eat in her own apartment. Robert had frowned at that, but only briefly, then he had held out his arm.

"Your coat, Madame?"

She had laughed at that too, said, "No."

"Very good, Madame," he had said, then made a show of holding her chair as she sat down.

She made no attempt to read his thoughts. She didn't need to. She could almost hear his thoughts over the sound of his voice. She knew he was composing and revising the story of this evening in his head. Even as he joked about another passenger seeing his skillet and having to explain that it was OK, he had received special permission due to his legendary culinary skills, he was reviewing the growing story in his mind about how he had popped the question to Soledad. She knew that her appearance and less-than-happy airport taxi service had already been incorporated. Those were the unexpected elements, the surprises, the spice. It would be a funny story, a story to entertain their friends and family and eventually their kids. As if her answer were a foregone conclusion.

She wasn't so sure. But the fish was really good, as were the avocados.

Part of her was sure. Another part of her was less sure.

Part of her was already regretting that she was going to tell him *no*. The other part reveled in his familiar presence, even his familiar romantic dinner.

His repertory of smiles, touches, kisses, laughs, it was all on display tonight. He was surrounding her with himself. He was laying siege to her in the most pleasant way possible.

It was fun. It was romantic. It reminded her of everything she loved about him. Yet it was everything she had moved back to Rio Cruces to be away from.

Why? asked the happy-he-was-there part of herself as she savored another bite of tuna. *He's perfect. Red hair. Six years older than I am. Funny. Good job. Good in bed. Good out of bed. And he can sear the hell out of a steak of tuna.*

Because distance had seemed the only solution, the other part responded, grabbing her glass for a quick swallow of wine.

Which was not what the happy-he-was-there part of herself had meant. At all. *And you know it. Why did I have to move away? Why did I run away from him? He obviously makes me happy. Look at me. I'm happy.*

The other part of herself started on the litany. *Graduated. No jobs. Be near my family–*

It's because you can read his mind. You know it is.

No. I can read the minds of a lot of guys that I want nothing to do with–

Stop trying to change the subject. Look at him. He's perfect. He likes me. He flew halfway across the country to make me dinner. He wants to marry me.

You don't know that–

Yes, I do. And so do you. He wants to make me happy.

He wants me to be a part of his story.

Exactly! Wait. You say that like it's a bad thing. Why is that bad? We could make a great story together–

His story. Not our story.

You don't know that–

It was her other part's turn to interrupt. *Yes, I do. And so do you. Mind reader. Remember?*

But he's such a nice guy.

Yes. He is.

So why do you want–?

It's complicated.

They had finished their meals, the single-minded Robert and the of-two-minds Soledad. They were on their second glass of wine, a dry white from one of her favorite Napa Valley vineyards, when his expression became serious. When he stood so he could retrieve a small black box from a pocket of his trousers. When he started to kneel beside the table.

The happy-he-was-here part sighed. The other part wanted to roll her eyes.

Fine. Spoilsport. But be nice to him.

She put her hand on his hand, closed his hand around the tiny felt box, and shook her head.

"No," she said. "Please. Please don't." Her eyes met his and she smiled at him to remove the sting of her words.

His expression faltered, but only for an instant. Then he was smiling again, and she knew he had just added a new line to the story in his head. He had misunderstood her smile.

He finished kneeling, his right leg forward, his left knee on the floor.

She added her left hand so she held his hand, with its tiny black box of promise, with both of hers.

"No," she said again. Softly, but firmly.

"But I haven't even asked yet," he said. His smile struggled to remain in place.

"I don't want you to ask."

Wimp, said the pouty side of her. *You know you would say yes.*

"You don't even know what I'm going to ask."

She smiled at him. "Yes, I do."

His face brightened. "That is an answer I will accept."

Part of her wanted to gloat. The other part shook her head. "But you haven't asked yet."

He took a breath. "Soledad Maria Winters–"

"No," she said. Louder now. She started to stand. "Please don't. You can't–"

"–will you marry me?"

She stood over him now, looking down at him. She still held his hand in both of hers. She took a deep breath and held it until her next word would not be *yes*. "You ... you can't just ask me that. Not now." Not after she had left him behind. Not after she had run away from him. Not just to get her to come back.

Because that was what she could see, if she looked. This was his Hail Mary play. One last, desperate–and desperately sweet–attempt to get her back.

He looked up at her. His eyes searching her face. "I don't understand."

"You can't ask me that."

"But I just did."

She sighed and nodded. "I noticed." She tried to smile at him, because it would have made a great story. She moved her right hand from holding his and touched his cheek. "Can we forget you asked? Can we go make love as if we hadn't seen each other in months? Can we get up in the morning like we used to? Maybe make love again, then some breakfast? Then I can go to work and you can–"

He pulled his face back, away from her fingertips. "I can what? Go back to the airport and fly home? I can't forget I just asked you to marry me. I can't forget you just said, 'No.'"

"But I didn't–"

"You said 'No' before I could even finish asking." He tried to take his hand–and his little box–back, but she wouldn't let him go.

"I wasn't saying 'no' to ... to your question." She still hadn't. She should. She should just say no- But she couldn't. But she also couldn't say *yes* either. For all the reasons she had told herself before, when she had decided to come home.

"I can't just ... unask," he said.

"I can't ... answer," she said. "Yes. Or no."

"But you're willing to go to bed with me-"

"To make love-"

He pulled his hand back, jerking it free of her grip.

"-like we used to," she finished, standing there, with both her hands empty. She watched him push himself back into a standing position, carefully, avoiding her hands. "Before." She wanted to reach for him, to comfort him, to tell him everything was still OK. That she stilled loved him, even if she knew she would never marry him.

She could see the turmoil of emotions behind his eyes. The pain. The love. The struggle to make sense of what had happened, to fit her words into the story he had been composing in his mind. She could already see the story beginning to twist and morph from his embarrassment. His humiliation. Her need to reach for him, to take him in her arms and comfort him faded, and a portion of her love for him became pain.

She drew her hands back, then pulled her robe tighter around her torso, the way she wanted to close her mind to him. She suddenly felt naked beneath the robe. She moved to step past him, toward the door to her bedroom. "I'll go," she said.

He could have stopped her. He could have stepped up to her, put his arms around her. Instead, he stepped back. "But it's your apartment," he said. Always the funny guy. He even managed a somewhat twisted smile.

She had been about to say *I'll go change.* Because she wasn't sure what else to do, and she wanted to give him time. It seemed he didn't need time. He had surprised her again.

"Then you can leave the dishes," she said as she went into her room. "I'll wash up later."

3

ROBERT WAS, OF course, still there when Soledad came out of her bedroom. Part of her had known he would be. And, of course, the other part of her pointed out that she had known he was, even before she opened the door.

She had meant it when she said she was going. She hadn't done anything with her hair, bur she was fully dressed in jeans and a t-shirt, with a full coterie of undergarments, including socks. She had even pulled on her hiking boots and had her trench coat over her left arm. She carried her bag by its strap in her right hand. Anyone could look at her and know she was leaving, and guess that she would stomp on toes on her way out.

Except Robert wasn't looking at her. He was sitting at the table, the empty, sauce-smeared plates still there with their unevenly unempty wineglasses. His back was to her, his head down. As she paused in the middle of her small living room, he looked up and she could see his face in the mirrored wall beside the table. His face looked as sad as the mind behind his eyes.

"It wasn't supposed to go like that," his mirror image said.

"I know," she said. She could almost see the bits of his story scattered on the floor around his feet, like scenes deleted from a movie and left on the cutting room floor. "But you weren't supposed to ask. You weren't even supposed to come here. You were supposed to-"

"What? What was I supposed to do, Soledad?" He turned to face her. She could feel his sadness transforming into irritation. "Please, tell me what I was supposed to do."

She had told him. More than once. She told him again, letting her own irritation-tinged-sadness into her voice. "You were supposed to move on."

He shook his head. "I couldn't. I can't. And you haven't either."

She turned her head away from his eyes. As if he could read her mind. "I was trying to–"

"Really?"

"Yes, really."

His hands took in her apartment. "You've been here how long? And you still don't have a roommate?"

"I wasn't feeling sociable. And there's only one bedroom. And what does that have to do with anything?"

"Just tell me why."

"I already told you why." And she had. And she thought she had done a really good job of not sounding as insane in words as it still sometimes sounded in her head. Maybe this time she should go for full-on crazy, and actually tell him she could read his mind. And that he had a nice mind, always trying to make stories out of everything that happened to him. Even when she first met him, and he was trying to get into her pants, the stories in his mind had been fun, and funny, and sexy. He had liked her because she always seemed to be laughing at his jokes as he told them. And he had misunderstood that as them being simpatico. Soul mates. Which was, of course, another of the stories in his mind. That he had found his soul mate after years of looking.

She didn't believe in soul mates or fate. And she had realized that she couldn't see herself spending the rest of her life as a supporting cast member in the stories Robert told himself. Not even romantic lead–

Which was not entirely true. A part of herself had no trouble imagining herself in exactly that role. And though Robert was as white as a white man could be, she knew her parents would like him. Once they realized the six years age difference was no big deal–

No. She stomped on that line of thought. Again. She had her own stories to live. And she knew the only way she would be able to live them was to put distance between her and the sexy, funny, Soledad Maria Winters-brand catnip that was Robert Schroeder.

She had told him nothing like that, of course. And she wouldn't tell him that now. Because she didn't like people thinking she was insane. Which she tried not to think might be her own mind protesting too much.

What she had told him, over and over in the weeks before graduation, was, "I'm moving home after graduation. I don't want us to drift apart, and I don't want us to feel stuck together, clinging to a long-distance relationship. So I think we should just call it done now, and move on." Short, to the point. The way communication should be.

She took a deep breath and prepared to launch into it again.

"Why are you so determined to move on?"

She looked at him, wondering again if he had read her mind. She let out the breath in a sigh. "It's complicated."

"Is there someone else?"

Dillon's face flashed in her mind. She shook her head to get rid of the thought as much to communicate a negative to Robert. "No. I said 'it's complicated.' Not 'I've met someone else.'"

"Is it that Dillon guy you mentioned?" Robert asked.

"What? No." She forced a laugh and shook her head again. "Dillon is ... no. He's almost my brother."

"Then why? What is so wrong with me that you had to run away–"

"I didn't run away. I moved home." This conversation was beginning to slip into the well-worn grooves of their arguments before she left. And since, on the phone.

"You could have stayed."

"I'm not going over this again."

"I think you're afraid of commitment."

"We dated for nearly two years, Robert. I'm not always happy being hugged, and I admit I have trouble with intimacy, but I think I've proven I have no issues with commitment."

"Two years is nothing. I'm talking about a lifetime here."

"No, you're talking about a lifetime *there*."

"I can move here–"

"No!" She held up her hands. "Don't even. Stop acting like ... like ..."

"Like what? Like I love you? Like I will follow you anywhere?"

"Like a martyr."

"But–" He stopped. "What?"

"A martyr," she repeated. "A longsuffering, selfless hero. Of your own story."

He stared at her, confusion in his eyes and behind them. And maybe a bit of fear. Of exposure.

Or maybe she was projecting now, instead of receiving. And being more than a little unfair. "I am not your reward. For anything. I am not a plot complication or romantic lead and I'm certainly not a plot point. I am not a shrew who needs taming or a kind hand or anything else. I have my own story. My own life."

"I don't," Robert started. Then stopped. "That's not ..."

Soledad met his eyes. She almost started telling him the story he had been composing in his mind since she had picked him up from the airport. She almost started reciting it, line for line, like a Homerian ballad or the oral history the story had been well on its way to becoming. Almost. She closed her mouth and clenched her jaw to keep it shut.

"I don't think of myself as a martyr–"

Robert, the table, the empty, sauce-smeared plates, the unevenly unempty wineglasses, and the wooden chair Robert was sitting in–plus the mirror behind him and the rest of her apartment–all leaped at Soledad as the floor under her feet changed its mind about where it wanted to be.

4

SOLEDAD FELT THE world–or at least the apartment below her–try to throw her off, backward. Or forward. No, backward. Except, maybe–

There was still some wishy-washiness in the decision, some back and forth and general indecision, but the net result, for Soledad, was that she fell backward as the world tossed and turned around her in what could only be an earthquake.

She knew her coffee table was behind her. Or would have been behind her, most days. She wondered if it was still there.

It was.

She had twisted to her right as she fell, so her right hip found the coffee table first, followed by her right elbow and right shoulder. She heard glass shatter, but it seemed too far away, and too high-pitched, to have been the heavy glass top of the coffee table.

The force of her fall and the continued instability of the floor rolled her off the coffee table and toward the center of her living room. In spite of the pain in her shoulder and elbow, Soledad kept rolling until she was face down on a glass free part of her carpet, and she covered her head with both arms. She resisted the urge to curl into a fetal position.

Then, as suddenly as it started, the world stopped. And, to Soledad's way of thinking, seemed to be pretending it had never moved at all. The lights flickered off, then came back on.

After a few, long seconds of silence and relative stillness, Robert said, "Wow. That was at least a six-point-oh."

His voice sounded cool, almost calm, like the veteran of central California's frequent tremors that he was. Behind his voice, though, Soledad could sense the surprise, the fear. Still, it was good to hear a calm voice. It helped her stay calm, as well. Or at least not panic.

Soledad rolled over and pushed herself to a sitting position. Her apartment, normally so neat, had been transformed into a reasonable facsimile of Dillon's daily existence. She saw that the glass top of her coffee table had–somehow–not been broken. The sheet of glass had fallen opposite to her and was leaning against her sofa. One of the panes of her sliding glass balcony door, though, had been flexed too far and shattered outward. The mirrored wall of her dining area had cracked, reflecting back at her the chaos of her apartment and the sight of Robert crouched beneath her table.

Robert smiled at her. "There's plenty of room under here if you want to wait out the aftershocks."

Part of her was tempted, but the other part resisted. Because of course they did.

Through the broken balcony door, she heard car alarms squawking, the high piercing shriek of fire alarms, and the shouts of people.

"Come on," she said to Robert. "Let's go see if anyone needs help–"

"What the hell is that?" The surprise in his voice made her look at him. He pointed past her, behind her.

Soledad turned to look and saw tentacles pushing through the cubic crystals that had once been her balcony door. As she watched, more tentacles appeared over the edge of her small balcony, swinging into view and lashing themselves to the concrete surface and the wooden slats of the railing.

"Good God in Heaven, Dillon," Soledad said. "How many times did you do that stupid shake trick?"

The nearest of the asterisk-squid-things jumped at Soledad in a shower of broken glass.

Soledad dodged to her left, rolling. She would have come up in a crouch except she got tangled in the trench coat she had dropped. The squid-thing landed with a rolling fluttering of tentacles, then pushed itself up on the tips of four tentacles, flexed, and jumped at her again.

Soledad untangled herself and caught the squid-thing in her coat, then threw both coat and captured creature at the next of the things to crawl through her window.

"I didn't think starfish could jump like that," Robert said. "Or climb."

"They're not starfish," Soledad said, scrambling back to where she had originally fallen to recover her handbag. "There are no species of freshwater starfish." This time she did come up in a crouch, her hand in the bag, her fingers searching for the grip of her pistol. The gun seemed to jump into her hand and she pulled it out of her bag as she stood and backed away. She held her bag in left hand, and kept the gun in her right hand pointed at the creatures. But she didn't shoot.

"What the fuck, Soledad?" Robert shouted. He was still crouched under her table. "Since when did you start carrying a gun?"

"Yesterday," she said. Then added, "And there's a lot you don't know about me."

She stared past the end of the barrel. She wanted to shoot. The *gun* wanted her to pull the trigger. But she didn't. Shooting the little bastards with a steel-jacketed .45 caliber slug seemed like overkill, and the sound of her gunshots would add to the post-earthquake chaos. Then there was the danger to the other people who lived in her apartment building. People she couldn't see in the darkness past her broken balcony door. She could almost hear Uncle Tio's voice in her head, drilling into her the rules of gun safety. *"Every time you pull the trigger, Sollie, there is going to be a bullet. And that bullet is going to go somewhere."*

Another of the creatures leaped at her. She swung the barrel of the gun, hit the creature at the mouthy intersection of its eight tentacles, and batted it away. It landed on her couch in a roll as another one leaped from the window.

Robert, still behind her and under the table, seemed to lose his qualms about her being armed. "Shoot it!" he shouted. "Shoot it!"

"No!" she shouted back as she reversed her earlier swing and knocked the next creature out of the air, this time in the direction of the front door. She didn't need a gun for these things. She needed a combination tennis racket and pole arm–

Not a chance.

The voice in her head that interrupted her thoughts was neither version of her divided self on issues of Robert, because it was a rough, masculine voice. And not Uncle Tio, who was the only man who's voice she had ever heard spoken in her head. Then she remembered the voice talking to her about how to kill Hlooth.

I am not a man, the voice protested, still sounding very masculine.

Soledad stood ready to bat away more of the leaping squid things, but they were no longer leaping at her. The ones she had struck remained where they had landed, still very much alive, their tentacles curled under them, poised to jump at her again. But they weren't jumping. They seemed to be waiting for something.

More of the creatures climbed onto her balcony. Some spilled through the broken glass door, but they didn't change her. Instead, they spread in an arc and assumed jumping positions.

She kept her attention on the creatures as she quickly glanced around her apartment, looking for whoever was mentally talking to her. Whoever it was, he–or she, or whatever–was close. Why couldn't she see him-her-it?

If you will not shoot them–

"I'm not going to shoot blind through an open window."

–then perhaps another form of weapon is required.

"You have to do something!" Robert shouted.

Soledad was about to tell Robert that she wasn't talking to him, then ask why it was *she* who had to do something, when he was quite capable of getting out from under the damn table and doing something–

The weight of the gun in her hands suddenly increased, interrupting her thoughts and dragging down her arm. The gun changed shape within her grip. She almost dropped the gun, or whatever it was. She stared as the short barrel seemed to melt and reform, extending up from her grasp. The grip morphed as well, oozing at first, then telescoping in the other direction. Within a second she was holding a wooden shaft an inch thick and more than three feet long. And still growing. The upward end sprouted a leaf-shaped head of black iron with long, curved edges that looked sharper than anything Soledad had ever seen. The downward end reached the floor then wrapped itself in more iron.

An hasta, the voice said. *A Legionaire's spear. This is as close as I will come to a combination tennis racket and pole arm.*

Soledad had to use both hands to grip the new weapon, so she threaded her left arm into her bag's strap. The hasta was at least eight inches longer than she was tall with the broad, leaf-shaped head nearly a quarter of that length. It was like a sword on a stick.

I resent that–

"Where did you get a spear?" Robert asked.

"Shut up," Soledad said to both of them. She took one step forward and adjusted her stance so she would be able to swing the hasta. "Robert, get your skillet."

"Why?"

"Just get it. Then we're walking out of here."

Behind her, Robert crawled out from under the table. In front of her, the creatures all leaped at the same time.

Soledad lunged forward and thrust into the center of the enclosing arc of tentacles and teeth. The point of the hasta disappeared into the maw of one creature, the widening blade slicing it in half. She planted her left foot firmly, then spun in a circle. The leaf-shaped blade cut through the creatures on her left as the blunt haft swept through those on her right and knocked them back toward the broken window and her thrift store sofa.

The heavy spear combined with the bag on her shoulder pulled her off balance as she tried to stop her spin, but she didn't fall. She planted her feet in the same positions as before, ready to do it again. She was closer to her front door, with various lengths of twitching tentacles on the floor around her. Robert was still in the kitchen.

"Get your skillet and get over here. We're leaving."

"I haven't washed it–"

A creature leaped at her. She thrust and stabbed it in midleap. Then stomped on one that had come skittering across the carpet at her.

"Fine," Robert said. "But watch where you're swinging that thing."

"Swing your own damn thing," Soledad said.

Just in time, Robert spotted the squid-thing jumping at him and batted it away with a cast-iron backhand.

"Now open the door," she said. "I–" She stabbed the next creature to come at her on the floor. The point of the blade scraped against the concrete beneath the thin carpet and rattled her teeth. "–will–" She stomped the next one. "–hold them off."

Robert gave her far more room than she needed as he went behind her. She took a step closer to the balcony–and her trench coat–stabbing and kicking as she went.

Robert pulled on the door behind her. "It's stuck."

"Then pull harder." She spun the spear in her hands and hooked the ironshod haft under a fold in her trench coat. Her coat flipped into the air. She held the shaft of the spear one handed, tucked under her right arm and grabbed her coat out of the air with her left hand. In front of her, a huge, writhing mass of tentacles pulled itself onto her balcony. The weight of the creatures splintered the wooden railing and caused the reinforced concrete of the balcony and her floor to groan in protest. Behind her, she heard Robert still struggling to pull the door open.

There were no longer individual squid-things. There was just the one, massive squid-thing on her balcony. As she watched, an arm-like appendage grew out of the mass and gripped the frame of the sliding glass door with finger-like tentacles of varying lengths. The "arm" flexed, glass shattered, and what remained of her sliding glass door frame bent outward.

"Got it!" Robert said. Then, with an odd change in his voice, he added, "What? Who are you?"

Soledad hoped he had opened the door wide and already gone through, regardless of who was there, as she turned and ran for it. She pulled up short. Robert had the door open, but only stood there, his skillet hanging useless from his left hand, his body blocking the exit.

A naked Cyd stood on the small landing in front of her apartment door. The curves of Cyd's body were accentuated by the light coming through the door. Her hair was a tangled mess, but eerily lit by the outdoor light that illuminated the wooden stairs to Soledad's apartment, turning what should have been a bird's nest into a brown halo. Cyd's eyes were wide open, glowing with a flickering, staticy light that looked like the mental white noise Soledad could now hear from the girl's mind.

Cyd didn't even glance at Soledad. Her eyes were locked on Robert's face. The girl was waiting, Soledad realized, for him to stop staring at her naked breasts and meet her eyes.

From behind Soledad came the sound of metal straining and wood breaking as what was left of her balcony door was pulled free, bringing with it some portion of the outer wall. Even that didn't seem to be enough to tear Robert's eyes from Cyd's exposed nipples.

"My eyes are up here, lover," Cyd said.

Soledad dropped her left shoulder and charged into Robert from behind, her shoulder catching him in the small of the back. She drove him into Cyd and sent both of them off the small landing and onto the stairs beyond.

She used the haft of her spear like a hockey stick to keep the pair of them rolling down the stairs as she followed them. They sprawled in a tangle of Dockers, pinpoint cotton, and naked limbs on the landing that separated the stairs to her apartment from those that led to the door of her next door neighbor. Somehow Robert hand managed to hold onto his skillet.

Behind her something soft, heavy and angry hit the doorframe she had just abandoned. She looked back to see the mass of tentacles now trying to squeeze itself through her front door. The mass of creatures bulged as tentacles gripped the wood of the door frame and sought purchase on the surrounding siding. In the center of the bulging mass was a pucker, a dark shadowy place like a black hole. But in the heart of the darkness Soledad saw a human eye, a nose, and a portion of cheek, like the mask worn by the Phantom of the Opera, in reverse.

From behind the eye, struggling against waves of static and a vortex of cold, flickering madness, came the glimmer of a mind she recognized. Phil Trichter. Dillon's uncle.

Cyd was hissing and the brown glow of her eyes was sweeping across the darkness like angry spotlights as she struggled to free herself from Robert.

Soledad hit the girl's head with the haft of her spear, then used her feet to kick Robert into motion down the last few steps. The animal control van was parked right at the base of the stairs. She hoped they could make it to the van before whatever it was that Phil Trichter had become managed to force itself through her front door.

She nearly dropped her jacket when she stepped on the trailing hem. Before she could form the coherent thought that a one-handed weapon–like a gun–would be useful again, the spear began to contract in on itself.

The doors of the animal control van were never locked. Soledad wasn't even sure the locks worked, which was beside the point. Uncle Tio had once joked that you never knew when you might need to get inside your animal control van in a hurry. Though, he had added, there hadn't been any bears wandering around Rio Cruces in decades.

Soledad stuffed the newly reformed pistol into her waist with only a quick hope that a magical gun included a magical safety, then yanked open the driver's door of the van. She threw her jacket into the gap between the front seats and climbed in, pulling the door closed as hard and fast as she could. Her left hand felt around in the dark for the emergency brake release while her right hand dug into her bag in a search for the keys. She watched Robert getting into the passenger side out of the side of her right eye, while she tried not to see the wiggling drip-drip-drip of squid-things pouring off her balcony.

Brake released, keys in the ignition and turned, she hardly waited for the engine to fire up before slamming the vehicle into reverse and pressing down on the gas. The van lurched backward, then bumped up and over something Soledad sincerely hoped was not one of her neighbors. She knew it wasn't Cyd. That girl was still back at the stairs, only just beginning to push herself to her feet again, to swing her glowing gaze in their direction.

"Don't look at her eyes!" Soledad shouted. Unnecessarily, since Cyd was still naked.

A squid thing landed on the windshield, tentacles splayed, circular mouth of teeth exposed. Robert jumped and shouted, "What the fuck-!"

Soledad flipped the wiper switch, put the van's transmission into drive, and gunned the gas again. Another squid-thing leaped and hit her window, but it fell away as the van surged forward. Another managed to land on her side mirror, obscuring the horrifying view of what was writhing and oozing out of her apartment via the gaping hole that had once been her balcony.

"What the fuck!" Robert said again, just as loud. "What the fuck are those things?"

Soledad had no useful answer to offer, and she could tell from the state of his mind he wouldn't have heard her anyway. So she said nothing and focused on navigating the parking lot. Some cars had been moved out of their parking spaces by the earthquake, and some of their drivers were stumbling around in the dark in a way people really shouldn't right after an earthquake. The van tilted back and forth on its old shocks as she swerved left and right around obstacles of varying mobility. She leaned on the horn to encourage more cooperation.

The throaty bleat of the van's horn helped her not to hear the wet, sticky thuds of squid-things leaping and attaching themselves to the outside of the van. The noise of the old engine mostly obscured the swirling, scratching sound of the creature's teeth against the metal skin. It was impossible, though, to miss the sudden, loud, thumping and clawing addition of weight to the van's rear end.

For a long, scared moment, Soledad thought the squirming mass that had once been Phil Trichter had already caught up to them. Then she had caught the backlit silhouette of a feminine shape through the murk that covered the rear window and she realized it was only Cyd.

Soledad turned out of the parking a lot sharper than she had too, causing the rear end of the van to fishtail. She wished she could see the naked Cyd flung from back of the van, but had to satisfy herself with only the thought.

"Where are we going?" Robert asked.

"To see Dillon," Soledad said, still focusing on her driving. The road was only slightly less obstructed than the parking lot had been. Her shouts telling people to get back in their damn cars were lost under the sound of her horn.

"I thought you said Dillon had nothing to do with this."

Soledad shook her head. "Dillon has nothing to do with me saying, 'no'," she said. "But he has *everything* to do with what's happening."

"But what's happening?"

"I have no idea. But I know it's his fault." She kept her left hand on the wheel while she felt around in her purse, which was still on her lap. She pulled out her phone and risked a quick glance at the screen. It took her three risky glances to find the right name and push it with her thumb.

"Who are you calling?"

"My uncle," she said as she listened to the call try to connect.

"Does he know what's going on?"

"I don't know. But he's got a lot more guns than I do." The call was taking longer to connect than she thought it should. "I just hope he has a flamethrower."

5

DILLON WOKE WITH the smell of sour milk burning the hairs of his nose. And the inside of his mouth. There was also something heavy pressing on his chest, but it wasn't heavy enough to stop him from breathing, which would have been an improvement. When he opened his eyes, the smell tried to melt them. He squeezed his eyes closed again just in time to prevent Hlooth's knotted tongue from licking them out of his skull.

He was lying on his back on a cold, hard surface, with Hlooth standing on his chest, licking his face and touching his cheeks lightly with the tips of his eyestalks.

Lying on his back fit with the last thing he could remember, which must have been an earthquake, combined with a head-on collision with Carlita's forehead. With the small portion of his nose that hadn't been overpowered by Hlooth's noxious breath, he could smell that he was still at the Buffalo Burger Pit. Which also made sense.

Which left the question, "What are you doing here?"

"Bark!" Hlooth said in his tapioca voice. Then he licked Dillon's face again. "Woof?"

Keeping his eyes closed for their own safety, Dillon discovered he could still use his arms. He felt up two of Hlooth's opposing legs, searching for the beast's neck.

"No pets are allowed in the dining room," Dillon said, failing to hold Hlooth's head away from him. "Ugh. Only ... service animals."

"Woof!" Hlooth replied.

"Dillon! You're awake!"

DAVID R. MICHAEL

His mother's voice made Dillon realize he could hear all sorts of things that he had been ignoring under the multisensual onslaught of Hlooth's tongue. People talking, most of them at the same time. Some of the voices he recognized, like Barbara and Coleman, some he didn't. Only one of the voices seemed to be talking to him so far.

He also heard the sounds of chairs being dragged across the tiled floor. Broken glass being swept up with a push broom. Distant sounds of fire trucks and ambulances, sirens wailing in nonharmony. Behind all of that, the wail of the Rio Cruces tornado and storm warning.

Hlooth tried to lick his face again. This time Dillon was able to push the beast off his chest, even if he couldn't hold Hlooth's head far enough away to be out of range of the knotted tongue.

"Dillonito! You are OK. I am glad."

He felt someone kneel beside him. Two sets of hands helped Dillon into a sitting position. He kept his hands in front of his face to fend off Hlooth.

"Let me help him," Mom said. "I'm his mother."

Carlita sniffed her one syllable opinion of Dillon's mother.

"Well I am."

Dillon opened his eyes cautiously. Hlooth sat just out of reach, his head and shoulders propped by his two front legs, his four back legs splayed on the floor. His eyestalks were in a constant flutter, each of them looking at him, then looking in a different direction, all around. It was dizzying, and hard to focus on, so Dillon shifted his gaze to Carlita's round face, the closer of the two women's faces. Carlita's eyes were also scanning him. She had a large, red bump on her forehead.

"I am holding up how many fingers, Dillonito?" Carlita asked, waving her hand in front of his face.

"All of them?" Dillon said.

"Good, good." Carlita looked satisfied. "It is as I always told my Juanito. 'Always be the head in motion,' I told him. Though, with his thick skull, it mattered less than for some."

Dillon stared at her. He seemed to remember she had told him something like that once too. For some reason.

"When butting heads," Carlita said, her voice taking on a maternal lecturing tone, "always be the head in motion. It will hurt either way, of course, but perhaps a bit less if you are the one giving the head butt rather than receiving it."

Dillon nodded and discovered that he must have a large, red bump of his on own. His head suddenly felt too heavy to keep lifted. He would have slumped backward, but both women held him up. All of Hlooth's eyestalks swung around to look at him. When he didn't fall over, the eyestalks resumed their sweeping, swinging motions.

"Are you sure you should be sitting up?" Mom asked.

"No," Dillon said, holding his body up with his left hand, and his head up with his right, "but I ... think ... this ... might be more comfortable than the ... floor." Mom put a steadying hand on his shoulder, so he devoted both hands to holding his head, which seemed to be trying to spin off his neck. "Though I might be wrong."

"You should lay back down."

He shook his head and wished he hadn't. Fortunately, with both hands he was able to keep it from splitting in two. "No." He said it again, just be sure, "No."

"Drink some water," Carlita said, thrusting one of the Pit's plastic water cups his nose. "You will feel better."

Dillon had no free hands, but the cup included a straw, so he was able to take a sip. After he took a sip and swallowed, he asked, "Is everyone OK?" He wanted to look around, to see past his mother and Carlita, but then again, no, he didn't. That would require moving his head. "And how did Hlooth get here?"

Carlita made a dismissive gesture with her right hand. "No, no, no, no one else was hurt. Just scared."

"I was not scared," Coleman said from somewhere nearby. "I was a goddamned tower of strength, like a mighty Tyrannosaurus Rex, watching calmly as those around him quailed. But with bigger arms."

"Whatever," Edward said. "Your scream was even more girlie than mine was."

"I thought that was me," Jorge said.

Carlita rolled her eyes. Seeing that made Dillon dizzy again.

"Look at me, Dillonito," Carlita said.

Dillon tried.

Then Carlita's right palm covered his face and pressed against the soreness on his head. He would have jerked his head away, but her left hand was behind his neck. Her two hands held his head like a vice. She muttered words he didn't recognize in what may have been Spanish- one of the words may have been "caliente"-then a warmth flooded out of her palm and washed through his skull. The pounding in his skull didn't go away completely, but most of it seemed to be gone as the heat dissipated.

"There," Carlita said, taking her hand back. "You will survive."

Dillon blinked and found he could focus now. "What was that?" he asked.

"How did you do that?" Mom asked.

Carlita put a finger to her lips in a shushing motion, then winked at Dillon. "Our little secret, no?"

Barbara appeared, completing the Circle of Maternal Concern that surrounded Dillon. She squatted so she could look Dillon in the eyes. Her hair was escaping its braid and her face was dirty. She no longer wore the drive-thru belt and headphones. For some reason, she was holding one of the long, stainless-steel bun spatulas. "We're all fine, Dillon," she said. "The restaurant needs a lot of new windows, but no one was hurt in the quake. Gil just called to make sure we're all right. He said he was fine. Then he said he was worried about you, but I told him you were fine. He said that was good, because he still wanted to kill you himself." She smiled one of her sweetest smiles.

Dillon opened his mouth to say ... something. But thought of nothing. So he closed his mouth again.

Barbara nodded, agreeing with him not saying anything. "I told him he might want to come on down here then, in spite of the mess on the roads, or he might not get the chance–"

"Here they come again!" Coleman shouted.

Behind Barbara, Hlooth scrambled to all six feet and charged out of view, his claws scritch-scritching on the tiled floor. Goose bumps went down Dillon's back.

"Once more into the breach," Barbara muttered, and stood. She transferred the bun spatula to her right hand. Dillon saw the long flat metal was dented, and covered in something slimy.

Mom stood up too. Carlita stayed with Dillon.

"What's going on?" Dillon asked. Now he could see that he had been laying next to the front counter with the dining room spread out in front of him. The tables and chairs that could be moved, plus a lot of empty plastic trays and milk crates and bun crates from the back, had been piled on the booths that lined the outer wall, creating colorful barricades for the windows that had been broken.

Dillon stared at Coleman. The man's face and the front of his shirt were a red mess. Then Dillon realized Coleman had painted his face with ketchup.

Coleman caught Dillon's eye and gave him a wide grin that made him look bat shit insane. He held the fire extinguisher in both hands, like a club. Still smiling, he swung the big red canister like a baseball player waiting for the pitch. Standing next to Coleman, Jorge held two of the bun spatulas, one in each hand. He had tied one of the damp towels around his head. On the opposite side, Edward held the push broom in both hands. His expression was the most serious Dillon had ever seen. The three of them turned to face north, looking like unlikely soldiers. Or two unlikely soldiers, and one prebloodied, animated corpse.

Facing west, which had only one broken window, Ronald held the mop, without the mop head attached. Just behind him, Andrew stood with the wide dust mop, looking lost and confused, but oddly determined.

Mom and Barbara and the Ghost of Autumn Present stood facing south. Barbara held the bun spatula with both hands. Mom had a makeshift spear created by duct taping one of the grill spatulas to the extra broom handle that had been in the cleaning closet for as long as Dillon had worked in the restaurant. The Ghost of Autumnn Present held what could only be a cane sword.

Hlooth was doing a six-legged trot in a circle around the circumference of the dining room, his eyestalks swirling in all directions, his knotted tongue lolling out of his mouth. He looked as happy as Dillon had ever seen him, except that the beasts claws were fully extended, and his mouth seemed to have grown some very unfriendly looking teeth.

Mom looked back at Dillon. "It's OK, Dillon. Just stay back there. We got this."

Dillon stared. "Got what? What have you got?"

"That trick you do with the shakes?" Carlita said. "With the squids, yes? The squids, they are all coming home."

The plastic trays and broken crates on the barricade rattled and shifted as tentacles thrust out, grasped and pulled. Thumps on the surviving windows became splayed, eight-legged forms. Dillon watched as tiny teeth appeared around the edges of the circular mouths and started spinning back and forth on the glass.

"They never did that before," Dillon said.

6

"IT'S THE END of the world!" Coleman shouted. A squid-thing leaped out of the rubbish at him. He swung the fire extinguisher and caught the creature in midleap with a meaty thunk that created a slimy spray. The limp creature flew back the way it had come. "Ain't it great?"

"No!" Edward shouted back in chorus with Jorge and Barbara.

Then the barricades came alive with tentacles and a tide of squid-things tried to force its way into the restaurant. Coleman was swinging the fire extinguisher back and forth, the muscles of his arms bulging from the weight of the fire extinguisher and the force of his swings. Edward and Jorge flanked him, pushing and batting and stabbing and slinging the creatures that managed to get past.

Coleman kept up a litany of profanity as he battled. "Fuck, yeah! Take *that*, you goddamned squid. Get the *fuck* out of my store."

"It's not your store!" Barbara shouted back.

On the opposite side of the store Barbara and Mom and the Ghost of Autumn Present faced a similar onslaught, but with far less profanity and a lot more accuracy. Mom showed a proficiency Dillon would never have guessed, stabbing with her makeshift spear, then pulling back to stab again, in a manner very similar to how the Ghost of Autumn Present used his cane sword. Thrust, parry, riposte, thrust. Barbara played backstop to them, catching those creatures who made it past the spear and the sword. She would bat the creatures out of the air with her spatula, or scrape them off the tiled floor, then throw them overhand back to the barricade.

Ronald and Andrew had only a single window to guard, and they focused on keeping the barricade standing, and pushing creatures back into it. When one of the creatures leaped and landed on Andrew's chest, he hardly flinched. He grabbed the knobby head of the creature and peeled it off, then threw it back outside.

Hlooth ran around and around the dining room, catching squid-things in his mouth, crunching them with his teeth and jaws, shaking them lifeless and flinging them away. That is, when he didn't swallow them whole.

Dillon pushed himself back against the wooden paneling of the front counter. He noticed then that Carlita was holding his right hand with her left. And she seemed to be praying, gesturing with her right hand in time with the strange words. There was a repetitive nature to the words, as if she were praying the Rosary. Except the words sounded neither Spanish nor Latin nor like any other language Dillon had ever heard. There were syllables–entire sentences–that Dillon was sure were not actually pro-nounceable. And there were portions vaguely reminiscent of Hlooth's tapioca warbling. Despite the alienness of the sounds and words, there was something oddly familiar about them, as well. As if, at some distant point in time and space, Dillon had heard them before.

The battle was noisy, but subdued. Only the combatants in the store made any sounds. Shouting. Swearing. Scraping. Stabbing. Thumping. Kicking. Stomping. Splatting. And behind it all, the sounds of a city in a state of emergency.

Through the portions of the west windows that weren't obstructed, Dillon could see the headlights of passing cars and trucks, the occasional whipping blue or red or white or yellow of emergency vehicles and utility trucks. Above the traffic, the bright brown-yellow sign of the Yellow Sign Buffet blazed as bright as ever.

Another set of goose bumps joined the first set, crowding and chilling the skin of his spine.

The yellow sign seemed to be looking back at him.

"Close your eyes, Dillonito," Carlita said.

The black and red letters that formed the words Yellow Sign Buffet never moved, but they no longer spelled coherent words. The lines of the letters swirled and morphed, forming new, impossible shapes even as they stayed perfectly still.

"Close your eyes!"

The battle in the dining room blurred until Dillon could no longer see it. His entire world had become a brown-yellow void.

He could not see Carlita's hands even as she pressed them over his eyes.

He heard the Voice of the Void. The Voice he had heard the night his father died. The Voice he had heard the night he and Cyd almost fell through his front door.

COME TO ME.

The words were heavy and hard and hit him like a jackhammer trying to split his skull.

I AM HERE.

The Voice was oddly muffled, though, as if talking from the far side of a long tunnel.

COME TO ME.

Dillon tried to stand, but could not. Something warm, heavy and smelling of dishwashing detergent fell on him, pinning him against the front counter and the floor.

OPEN THE DOOR.

Through the yellow-brown light Dillon saw a massive stainless-steel door. A familiar door. A door he had opened so many, many times, but as infrequently as he could manage through procrastination, delegation and avoidance.

Dillon realized he did not need to stand up or walk or even move. He could just reach and grab the big, cold latch on the freezer door–

His fingers suddenly stung from something or someone he could no longer see slapping his hand.

"Oww!" he said. Or thought he said. He could no longer hear his own voice. Only the Voice of the Void.

I AM HERE–

The light of the sign disappeared, taking with it the vision of the freezer door and the red and black markings and the Voice of the Void.

The last word of the Voice echoed in his head. *HERE ... Here ... here* –

Or maybe that was gunfire.

Dillon's vision returned as the yellow-brown film of wax that covered everything melted away. His head pounded, and with Carlita's face right in front of his, he wondered if she had head butted him again. On purpose this time. He noticed he had the fingers of his right hand in his mouth, sucking on them. He took his fingers out of his mouth.

Beyond Carlita's face, he saw that something large had blocked his view of the Yellow Sign Buffet. A truck or a van of some sort had pulled up next to the front windows. Barbara was going to be upset–

What could only be gunshots exploded on the far side of the barricade defended by Ronald and Andrew. The two young men pulled back and ducked. So did everyone else in the dining room. Except Hlooth, who bounded over to the broken window and its pile of junk. His eyes fluttered, seeking lines of sight through the broken crates.

"Bark!" Hlooth said. "Woof?"

Dillon noticed that the barricades on all sides of the dining room had stopped moving. No more squid-things seemed to be trying to get in.

"Don't shoot!" a man shouted from outside the restaurant.

"You're the only one shooting!" Coleman shouted back.

"It's not me–"

"Is that you, Coleman?" A woman's voice.

Dillon and Coleman recognized Soledad's voice at the same time. Coleman let his extinguisher-club drop to his side. His ketchup-covered face smiled. "You damn skippy."

"If you don't let me in right now, Coleman–"

"Soledad?" Barbara said. She left her dented, ichor-covered bun spatula on the floor as she stood. A length of tentacle near her foot squirmed and she stepped on it. "Soledad Winters?"

There were the sounds of someone climbing up the far side of the barricade. Soledad's head appeared in a gap.

"Hey, Barbara," she said. "Sorry about not parking in the employee spots."

Barbara nodded and made a dismissive gesture with one hand.

"Hey, Hlooth," Soledad said as the not-a-dog leaped into the air to get a view of her. "If you're here, I'm going to assume–" Her eyes searched the dining room as she talked until they stopped on Dillon. "There you are." She interrupted herself and pointed at Dillon. "Don't move. I'm coming in. And when I do, I think I'm going to kill you."

7

"I thought we had removed killing him as a possible option," the Ghost of Autumn Present said.

"Yes," Mom said. "We did." She kept her spatula-spear as she came to stand in front of Dillon.

The Ghost of Autumn Present shrugged and sheathed his cane sword. He grabbed a chair from the part of the barricade he had been defending and set it upright. He pulled a handkerchief from a sleeve, wiped the seat of the chair clean, and sat. Dillon noticed that the man still had his top hat on.

Tired of looking up at everyone and everything happening around him, Dillon managed to achieve a standing position, but only because Carlita helped him. He looked behind him, thought about sitting on the stainless-steel top of the counter, then remembered that Barbara was standing nearby. And she was armed, if only in a manner of speaking. So he leaned against the counter.

He watched as Coleman and Ronald dismantled the barricade barring the north door of the dining room. There was no need to actually open the door, as the heavy, dual-layered safety glass had been shattered and pushed inward. Soledad stepped under the push bar and into the dining room, bits of glass and broken plastic crunching under her hiking boots. She wore her trench coat over jeans with her big bag draped across her body. She carried a pistol in her right hand, the barrel pointed down.

Hlooth bounded over to her, then pulled back, all his eyes shaking as they regarded the gun in her hand.

Mom stepped to put herself between Soledad and Dillon as a man Dillon only recognized from pictures from Soledad's phone came through the dining room door behind her. Instead of a gun, he carried a cast iron skillet.

"You can't kill him," Mom said, holding her spatula-spear in a manner that didn't exactly threaten Soledad, but that could have very quickly been adjusted to make that happen.

Soledad started to raise her gun, then stopped and let it fall back to her side. "First," she said, "he's my best friend. I'll kill him if I want to."

"Sounds fair to me," Coleman said.

"Shut up, Coleman. Second–"

"You have Phil's gun," Mom said. Now the spatula-spear was aimed directly at Soledad's heart. "Why do you have Phil's gun?"

"She has the Weapon?" the Ghost of Autumn Present asked, standing again.

"Where is Phil?" Mom asked.

Soledad's eyes looked from the slimy blade of the spatula-spear to Mom's face.

The footsteps of a third person crunched through the dining room door. Dillon recognized Detective White just as the woman pointed a pistol at Soledad. "Yes, Miss Winters, please tell us where Phil Trichter is. First, though, please drop the weapon."

8

SOLEDAD TENSED. SHE had been so focused on Dillon–and distracted by his Mom going all Amazonian warrior princess with that Lord of the Fries spatula-spear–she had not noticed Detective White coming up behind her. On the other hand, with Robert and his mental baggage crowding everything else that had already happened this evening, she wasn't sure she would notice another earthquake.

"Drop it, Miss Winters," the detective said.

The gun in her hand did *not* want to be dropped. She dropped it anyway, and took some satisfaction with how hard it hit the tiled floor. She raised her hands, palms forward. She smiled at Dillon's mother, and the woman shifted her grip on her spatula-spear.

"You too, Ms. Offner," Detective White said. "Drop it. All of you, show me your hands. Yes, I mean you too, Top Chef. Drop the skillet."

There was a loud clatter as bun spatulas, brooms, mops and one cast-iron skillet fell to the tiled floor. With Dillon's mother no longer armed, Soledad turned to face the detective.

Hlooth chose that moment to bound to Soledad, stand on his rear legs while his forward four legs grabbed her shoulders and waist, then lick her in the face with the entire length of his knotted tongue.

"I'm–" She coughed and blinked tears out of her eyes. "Happy to see you. Too." She coughed again, then managed to get her hands on what might be described as Hlooth's shoulders, just below his eyestalks. She pushed. "Down boy."

"Woof!" Hlooth said, but he let her push him away. He settled into a seated position, most of his eyes staring up at her face, the rest bent to watch Detective White.

"Madame Officer–" the man in the top hat started.

"Detective," Detective White said, her voice sharp. "Detective Ellen White, Rio Cruces Police Department. And who are you?" Before the man could answer, she added, "All of you need to step over there, and keep your hands where I can see them."

The detective gestured with quick movements of her pistol, indicating the opposite side of the dining room. Soledad glanced behind her and saw the man in the top hat sitting again in the only upright chair. She doubted Detective White would be happy if anyone else picked up a chair from the barricade, and there was no way she was going to sit on the floor, so she turned around and stayed where she was.

From where it lay on the tiles amid the various makeshift weapons, the gun projected mental images at Soledad. She could see the gun appearing in her hand and her finger squeezing off a shot.

"I'm not going to shoot a police officer," she told the gun. Then realized she had said it out loud.

"No, you're not," Detective White said. "No one is going to shoot anyone."

Soledad glanced at the detective's gun, recognized it as a Glock 22 .40 caliber, then looked back at the detective's face. The detective's gun remained steady, pointed at Soledad's center of mass, as the detective glanced down at the floor where Soledad's newly acquired gun lay. To Soledad, the gun was seething. She wondered if the detective could sense that.

"So that's the missing gun, is it?" the detective asked. "The one Phil Thrichter kept in his safe?"

Soledad thought about saying she wasn't entirely sure, that the gun had just appeared in her bed–under her pillow, actually–a couple nights ago, but she was pretty sure, yes, that this was Phil Trichter's famous gun. Instead, she just nodded.

"Bit of a relic, isn't it?"

Soledad shrugged, then smiled at the new blast of outrage from the gun on the floor. She was surprised the gun wasn't hopping around on the floor instead of just laying there.

"You have no idea, detective," said the man in the top hat behind her.

"Someone's grandpa bring it back from World War Two, maybe?" the detective asked. "That why it's not registered? No, don't tell me." She focused on Soledad again. "You. Miss Winters. Tell me where Phil Trichter is."

Soledad pushed the image of Phil's face within the mass of tentacles from her mind. "I don't know." Then she glanced over at Dillon, who looked even more lost than usual.

"How do you have Phil's gun?" Dillon asked.

"I don't know," she said again.

"She is the new Bearer," the man with the top hat said. By his tone, nothing could have been more obvious.

Soledad turned to face the man. "What are you talking about?" she asked, even as she realized the gun had been referring to her as "the Bearer" all night. And probably the day before, as well. Soledad's mind had just interpreted it as "you." "And who are you? I'm tired of thinking of you as 'the man with the top hat'."

The man smiled at her and looked to be about to stand, but the detective interrupted him.

"Hey," the detective said. "I'm the one asking questions here."

The man with the top hat shrugged and continued sitting in his chair. Soledad turned to face Detective White again.

"Where is Phil Trichter, Miss Winters?"

"I don't know," Soledad said. Then she added, "But I think I saw ... what was left of him ... earlier tonight. Right after the earthquake."

Dillon's mother gasped. "Phil's alive?"

Soledad wasn't sure how to answer that, so she repeated her earlier statement of ignorance. "I don't know."

The man with the top hat said, "No, Molly." There was no hint of a question in his voice. "*She* is the new Bearer."

"But you saw him? You saw Phil?"

"I saw ... part of him?" Soledad said. She pointed to the bits and pieces scattered over the floor. "He was covered in those ... squid-things. And he was taking apart my apartment building the last I saw him." She glanced over at Dillon. "And Cyd was there too."

"Cyd?" Dillon said.

"Yes, Cyd," Soledad said, letting her voice get sharp. "Jay-Bee Cyd. Baby Cyd. The cradle you robbed? That Cyd? Do you remember now?"

"Was she OK?"

Soledad squinted at him. "She was naked. And she attacked us too. So I don't think so, no."

"You too?" Coleman asked. "God *damn*, how did I miss out on all this naked Cyd action?"

"What is going on?" Barbara asked. "Why is everything and everyone going crazy? And what are these *things* that attacked my store?"

"It is the nature of these times, Madame," said the man in the top hat.

"And which times are those, Mister Top Hat?" Soledad asked, turning to face him again. As she turned, she caught a glimpse of the exasperation behind the detective's sternly unemotional face.

"The End Times, baby," Coleman said. "Ain't it great?"

"No!" shouted Barbara, Jorge, and Edward.

The man in the top hat smiled and nodded, once, at Soledad.

"Hey!" Detective White shouted.

Soledad ignored the woman. She focused on the man in the top hat. She opened her mind, just a sliver, wanting to take a quick look behind his eyes, ready to slam the door in a hurry. But he was as closed to her as Dillon. No, not like Dillon. He was like Uncle Tio, or like Phil Trichter had been. He wasn't just closed to her, though, he had shut her out. The man smiled at her, as if he knew what she had tried–and failed–to do.

"Who are you?" Soledad asked him.

This time the man did stand, in spite of the detective's repeated protest that *she* was the one in charge. Then he doffed his hat and bowed low. "I," he said, "am at your service, Weapon Bearer."

Soledad glared at him, opening her mind wider. Even with her mind's eye, though, she saw only the man in front of her. Even with her mind's eye, he glowed brown and orange. "That's not an answer," she said.

He put his hat back on his head and smiled. The brown eyes twinkled beneath the brim of the top hat. "As you say, Weapon Bearer."

Soledad formed her own mental images of the gun appearing in her hand and shooting this man– Or tried to. This time the gun refused to cooperate. The man smiled at her.

"Let it go," Dillon's mother said. "He does that to everyone."

"What is that humming?" Dillon asked.

"I don't hear anything," Coleman said.

"Me either," Edward said, "though it pains me to have to agree with him. About anything."

Soledad was about to say the same thing, then realized what she heard was almost total silence. Except for the people around her talking and Hlooth's heavy breathing. "Where did the sirens go?" she asked.

Beyond the broken windows of the dining room came ... nothing. No sounds at all. No sirens. No traffic. No sounds of people. And no light.

No street lights. No headlights. Just ... nothing. The dining room of the Buffalo Burger Pit seemed to float in the center of ... nothing.

Then she did hear a humming, but not with her ears. The sound was not sound. It was more like a low-frequency vibration grating against the edges of her mind. Like the feedback between a microphone and a subwoofer, just before it got painful.

"I would close that wide open mind of yours, Weapon Bearer," the man in the top hat said.

At her feet, Hlooth's eyestalks spread like a flower, trying to watch in all directions. He got up and turned his snout to face the outside. "Growl," he said.

"What's the matter–" Soledad started to ask.

Then it got painful.

9

DILLON SEARCHED THE faces looking at him. None of them seemed to hear it. "It sounds like ... monks?" he said. He was going to add, "Chanting," but Soledad let out a cry of pain and fell to her knees, her hands pressed against her ears.

Dillon stepped toward her from her right as Coleman came from the left. Hlooth turned his snout and two eyes to face Soledad, but the rest of his eyes remained spread, waving around, as if trying to see in all directions at once.

"Stop!" Detective White shouted.

Dillon froze in place. Coleman knelt beside Soledad and put his right arm around her shoulders. She would have pitched forward into Hlooth if Coleman hadn't grabbed her.

The hum continued to buzz in Dillon's ears. As the volume grew, the hum and buzz resolved into long, rolling syllables of words he couldn't understand, spoken by mouths he couldn't see.

The man who had come in with Soledad took a step toward Coleman. "What are you doing?"

"I said *stop*," the detective shouted.

Soledad, her hands still pressing against her ears, mumbled something through clenched teeth.

"What?" Coleman asked, leaning closer.

The rising volume of the chant obscured what Soledad said next, but the deadly intent was very clear in her eyes. Coleman reluctantly took his hands back, but he was still smiling.

"How can you guys not hear this?" Dillon asked, hardly able to hear his own voice. So he asked it again, louder, almost shouting.

"Stop shouting, Mister Offner," Detective White shouted at him. "There is no need to shout," she added in a softer voice that he almost could not hear. "Everyone just needs to calm down ..."

Dillon stared at her as she continued talking. He could no longer hear her. Her lips moved without sound.

The words in the chanting became more distinct, staccato shouts of incomprehensibilities that echoed in his skull, bouncing around in the bone chamber of his mind. Before he realized he had done it, he had copied Soledad and put his hands over his ears. The volume of the chanting was unaffected. The sound waves passed through the flesh and bone of his hands and through his ears straight into his head.

The volume continued to rise. The faces of the people around him began to shake, but it was not another earthquake. It was his eyes, picking up the frequency of the chanting and vibrating within their sockets.

He didn't remember falling to his knees. His hands were still pressing against his skull in their futile attempt to muffle the shouting in his head.

The words of the chanting roared over him and tried to crush him like a waterfall. He tried to squeeze his eyes closed, but the force of the words in his head battered them open again. The words also pushed his hands away from his ears and pried open his clenched jaw.

The words exploded in his skull, one after the other, and poured out of him through his eyes and ears and mouth.

He had never heard the words before. They were not words in English, nor Spanish, nor Latin, nor any other European or Asian language he had heard spoken.

He could no longer see anything inside the dining room of the Pit. The shaking of his eyes, the pounding of the words in his skull, made everything blur. Beyond the haze, though, he spotted a point of stability, a piece of his reality that wasn't vibrating out of control. A man.

One of the monks who had been sitting so still in the dining room at the time of the earthquake, was now standing still directly in front of Dillon, chanting. He stood so far away, though, that he could not be standing in the dining room. He had to be standing in the middle of Harvard Avenue. Except there was no way Dillon should have been able to see him, because of the intervening barricade on the window and Soledad's animal control van. The monk stood there, chanting, seemingly unconcerned with any traffic that might come along or any laws of physics he might be breaking.

Only the monk's lower jaw moved, opening to emit the next word or phrase, then closing again, his teeth chopping the sounds off like a chef's knife chopping carrots. His eyes were open, but focused past Dillon, as they always seemed to be. His arms were spread wide, making a tent of his robes. No hands extended from the ends of the sleeves, only finger-like beams of hard brown-yellow light.

More beams of light emanated from both Dillon's left and right, alerting him to two more monks. These monks were in the same pose as the first, their jaws also chopping out the incomprehensible words that flooded over Dillon. The brown-yellow beams from their outstretched arms criss-crossed with those of the first monk, creating neon webs across the blur-obscured darkness.

Dillon twisted his head to the left, then right, and saw the last two of the five monks, all of them positioned equally around him. The net of their beams surrounded Dillon and extended above him, into the infinite night sky.

The Buffalo Burger Pit and his friends no longer seemed real. He could see them, but they were faded, transparent. He saw the man he didn't know helping Soledad to her feet. He saw Hlooth coming to him, tongue ready. He saw Carlita trying to grab him, to pull him to her, but her hands passed right through him. He saw a car driving north on Harvard Avenue pass right through the monk in the middle of the street. Neither monk nor car seemed to notice.

"You are the Opener," said a voice that did not thunder anywhere near as much as Dillon would have expected for him to be able to hear it.

The chanting of the monks was as loud as ever. Louder, maybe, and still increasing in volume. But the voice cut through their chanting with no apparent effort.

"You were born for this night."

Dillon managed to turn around. Or maybe the chanted words pushed him, turned him. An old man had joined one of the chanting monks. He stood behind the monk, just outside the circular net of brown-yellow light.

"You have lived your life so that might be right here."

Dillon recognized the old man as the one he had called the Ghost of Autumn Future, the one who had wanted Dillon to open his shake. He wore a robe similar to the monks now, but it did little to make him look less like a scarecrow.

"You have legs so that you might stand where you are standing, feet so that you may walk the last few steps."

Dillon looked down to see what might be special about where he was standing, and saw that the ground beneath his feet had become as ghostly as the Pit around him. He stood–or floated–over an infinity as dark as the sky above him. He would have jumped, but his feet stayed where they were.

Brown-yellow light traced footprints in the nothingness, beginning around his own feet, and extending in uneven steps toward the old man. Dillon had no intention of taking any steps, forward or backward, but the nothing under his feet tilted abruptly and he stumbled forward. His feet came down precisely in each traced footstep, carrying him forward until the nothing tilted back to an even keel and he stopped.

"You have hands so that you might reach out and take hold of your destiny."

Dillon looked at his hands, then back at the old man. He was about to ask if there was a reason he had a small mole on his left hip, which seemed to have been precisely positioned that he would scratch it while pulling on his boxers, but a new, brown-yellow shape had been drawn in the air, this time directly in front of him.

A door. A large door, with massive hinges and a single pull latch.

The Ghost of Autumn Future stood alone on the far side of the door. The monk he had been standing next to was no longer visible. Nor were the other monks. Dillon and the old man stood in a void with the outline of a door between them.

The old man pointed at Dillon, a beam of brown-yellow light extending from his finger like a laser that struck Dillon in the middle of the forehead. Dillon would have flinched, but the cold touch of the beam held him. He seemed to dangle from the end of the shaft of light.

"You are the Opener," the old man said. "This is your destiny, to Open the Door."

The void tilted around Dillon in a way that didn't seem entirely geometrical. He felt like a rag doll being tossed around by a child, but only his right arm extended. His hand, limp at the end of his arm, struck painfully against the cold latch of the door.

"Oww!"

"You are the Opener. Grasp your destiny!"

A familiar feeling worked its way up Dillon's arm. He couldn't move his head, so he moved only his eyes as he examined the outline of the door. He knew this door.

"Why is it my destiny to open the big freezer?" he asked. "Why is it my destiny to open any door? I hate opening doors. You never know—"

Then white light exploded in the back of his head, and everything went dark.

10

Soledad managed to visualize the vault door of her mind slamming closed, but with no control. The purely mental exercise hit her with enough energy that her whole body jerked, as if a heavy metal door had actually struck her. If Coleman had not been there to catch her, she would have fallen on Hlooth, then on her face.

She hoped Coleman enjoyed the memory, because she had no plans to let him touch her again. When this night was over–assuming that ever happened–she was going to get her trench coat dry-cleaned. Immediately. Maybe with fire.

She tried to open her eyes, but they were still crossed from the mental pain of the inaudible chanting that Dillon was yelling about. She closed her eyes again. She could no longer hear the chanting, at least.

"Let go of me," she said through clenched teeth. Like her eyes, her jaw wasn't quite ready to believe the pain had stopped.

"What?" Coleman asked, leaning close.

"If you do not let go of me, Coleman," she said, "I will chop off your hands and feed them to you."

On the floor, ten feet away, the gun seemed to twitch in anticipation of transforming into something with a very sharp edge. Soledad forced her eyes open and glared at the gun, willing it to remain exactly where it was, and in its current shape. She turned to face Coleman, who was close enough she could smell his breath, and the vinegary mixture of his sweat and the ketchup he seemed to have painted himself with. Then Hlooth pushed his snout closer and sour milk was all she could smell.

Coleman smiled in a way that made her almost want to follow through on the threat even after he released her.

The gun really moved this time, jerking toward her and knocking against one of the kitchen tools-cum-weapons scattered on the floor.

Soledad ignored it, but Detective White frowned and glanced down at the floor.

Robert replaced Coleman, his hands on Soledad's shoulders. "Are you OK?"

"I'm fine," she said. She twisted out of his grip too and forced herself to stand without anyone's assistance.

"How can you guys not hear this?" Dillon shouted. "Seriously," he added, even louder than before, "how can you guys not hear this?"

"Stop shouting, Mister Offner," Detective White shouted back at him. "There is no need to shout," she added in a–slightly–softer voice. "Everyone needs to just calm down. Take a deep breath and calm the fuck *down*. I don't know what's been going on here, but I intend to get to the bottom–"

Dillon cried out and fell to his knees, copying Soledad's hands-on-ears pose from a minute earlier. The expression on his face was one of pain, as if someone was crushing his skull. Soledad recognized that from her own experience as well.

With the door of her mind closed, she could not "hear" what Dillon was hearing, but she could still sense it. It was like a psychic waterfall crashing down on him, knocking him to his knees, then forcing him to bend over still further. As if it wanted to him kneel. Or to crush him.

"Dillonito!" Carlita shouted as she fell to her knees beside him. She put her arms around him. She winced as she touched him, but she didn't let go. The psychic waterfall continued unabated.

Dillon's mother ran to him as well, but she could only stand there awkwardly, as Carlita did not make room for her. With a last glance from one of its eyestalks, Hlooth left Soledad to go to Dillon.

"Whimper?" Hlooth said.

Dillon's mother looked at Soledad. She recognized the woman's need to do something and felt the same frustrated inability to do anything. She looked at Barbara, who hadn't moved, and who was also looking back at Soledad with a helpless expression. Soledad turned to the man with the top hat.

"What is going on?" she asked. "What is happening to him?"

The man took off his top hat and held it in both hands. He stared into the depths of the hat, as if there were answers there. Then he looked at Soledad. "His Destiny, Weapon Bearer. Unless you still wish to intervene?"

"How?" she asked. "How can I intervene?"

"Use the Weapon," the man said, nodding to where the gun was on the floor. "Kill the Opener. This may be our last opportunity–"

"That's not funny," Soledad said.

"I am not speaking in jest, Weapon Bearer. This has been the Opener's Destiny since the day he was born into this world. To Open the Door, to bring forth into this world the Devourer God–"

"Stop!" Soledad shouted. She was shouting at the gun, but the man with the top hat stopped as well. Somehow the gun had been able to bypass her mental defenses. As the man had spoken, the gun had sent her a slide-show of images. Her shooting Dillon in the head. Her chopping his head off. Her bashing his head in. Her stabbing him in the heart. All the images featured the gun–the Weapon–*the* Weapon, it insisted–in its myriad lethal forms. All with her hand delivering the killing blow. Because the Weapon needed a Bearer, and she, Soledad Maria Winters, was the Bearer.

"If the Opener is to be prevented," the man with the top hat said, almost word for word what the gun was also saying in her mind, "he must be killed. And there is only one Weapon that will–"

"Stop!" Soledad said at the same time Dillon's mother shouted the same thing.

Dillon's mother said, "You said we weren't going to kill him, that to kill him now would be tantamount to offering him as a sacrifice to–" She stopped talking, biting down on whatever she had been about to say. "To the Devourer."

The man positioned his top hat back on his head. "I fear we may be running out of options, Molly. Excercising a potentially disastrous option may be better than a catastrophically disastrous lack of action."

Soledad turned to look at Dillon again. He was hard to see. His whole body seemed to be vibrating, blurring at the edges, making focus impossible. His face had become a caricature, the eyes only black holes in a vaguely human shape, the mouth and nose lost in the blur of motion. His face lengthened and shrank as Soledad watched, and she realized he was talking. Whatever he was saying, though, was beyond her ability to hear or otherwise sense.

"Dillonito!" Carlita said as he twisted around in her grasp in a way that did not seem physically possible.

Dillon stood up. Carlita tried to pull him back to her, but her hands and arms passed right through him. Then he stumbled through her. Hlooth pulled back before Dillon could walk through him as well.

"Everybody stay right where you are!" Detective White shouted.

Everyone but Dillon did as they were told.

Detective White pointed her pistol at Dillon. "Mr. Offner, that means you too."

If Dillon heard her, he gave no indication.

Though he had just walked through Carlita, Dillon walked along the edge of the front counter until he came to the gap, then he turned and walked behind the counter, and through the French fry pass through.

"Mr. Offner," the detective shouted again.

Soledad decided that if the detective wasn't going to shoot Dillon, the detective wouldn't shoot her either. So she followed Dillon. Hlooth fell in step behind her. After a look from the man in the top hat to the detective, Dillon's mother did too. Then the man in the top hat, and Carlita.

"Miss Winters," the detective started.

"Join the parade, detective," Soledad said over her shoulder. "Maybe we'll all learn what the hell is going on."

Soledad walked through the grill section, past the manager's nook and around the corner of the dive area. Unlike Dillon, though, she wasn't able to do it quietly, stepping soundlessly through the scattered stainless-steel basins and bowls the earthquake had dumped on the floor. She noisily kicked everything out of her way as she walked, taking a certain satisfaction from both the action and the racket. She noticed Hlooth staying well back out of the range of her hiking boots.

Dillon stood in front of the door of the big freezer. He was even harder to look at now. It was as if he stood in plumb with a different line of gravity than Soledad or the rest of the world. He wasn't leaning over. He appeared to be standing as straight as he ever did. Just at an angle. His blur-distorted, alien-like face very nearly touched the stainless-steel sheeting that encased the freezer, but his feet were where not they would normally be. Maybe the blurry tips of his shoes disappeared into the floor. Soledad blinked and looked away.

The rest of the parade had spread out behind her, giving Soledad a sense of *deja vu*. She had only worked at the Pit a few months. She had witnessed the ritual of Dillon "breaking in the new guy" only a handful of times, with his stupid squid-from-a-shake trick, followed by a glimpse of the Nothing that always seemed to lurk behind the big freezer door when Dillon opened it. Just like all those times, though, the people behind her positioned themselves so they could see Dillon, but wouldn't be able to see what was behind the door. Assuming Dillon opened it–

As Soledad watched, Dillon's right arm swung limply forward. Unlike when Carlita had tried to grab him and her hands passed through him, his knuckles thumped against the shiny metal latch that would open the door.

Kill him! Kill him! Kill him!

Soledad staggered under the mental onslaught of the gun as it renewed its earlier slideshow with surprising urgency and even more violence.

Kill him! Kill him! Kill him! Each order came with a new image of a new form of the Weapon and a new way to kill Dillon before he opened the big freezer door.

Soledad felt the weight of the gun in her hand, her fingers wrapping themselves around the carved wooden grips, her index finger extending along the cool metal of the trigger guard, before she realized the gun had come to her, bypassing the space between where she stood and where it had been on the floor in the dining room.

"No!" Dillon's mother screamed at the same time the man in the top hat appeared at Soledad's right shoulder and said, "Now would be our last chance, Weapon Bearer."

Soledad quelled the surprise at the man's sudden appearance. Had he just done the same trick as the gun in her hand? Or had she just not seen him walk there?

She noticed Hlooth was at her feet again, on her left side, away from the gun in her hand. His eyes looked up at her. She could tell he was trying to project a question at her, to ask her something. But she had her mind closed, and the gun was shouting too loud.

Now! Now! Now! the gun shouted in her head. She could feel it trying to will her to raise her arm and shoot Dillon through where his ear would be if she could see his head clearly.

"No," she said, because she couldn't think of a faster way to tell everyone that there was no way she was going to shoot her best friend. Even if he was about to cause the end of the world. Still, something needed to be done before he did exactly that. Or at least before he opened the big freezer, which might be the same thing.

Soledad visualized the weapon she needed, and forced the form on the gun, the Weapon, as she stepped forward. She clutched the stitched leather haft of the sap as she brought her right arm up and across her body. With a measured amount of force and an accuracy that would have made Uncle Tio proud, she swung the flat, round, lead-weighted face of the sap so it hit just behind where Dillon's ear should be.

Dillon snapped into focus and slumped forward. His forehead bounced against the stainless steel and left a smudge as he slid down.

Soledad caught him, but his weight was too much for her. He dragged her down to the floor with him and, somehow, came to rest with his head in her lap.

"See?" Coleman said behind her. "How has he been so lucky lately?"

Appearing above her as suddenly as he had appeared at her shoulder, the man in the top hat looked down at Soledad with a bemused expression that became a nod. "That is an option I had not considered, Weapon Bearer."

Hlooth's long snout split in what might have been a smile. "Bark!"

Before anyone else could say anything, the world shook again.

PART X
Who's There?

The Gun

THE GUN TOOK a certain satisfaction in a job well done. A certain satisfaction that it felt was not available in the current circumstances. Not the least because it hardly felt like a weapon, much less a Weapon, in its current form.

It felt ... limp. And droopy.

The Gun did not wish to be limp, or droopy, and had never been either one, not even during the brief period when bullwhips had been popular. Which had been troublesome, but in a very different way. The Gun had not appreciated being used as a *swing*. Still, even a bullwhip was a weapon, and the Gun had been *the* Bullwhip, and quite lethal in its own way.

But this, though ... this was ... unacceptable.

Where was the satisfaction in being the Weapon if it were incapable of actually *killing* something?

The God

THE GOD DID not like being teased.

The Phone

The Phone rang.
    The call was coming from outside its service area.
    Way, way, *way* outside its service area.
    No one answered. Which did not surprise the Phone at all.
    The Phone rang again.

1

Soledad hugged Dillon to her and curled up into as tight a ball as she could manage as she experienced the second freak earthquake of the night. Her current definition of "freak occurrence," though, was beginning to feel quaint and outdated. For instance, the big freezer seemed to be trying to break free of the floor and roll on top of her. She could quite clearly sense the malice and the cold, hungry intent pushing on the steel door from the far side. Between that and Hlooth falling all over her and Dillon in a haystack of legs and eyestalks, she wished she could move away, but she was stuck where she was for the duration.

Beside her, the man in the top hat stood as if the earthquake did not affect him. He didn't even put out a hand to steady himself. He just stood there. Beyond him, Dillon's mother and Robert and Detective White and the remaining crew of the Pit were thrown about in the more traditional manner of earthquake victims. A large stainless-steel shelf that had remained during the first earthquake fell over this time. Coleman managed to jump out of the way, pulling Edward to safety with him. Carlita disappeared under a toppling tower of plastic bun trays and an avalanche of plastic-wrapped buns as Barbara and Detective White hugged each other and fell in a heap when Robert stumbled against them.

Through the whole experience, Soledad thought she heard Dillon's phone ringing and buzzing in his pants pocket. Where it would stay, so far she was concerned, until he could pull it out himself. They might be best friends, but they weren't *that* friendly.

She thought she had dropped the Weapon when she caught Dillon, but she saw that it had created a leather wrist strap for itself and hung from her right wrist. As the earth shook, the Weapon bounced up and down and around, as if it were still trying to attack–and kill–Dillon or trying to strike her in some kind of blunt revenge. The flat face of the sap only bounced off them harmlessly.

Beneath her and Dillon, tiny cracks appeared in the grout between tiles. Then the entire section of floor gave way and dropped several inches as the earth finally went still again.

The cold, hungry presence just out of reach beyond the freezer door was suddenly much colder, much hungrier and much, much more present. Soledad's breath crystallized in front of her face, showering Dillon with tiny, glittering frost.

"Perhaps we should move away from the freezer door, Weapon Bearer," the man in the top hat said and offered her a hand up.

Soledad ignored his hand and dragged herself and Dillon up the shallow slope of broken floor tiles, away from the freezer and whatever was inside. Hlooth bit toothlessly on Dillon's left elbow and helped her drag almost as much as he got in her way. Still, they managed to put a few feet of distance between them and the freezer door. If there had been room, she would have dragged all three of them under the deep sinks of the dive station.

The big freezer had sunk into the floor. There was a shallow crater around it, and there was a gap where it had been attached to the roof above. The dirty white tiles of the drop ceiling were warped. More than one had dropped free. Fog formed around the walls of the freezer and floated down to the floor, where it pooled in swirling eddies.

Buns and plastic trays were pushed aside and Carlita appeared. She looked dazed, then her eyes focused on Dillon, then Soledad. Soledad nodded in response to the unspoken question. Dillon seemed OK. As OK as could be expected after being knocked unconscious. Then shook her head twice. No, he was not awake. Carlita nodded once in reply, then settled back into a sitting position among the buns as Soledad tried to remember ever having such a silent, eyes-only conversation with the woman before.

There was the meaty, clanking sound of someone big hitting a floor covered with metal items. "God damn it!" Coleman shouted. "The fry vats sloshed over. I slipped."

"I'm not cleaning that up," Edward said. "The grease I'll do, but not the big oaf stain."

"I will take that to mean you're both OK," Barbara said, sitting up. She and Detective White had fallen to the floor, but nothing seemed to have fallen on her. Besides Robert.

"Damn near cracked my head."

"Be more careful, Coleman," Barbara said. "I'm not sure how much more our insurance will cover." The detective sat up now. "Are you OK, detective?"

"No!" Jorge shouted. "Not my grill! No! Damn it. It's cracked!"

Barbara sighed. "Probably not enough insurance in the world. Check for a gas leak," she added. "All of you. Fry vats. Grills."

"But we turned off the all the pilot lights," Coleman said.

"That was before the foundation gave out. See if any pipes broke."

Edward giggled. "I'm pretty sure Coleman's pipe was already broken."

Carlita pulled herself to her feet using the counter of the dive station. "I will check the back door," she said.

Detective White looked dazed, then started feeling around on the floor for her lost firearm.

"Here, detective," Robert said. He picked up the detective's pistol by the grip and handed it to her in a way that would have made Uncle Tio apoplectic.

Detective White looked warily at Robert, then took the gun from him carefully, making sure to the turn the barrel so it wasn't pointed at anyone.

Dillon's mother squatted next to Soledad. "Thank you," she said. Before Soledad could decide how to respond, the woman went on. "We need to ..." She glanced at the big freezer, and the metal door that was becoming wrapped in frost. "We need to get away from that door."

"Good idea," Soledad said. She would have agreed more if she could.

The two of them were able to pick up Dillon's limp form by his arms. Then they dragged him the opposite way around the big freezer to avoid the fallen shelf and the crowd of Barbara, Detective White, Carlita and Robert. Hlooth followed them. On this side of the freezer, the four smaller doors of the refrigerators were still closed. Which was good. Because the so-called refrigerators were just metal shelves that opened into the freezer behind them. Only thick plastic flaps that hung from the ceiling inside separated fridge from freezer. Whatever was waiting behind the big door was also waiting behind them.

Dillon came to as they pulled him out of the broken grill section, past the shake machine. Which was too bad. Soledad had planned to have Hlooth lick his face to wake him up.

"What happened?"

"I saved your life," Soledad said. "And maybe the world. But mostly I saved your life."

"Why does my head hurt?"

"I saved your life," Soledad said again. She eyed the sap still hanging from her right wrist.

"I can walk," he said.

He couldn't.

They had to go single-file through the gap in the front counter, so Soledad dragged him while his mother pushed from behind.

"Can you help me get him in my van?" Soledad asked his mother.

"Where would you take him?"

It was a good question. One she had no answer for. Her apartment no longer existed. "A long way from here?"

"I do not believe that will be possible, Weapon Bearer," the man in the top hat said. To Soledad's unspoken question, he replied by pointing.

The barricade blocking the front door had not been replaced since she had come in, providing a view of the parking lot. Under the flickering streetlights, Soledad could see a line of people, men and women of varying heights and ages, evenly spaced, standing so they faced the Pit. She saw one of the monks she had seen the night before, distinguishable by his robes and bald head. Many of the others wore uniforms that looked familiar.

"They're all around us," Coleman said, looking through the gaps in the barricade on the south side of the lobby. The second earthquake had made lots of gaps, all the way around. "Fucking Yellow Sign employees. Who knew they had so many?"

Soledad recognized the uniform then. Yellow shirts and brown slacks, almost as shapeless as the monk's robes. She had only been to the restaurant once. Which had been enough. A sprawling buffet of highly varied and multiethnic cuisine that all tasted exactly the same. Broccoli beef should *not* taste like General Cho's chicken, which should *not* taste like curry chicken. And soft serve ice cream shouldn't taste like any of those things. Soledad shuddered at the memory.

"What do they want?"

"They want Master Dillon to Open the Way, Weapon Bearer," the man in the top hat said. "And I do not think they will allow us to leave the premises until he does. Or, I suppose, even after, because then we will be the first sacrifices. The appetizers, if you will, before the main course."

"So what do you expect me to do, Mr. Top Hat?" Soledad asked. "I'm not going to just open fire on a bunch of people I don't know, even if they are acting weird." On her wrist, she could feel the Weapon wanting her to do just that, and for exactly that reason.

Dillon suddenly stood straight and took his arm from Soledad's shoulders. He stepped forward, peering out at the line of people. He swayed back and forth, as if drunk, until Soledad put her hand on his shoulder to steady him. "Tina?" he said.

"OK," Soledad said. The Weapon in her hand became a M1911A1 .45 caliber semiautomatic pistol again. "Maybe."

2

DILLON'S FOCUS SWAM and bobbed, struggling to fix on any one object. Or face. The faces of everyone in the line outside the Buffalo Burger Pit were in shadow, but one was very familiar.

"What are you doing out there, Tina?" he asked. He stepped through the mess on the floor, broken glass crunching under his feet, until he was standing just inside the empty frame of the door. "Is that Ricky?"

Neither Tina nor the man standing next to her in the brown slacks and ecru buttoned-down shirt that marked a manager of the Yellow Sign Buffet replied. At least, not in a manner Dillon found meaningful. As one, all the people in the line abruptly started chanting, their mouths opening and closing in unison, their voices mixing with no harmony.

Dillon winced, and took a step back, but the chanting didn't get louder this time, or try to crush him. Static and clicks and pops like a radio trying to play while spinning in a microwave rose from their throats and created yellow-brown sparks in the air. The sounds made Dillon want to clear his throat.

Behind him, Barbara said, "Edward, make sure the drive-thru window is still secure."

"Why? All the other windows are, well, not there."

"Just do it. Carlita?"

"The back door is locked, yes."

The phone in Dillon's pocket vibrated and rang.

Dillon tried to retrieve his phone from his pocket, but his fingers failed to get a firm grip. It was almost as if the phone were pushing itself into his hand, maybe even trying to help him answer it. The usually simple task would have been easier if the phone hadn't been trying to help. Finally, though, he had the phone out and pressed the button to answer.

"You have to close the door, Dillon," a man's voice said, then repeated itself. "You have to close the door, Dillon."

Dillon pulled the phone away from his ear as if it were burning him. He almost threw the phone away, but he finally saw the name displayed for the caller.

"Daddy?" he said, feeling at once very small, and too tall. He would have fallen except two sets of hands grabbed him and held him upright.

The phone's screen showed "DADDY", all caps, the letters slightly askew, as if written by a six-year-old still struggling with straight lines and margin control and more interested in drawing pictures of dinosaurs and squid than angular letters.

"You have to close the door, Dillon." The voice from the phone was fainter, but Dillon could still hear every word. Louder now, as if the voice on the end of the impossible phone call realized Dillon was only staring at the phone and no longer held it to his ear. "You have to close the door, Dillon."

He looked past the phone, to the glassless door in front of him. There was no way he could close that door now.

The phone switched itself to speaker mode. "You have to close the door, Dillon." His father's voice repeated itself word for word, tone for tone, as if it were only a recording, playing over and over.

"Keith?" Mom's voice.

Through the empty frame of the door, Dillon stared at the memory of his father rushing out of the kitchen. He held a spatula. He had been making pancakes. Dillon remembered that now. The small house had been filled with the smells of buttermilk pancakes and maple syrup. And he had been watching Bugs Bunny–

"You have to close the door, Dillon."

Except Daddy hadn't been able to say anything that night. He had rushed into the living room and the light from the open door behind Dillon had claimed him, hitting across the eyes, making his face look as if he had been caught in a bad photograph with the flash on full, the shadow of the spatula across his face, covering one eye, trying to shout–

"You have to close the door, Dillon."

Except it hadn't been Daddy who shouted. Not that night. That had been Uncle Phil. All Daddy had been able to say that night had been, "Dill–" Then his words had become incomprehensible clicks and static.

"Keith?" Mom said again. Then she was grabbing for the phone. "Oh my god, Keith!"

A wave of cold washed over Dillon from behind, from the direction of the big freezer, as if someone had opened the door right behind him. The cold took his breath away in a cloud of crystal fog and froze the tears on his face. His fingers holding the phone went numb. He would have dropped his phone, but his mother had already grabbed it out of his hand.

"Keith!" she shouted into the phone, but Dillon could see the display already showed, "Call Disconnected." She seemed unaffected by the cold, even when Dillon let out another breath and it fogged in front of his face.

The streetlamp behind the line of chanting Yellow Sign Buffet employees and the one monk Dillon could see jerked back and forth with the sound of stressed metal and breaking concrete. Then the light went out and darkness rolled forward.

Black tendrils appeared between the chanters, swelled to become thick tentacles that twisted around them and engulfed them, even the monk. The tentacles did not pull or push, they only encompassed. The chanting went offbeat. Dull, empty gazes registered confusion for an instant as faces and bodies were subsumed into the mass of blackness that had eaten the streetlamp. Tina's face disappeared. So did Ricky's. It was as if the night itself was swallowing them whole. Then the chanting continued as before, as if nothing had happened.

Uncle Phil's face appeared, thrust forward, out of the darkness. A tiny fraction of a face still recognizable even across the distance between them. The one eye looked at Dillon.

Behind Dillon, Hlooth's growl sounded like an angry bowl of pudding.

The darkness swirled again, and another figure emerged. Cyd, still naked, stepped out of the darkness and walked toward Dillon.

"Not again," Soledad said.

"Yes!" Coleman shouted behind Dillon. "Finally."

3

"Cʏᴅ?" Dɪʟʟᴏɴ sᴀɪᴅ. He would have stepped forward again, but Soledad's hands pulled him a step in the opposite direction. "Are you ... ?" He stopped, because the question seemed unnecessary. Cyd was definitely *not OK.*

Her hair was disheveled, and her right shoulder and arm were scraped, and blood seeped from the worst of the abrasions. Her skin was dirty. She limped, favoring her right leg. The same yellow-brown light as from the Yellow Sign Buffet sign across the street shone out of her eyes, tinged with black sparks that flared in time with the static and popping noises that came out of her open mouth.

"Don't look at her eyes," Soledad shouted, her voice loud in Dillon's left ear.

"No problem here," Coleman said.

"You are so gross," Edward said.

"Not that gross," Jorge said. "Though, yeah, she has looked better– Oww!"

Soledad's arms came up, her hands holding a pistol that looked huge, especially for being so close to Dillon's face, even if it wasn't pointed at him. "That's close enough, Cyd."

"What are you doing?" Dillon asked.

"Drop the weapon, Miss Winters." Detective White's voice.

Soledad ignored the order and kept the pistol pointed at Cyd.

Cyd stopped less than ten feet from Dillon, the broken door with its now pointless push-to-open bar dividing the space between them. Her eyes blinked, and the light behind them went out, replaced by a darkness even more disturbing. Her mouth closed. The corners of her lips twitched, then pulled up into an uneven smile.

"I said drop it." Detective White.

"I'm not going to do that," Soledad said.

Soledad stepped forward so she was even with Dillon. Dillon looked from her to Cyd, then to the gun again. It was Uncle Phil's gun. He looked past Cyd's face to the writhing darkness with Uncle Phil's single eye looking out. At him.

You have to close the door, Dillon. You have to close the door.

Not Daddy's voice this time. It was Uncle Phil's voice. Dillon's memory from the night his father died. Uncle Phil holding him, his face covered by a pillow, Uncle Phil swinging his legs to catch the door and force it closed.

The night Uncle Phil had killed Daddy.

He had to, Dillon. There was no other choice.

His mother's words, from earlier this afternoon. "Phil?" Mom still held Dillon's phone.

Dillon wanted to ask Uncle Phil if she had told him the truth.

The eye only looked back at him. Dillon could see no answers there.

"I do not think you will shoot me, Weapon Bearer," Cyd said. The voice was Cyd's, but not quite. Pops and static sounded behind the words.

"I will if you call me 'weapon bearer' again."

The pits of darkness that had been Cyd's eyes shifted their focus back to Dillon. "You are the Opener," she said. "He who Opens the Door. You have inserted the Key, and you have Opened the Lock–"

"Way to go, Dillon," Coleman said. "Oww! What?"

"The Door stands ready," Cyd went on. "The Way has been prepared. This is your Destiny. This is the Destiny of your world." She spread her arms, as if ready to embrace the world. "You are the Opener," she said again, and took a step forward.

"I said that's close enough!" Soledad shouted.

"And I said 'drop the weapon'!"

Cyd smiled, then took another step.

"Damn it," Soledad said. "You're right." She let her arms drop, but she didn't release her grip on the pistol.

Cyd took another step. She stood just outside the door now, the bar across her chest, hiding her nipples. Dillon saw that her feet were bleeding now from the glass on the ground. She didn't seem to notice.

Soledad stepped in front of Dillon. She raised the gun again, but she didn't point it at Cyd. She aimed past her, over the girl's shoulder.

"Soledad-" Dillon shouted.

"Miss Winters-"

The three shots were loudest thing Dillon had heard since the night his father died.

Boom-boom-boom!

Dillon flinched at the first shot. Before he could recover, before he had realized she had stopped shooting, Soledad had spun around and grabbed him and was pushing him back, away from Cyd and the now-screaming blackness she had shot.

Dillon looked past Cyd, who no longer smiled but who had not moved, not even flinched despite the gunshots that had exploded so near her face. In the darkness beyond Cyd there was no longer any sign of Uncle Phil, only tentacles waving about and clutching each other. Whatever had been left of Uncle Phil was gone.

"What happened?" Dillon asked as Soledad pushed him backward.

"She released Phil," Mom said.

4

SOLEDAD WISHED SHE had a better plan. The Weapon had a plan, but it was the same plan the Weapon always had: Shoot something! Stab something! Hit something!

She briefly wondered if it was progress that she was arguing with herself less now, and was instead arguing with the Weapon. At least there was someone–or something–on the other end of the conversation, even if it was a bit single-minded. Then she focused on pushing Dillon back, away from Cyd and whatever it was that Phil Trichter had become. Away from whatever the hell was going on out in the parking lot of the Pit.

She released him, Dillon's mother had said.

Release the former Bearer, the Weapon had said, with the same plan it always had. This time, Soledad went along. She had never shot a person before. She wasn't entirely sure she had shot one now. She wasn't sure of anything. At least Dillon's mother and the Weapon approved. And, somehow, she knew that Phillip Trichter had been, for lack of a better word, *released*. Whatever that meant.

Soledad focused on getting Dillon safe. In the current situation, unfortunately, with the new open-air concept doors and windows in the Pit's dining room, that meant going toward whatever waited for them in the big freezer.

She bulldozed Dillon back through the gap in the front counter, leaving his mother standing there with his phone, and nearly bowled over Detective White. The detective still had her Glock out and was yelling at Soledad to freeze and demanding to know what the hell was going on.

Soledad was not going to do one and she wasn't sure she knew any more than the detective about the other. She knew only that she needed to protect Dillon from the women in his life. And that might include her, if the Weapon ever got its way.

Dillon's feet went out from under him and took hers with them as they stepped in the congealing grease that had been spilled from the fry vats.

Dillon managed to keep his head up and avoid bouncing it off the ceramic tiles of the floor, even with nearly the full weight of Soledad–plus her bag and the pistol–landing on his chest. Soledad managed not to trigger a shot. She didn't have time to wonder if the Weapon had been looking for one last chance to remove Dillon from the equation.

The narrow pass through, with the fry vats on one side and a stainless-steel prep station and load-supporting pillar on the other, made a graceful recovery impossible. Soledad couldn't get off Dillon without climbing over him. So she climbed over him. It would have been easier if her right hand hadn't been holding the Weapon, but she wasn't going to let it go. Dillon grunted as first her knees then her boots found purchase on his chest. Then her bag swung free and struck him on the face.

When she was finally off him, she stood, or tried to. The soles of her boots were slick with grease now, and wanted to slip out from under her again. She caught her balance, then got a quick view of what was happening up front.

Dillon's mother had grabbed Cyd's shoulders as the girl knelt to come through the empty door, and the two of them were pushing against each other. Around them, the rest of the Pit crew and Detective White fought against a new, rising tide of squid things.Hlooth had positioned himself in the gap of the front counter, jaws and claws tearing at the squid-things trying to come that way. One of his eyestalks swung around to look at her, and Soledad felt a question projected at her that seemed a lot like, *What the hell are you waiting for?* It sounded like, "Bark!?"

She resisted the urge to point out all the spilled grease–ignored the Weapon's urge to open fire on Hlooth and all the other "outsiders" it was gibbering about–and grabbed the back of Dillon's collar as he was trying to sit up. He made choking sounds as she pulled him back, but she could hardly hear them over the sounds of the fight and the clanging of metal basins, bowls, and utensils on the floor.

"Everybody get behind the counter!" Detective White shouted.

Gunshots echoed through the store as Soledad pulled up short at the fallen metal shelf. She braced her still-slippery feet against the heavy shelf and pulled Dillon to his feet. Up front, Detective White stood shoulder to shoulder with Coleman, Edward, Jorge, Ronald and the new guy as Barbara and Carlita climbed over the counter to get behind it. The men of the closing crew were pounding, stomping and stabbing as the detective squeezed off shot after shot. Beyond them, Soledad could see the man in the top hat, cane sword out again, walking through the chaos as if nothing much were happening, stabbing squid-things on the floor or threading his blade through multiple creatures as they jumped at him. There was no sign of Dillon's mother, or Cyd.

"Come on," Soledad shouted into Dillon's ear between gunshots, and stepped into the space between two shelves. She moved her hand to his left elbow.

"We have to help them!" Dillon shouted back, and pulled against her grip. His shoes were still slick, as well, and he nearly fell.

"No! We have to–" She stopped. Because the words she was about to shout weren't hers. And they were in a voice she had never heard until a few minutes ago. "You," she said, and stopped. Suddenly she couldn't breathe. "You have to." Her voice was not her voice. Not completely. It sounded wrong in her own head. "Dillon."

Dillon turned to stare at her. His eyes were wild, and there were tears. "I can't!" he said.

Soledad could only stare at him as she tried to regain control of her mind. She started to pull on him again, but the battle in the dining room drew her attention.

"Fall back!" Detective White shouted as she paused to reload. "All of you."

Coleman just laughed as he continued to swing his fire extinguisher club back and forth. Ronald and Andrew needed no additional encouragement.

"Damn it," the detective said, squeezing off another two shots. "I said *fall back*."

"I could not agree more," the man in the top hat said, appearing beside her, though he had been across the dining room an instant before.

He sheathed his cane sword as he leaped lightly over the counter. He landed facing the dining room in a way that made Soledad's head hurt to consider. Then he reached across, grabbed Detective White with his left hand and Edward with his right, and pulled them bodily over the counter.

Coleman stepped forward, out of the man's reach. "I got this, bro!" he shouted over his shoulder. He stomped and swung. The fire extinguisher smashed against the floor with a muted, squishy thud.

With a sound like a tornado, what was left of the north door, and a good portion of the wall, from just in front of the counter to the first booths, was pulled away. Long tentacles as thick as tree branches with suckers the size of golf balls appeared in the gap, writhing and grabbing anything they came in contact with, pulling it out through the hole to disappear into the darkness. Then the darkness seemed to pour in.

Coleman paused, panting. "Fuck a duck," he said. Then, with the biggest smile Soledad had ever seen, he added, "Welcome to the Buffalo Burger Pit, motherfucker. Could I interest you in a Meatgrinder End of Days Holiday Special?"

One thick tentacle knocked his extinguisher aside as another snaked out of the darkness and wrapped around his torso. He struck at the tentacle to no visible effect. It lifted him off the floor.

"Coleman!" Edward shouted. He started to climb over the counter again, but the man in the top hat pulled him back.

The sound of a truck horn crescendoed and culminated in a crash that shook the building almost as much as another earthquake. The south door of the dining room exploded inward, spraying broken chairs and tables, followed by the iron-pipe-reinforced front grill of the Rio Cruces Animal Control military surplus Humvee known as the Lion Catcher.

The Lion Catcher plowed through the dining room until it was even with the front counter, with its hood directly beneath the Coleman. Jimmie the Wrangler came sliding over the roof of the cab with a catchpole held in both hands as Uncle Tio came out of the far side of the cab with an AR-15. Jimmie planted his feet on the hood and swung the loop of his catchpole over Coleman's head and chest. Uncle Tio opened fire, shooting multiple 3-shot bursts into the darkness beyond Coleman.

Jimmie yanked the loop tight, then heaved. The tentacle heaved back, nearly pulling Jimmie off his perch. Another burst of fire from Uncle Tio, this time aimed at the tentacle, and the tentacle dropped Coleman and pulled out of view. Jimmie swung Coleman as the young man fell so he landed on the counter. Coleman slipped on the stainless-steel surface, but managed to keep his hold on his fire extinguisher and not fall. He braced his feet against one of the cash registers. He was still smiling, if looking a bit dazed.

"Sollie?" Uncle Tio shouted. He kept his rifle pointed north but held his fire. He glanced at each of the people in front in rapid succession.

"I'm back here, Uncle Tio," Soledad shouted. "I'm OK."

Jimmie loosened the loop and lifted it off Coleman with a practiced ease that Soledad decided she never wanted to think about again.

Coleman looked at her, then at Uncle Tio and the Lion Catcher, then back at her.

"Fuck yeah," he shouted. "I want to marry into your family so bad."

"Frank?" Detective White said, letting her arms fall to her side.

"Ellen," Uncle Tio said, nodding to the detective.

"You have another one of those?" she asked.

Uncle Tio gave her a lopsided smile. "*Absolutamente*, Detective."

Detective White reholstered her pistol and caught the AR-15 Uncle Tio tossed over the counter to her.

"Do I get one?" Coleman asked.

"No," said Uncle Tio, Detective White, and Barbara all at the same time.

"What do you need, Sollie?" Uncle Frank asked loudly. "I brought the arsenal."

Soledad looked at the pistol she gripped in her right hand, then she looked at Dillon again. His eyes were wide with fear. "Time," she said. "I need time."

"Roger that. I hope I brought enough."

Uncle Frank walked back to the cab of the Lion Catcher and returned with a second AR-15, this one painted in forest camo colors, and a pump-action shotgun. He tossed the shotgun to Jimmie, who let his catchpole drop out of sight on the far side of the front counter. Jimmie pumped a shell into the chamber as Uncle Tio pulled back the operating rod and made the AR-15 ready to fire.

"Start the clock," Uncle Tio said.

5

DILLON DIDN'T TURN around, even when Coleman shouted, "Here they come again!" Not even when a shotgun blast started a thunderous new barrage of weapons fire.

"Come on!" Soledad shouted at him. She had her hands on his shoulders, shaking him, yelling in his face to be heard over the noise. "You need to close the door, Dillon!"

He knew what he had to do. Dad had told him. Somehow.

He felt four years old again. Or six. Or ... he didn't know.

He felt like a child, standing on the edge of nothing. On the threshold of infinite darkness. Alone. He would not have been surprised to discover he had wet himself, as he had all those times before. He didn't check, though, because Soledad was standing in front of him, shouting at him, pulling on him.

"How do you know?" he asked.

"Know what?"

"How do you know what I need to do? Did Dad ..." His voice choked before he could ask if Dad had told her. He had heard her speak with Dad's voice. Seen her look at him with Dad's eyes. Which had been so startling, because he had to look down into those eyes, which had always been so far above him. "Did Dad tell you?"

Soledad shook her head. "No. He told *you*." She pulled him forward.

"Come on, Dillonito, there is work yet to be done." Carlita was suddenly behind him, pushing him.

Pushed from behind, pulled from in front, he tripped over the shelf. Soledad caught him. "Look where you're going."

Dillon nodded as he stood again. He followed her, stepping carefully along the narrow confines of the overturned shelf and its scattered, fallen contents. He heard Carlita coming the same way behind him. He managed to step out of the shelf on his own, before either woman could help him.

He heard Coleman shout and Barbara scream, and he would have turned to see what was happening, but Soledad grabbed his arm and pulled him around the corner with Carlita pushing him again for good measure.

He stood in front of the big freezer door, just past the broken tiles and their treacherous slanting. He had his back to the dive station. He didn't need to touch the door this time to feel the Cold Wrong on the other side. He could feel it where he stood. It was waiting for him.

His Destiny.

He knew what he had to do, but he did not think he could do it alone. To close the door, he had to open it first. And when he did, the Cold Wrong on the other side would be waiting for him. He didn't think he was strong enough to keep the door from being pushed wide open from the other side. The Cold Wrong would push him aside and devour him. Dillon would never get the chance to close the door. The door would remain open and the world would die.

The only consolation was that anyone who would know to blame *him* for the End of the World would have to do it in a real hurry, before they too were devoured.

You opened the door, Dillon, so you have to be the one who closes it.

His father's words.

Dillon glanced at Soledad to see if she had spoken with Dad's voice again. She wasn't looking at him. She had turned to face the door that led to the break room and raised her pistol with both hands.

Somehow, through the noise of the battle up front, Dillon heard his phone ring.

Cyd stepped into view. She was still naked, but dirtier than before, with fresh, parallel scratches across her left cheek and new abrasions on her knees and elbows. Behind Cyd stood Tina. Tina's face was blank as she stared at him. Cyd was smiling. She held Dillon's phone in her left hand and a shiny, freshly cut key in right hand. The phone rang again.

"Where's Mom?" Dillon asked. "How did you get in?"

"It is for you, Opener," Cyd said, and threw Dillon his phone as it rang a third time.

Soledad looked up at the phone. In that instant, Cyd charged and tackled her against the dive station. Soledad's gun fired, striking the door frame near Tina's head. Neither Cyd nor Tina flinched. They rushed forward and engulfed Soledad in arms and legs as Carlita ran to help. The combined weight of the three women dragged Soledad to the ground. Another shot punched a hole in the drop ceiling.

Dillon caught the phone. As he fumbled with the phone, trying not to drop it, his thumb brushed against the Take Call button.

"Daddy?" he said, pushing the phone to his ear, stepping back from where the women wrestled on the floor. Carlita had her thick arms around Tina's body, trying to pin Tina's arms. Tina was sitting on Soledad, holding Soledad's right arm upright with her both hers while Cyd tried to pry the gun from Soledad's fingers.

"If you're not going to help," Soledad shouted at Dillon, "close the fucking door!"

Dillon shifted the phone to his left hand as he stepped up to the door. He put his right hand on the latch. The cold immediately raced up his arm, but with Daddy's help, maybe he could do this—

"No, honey," his mother's voice said in his left ear. She sounded weak. He could hardly hear her over the static and popping that filled the air where she was and the women fighting where he was, not to mention the gunfire and shouting from the dining room. "It's not Daddy. Daddy's—" Her voice choked. After a second she went on. "It's just you and me this time, honey."

"I need Daddy," Dillon said. He would have pulled his hand from the latch, but the skin of his fingers and palm had frozen to the metal. "Or Uncle Phil. I can't do this alone. It's *waiting* for me."

"That's why I'm here, honey. Now come on."

Something brushed past Dillon's face, dented the stainless-steel surface of the big freezer door and ricocheted away before the sound of the gunshot hit Dillon from behind. He jerked back from the door, dropping the phone as he did. He tried to grab for the falling phone with his left hand and turn to see why Soledad was shooting at him at the same time, but his right hand was still frozen to the door latch. He barely heard the phone hit the floor.

"It is his Destiny," Cyd said.

Soledad still held her pistol, but Carlita and Tina wrestled on top of her, and Cyd had forced Soledad's right arm to point at him. Cyd had her hand over Soledad's, and forced her finger into the crowded space of the trigger guard.

"You have Opened the Way, Opener," Cyd said.

"No, I haven't–" Dillon started to say. Then the door hit him in the shoulder. He flinched, but the door did not hit him hard. It didn't sweep him away. It just ... opened.

From the corner of his eye, Dillon could see the light spilling around the sides of the door, and he felt the Cold Emptiness inside sucking all the heat from the air.

Cyd smiled at him along the length of the pistol barrel. "Now your Sacrifice will bring forth the Devourer God–"

Dillon flinched again at the gunshot, but he had no idea where the bullet went. Soledad had jerked her arm out of line.

"Stop," Soledad said, struggling to keep her arm out of line with Dillon and twisting against the weight of Carlita and Tina. "Trying. To shoot. My. Dillon!"

As Dillon watched, unable to take his eyes off the muzzle of the gun jerking back and forth across his center of mass, the gun changed. The muzzle closed, the barrel pulled back and seemed to wrap itself around Soledad's hand.

"Dillon!" Soledad shouted again. "Shut." Her fingers were now encased in what could only be brass knuckles. "The Fucking." They didn't look like brass, though. They were gunmetal gray, and the hard edges gleamed. "Door!" she shouted and hit Cyd in the face.

With a wince at the blood that sprayed from Cyd's lower lip, Dillon turned to face the door. His right hand was still frozen to the latch, and ice was forming around open edges of the door. He saw the light spilling around the left and top edges of the door, bending in a way that light was never supposed to do, looking for him. He closed his eyes just before it found him.

YOU HAVE OPENED THE WAY!

The Voice of a God, shouting in triumph. The sound of the Voice was noise, white and cold, hard and sharp. It stabbed at him from all sides. It burned him as it pulled at the heat of his body.

Dillon put his left hand against the door. He felt the skin of his fingertips freeze to the metal. He tried to push the door closed. He failed. The way his hands were frozen to the door, he could not get proper leverage. He braced his feet as best he could on the uneven floor and pushed with all his weight. He failed again.

COME TO ME, OPENER, AND I WILL COME TO YOU!

The door pushed against him, and with the strength of the light behind it, it pushed Dillon back. His feet slid on the tiles. The door would have opened fully except for his heels coming up against the broken part of the floor.

YOU ARE MY CHILD!

You have to close the door, Dillon. You have to close the door. Uncle Phil's voice. In Dillon's head, somehow audible over the noise of the god.

Dillon shook his head. Couldn't Uncle Phil see he was *trying*? It wasn't like Uncle Phil was there to pick him up again and almost break his ankle forcing the door closed. Or maybe, just, you know, help push.

EMBRACE YOUR DESTINY!

You opened the door, Dillon, so you have to be the one who closes it. Daddy's voice.

Dillon shook his head, his eyes still squeezed close. Tears leaked out. Because Daddy wasn't there either. He felt the tears freeze on his cheeks. He would have to close the door by himself this time.

YOU ARE THE DOOR!

Dillon tried to pull his hands back, but the ice wouldn't let him go.

On three, Dillon. One. Two. Three!

Dillon pushed.

The door refused to budge.

YOU ARE THE WAY!

Dillon braced his feet as best he could against the broken floor. He clenched his teeth and pulled his right hand free of the ice that held it to the door's latch. He tried not to think about how much frozen skin he was leaving behind, how much his hand was bleeding.

The Voice of the God rose in ecstasy at the taste of Dillon's blood.

THIS IS YOUR DESTINY!

Dillon ignored the pain in his hands and shifted his stance so he could put his full weight against the door, pressing with both hands at chest level, the skin of his cheek tingling from the nearness of the metal. He pushed.

The door moved, ever so slightly.

YOU ARE THE OPENER!

The Voice of the God lost its ecstasy. Maybe it even sounded a little desperate. The door pushed back, but less than before. Dillon kept up the pressure. He had opened this door, even if-sometimes-by accident. And if he could open the door, he could close it, as well. On purpose. Or he hoped he could.

YOU ARE THE DOOR!

The door moved again, enough that Dillon had to move his feet. He took a small step. The soles of his shoes slipped, some, then found new purchase. He had gained maybe an inch.

YOU WERE BORN TO OPEN THE WAY!

Something heavy hit the door next to Dillon. He would have opened his eyes in surprise, but the tears on his cheeks had frozen his eyes shut. And since whoever or whatever it was seemed to be helping, Dillon continued to focus on pushing.

THIS IS YOUR DESTINY!

The Voice of the God sounded shrill and the door moved faster. Dillon felt as if he was running, pushing against the door, but the door was infinitely wide open and he had to push it all the way across the night sky.

YOU ARE MINE!

He didn't know how much further he could run. How big was this damn door, anyway? Then someone or something else joined him in his effort, added their weight and the strength of their will.

I WILL BE WAITING!

The door slammed closed with a force that knocked Dillon back, away from it. For an instant, Dillon thought he smelled pancakes.

6

DILLON LANDED ON his butt hard enough to knock his teeth together and make his spine feel like it was trying to punch through the top of his skull. He opened his eyes as the cold began to dissipate and the icicles on his eyelashes melted. He held his hands in front of his face. Both of his palms were bloody and looked ... peeled. He looked at the freezer and saw four bloody hand prints on the door. His throat tightened as he realized he had expected at least two more.

He saw Andrew sitting on the floor next to him, looking as stunned as Dillon felt. Dillon swallowed the lump in his throat and tried to smile at Andrew before the young man realized he had been about to cry.

"You looked like you needed some help," Andrew said, panting.

Dillon nodded. He reached out and patted Andrew on the shoulder, leaving a bloody handprint on Andrew's uniform. "Way to pay attention, Andrew. Good job."

"So there was ... something ... in there? This time?" Andrew shivered.

Dillon nodded again.

"So do we ..." He stopped, looking uncertain. "Do we flip it off now?"

"Fuck, yeah," Dillon said, and raised both bloody middle fingers to the big freezer. Andrew copied the gesture.

Soledad stepped up from their right and loomed over them. She had a welt under her left eye beginning to swell. Blood had splattered on her trenchcoat and shirt. She still had the gunmetal gray brass knuckles on her right hand. There was blood on her hand, but none on the brass knuckles. Dillon wondered how that was even possible. She held out her left hand for Dillon, as if he wanted to stand up. He just looked up at her. After a few seconds, she shrugged, let her hand drop. She stepped across in front of them and sat down next to Dillon.

"Where's–" Dillon started to ask.

Soledad held up her fist with the brass knuckles. "If the first thing you ask me is 'where is Cyd'," she said, "I will punch you in the mouth."

Dillon closed his mouth.

"She's in the break room," Soledad said, letting her fist drop. "Carlita's taking care of her."

"What about–"

Soledad raised her fist again and Dillon closed his mouth. "Tina ran off." She let out a long breath. "I never liked her, anyway."

Dillon also wanted to ask about his mother, but it seemed like the best choice to wait.

"Bark?" Hlooth's tapioca voice came around the corner just before his eyes and the rest of him.

"Yes," Soledad said. "I saved him. Though I'm not sure I should have."

Before Dillon could raise his hands to protect himself, Hlooth was on him, licking his face with all three feet of rough, knotted tongue and trying to melt Dillon's eyes with the worst breath ever.

"Woof!" Hlooth said, his eyestalks bouncing around happily.

PART XI
Orange

The Gun

THE GUN WOULD have smiled if it could.

The War was not over, of course. The War would never be over. But another Battle had been fought and won.

And the Bearer had never once shoved the Gun down the back of her pants.

The God

THE GOD WAITED.

The God did not like to wait, but It could. It was, after all, a God.

New Doors would Open. Doors to new Universes. Doors to new Places to Feed.

Though hunger and anger ached and raged through Its Being, the God exercised Patience, and waited.

The Phone

ITS FINAL CALL answered, its last message delivered, the Phone slipped into oblivion. It wondered if the Opener would even notice it was gone.

1

"HERE'S YOUR PHONE," Soledad said, and handed the pieces to Dillon.

Dillon sat on the front counter next to Andrew, where Barbara had told them to sit. Barbara had wrapped their hands in gauze from the restaurant's first-aid kit.

Barbara looked at the pieces of broken display, case and battery that Soledad had dropped into Dillon's upturned hands and sighed. "Now you're going to need a new phone as well as a new job."

"I'm fired?" Dillon asked.

Barbara's gesture included the wreckage of the Buffalo Burger Pit's dining room behind Dillon and what was left of the front counter. "I think we all are."

Andrew's shoulders slumped. "But I just started."

Barbara patted him on the knee. "Don't worry, Andrew. I'll give *you* a good reference."

Before Dillon could protest that he deserved a good reference too, Barbara's phone played "Hail to the Chief" and she answered it, crying, "Oh, thank god, Gil, are you all right?" She turned away from Dillon and Andrew.

Dillon dropped the remains of his phone on the counter. The broken battery case caught in the gauze of his bandages and took three tries to shake off. He looked at Soledad.

"There's nothing in the freezer," she said. "Not anymore."

"Then what was all the shooting about?"

"Just being sure."

Behind Soledad, her uncle smiled. He had slung his AR-15 on his back, and had his hands on her shoulders. "No kill like overkill," he said. "Right, Sollie?"

She shrugged and gave a wan smile. "Why not?"

"Hoo-ah."

"Dillon!" Coleman's shout drew their attention to the gaping hole where the north door of the dining room and several plate-glass windows used to be. Out in the parking lot the still-twitching tentacles of an enormous squid-thing sprawled across the pavement and more than a few cars, including the red convertible Dillon's mother had been driving. There was very little light. The Yellow Sign Buffet's sign was out. None of the Yellow Sign Buffet employees, nor the monks, could be seen.

"I found your mom!" Coleman stepped into view with his arm around the shoulders of Dillon's mother, half dragging her as she leaned against him. The condiments on Coleman's face had streaked from sweat, but there was also drying blood from a circle-shaped bite mark on his left cheek. A line of sucker marks extended down his right arm. "I think she likes me. So now I can be your replacement here at the Pit *and* your new daddy. You can be my best man at the wedding. Edward Poofyhands can be the Maid of Honor."

"In that case," Edward said, "*I* would be the best man at the wedding."

Dillon pushed himself off the counter. He landed awkwardly on the remains of a bun tray, then limped to his mother.

Hlooth, who had been lying on the floor while Jimmie the Wrangler rubbed his belly and called him Lassie, rolled over, licked Jimmie's face, and followed Dillon.

Mom let go of Coleman and fell into Dillon's arms once he was close enough.

"You did it, honey." She seemed so small as she hugged him. He had to lean over, and hold her up. "You did it."

Dillon hugged her close. "Does this mean you're leaving again?"

"No. Never again." She paused. "Well, I will have to go get my stuff."

"Can I come with you?"

She smiled. "I would like that."

The Ghost of Autumn Present appeared beside them. His brown suit and orange ruffles were as immaculate as ever and showed no sign of the battle just fought. He doffed his top hat and bowed to them.

"Until next time, Opener," he said. "Molly," he added with another bow.

"Next time?" Dillon asked, but the man was already walking away, fading into the darkness outside the tiny island of light that was the dining room of the Buffalo Barbecue Pit.

2

Soledad watched Dillon and his mother hug and felt some of her resentment toward the woman slip away. If Dillon could forgive the mother that abandoned him, Soledad could at least consider the option.

Robert approached the front counter. He was carrying his prized cast-iron skillet in both hands. The black, seasoned iron was covered with ichor and a mix of splattered condiments. One side had been bent almost flat, and there was dent where it looked like a bullet had hit it. He put the wounded pan on the counter after brushing away the bits of Dillon's dead phone.

Andrew, still sitting on the counter where Barbara had told him to sit, looked at Soledad, then at Robert. He excused himself in a low voice and pushed off the counter. He walked over to join Edward in the drive-thru station. Uncle Tio squeezed her shoulders once more, then left her with Robert.

"I could strip it and reseason it," Robert said, still holding the pan, looking down at it, "but ..." He stopped. "Maybe I can hammer it back into shape?"

Soledad shook her head. She leaned against the counter, letting it support her and keep him at arm's length. "No. I think it's ... I think it's just recycling now."

He ran his fingers across the metal. "It was a good pan."

She nodded this time. "Yes it was."

He looked up from the pan, met her eyes. "So that's it then?"

She nodded again. "I think so."

Robert glanced over at Dillon. Then back to her. "So is it OK if I stay ... here?"

"It doesn't look like anyone's leaving. We certainly can't go back." She added, "To my apartment, I mean."

It was his turn to nod.

"I'm going to need a ride to the airport," he said after a minute. "My flight is tomorrow afternoon."

"I can stand it if you can," she said. Then added, "The van, I mean. It isn't any cleaner than it was today."

Jimmie the Wrangler stood up from where he had been sitting on the floor. "What's wrong with the van?"

3

DILLON HELPED HIS mother walk back into the dining room.

Detective White walked from the south side of the dining room, picking her way through the wreckage and around the huge, sand-colored Humvee Soledad's uncle had parked there. She carried a black AR-15 in the crook of her right arm. She had her phone in her left hand, its screen dark. She nodded to Dillon, then faced Soledad's uncle as he came around the front counter.

"Frank," she said, then, "Thanks." She pushed her phone into a pocket of her blazer, then presented the rifle with both hands. "I'll pretend only one bullet ever came out each time I pulled the trigger."

The man took the rifle with a big smile. "But of course, Ellen." They shook hands. "In return, I will mention you kindly in my report to the mayor about this unusual animal control issue. I suspect I will need to ask for a bigger budget next year. Maybe a new animal control van. Or a new Lion Catcher if this sort of thing happens again."

"Animal control issue?" The detective shook her head. "I was thinking I would call it in as looters, and you happened to be in the neighborhood and were generous enough to offer a hand."

The man looked out at the parking lot. "Does that mean you're going to help carry away that immense ... dead thing? It doesn't look like any looters that I've seen."

Detective White smiled. "Animal control issue it is."

She stepped past the man and walked up to Dillon. "Mister Offner," she said, sticking out her hand. Then she saw the bandages and took her hand back. She looked around the dining room, then over Dillon's shoulder at the monstrosity in the parking lot, then back at him. "If you hear from your uncle again, call me. You have my number."

"My uncle ... Uncle Phil ... is dead, detective." He didn't add, *I talked to his ghost.*

"Hmm," the detective said. "Without a body, he's still just missing, officially. But if I hear anything, I'll let you know." After another glance past Dillon, she said, "I better go."

Soledad was coming from behind the counter as the detective walked away. "Get that weapon registered, Miss Winters," the woman said as she passed. "Antique or not, I do *not* like unregistered firearms in my town."

Soledad nodded, then added, "Will do, detective."

Soledad stopped in front of Dillon, just out of arms reach. She met his eyes. Her expression was disapproving, but there was a smile trying to pull up the corners of her lips. She glanced at his mother, then back at him.

"Mom," Dillon said. "This is Soledad. Soledad, Mom."

"Nice to meet you–" Soledad started.

"Thank you," Mom said and hugged her.

After an awkward few seconds, Soledad put her arms around Mom and patted her on the back. Then Dillon hugged them both.

Dillon stepped back to let Soledad disentangle herself when Mom finally let her go.

After what he thought seemed sufficient time, he asked, "Carlita?"

Soledad rolled her eyes. "Carlita is still in the break room, yes," she said. "And she's still taking care of Cyd, yes. Fortunately, Cyd's uniform was still there from before, so that's no longer an issue."

Dillon nodded, then kept his mouth shut as he didn't ask if–

"No," Soledad said, "Cyd doesn't remember anything since walking home with you two nights ago." She paused, then added, "Let's leave it that way, shall we?"

Dillon glanced at the handbag on Soledad's hip, then nodded. Some parts of the past two days were better left ... unremembered.

"Thank you, Mary, Mother of God," Jorge shouted from the grill section. "My grill, she works! Ronald, fetch me a clean apron and grab that box of patties out of the lowboy. Pick out the bullets if you need to, but we are going to have ourselves some postapocalyptical buffalo burgers."

"I'll find us some buns," Edward said.

"I got your buns right here," Coleman said.

"Not in this lifetime."

"How about it, Mom?" Dillon asked. "Would you like a bacon cheese-burger-no-cheese?" He looked at the chaos of the dining room. "Though I would understand if you still don't want to eat here."

Mom bit her lip, then said, "Why wouldn't I eat here? My son works here."

She smiled. Dillon smiled. Soledad rolled her eyes again, then looked away.

THE END

About the Author

David R. Michael finds it endlessly fascinating that the city names of both Tulsa, Oklahoma, and Tallahassee, Florida, come from the same Native American root word meaning "river crossing." Rio Cruces is Spanish for "riving crossing," as well. Make of that what you will. David lives in one of those three cities with his wife, kids, and cats.

To know when new books by David R. Michael are available, and get a taste of what's coming up next, sign up for David's email newsletter here: **www.gunsandmagic.com**

About the Cover

Cover painting, *Super Size Me*, by Don Michael, Jr.

See more of Don's artwork here: **www.donmichaeljr.com**